Murder at the Wedding

GREG MOSSE is a 'writer and encourager of writers' and husband of internationally bestselling author Kate Mosse. He has lived and worked in Paris, New York, Los Angeles and Madrid, mostly as an interpreter and translator, but grew up in rural south-west Sussex. In 2014, he founded the Criterion New Writing playwriting programme in the heart of the West End and, since then, has produced more than 25 of his own plays and musicals. His creative writing workshops are highly sought after at festivals at home and abroad. His first novel, *The Coming Darkness*, was published by Moonflower in 2022, followed in 2024 and 2025 by *The Coming Storm* and *The Coming Fire*. *Murder at the Wedding* is the sixth book in his successful 1970s cosy crime series featuring the charming and perceptive amateur sleuth Maisie Cooper.

Murder at the Wedding

Greg Mosse

**HODDER &
STOUGHTON**

First published in Great Britain in 2025 by Hodder & Stoughton Limited
An Hachette UK company

The authorised representative in the EEA is Hachette Ireland, 8 Castlecourt
Centre, Dublin 15, D15 XTP3, Ireland (email: info@hbgi.ie)

1

A CIP catalogue record for this title is available from the British Library

Paperback ISBN 978 1 399 74070 8
ebook ISBN 978 1 399 74071 5

Typeset in Monotype Plantin by Manipal Technologies Limited

Printed and bound in Great Britain by Clays Ltd, Elcograf S.p.A.

Hodder & Stoughton policy is to use papers that are natural, renewable
and recyclable products and made from wood grown in sustainable forests.
The logging and manufacturing processes are expected to conform
to the environmental regulations of the country of origin.

Hodder & Stoughton Limited
Carmelite House
50 Victoria Embankment
London EC4Y 0DZ

www.hodder.co.uk

For Saira

Maisie's Map of Framlington

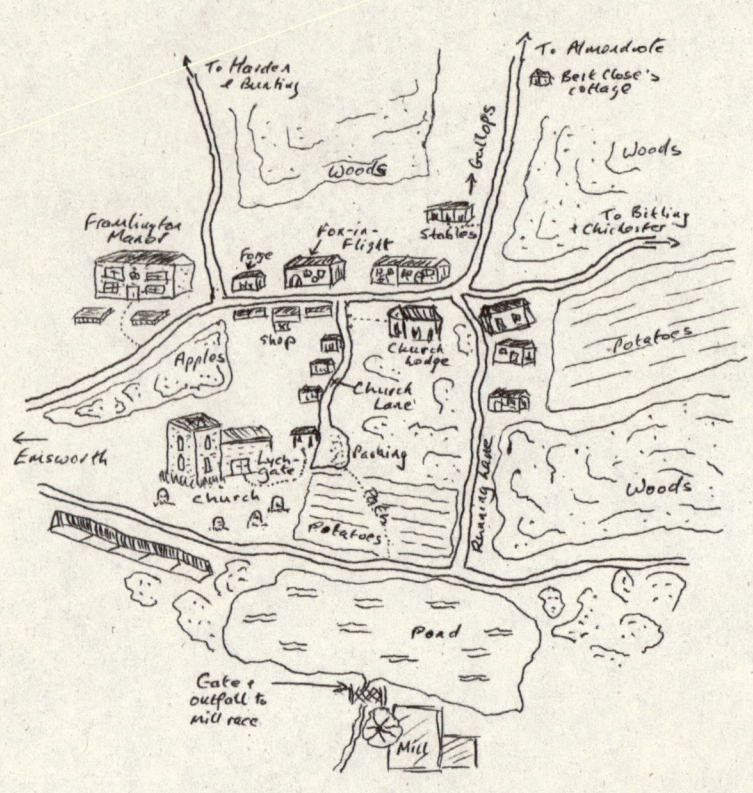

Cast of Characters

Maisie Cooper
Florence Wingard, Sergeant Jack Wingard's grandmother
Kinori Osaka, Florence's friend, an expert florist
Sergeant Jack Wingard of the Chichester police
Reverend Millns of St Mary's, Framlington
Madame de Rosette, Maisie's Paris boss
PC Donaldson of the Newcastle police
Sergeant Gary Naylor of the Bristol police, on the same Newcastle training programme as Jack
Peggy Kemp, also known as 'Esmeralda', confidence trickster
Ronan Kemp, her dangerous son
Mick and Jez Carter, scrap dealers
Phyllis 'Phyl' Pascal, owner of Bunting Manor, Maisie's mother's sister
Archie Close, Phyl's farm manager
Zoe Pascal, Phyl's ward
Inspector Fred Nairn of the Chichester police, Jack's best man
Mavis Nairn, his dissatisfied wife
Commander Kimmings, retired naval officer
Liz Petter of Petter Farm, cultivator of roses
George Petter of Petter Farm, her father, also chairman of the Rotary Club
Charity Clement, assistant to and wife of Maisie's solicitor
Maurice Ryan, Maisie's solicitor
Arthur Tate, confectioner
Daphne Fieldhouse, owner of Framlington Manor
Derek Fieldhouse, her estranged husband

Sergeant William Dodd of the Chichester police

Harold Farr, impoverished farm labourer

Adam Farr, his nephew

Mohammed As-Sabah, once Maisie's brother Stephen's best friend

Dorothy Dean, general manager at Chichester Festival Theatre

Russell and Audrey Savage, Maisie's friends, ten years previously her employers, owners of Sunny View Guest House

Canon Greig, of the 'Collegiate Church of the Holy Cross and the Mother of Him Who Hung Thereon', in Kirton

Pawlu (known as Paul) Linton

Police Constable Barry Goodbody of the Chichester police

Cedric Tate, Arthur's brother

Alicia Knight and Beatrice Otterway, Framlington shopkeepers

PROLOGUE

On the last Friday in September in the year 1972, in St Mary's church in the village of Framlington, the brass of the candlesticks and the carved timber of the pulpit were being polished by practised hands. Flowers had been delivered. Other hands – equally expert – were arranging them in bunches, plunging them into vases full of the chalk-rich water of the Sussex Downs.

The squat house of worship stood at the end of a narrow cul-de-sac, Church Lane. The building had no special architectural features, no historical oddities, but it had served sixty generations of local people in their weekly devotions and important life-changing ceremonies. Their births, marriages and deaths – hatch, match and despatch.

The following day, the last day of the month, Saturday the 30th of September 1972, would be match. Maisie Cooper was to marry Sergeant Jack Wingard of the Chichester police and – perhaps – the cycle of Maisie's accidental murder investigations would thereby come to an end.

The wedding flowers came from the glasshouses and the gardens at West Dean House, gifted by its noble owner, Edward James, to a foundation that bore his name, an extraordinary stately home converted into an 'Eden for the arts'. West Dean produced blooms year-round, tended by a team of devoted horticulturalists, many of them volunteers, including Florence Wingard, the grandmother of the groom.

Florence and Jack Wingard lived in a small but pleasant bungalow on Parklands Road, Chichester. The wedding would be the culmination, for Florence, of months of hoping and impotent scheming, while the murders at Church Lodge, Bunting Manor, the theatre, the fair and Sunny View slowly played out, with Florence wondering why her grandson was taking so long to seize the glorious opportunity life had presented to him in the person of Maisie Cooper.

Today, Florence was busy helping the Edward James Foundation's chief florist, a small woman of similar age, of Japanese descent, called Kinori Osaka. Kinori, by a quirk of twentieth-century history, after a lifetime buffeted by oppression and war, had found a haven in south-west Sussex. And it was she – an expert in such things – who had chosen and designed the floral displays, selecting them for their symbolic meanings, as well as their appearance and scent.

The other ladies, those armed with Brasso and Mr Sheen furniture polish, drifted away, leaving Kinori and Florence alone in the vestry, a private space, conducive to shared secrets. Arranging a bouquet of peonies, Florence prompted: 'Your family were farmers in California. It's astonishing to me that you've washed up here, in south-west Sussex.'

'We were happy on the West Coast, integrated. But, with the attack on Pearl Harbor, everything changed. My parents and I were removed from our land, leaving our crops to wither and die, and placed in an internment camp.'

'How awful.'

'I was quite fluent in American English, as well as my parents' mother tongue, able to speak, read and write in both languages. Some weeks later, I was recruited from the awful detention centre for the ATIS, the Allied Translator and Interpreter Section, a subdivision of the American military intelligence service.'

'What happened to your parents?'

'They remained in captivity.'

'Oh, dear.'

'After some basic tests and training, I was shipped out to the Pacific Ocean theatre of war, translating sensitive Japanese military communications, intercepted or captured by the US and Australian forces. Each week, I was allowed to send a bland, heavily censored letter to my parents, wishing them well, reassuring them that I was safe. I never received a reply.'

'Not knowing how they were getting on must have been very hard.'

'It was, and time passed extremely slowly.'

Kinori snipped an inch or two from several stems to help them draw up water.

'What did your intelligence work comprise?'

'The Japanese military commanders presumed that the Allies would be unable to read the contents of their orders and strategic documents. They worried little when, inevitably, some were lost or captured. At first, they were right. Only three bilingual Americans were known to US military intelligence before they came recruiting in the internment camps. Then the focus shifted. The Japanese forces began to retreat and I had to devise devious anti-Japanese propaganda to be dropped as leaflets or to be broadcast by radio, part of a programme of psychological warfare that only came to an end with the dropping of the atomic bombs on Nagasaki and Hiroshima.' Kinori's busy hands became still. 'But I don't want to talk about that.'

'No, Kinori, I quite understand.' Then, stripping the lower leaves from some magnificent white roses, Florence asked: 'Were you ever in danger yourself?'

'There were ATIS linguists attached to every assault force. Many of my friends died.'

'How distressing.'

'Some of them worked under duress, motivated by the promise of preferential treatment for their interned families.'

3

'Did those promises turn out to be true?'

'Not in every case,' said Kinori.

'You must have felt conflicted, yourself, working for the war effort of an adopted country that had, effectively, rejected your family, destroyed your livelihood and then exploited you?'

Kinori sighed then told her: 'Yes, I did feel conflicted, not least because my parents died before they were released – but that might have happened in any case. I mean, they might have died young on the farm . . .'

Kinori's voice drifted off and Florence regretted probing her friend for details of her traumatic past. She racked her brain for a more neutral subject of conversation to accompany their work.

'Can you show me how to write your name?'

'In Japanese characters?'

'Yes. I expect it's very beautiful.'

Kinori looked round for something to write with. There was a pad of Basildon Bond writing paper on the vestry desk and a Paper Mate felt-tip pen.

Florence said: 'Write them big because I don't have my reading glasses.'

The nib of the felt-tip pen flexed a little in Kinori's grip, meaning each stroke narrowed as she lifted the pressure in a clumsy imitation of brushstroke calligraphy.

希紀

'So, it's made up of two characters?' asked Florence. 'Or is that three?'

'That's two but it can be written in other ways.'

Kinori drew another example.

季乃凛

'How complicated,' said Florence, 'but, I suppose, English must seem so if one isn't used to it. Does your name have a meaning of any kind?'

'It's very boring. It means something like "the wish for regulation" or "the hope for order",' said Kinori with a self-deprecating smile.

'No, that isn't very poetic,' said Florence with a laugh. 'Languages are such fascinating things.' She gestured to the roses that she had finished preparing for the display. 'There's a language to flowers, too. You know all about that.'

'There is,' said Kinori. 'A symbolic language. But symbols are slippery. The "language of flowers" isn't fixed and universal. For example, peonies are a beloved wedding flower in England today but, historically, they used to denote anger and resentment. Meanwhile, in Japanese culture, they signify bravery, courage and good fortune.'

'How fascinating,' said Florence, a little unnerved at the idea that the wedding of her grandson, Jack Wingard, to his childhood sweetheart, Maisie Cooper, might be decorated with a flower with such negative connotations. 'What about the others?'

'It's often a question of colour. Red roses are a symbol of love, of course. White roses are for purity. Yellow roses imply jealousy or infidelity.'

'I think I knew that.'

'Peonies are supposed to soothe and encourage relaxation, but they have been used to represent resentment and anger. Were we earlier in the year, we might have had daffodils for "respect", but they also signify unrequited love.'

'It's an unexpected minefield,' said Florence, intending to change the subject because she was beginning to feel an odd disquiet. 'Do you—?'

'Lotus flowers can symbolise estranged love,' persisted Kinori. 'They are marvellous. I have a small artificial pond at West Dean devoted to their cultivation. You know about their daily cycle of life, death and rebirth? They come, like me – by descent, at least – from the East. The white ones represent

5

purity and beauty, serenity and self-knowledge. The yellow lotus suggests spiritual ascension and a pink one evokes the essence of Buddha.'

Florence indicated her glass vase of white roses.

'Is this satisfactory?'

'Beautifully done,' said Kinori. Then she frowned. 'I need to tell you something.'

'What is it?' Florence asked.

'You remember, in the design we discussed in your kitchen, we decided we would have bunches of red carnations by the door because, in the greetings cards and so on, they mean "I love you"?'

'Of course.'

'When I arrived here, the delivery from West Dean was waiting for me in the shelter of the porch, outside the south door of the church, including some lovely sheaves of wheat for contrast. But there was a bunch of yellow carnations in there as well.'

'Is that important?'

'They shouldn't have been there.'

'You didn't request them?'

'No, of course not.'

'Perhaps someone added them from their own garden,' said Florence. 'Maybe a kindly neighbour who meant well? Will they upset the balance of the design?'

'No, that's not it. Florence, the yellow carnations represent a slight, you know – taking umbrage. Or, worse, a desire for revenge.'

'Oh.'

'I felt . . . odd, on seeing them, you know?'

'But do people know that?' asked Florence. 'Generally, I mean?'

'I suppose not,' said Kinori, sounding unconvinced.

'And who could possibly bear a grudge against Jack or Maisie? Everyone likes and respects them. They are universally well thought of.'

'Are they?' asked Kinori. 'Even by the people they've brought to justice?'

'That's absurd,' said Florence, more abruptly than she meant.

A little stiffly, the two women completed their preparations, placing the last displays in their niches and checking that all the vases contained sufficient water to sustain the blooms until the following morning at eleven, sharp, when the celebrated tune by Mendelssohn would accompany Maisie up the aisle. Florence thought once more about the murders at Church Lodge, Bunting Manor, the theatre and the fair.

And at Sunny View, the Devon guest house – Maisie was actually summoned by the owners to look into it.

★

Kinori had not been offended by the sharpness of Florence's tone. Her life had been sufficiently filled with drama to know that taking umbrage at the slightest impertinence was foolish in the extreme. Their work done, they stepped outside into the lovely autumn afternoon. The leaves on the beech hedge at the far side of the graveyard, beyond the ancient yew tree, were just beginning to turn from green to gold.

This is a lovely place, thought Kinori, *and I don't want to spoil things by telling Florence what happened when I met Maisie here. She's already on edge.*

'Forget I mentioned it,' Kinori told her friend. 'After all, what importance should we attach to symbolic meanings?'

★

Lost in her own thoughts, Florence was too distracted to reply. She knew that Jack and Maisie were both worried and she was uncomfortable that they hadn't shared their reasons with her, presumably in order not to spoil her own pleasurable anticipation of their big day.

But their unhappy silence is spoiling it anyway. They have no reason to keep their secrets. I'm not a hot-house flower, am I?

Florence and her friend walked down the gravel path to the lychgate.

And it's not just against Maisie that people might bear a grudge. There's Jack, too, and the enemies any police officer inevitably makes.

Kinori was carrying a large cardboard box of damp paper wrappings, multiple lengths of string, secateurs and so on. Florence held the gate open and told her: 'I have to make a repair to Maisie's wedding dress. She stepped on the hem, trying it on. Do you still have time to give me a lift home?'

'Of course.'

Once her friend had passed through, Florence looked back at the squat Norman church, its grey stonework mellowed by the lowish sun.

All will be well, she told herself. *Tomorrow will be a wonderful day, the start of a new chapter in Jack's and Maisie's lives – the first chapter of their shared life.*

★

In one way Florence was right. In another, she was very, very wrong. But there was no reason for her to know that, not far away, at the edge of the village, there was a dead body lying on damp, straw-strewn concrete, the disgusting processes of putrefaction already under way.

More than a week before the celebratory bells were to begin pealing, there had already been a murder at the wedding.

I

Lotus Flowers

Signifying life, death and rebirth

ONE

One week earlier, on Friday the 22nd of September 1972, Maisie found herself on a rickety slam-door British Rail train, her small travel suitcase in the net luggage rack above her head, heading north up the east side of England, watching the towns and cities, fields and rivers go by through smudged and dusty windows. It reminded her of Philip Larkin's poem 'The Whitsun Weddings', in which lots of passengers, all packed in together on a holiday-weekend service, travelled with a single destination but many purposes.

I wonder how many of my fellow travellers are lucky enough to be as happy as I am?

At the conclusion of her investigation into the murder at Sunny View, back in July, the events all packed into just a couple of days as the schools broke up for the long summer holidays, she had taken a decision. It had seemed easy at the time.

I'm not going to wait for months and months of engagement and dress fittings and banns and preparations. I've decided that I'm going to marry Jack Wingard before this summer is out.

Having no sisters or female cousins – and only a dissipated murdered brother – Maisie had no experience of the multiple complications of planning a wedding. And she had underestimated Jack's grandmother Florence's determination that 'if it's worth doing, it's worth doing right'. At every step, she felt, there had been hindrances and hiccups.

Not least among these had been the availability of the church. It turned out that September – like May – was a prime month in the seasonal cycle of marriages. She, of course, had wanted to celebrate the occasion in the village where she grew up, walking up the aisle of St Mary's, Framlington, with her parents lying patiently under the ground outside, in eternal rest in the millennial churchyard.

Discovering that St Mary's was already booked for another happy couple's 'special day', she had got in touch with her fiancé at his police posting in Newcastle. To her surprise, Jack had suggested Chichester's enormous cathedral, home to a choir school, a bishop and any number of important ceremonial priests.

'Surely that will be more difficult still?'

'Maybe, but if it's already booked for the matinée,' he told her, with a smile in his voice, 'we can make ours a morning wedding and be done in time for the more important people to have the afternoon.'

'Is that even possible?'

'I'm sure I can swing it. Other officers have done the same. Fred's organised a guard of honour from the lads at the station, all polished up and in white gloves.' Jack was referring to his colleague and best man, Inspector Fred Nairn, with whom Maisie was also friends. 'The cathedral loves that sort of thing. And you're famous in the city.'

'But I'm an orphan,' she had objected. 'And I've been living abroad. There'll be hardly anyone there on my side. It will look ridiculous – a sea of empty chairs.'

'Then we won't use the nave. We'll make it a small wedding on both sides. Everyone can sit in the choir stalls up close to the altar, all mixed in together. My people are your people, now.'

'I'm not sure—'

'Or we can simply go to the registrar's office in North Street,' Jack had insisted, 'like in those pictures in your Aunt

Phyl's wartime photo album. We just need two witnesses and an official to say it's legal.'

Maisie had taken Jack's call early one morning in the front hall of Phyl Pascal's ugly Jacobean manor house in Bunting, with the front door open onto the gravel drive, the sun poking its way through the small leaded windows either side, filtered by the close-looming trees. At Jack's end, the pips had begun sounding. When they stopped, in the tiny gap before his money ran out, he had quickly told her: 'I'm at the hostel where they've been putting me up for the duration. I don't have another tuppence. I'll call you again this evening.'

The connection had cut, leaving Maisie alone with the receiver in her hand, hearing the distant continuous whine of the 'disconnected' tone, feeling foolish and abandoned. After she had hung up, however, the telephone had immediately launched into a second raucous metallic ring. Picking up, Maisie had announced: 'Bunting Manor.'

The news had been as good as it was unexpected – from Reverend Millns of St Mary's, Framlington.

'The couple in possession of Saturday 30th have cancelled.'

'Really? Do you know why?'

'In the course of our interviews – a normal practice in the Church of England in preparation for their spiritual and legal commitment to one another – they say that they have discovered that their desires are not so tightly aligned as they previously thought.' Reverend Millns' tone had been wry and she had heard him strike a match to light one of the crafty cigarettes of which he seemed ashamed. 'But, perhaps, you have made other arrangements, Miss Cooper?'

'No, I haven't – not yet.'

'Shall I pencil you in?'

'Ink us in, please. How marvellous. But there is one other thing.'

'Yes?'

'I don't know precisely the form, but I wonder if another priest might be empowered to conduct the service?'

After a pause, Millns had replied: 'It is not entirely unheard of.'

'I have a close connection to the church – once a cathedral – in Kirton in Devon. I would very much like the minister there, Canon Greig, to conduct my marriage service. Would that be possible?'

Millns had left another pause before replying. Bunting was only a few miles from Framlington, tucked into a little-frequented valley in the Downs – a place people only went to if they had business there – but the distance had seemed to stretch out further, along with the empty seconds of silence.

I wonder if, somehow, he knows that Canon Greig isn't really a 'close connection'.

'It would be possible,' Millns had finally replied, with an icy formality. 'Perhaps you would care to drop in and provide me with his address.'

'I will, later today,' Maisie had promised.

That had been two weeks before and ought to have forced Maisie into more concentrated action. But, she judged, the small wedding both she and Jack desired didn't demand enormous preparation. Instead of thinking about a choir or flowers to decorate the nave or a reception, she had chosen to slip away from Sussex for a couple of days of solitary gallery- and theatre-going in London. And, now, she was on her way to visit her fiancé, the rickety northbound train meandering through the suburbs of Durham, interrupting her thoughts with a series of glimpses of historical stone buildings, including ancient colleges and an impressive Gothic cathedral.

They came to a stop. Outside, on the station platform, a guard cried out, promising a 'four-minute halt'. Maisie opened the door of her six-person compartment – shared with two mature men who looked like travelling salesmen, and three younger ones wearing overalls spattered with white plaster who clearly worked in the building trade.

Maisie climbed down. She was wearing quite a narrow jacket and skirt in powder-blue wool because she wanted to make a good impression, should she be introduced to Jack's superior officers. She had to take care, therefore, descending the high step, finding it a relief to be outside in the fresh air. Despite the fact that the warm day allowed them to travel with the window down a few inches, the compartment was very close and choked with a fug of smoke from several of the men's cigarettes.

Maisie strolled to the end of the platform, looking up the line at the rails narrowing with perspective, distantly merging in the direction she was travelling.

My entire life is narrowing down, becoming more focused. Will it open out again, after the wedding? I hope so.

Maisie had been in England since February when, quite unexpectedly, coming home to her flat on the Place des Vosges after a day's work in Paris, her flatmate had passed on a message from her dissipated older brother, Stephen. It had asked her to drop everything – meaning her busy life as a respected and sought-after tour guide – and revisit their childhood home in Framlington. On arrival, she had discovered that she was too late, that Stephen was dead.

Later, she had learned – from Sergeant Jack Wingard himself – that Stephen had been murdered. Out of that strange and unhappy set of circumstances, she had been drawn into several murder investigations.

Each time it's happened, there have been good reasons. I've not sought out tragedy. It's not my fault there's so much unhappiness and resentment and jealousy in the world. And it's changed me. I hope I'm not becoming jaundiced or pessimistic.

Maisie strolled back to the open door of her compartment. She climbed aboard, pulling her narrow skirt up above her knee to the delight of her gentlemen travelling companions. She slammed the door closed, glad to be sitting next to the window, thinking about Reverend Millns, relieved to have found a way of sidelining him from the wedding. Trying to find out about Stephen's death, she had discovered information much to his discredit. In the investigation into the murder at Church Lodge, it had emerged that Maisie's brother, Stephen, had an affair with the barmaid at the Fox-in-Flight, June Strickland. When June was a little girl, Reverend Millns had done nothing to protect her from the cruelty of her father, Old Man Strickland, despite knowing all about it.

The train pulled away, heading out of Durham city centre, through the suburbs into the beautiful countryside. Looking forward to catching a glimpse of the penultimate stop, Chester-Le-Street, Maisie turned her mind to the guest list for the wedding. As it turned out, despite being an orphan with no brothers or sisters with whom to 'share her special day', her side of the church wouldn't be so badly attended. There was her mother's sister, Phyl Pascal, of course, from whom Maisie and her parents had been estranged for many years.

But that's all fixed, now.

And there was Phyl's ward, Zoe, a sparkling young woman of just sixteen years old. Since Phyl had taken steps to officially become Zoe's adoptive parent, Zoe had begun referring to Maisie proudly – though not entirely accurately – as 'my sister'.

Maurice Ryan, Stephen's solicitor and now her friend, would also be there with his delightful wife Charity – née Charité Clément – a vibrant and determined woman of Guadeloupian heritage. There would also be some of her charming childhood neighbours from the village of Framlington, many of whom had been helpful – knowingly or unknowingly – in solving the mystery of Stephen's murder. And she had made a good handful of excellent new friends in Bitling, where she had been instrumental in solving the murder at Bitling Fair. Plus, there would be the small contingent travelling up from Devon on a slow train from Kirton.

There might be one or two from the theatre as well. Yes, all things considered, my side won't look too sad.

Maisie was still hoping that her closest Paris friend, her former flatmate Sophie Labeur, might be able to attend, but that would depend on Maisie's fierce Paris boss – now ex-boss – Madame de Rosette, who had been less than pleased when Maisie had called her to say she was not coming back to work.

'*Mais qu'est-ce que vous faites, Mademoiselle Cooper? Vous changez entièrement de trajectoire comme ça, pour un homme?*'

Maisie had explained that, no, she wasn't 'entirely changing her life's trajectory for a man', but 'in order to marry my childhood sweetheart', continuing in her impeccable French: 'In any case, you already have an ideal replacement. Sophie has proved invaluable in the past on temporary assignments.'

'Mademoiselle Labeur is good,' Madame de Rosette had allowed, 'but – for obvious reasons – she doesn't have your ease or charm in English.'

'Sophie is quite competent and, with practice, her accent will improve.'

Maisie had heard a sigh at the other end, then Madame de Rosette had pulled herself together and wished her well in her new life, enjoining Maisie 'not to forget us'.

'*Jamais, chère madame.*'

Never.

Lost in these reminiscences, Chester-Le-Street went by almost without Maisie noticing and she was finally on the last leg of her journey to one of the nation's most northerly outposts, where Jack had been working hard in preparation for his promotion from uniformed sergeant to plain-clothes inspector.

He's been away for two months. What will he think of me? That I've changed? I hope not. But I'm worried that I have ... and not for the better.

Before she knew it, Maisie's train was slowing, crossing the River Tyne via an arched bridge built from enormous iron girders, an impressive relic of Victorian infrastructure. The train entered the city proper with the tall, frail-looking floodlights of a sports stadium visible beyond the rooftops. Maisie saw more evidence of the era of industrial revolution, with sooty deposits on the grey stone and bricks, lending everything a depressing, unwashed air. The view reminded her of a story Phyl had told her about Queen Victoria instructing a footman to close the curtains of the royal train on her processions north to Balmoral, in order not to witness William Blake's 'dark, satanic mills' – the chimneys and colliery wheels, the slag heaps and the tenement towns.

It all needs a good spring clean.

The brakes of the train began their work with a squeal, just as Maisie imagined it in Larkin's 'The Whitsun Weddings'. The three plasterers were soon on their feet, leaning across her to open the door and jump down while the train was still in motion. Maisie stood to retrieve her small suitcase from the net luggage rack above her head, then she helped the shorter of the two travelling salesmen – the only other passenger who hadn't smoked – with a very heavy holdall whose zip had burst, revealing hundreds of copies of a commercial pamphlet for Target Insurance and many tiny books of branded safety matches. The second salesman – who looked like he needed a shave – had a small PVC holdall with a long strap *en bandoulière*, diagonally across his chest.

The train came to a complete stop and Maisie got down, finding herself lost in a crowd of people, all of whom – it seemed – knew precisely where they were going while she tried to orient herself. She joined the flow, heading for the ticket barrier, preparing her ticket for the British Rail employee to clip, indicating that her outward journey had been accomplished.

She stepped through onto the concourse and stood still, causing the crowd to flow around her, like water either side of a boulder dropped in a stream. Little by little, the mass of northbound humanity dispersed and, to her surprise and disappointment, she was left isolated and alone.

What's happened, Jack?

★

Maisie was less alone, however, than the cold body, left concealed beneath a scattering of straw, in the unused agricultural building on the edge of Framlington.

The victim was a well-liked man who had lived alone in a tiny cottage outside the village. As an odd-job labourer for the wealthy Fieldhouse family, he had also worked mostly alone. And he had recently been unwell so no one had missed him, assuming he had taken to his bed.

All this was a great shame for Maisie and for Jack. It would have been so much better if someone could have said: 'Where's he got to? I'll go and check up on him.'

But, in the farming milieu, it was a very busy time of year, with harvests to bring in and everyone short-handed. So, no one did 'check up on him' and, therefore, no one knew that he was dead.

Which meant that no one knew, either, that the person who had killed him – who had been using the building as a place to hide, out of sight of prying eyes – bore both Maisie, the accidental sleuth, and Jack, the professional, the bitterest and most deep-seated of grudges.

Two

Newcastle Central felt very much like a terminus and Maisie had arrived, it seemed, at a relatively quiet time, before the evening rush of city workers heading out into the suburbs. Opposite where she stood, on a high façade, were the white-neon letters of the W H Smith & Son shop sign where she thought she might buy a book, if Jack had time for her to browse. Alongside – incongruously she thought – was a sports-goods shop selling skiing equipment, among other splendid things. Beyond that was a Finlay's tobacconist with an advertising panel in curly script promoting a popular brand of cigarettes: *Player's, please.*

Frowning, because it was unlike Jack to be late, she checked her lady's wristwatch and compared the time with a large round clock hanging from metal stanchions in the curved roof. The circle of Roman numerals on a white background was illuminated by slanting sun through a grimy half-barrel of glass. The clock and her watch matched, as if synchronised: four o'clock on the dot. Because she had expected Jack to come and meet her at the barrier, Maisie had no further clue how to find him.

Should I ask directions for the hostel? But it isn't certain that Jack will be there. Could he have been called away to some emergency?

Though officially in training, Jack was also on duty in the city, alongside his programme of seminars and theoretical assignments.

If called away, surely he could have found someone to pass on a message?

Then, Maisie felt a lurch as she saw what she half expected but also half feared. A uniformed constable was making his slow way across the concourse towards her, his eyes down, as if he had bad news to impart and was reluctant to meet her gaze.

Unwilling to simply stand still where she was, beneath the clock on the station concourse, and wait for the constable, Maisie picked up her suitcase and went to confront him. Coming closer, she understood why his eyes were down. He was examining, in the palm of his right hand, a photograph – a small square of glossy paper in slightly wishy-washy colours. Becoming aware of her presence just a few feet away, he looked at her, glanced back at the photograph, then up again.

'Miss Cooper?'

'Yes.'

'I'm PC Donaldson. Would you come with me, please?'

'Of course.'

He turned and walked away and Maisie followed, aware that the tobacconist, standing outside Finlay's was following her closely with an interested eye, wondering in what way she might be 'helping the police with their enquiries'.

PC Donaldson hurried on, through a preposterously grand internal colonnade and out into the sunlight where the traffic was busy but not oppressive. On an island between two converging roads, Maisie saw a neo-Gothic church or, perhaps, a cathedral with a very pointed spire. PC Donaldson was already crossing towards it.

'Excuse me,' she called after him. 'Could you wait a moment?'

The young man stopped, turned and held out a hand for her suitcase.

'I'm sorry, miss. Let me take that for you.'

'That's not what I meant. I would like to know where we're going and what's happened.'

'In what sense, miss?'

'First of all, why isn't Sergeant Wingard here to meet me?'

Maisie realised that she had asked the question with a horrid tightness in her throat and her voice had come out reedy and thin.

'Who is Sergeant Wingard, miss?'

'The person who gave you that photograph of me.' The square of glossy photographic paper was still in his hand. It depicted Maisie in one of her summer dresses, standing reluctantly on the medieval flagstones of the Market Cross in the centre of Chichester, one hand half raised to shield her eyes from the glare of the sun. Even to her own eye, she thought the pose becoming. 'Could I have that, in fact?'

He handed it over with a kind of reluctance and she put it away in her handbag.

'I'm sorry if there's been some confusion,' he told her. 'I was given instructions to find you at the railway station and that's really all I know.'

'Who by?'

'My station sergeant.'

'And you've not met Jack Wingard?'

'No, miss.'

'And you don't know what might have happened to him?'

Donaldson frowned, looking confused. 'What might have happened to him?' he repeated, looking worried that he had made some kind of *faux pas*. 'What does that mean?'

'I don't know,' said Maisie, her voice becoming tight once more. 'I've not seen him for two months and, here I am . . . and he isn't.'

'I see,' said the young man. He had a pale, raw face as if his cheeks were not yet used to the daily scrape of his safety razor. 'It's not far.'

'What's not far?'

'The hospital.'

The word was like a cold draught on the back of Maisie's neck but, before she could react, he gave her a nod and was on the point of turning away when she put down her suitcase and took hold of his blue uniform sleeve.

'What do you mean, the hospital?'

'Newcastle General, up Arthur's Hill, not much more than a mile. Can you walk? Or, if you've the necessary, we could take a taxi and be there—'

'Why the hospital?' Maisie insisted. 'You must know what has happened – something, at least.'

'I'm sorry, miss. I'd just come on duty at the station and my sergeant gave me your photograph, told me what time you were expected and to bring you to the hospital. That's all.' He looked sheepish, clearly also wishing that he knew more. 'Sergeant was in a dreadful bate with other things and I'm new,' he explained apologetically, 'so I didn't dare ask questions.'

'Fine. Wait here and look after my bag.' Without a care for the nosy glances of the passers-by, Maisie ran back across the road and waved to a taxi driver who had just dropped off his fare. He wound down his window and she asked him: 'Can you take me and that constable over there to the hospital?'

'Which one?'

'Newcastle General. Just swing round, would you? He's got my suitcase.'

Maisie ran back across the road to rejoin Donaldson as the taxi driver completed his manoeuvre. They got in and the constable repeated the instruction.

'Newcastle General, top of the hill.'

'Yes, I got that.'

The driver pulled away between impressive civic and commercial buildings in dark-red brick and grey stone. Then the road narrowed between shops and then terraced houses. On the left, a park opened out with mature trees and lush green grass. Maisie decided there must have been even more rain 'up north' than she had seen in a wet September in Sussex.

They took a right turn off the main road, entering the scruffy grounds of Newcastle General. The hospital was a sad combination of impressive Victorian architecture in dressed stone, plus a haphazard handful of extensions in more modern, less durable materials, already showing signs of wear and weather damage. On a blank, rendered wall, someone had painted a mural – sadly faded from exposure to sun and weather – of a lotus flower. Maisie found it disconcerting, the image of a transient bloom, well known for its brief lifespan, on the wall of a hospital.

The taxi driver pulled up at the main entrance and asked for a very modest fare for the short journey. Maisie paid with a few coins from her purse, including a tip, and she and Donaldson got out.

'Which way?' she asked.

'Reception, I suppose?'

The taxi pulled away and, with an unfair feeling of irritation at the constable's vagueness, Maisie led Donaldson inside. The reception desk was staffed by a nurse with very masculine features in a starched blue uniform and an odd white cap in the shape of a pillbox.

'I'm looking for Jack Wingard, Sergeant Jack Wingard. He's a police officer.'

'Are you Miss Cooper?'

'I am. Good afternoon.'

'I was told to expect you. Do you have a case?'

'Yes.'

'Pass it over. I'll put it behind the desk for you to fetch later.'

'Why?'

'Well, you won't want it on the ward, will you?'

Maisie's heart sank.

So, Jack's on a ward somewhere. What on earth could have happened?

'Can I speak to him?'

'I don't know, miss. I expect you'll find out soon enough.' The reception nurse summoned a porter in green overalls. 'Please take this lady to St Nick's, the post-op ward.'

Oh, no, thought Maisie.

'I'll leave you to it,' said Donaldson.

Rudely, not feeling proud of herself, Maisie paid him no attention. She followed the porter across the lobby, into a corridor with wooden panelling either side to protect the walls from inevitable collisions with wheeled stretchers and other equipment. They passed by smooth modern doors labelled with the names of different practitioners and their specialisms, until they came to staircase that led up the rear of the building, the air feeling cooler away from the sunnier façade. On the first-floor landing, the porter told her: 'In there.'

Then he left her, too.

The door was pinned back, with a plastic sign that read: *St Nicholas Ward – Men*. Just inside was an unattended nurses' station with an open ledger. Maisie leaned over to try and find Jack's name. As far as she could see, it wasn't there.

If he's only just come out of surgery, though, perhaps the ledger hasn't been updated.

Aware that she was intruding without proper authority, she advanced between the first two sets of flimsy curtains, glancing left at a man with a very creased, elderly face whose broken arm was elevated under traction. On the other side, a young man with both legs in plaster was reading a motorcycling magazine.

She moved on, between the shrunken forms of two older patients, one of whom was being helped to sit up by a nurse – once again in the starched blue uniform and pillbox cap. The nurse told her: 'Visiting hours are later. You can't be here.'

'I understand, but could you help me?' she began. 'I'm looking for—'

To her surprise, she was interrupted by a voice she recognised – her favourite voice, in fact. It came from the very end of the ward, sounding weak and distant. Without any further preamble, she advanced between two more sets of curtains, closed on their occupants.

What will I do or say if Jack has lost an arm or a leg or his sight or is horribly disfigured or—

All at once, there he was, standing in front of her, in uniform, looking very serious but apparently unharmed. In the hospital bed alongside was a man whose head was wrapped in a swathe of bandages that finished just above his eyebrows, his eyes vague and dreamy.

'I thought—' Maisie began.

'I'm sorry—' Jack started to answer.

'When you weren't at the railway station and Constable Donaldson didn't know anything, I worried that—'

'It was all a terrible rush, Maisie. You look lovely in blue, you know.'

'But you're all right?'

'I'm absolutely fine. Don't worry. It's Gary, here, who needs your sympathy. It's not too much to suggest that he might have saved my life.'

THREE

Maisie felt foolish and ashamed at her rush of anxiety and, simultaneously, unfairly resentful at the constable, PC Donaldson, for not knowing what was going on. Above all, she wanted to fold Jack in her arms and feel reassured by his presence.

'Thank you for whatever you've done,' she told the injured man. 'My name is Maisie Cooper.'

'Gary Naylor,' he replied in a vague voice that told Maisie he might be woozy from painkillers.

The nurse – who had followed Maisie – respectfully told them that they needed to clear the ward. 'Visiting hours are not till later and the doctor will be through on his rounds and he's a tartar for anyone unauthorised.'

Jack wished his colleague well and led Maisie back out, down the stairs and along the corridor. Arriving in reception, Maisie realised she had been so overwhelmed with relief that she had said nothing since leaving the ward.

'Let's sit down,' Jack said.

To one side of the lobby was a miserable tea shop. A few tables were occupied by two older couples and a young mother with three children under the age of ten. The mother was smoking Embassy cigarettes, the packet on the table in front of her, knocking the ash into an empty teacup, something Maisie hated.

'Are you definitely all right?' she heard herself repeat, foolishly.

'Absolutely.'

'Could we go outside? There must be a bench or something.'

Maisie reassured the reception nurse that she would shortly come back for her suitcase. At the foot of the front steps, they waited for an ambulance to go past then crossed the access road onto a stretch of lawn, drier and less well kept than the lush green park. There was no bench. Jack suggested that they simply sit and Maisie did so, tucking her legs sideways under her in her narrow blue skirt. He half lay on his side, propped on one elbow.

'What happened, Jack? I was so worried.'

'I know. I can see that. I'm so sorry. I couldn't think what else to do. It's very kind of you to come up and meet me. It seems a terrible waste of your time.'

'Never mind that,' she told him. 'You know I have more time than I know what to do with.'

'Up and back in two days, though.'

'Jack, please, tell me.'

'It happened on the pavement next door to the hostel. Some building materials fell from a platform on the scaffolding around the building site: a few lengths of timber, a coil of rope and a handful of heavy iron clamps. Gary pushed me out of the way and, in doing so, was struck himself. He got a nasty gash to his forehead – from one of the metal clamps, I think. And – you won't have seen this because it was under the covers – he's awaiting surgery to set some broken metatarsals where a length of timber landed end first on his foot.'

'How awful,' said Maisie.

'It made a terrible crack,' said Jack with a sympathetic smile for his colleague. 'I can still hear it. I radioed for an ambulance to take Gary to the hospital, getting them to drop me off at the city-centre station where I found a harassed sergeant dealing with an afternoon drunken brawl – three of them, kicking up the most dreadful fuss. Giving the sergeant the photograph of you that I always carry seemed the obvious thing to do and I told him to insist to you that I was unharmed but, I suppose, he wasn't paying attention.'

Maisie took the photo out of her handbag and gave it back to him, feeling a surge of affection as he replaced it tenderly in his wallet.

'The sergeant you spoke to,' she explained, 'sent someone else. The man who came to meet me was a constable.'

'Of course. That makes sense.'

'But how could it have happened. I had a dreadful . . .'

Maisie stopped, realising that she was embarrassed to tell Jack that she'd expected some kind of terrible drama. Jack didn't seem to notice her indecision and went on: 'Gary is another uniformed sergeant on the same programme as me, from Bristol. He's also staying at the hostel – a dreadful place, by the way. I've been jealous of you in your lovely room in Bunting Manor.'

A starling came hopping over towards them, perhaps thinking that they were picnicking on the grass, wondering if there might be crumbs. Jack reached out a hand, optimistic that the bird might perch on his fingers. Maisie looked at his profile. His face was unworried and quite relaxed. He turned back towards her.

'Now,' he said, 'I should kiss you.'

'Yes,' said Maisie, 'you should.'

He leaned forwards but with a little distance still between them.

'Have you missed me? I've missed you every day. I'm so glad you brought the whole wedding rigmarole forward. You are perfect in every way.'

'You're not so bad, yourself.'

They kissed at last and Maisie felt the knot of anxiety in her throat begin to untangle. Jack pulled away, but only to say: 'Once is not enough.'

He kissed her again and then shuffled closer so that he could hold her in his arms. Maisie felt warm and reassured. Her head on his shoulder and her eyes hidden from him, she felt a huge wave of gratitude to Gary Naylor, Jack's new friend, who had pushed him out of the way of a potentially terrible accident. Jack released the delightful pressure of his strong arms and sat back.

'You feel like home,' he told her.

'You've said that before. It's the most wonderful compliment.'

'Not a compliment. The truth.' Maisie dropped her gaze. As usual, Jack read her mind. 'I know what you're thinking, Maisie. You're wondering if there was more to it.'

'I am. Will you show me the place?'

'Of course. What else?'

'Just that we're so very happy, and I don't want anything to get in the way of that. Maybe it's irrational but I just want to look, to get a sense of what happened.'

He took hold of her hand and kissed her palm. It sent a tingle up her arm and deep inside her, too. 'What do you feel?' he asked.

'It's a kind of shadow – over us. Perhaps I'm making it up.'

'Of envy? Of resentment?'

Maisie shook her head. She didn't want to say it out loud, but she felt she had no alternative.

'Of vengeance. But that's ridiculous. I'm becoming paranoid. You think it's ridiculous, too, don't you?'

'I think, Maisie, that you've seen too much unkindness and violence in the last six months and it's made you extra vigilant.' He smiled. 'Like a superhero in a comic.'

'But don't they all have tragic home lives and pasts?'

'Yes, they do. But you're different,' he told her smiling.

'Because?'

'You've got me.'

30

FOUR

On her release from East Sutton Park, a women's open prison near Maidstone, Peggy Kemp had gone straight to the town centre, looking for a branch of her bank, Barclays. The one she had used before being locked up was in Selsey, eight or so miles south of Chichester, and looked like a converted country cottage – which it was. The Maidstone branch was much less homely, built in brick and stone and topped by multiple office floors where the arcane mysteries of finance were accomplished in sober privacy.

On entering, she had attracted attention because of the clothing returned to her by the prison authorities, in particular her scarves and shawls, which seemed incongruous on a late-summer day. The branch had been busy and she had been obliged to queue before being able to address a cashier.

'Good morning. I'm here to make a withdrawal.'

'Do you have your cheque book, madam?'

It had been in Peggy's hand, but covered by one of the drapes of her beaded shawl, the slip already filled out requesting a payment 'To cash'. The bank employee had processed the transaction and placed the money on the smooth counter. Peggy had collected up the notes with a sense of deep satisfaction – because money meant independence and freedom. There wasn't much of it, however.

From the bank, Peggy had gone to find herself lodgings for the night in a cheap bed and breakfast that smelt of boiled cabbage and Vigor cleaning fluid. The next day, she had made her way by several connecting trains from Kent to

Sussex, a torturous journey on slow and stopping services along the south coast. Arriving in Chichester, she had taken care not to be seen, walking out of town to pick up a Selsey bus, well away from the prying eyes of the officials at the police station.

In Selsey, she had found her home – a converted railway carriage close to the promenade and the sea – intact but dishevelled, the bunting round the door faded and torn, the timber porch crumbling. She had gone inside, brushing cobwebs out of her eyes, to sit in the dark and the damp – without electricity because the service had been cut off – thinking dark thoughts.

The next morning, Peggy had abandoned her fortune teller's costume, dressing more soberly, going out to find a salon where a garrulous hairdresser had cut her unkempt grey hair into a tidy bob, dyed a deep chestnut brown. Pleased with the transformation, she had sought out a collier for a delivery of coal for her stove. Back at home, she had lit it with all the windows open to drive out the damp.

Several days had passed with nothing much to differentiate them.

I need my boy.

Her 'boy' was a combustible young man in his twenties by the name of Ronan Kemp, still himself detained 'at Her Majesty's pleasure', as the saying went.

Never mind. I've waited years. I can wait a few more weeks.

More time had passed and, finally, the desire for action had become too urgent to be denied.

Perhaps I'll not wait for Ronan to be out?

A fluent and persuasive liar, Peggy had found it quite easy to discover the whereabouts of her target. In particular – dressed in her different clothes and barely recognisable with her different hair – an elderly sergeant she found on duty at the front desk of Chichester police station had been extremely sympathetic about her report of a peeping Tom and, with a little encouragement, was only too pleased to tell her about his 'good friend Sergeant Jack Wingard' and his 'remarkable fiancée Maisie Cooper'.

The knowledge of Jack Wingard's happiness had been the final straw, building the hot coal of resentment in Peggy's chest into a raging fire.

FIVE

Maisie recovered her suitcase from the hospital reception and Jack insisted on carrying it. He led her back outside and along the drive to a bus stop built of elderly creosote-stained timbers on the main road. Maisie felt suddenly weary from her long journey and from the unexpected drama – the anxiety bubbling up into fear, then evaporating into relief.

It was gone five o'clock and the traffic was heavier. They could see the bus that Jack said they wanted in the distance, but it was trapped beyond two sets of traffic lights and a platoon of merging cars. Because, she thought, he could sense her mood, Jack kept his conversation light, describing his superior officers and tutors, and the many fanciful policing scenarios that he had been obliged to evaluate and respond to on the theoretical part of his programme.

'It sounds like you've done incredibly well,' said Maisie. 'I'm not surprised.'

She went on to tell him – in person for the first time, not on the phone – the story of how St Mary's church in Framlington had become, unexpectedly, available and the way she had sidelined Reverend Millns. Jack shared her distaste for the character of the local priest and approved her actions.

'What's Canon Greig like?'

'A bit of a wet fish, if truth be told, but it has to be somebody and it's only a formal role after all. We don't necessarily need someone who knows us well.'

'Agreed. Did he have a role to play in the investigation into the murder at Sunny View?'

'A small one,' she began. 'But—'

Before she could complete her answer, the bus arrived with an imprudent surge of acceleration followed by a sudden stop. They climbed on board and, as luck would have it, found seats together, surrounded by people speaking in the characteristic – and very musical – local accent. The conductor approached and took their fares. Then Jack gave her a glance that meant: *Aren't their patterns of speech wonderful?*

In the seat in front, two middle-aged men in labouring overalls were sharing opinions on the sporting issues of the day. First, there was the 'unparalleled prowess' of the Newcastle United centre forward Malcolm Macdonald. Next came the miracle of the Brazilian racing driver, Emerson Fittipaldi, winning the Italian Grand Prix and, with it, becoming the youngest ever Formula One world champion.

'If you want proper world champs, though,' said the second man, dogmatically, 'there's that Bobby Fischer teaching the Russkies a thing or two in the chess.'

'Terrible hard game, chess,' his friend replied.

'Aye, it is, for those that don't understand it.'

At the stop by the railway station, the two sports fans got off. In fact, the bus half emptied, meaning two other conversations became audible. In the seat behind, a housewife carrying a wicker shopping basket was complaining about inflation.

'It's not just that you have to work out the prices in proper old money, but everything's on the up, and not in a good way. Soon we won't be able to afford baked beans and then where will we be? Petrol's seven shillings a gallon.'

Her friend, a big woman with horn-rimmed glasses, replied: 'And every pint my Alan drinks sets him back thirteen new pence, if you please.'

On the other side of the aisle was an earnest-looking student type, little more than a boy, with a first attempt at a moustache barely covering his top lip. Maisie thought perhaps he was an admirer of Che Guevara. He was analysing the recent upsurge in tension over fishing rights between the United Kingdom and Iceland, lecturing a wan-looking friend.

'The papers are right to call it the Second Cod War, but it's a war between classes, not nations, between the self-interest of the rich and the livelihoods of the poor. Take the Munich attack by Black September . . .'

The boy began elaborating an analogy – which Maisie found in extremely bad taste – between 'the struggles of working people, especially in the Third World', and the recent murders of eleven Israeli athletes at the 1972 Summer Olympics in Munich. Jack was on his feet and moving forward down the bus as it was time to get off, but Maisie couldn't help herself.

'Excuse me,' she said, politely.

'Yes, pet?' said the boy, looking her up and down.

'I overheard your conversation. I wasn't eavesdropping. You were speaking quite loud enough for everyone to hear. I just wanted to say . . .' She stopped, wondering what it was that she felt a sudden need to explain.

'Go on, then. Speak your mind, pet,' said the young man, more amused than offended.

'Just this. I've served in the army. In civilian life, too, I've seen death. Even though there's sometimes no alternative, it's always the worst of desperate answers. In the case you were referring to, there was no excuse. There's nothing violence can put right that talking and understanding and compromise can't do better. That's all. Good day to you.'

The boy's mouth gaped open as he sought a suitable reply. Maisie turned and joined Jack at the door at the front of the bus. Smiling, he told her: 'Well said, Maisie. I was on the point of butting in myself.'

36

'I feel like an idiot,' she murmured. 'Is he staring after me.'

'He is,' said Jack. 'But that's not unusual for my beautiful fiancée, is it?'

The bus came to a lurching halt and Maisie was pleased to get off. They were only a few blocks east of the railway station and the city centre, but the atmosphere in this new neighbourhood was almost suburban. They took a side street to Jack's hostel, a sprawling red-brick building that looked like a converted Victorian rectory or, perhaps, a school. Jack put her suitcase down in the doorway, then led her next door to a more modern structure, presumably in-fill replacing houses damaged or destroyed in Luftwaffe bombing raids in World War II.

As Jack had mentioned, it was clad in scaffolding and the upright tubular steel posts were set on blocks of wood to keep them level. Maisie thought it looked like the timber-clad façade needed to be rubbed down and repainted. There was no one at work because, she supposed, it was quite late in the day.

'This is where it happened,' said Jack. 'Look, there's even a crack in that slab.'

It was true. One of the pavement stones was broken with lines radiating out from a heavy impact in its centre.

'Where did it all fall from?' asked Maisie.

'You see up there?' said Jack. He pointed to a platform of planks at the level of the third floor, about twenty-five feet up, where a heap of equipment had been stacked, including ropes, paint pots, spare lengths of scaffolding, some of them extending slightly over the edge, some of them secured with heavy clamps. 'I think a rope must have become dislodged and, as it fell, dragged down some other bits and pieces.'

'Do you really think a rope could have overtoppled a length of timber, heavy enough to break your poor friend's foot?'

'It was the fact that it landed end first, not because it was heavy. Gary was just unlucky.'

'Perhaps,' said Maisie. 'I'm going to have a look.'

Before he could argue, she gave him her handbag to hold and shinned up a narrow wooden ladder, set at a steep angle and tied in to the scaffolding with more rope. Normally, she would have found it easy but she was impeded by the narrow skirt of her posh blue suit.

'You're unique, Maisie,' Jack called after her.

'I'll take that as a compliment,' she called back, arriving at the level of the platform. 'Is this what it looked like earlier on today?'

'More or less, I think.'

Maisie scanned the assorted decorator's and builder's paraphernalia, not certain what she was looking for.

Evidence of evil intent, I suppose. Is it the stress of the wedding that's making me worry like this?

Contrary to Jack's suggested scenario, everything was positioned very tidily and nothing looked easy to dislodge. The heavy clamps were linked into one another and half tightened, making them almost impossible to move.

Maisie climbed back down, frowning, wondering what to think. Jack, she knew, would be keen to assuage her anxiety, but . . .

I refuse to be an ostrich and stick my head in the sand. It's always better to face the truth. If there's a threat to us and to our wedding, I'd rather go out and meet it.

Six

Back on the pavement, Maisie brushed some dust from her skirt and retook possession of her handbag. On the opposite side of the residential street, a woman in curlers, only partly hidden by her headscarf, was watching them with undisguised interest from behind a tightly clipped privet hedge.

'Good afternoon,' called Maisie. 'Could we have a word?'

The neighbour didn't refuse, so Maisie crossed the road, half aware of an amused expression on Jack's face. He joined her by the neighbour's gate.

'Get a good view from up there, did you?' asked the woman.

Maisie smiled her brightest smile. 'I wonder, have you been watching the workmen going about their business at all?'

'No, I haven't.'

'Oh, that's a shame. I thought you were perhaps a noticing sort of person. It often pays to know what's happening on one's front step, don't you think?' Maisie felt a little queasy, trying to butter the woman up, but it seemed to work.

'I've been out here in the garden, pruning, as you can see.'

'You've done a wonderful job on that privet,' said Jack.

It was true. The top of the hedge was clipped almost as smooth and flat as a table.

'My old pa planted it and I'll not let his memory down.'

'Excuse me,' said Maisie, 'but why did you say you haven't been watching the workmen, I mean, if you've been out here for some time?'

39

'Because there hasn't been none. Them scaffolders came yesterday, and don't tell me I'm wrong, because I remember because it was Thursday and that's my pension and today's Friday because we had fish.'

'We wouldn't dream of arguing,' said Jack, looking amused.

'Please, go on,' said Maisie.

'I'm telling you, aren't I. The scaffold went up Thursday and the decorators came this morning with their things and we had a word and I made them a cup of tea because one of them sits near our George, meaning my brother, in the Gallowgate End.'

'That's the football ground, St James' Park,' said Jack for Maisie's benefit. 'You probably saw the floodlights as you crossed the river on the train.'

'I did, yes,' said Maisie. Then she added to the neighbour: 'So, you kindly made them tea and then they left without starting work? Was there a problem?'

'They only dropped off their stuff because they'd finished their previous job early. This one was always set for Monday.'

'I see,' said Maisie. 'That makes sense. Did no one at all go up there afterwards, once the decorators had brought in their equipment, drunk their tea and left?'

'I didn't say that, did I?' asked the neighbour.

'No, you didn't,' said Maisie, patiently.

'There was you for a start.'

'Yes, I see that. But you're suggesting that someone else shinned up there, earlier on, like me?'

'Well, I assume they must have done, because I saw them come down.'

Maisie left a pause. She didn't think the neighbour was being wilfully obstructive, just enjoying herself at their expense.

'I would be grateful, madam,' said Jack, changing his tone to something much more formal, straightening his dark-blue jacket, 'if you would put your thoughts in order. It might be more important than you imagine.'

The neighbour seemed to take Jack's status into account for the first time, looking at his broad shoulders, handsome face and well-kept uniform. Maisie noticed there was a blemish in the woollen fabric on his shoulder.

'Not local, are you, either of you,' the neighbour told him.

'No, madam. I'm from Sussex but I'm working with the very best metropolitan police force in the country here in Newcastle and I'm learning a great deal.'

'I see,' she said, apparently mollified. 'They do say our boys are not too bad.'

'Please share what you saw,' he insisted in the same formal tone.

'Here it is, then. I had my washing to put out so I broke off from the garden and the clippers and the hedge to get things on the line while there was still some sun. I heard the commotion of the police siren – or it might have been an ambulance. I didn't see because I couldn't leave my sheets trailing on the ground. By the time I got back around here, there was no vehicle in the street but just the sound of an engine pulling away round the corner.'

'And?' asked Maisie, deploying her bright smile once more.

'Someone was just hopping down off the bottom rungs of the ladder and they skipped away sharpish.'

'You mean they ran? As if they didn't want to be seen?'

'Like a rat down a drainpipe, he was.'

'Definitely a man?'

The neighbour put her head on one side and pondered aloud: 'I suppose I assumed. You would, wouldn't you?'

'Could you describe this person?' asked Jack.

'I could, but I'd be making it up because I'm short-sighted like a mole and that's God's truth.'

41

Maisie asked a few more questions but there was nothing else to learn. She and Jack returned to the hostel, taking her suitcase inside. Jack showed Maisie the grey coin-fed telephone on the wall from which he had called her every third evening or so. The hallway smelt of cabbage and unwashed feet.

'Stay here,' he told her. 'I'll just run up for my bags.'

He took the stairs two at a time. Masie contemplated the peeling wallpaper with its depressing pattern of drab, green-brown leaves. The white paint on the architraves around the closed doors – leading to unknown ground-floor rooms – was chipped and yellowing. From the grubby plaster ceiling rose above her head, a braided cable ended in a bare light bulb.

Unhappy indoors, she stepped back outside. The front garden was only a couple of paces deep, shared between small stone slabs and flourishing weeds, ending in a low brick wall. The early evening air had begun to feel fresher or, perhaps, damper with falling dew. An Austin Seven car went past, looking very old-fashioned, like a little black lorry, almost a relic of another age.

Jack came out to join her, carrying his own suitcase and hers in his two hands, plus a khaki kitbag over one shoulder.

'The trouble with wearing a uniform for your job of work is having to lug around several changes of clothes in order to keep up appearances. Shall we go?'

'Where to?' asked Maisie. 'I'm sorry, I feel I've sort of steamrollered everything since I got here. I haven't asked what your plan might be?'

'Back on the bus into the centre of town. There's a lovely hotel I've booked next door to the Theatre Royal.'

'Oh, dear,' said Maisie. 'That sounds extravagant.'

'Not at all. I did the manager a good turn a couple of weeks ago with a bit of a disturbance and he's promised me his finest accommodation at bog-standard prices.'

'How lovely.'

Maisie obliged him to let her carry her own case and they set off, seeing the bus coming and running the last twenty paces so as not to miss their ride. Once on board, Maisie realised there was something she ought to have asked. She did so, uncertain what she hoped his reply might be.

'Did the grateful hotel manager offer you one splendid room or two?'

SEVEN

Maisie wasn't a prude but she thought that she was – on balance – pleased to discover that Jack had booked two rooms at the hotel. He explained: 'I suppose it was the idea that we're getting married in a week and a day. I told myself: "That shouldn't be too long to wait." What do you think?'

'Agreed,' said Maisie, but not without a pang of doubt. 'I suppose.'

He frowned and asked: 'Have I done the wrong thing?'

'No, the right thing. It's just that the two months we've been physically apart have been unexpectedly difficult.'

'Because of the distance or was it the drama of the murder down there in Devon?'

'I would rather be with you and getting on with life. I actually found myself so much at a loose end that I went up to London for two days to visit some galleries and see a Wednesday and a Thursday matinée. Then I came on north.'

'That's a coincidence. I've made plans of a similar sort for our evening. On the question of rooms, it's probably best not to offend the provincial morals of this puritanical city.'

'Agreed,' said Maisie again, still distracted by the enticing idea of the alternative. 'I'm sure that's right.'

'I don't make a habit of inviting lady friends to provincial hotels.'

Maisie laughed and asked: 'Do you ever think about the fact that we know very little about one another, about our separate lives – the ones we've both lived since going our separate ways from school, you in the Chichester police and me away in the army and the West Country and then Paris? Since I've been back, we've been so caught up in bigger events. I've never even asked if you've been engaged before.'

To her surprise, he looked momentarily shocked as if he had been caught out. Then he said, firmly: 'I haven't, because there was only ever you.'

They were back in the heart of the city, getting off the bus at the railway station to walk uphill, away from the River Tyne. Maisie carried her small grip and Jack his larger suitcase and kitbag as they made their way to Grey Street where Maisie was impressed by an imposing row of columns in front of the Theatre Royal, set on square pediments almost as tall as she was.

This colonnade is much more appropriate than the one at the railway station.

They turned right onto the short but aptly named Shakespeare Street, finding their hotel, the Northumberland, in the middle on the right, effectively a continuation of the theatre's grandiose architecture from a period when the city must have been awash with cash from industrial prosperity. They met the manager, a dapper man in a dark-blue blazer who seemed to Maisie a higher-class version of his counterpart, Mr Hume, at the Dolphin & Anchor Hotel in Chichester. He greeted Jack as an old friend and showed them personally to the first floor where a palatial landing overlooked the lobby. The doors to their adjacent rooms were right there. He gave them their keys and they each went inside.

Maisie was delighted. Her room had tall picture windows that opened onto the quiet road, a pair of twin beds covered with chintz counterpanes, a rather chichi desk with delicate curved legs, a masculine leather armchair and a fireplace that had been bricked in and fitted with an electric bar heater.

She hung her few clothes in the wardrobe and went next door. Jack didn't hear her open it because he had flung his windows wide and a truck was going by. He was in the process of changing into a lounge suit in a pleasant pale grey, suitable for a summer evening. He had done up his trousers but hadn't yet put on a shirt. Maisie noted a dark bruise on his left shoulder.

'So, you were struck by the falling—'

'Good heavens,' he blurted, turning to face her. 'You did give me a shock.'

'I noticed the blemish on your uniform but I didn't make the connection. What else have you been hiding from me?' she asked.

'It was nothing. I barely felt it. But it has come up impressively, hasn't it?'

Maisie approached and put a hand on the darkened flesh. 'It didn't break the skin.'

'It was the length of timber. It hit me falling horizontally then spun into the vertical, if you see what I mean, to break poor Gary Naylor's foot.'

Maisie found she wasn't very interested in the precise order of events any longer. She put her spare arm round Jack's back and pulled him closer till her face was in his neck, her mouth just below his ear.

'I do love you, Jack Wingard,' she said, her voice a whisper.

'You are everything to me,' he replied, equally quietly.

They stayed there for a minute or so, not speaking. Maisie wondered what she would say if Jack changed his mind about sharing one of the two rooms. Through the open window, she heard someone singing a folk song as they walked by below, on the pavement of Shakespeare Street, a man with a pleasant tenor voice, perhaps an actor heading for his dressing room to prepare for curtain up at eight o'clock at the Theatre Royal.

One minute became two and Maisie realised that this closeness was exactly what she needed. There was a lingering niggle in the back of her mind, though, something about propriety and marriage. She forced herself to make a small move to pull away, but he told her: 'Just a moment more.'

Suddenly, her mind was made up.

'More than a moment,' she replied.

★

Sometime later, Maisie was in Jack's bathroom, washing and dressing. She felt strong and sleek.

We are so very lucky.

Emerging, she found Jack eating a sandwich provided by room service. There was one for her, too – ham with mustard and an enormous thick smear of excellent creamy butter.

'Eat up. I didn't know what you'd want to do this evening so, as I hinted, I booked theatre tickets. It's only next door – a touring show. I hope it's all right.'

'I'm sure it will be.'

Maisie wolfed her sandwich while Jack, who had finished his, told her: 'I know what you're thinking. We've discovered that there was a mysterious person, call him or her Mr X, who ran from the scene of the accident or crime. I wish that neighbour wasn't so short-sighted. But perhaps someone else might have seen? If I wasn't expected at the station back in Chichester, I might consider staying on tomorrow and going door-to-door. Oh, I wonder if we could ask that constable, the one who came to meet you. Was it Donaldson?'

'You have an excellent memory,' said Maisie, swallowing her last morsel. 'But I'm afraid I was so worried that I snubbed him when we arrived at the hospital.'

'No one bears a grudge against you, Maisie. You're far too lovely.'

He reached out and touched her cheek, then ran a fingertip along her lower lip.

47

'Are you thinking you'd rather stay in?' she asked, quietly, thinking that wouldn't be such a bad idea.

'No,' he said, standing. 'Let's get ahead of married life and go out to the theatre with the great and the good.'

Maisie got up, too, and insisted on carrying the room service tray down to reception where the manager greeted them enthusiastically for a second time and told them they ought to hurry.

'I think I heard the five-minute bell.'

Luckily, the play was a few minutes late 'going up' – as Maisie knew the correct theatrical expression to be from her time investigating the murder at the theatre – because of the late arrival of a coach party. That gave her time to peruse the programme, learning that the Theatre Royal had several times been a victim of fire, explained by the dangers of illumination by limelight, jets of burning gas focused on lumps of chalky rock, producing a bright white luminescence.

The rebuilt auditorium was magnificent – 'Italianate' was the word used – designed by a man called Matcham who Maisie thought she had heard of. The play was called *The Secretary Bird*, but Maisie refrained from reading anything about it so as not to spoil the suspense of the story.

As it turned out, she needn't have bothered to take such precautions. It was a generic 'sex comedy', a kind of farce with dropped trousers and multiple moments of toe-curling comic embarrassment about a married man who, worried that his wife was having an affair, tries to make her jealous by embarking on his own adventure with his secretary.

In the interval, Maisie was interested to read that the first actor to have made a success of the part was Kenneth More, an actor Maisie admired. Noël Coward saw him and compared More's performance to the one he might have given himself. This made Maisie smile at Coward's – almost certainly justified – arrogance.

The play was well received by the audience – in particular by the delighted coach party. Maisie and Jack clapped politely and were glad to step out into the street for a walk through the city before returning to the Northumberland.

'The police station's just along here. I'm going to pop in.'

'To see if Donaldson's there?'

'He might well be. It's not yet ten and you say he came on about four.'

Jack strode inside and Maisie heard his lovely warm voice greeting a colleague. She stayed on the pavement, watching the busy city: two buses, several taxis and half a dozen private cars; a gaggle of young women in skimpy minidresses, laughing and clinging to one another, perhaps for support because they'd been drinking, or perhaps with simple affection.

Jack came back out with Donaldson and Maisie apologised, concluding: 'I was in a rush to find out what had happened, but there was no call for it.'

'All in a day's work,' mumbled Donaldson, looking dazzled by her earnestness and charm.

'PC Donaldson has agreed, very kindly,' said Jack, 'to ask around the neighbourhood.'

'The Toon aren't playing at home,' said the constable. 'Perhaps people will be in. I'll do the south side of the street in the morning and, if I need to, go back in the afternoon for the north side. People don't like to be disturbed while they're eating.'

'Excellent, Donaldson,' said Jack, warmly. 'You've already grasped one of the fundamentals of investigative work. You can only collect information from those willing to share it.'

Maisie was touched to see Donaldson's raw cheeks blush with Jack's keen praise.

'Tomorrow evening, Sergeant, will you call me at the station, when I come in again for the late shift?'

'Assuming our trains run on time and we make our connections back to Sussex, yes. Thank you, Constable.'

Maisie and Jack did another circuit of the town centre, ending up down by the river.

'The Tyne reminds you that Newcastle is an industrial city,' she told him. 'It's not at all romantic by the water, is it.'

'Anywhere with you is romantic.'

He took her hand and she felt that he was about to kiss her but a gaggle of young men – perhaps in search of the gaggle of young women Maisie had seen outside the police station – went past, calling out indistinctly and wolf-whistling.

'Thank heavens you're no longer in uniform,' said Maisie. 'That might have got you a black mark. When will you find out if you've passed?'

'It's not just whether I've done well. It's also about whether there's a job for me anywhere. They won't promote me if there isn't a post I can go and occupy.'

That was something that Maisie had been worrying about ever since Jack had embarked on the 'plain-clothes pathway'.

'So, you might be posted more or less anywhere and—?'

He completed her thought.

'Anywhere there's work to be done and a gap to fill. And, of course, I'm worried about Grandma. I know she says she can cope on her own, but you remember she had that hospital visit while you were being brilliant over the Festival Theatre business.'

'Yes,' said Maisie. 'That was very worrying.'

They completed their post-theatre amble, talking through the things they had liked about the show. Maisie found it had grown on her, in memory, despite the clichéd presentation of the female characters.

Back at the hotel, they found the lobby of the Northumberland crowded with a retirement event. One of the older men in attendance greeted Jack by name and Maisie soon worked out that he must be a senior officer in the local police force. Jack introduced her as his fiancée, making her glad that she had chosen her prim powder-blue suit in order to make a good impression, rather than something more casual.

The conversation was lively and they were drawn into a polite circuit of the room, from which Maisie deduced that Jack was much appreciated by every one of his – self-important, if truth were told – senior officers, and by their smiling and very attentive wives.

The circuit complete, pleading an early start, they climbed the stairs together, separating demurely on the landing because they were in full view of the perhaps puritanical Geordie 'great and good' below.

EIGHT

Breakfast the next morning in the Northumberland was a sumptuous affair. They both packed their bags to leave in reception, already checked out, while they drank coffee and ate their sausages, black pudding, bacon, scrambled eggs, grilled tomatoes and thick white toast. Jack was wearing his lightweight grey suit and Maisie had chosen one of her favourite dresses, white with polka dots and a narrow waist, glad to have shed her prim woollen jacket and skirt.

The manager came over as they were finishing and – clearly considering his debt to Jack not fully repaid – told them he had a taxi waiting, 'on the house', for the short hop down the hill to the railway station. They accepted his kind offer and that meant, on arrival, that Maisie had time for a quick browse of the bookshelves in the W H Smith & Son on the concourse.

Maisie was pleased to discover a section devoted to her favourite mystery writer, the New Zealander Ngaio Marsh. There was a paperback copy of one of Marsh's novels that Maisie hadn't read because it had only come out a couple of years before. It was called *When in Rome* and, from reading the blurb, she was glad to see that – despite its foreign setting – it featured Marsh's punctiliously polite but ruthlessly perceptive hero, Chief Inspector Roderick Alleyn.

Maisie and Jack walked the length of the platform to find an empty compartment at the front of the train, not expecting to occupy it alone for the entire journey, but pleased to begin the long trip unflustered by the conversations of strangers. They sat opposite one another so both could enjoy the view from the window. The train pulled gently out, giving Maisie the queasy sensation that the world was slipping away outside the windows. Then, they picked up speed and crossed the impressive arched iron bridge over the Tyne.

Jack had some paperwork to study, sent to him at the hostel by post from his friend and best man, Inspector Fred Nairn. Maisie opened her book and was immediately engaged by the story of a British author called Barnaby Grant whose briefcase – containing the sole typescript of his most recent novel – had been stolen. Maisie became so absorbed that, for a second time, she missed Chester-Le-Street, only looking up as they pulled in at Durham.

A tea trolley came by but neither of them wanted anything. Once the tea lady had gone, Maisie realised that there was an expression of disquiet on Jack's handsome features. She asked: 'What's the matter?'

Without a word, he folded one of the sheets of paper and put it in the inside pocket of his jacket. Then he passed her a second sheet, a one-page summary of some recent events, clumsily typed with several mistakes and corrections. For a minute or so, she read in silence.

'It's from Fred, as you can see,' Jack told her. 'He thought I should be aware.'

'Yes,' she said, the knot of anxiety tightening once more in her throat. 'I begin to see.'

The news related to several wrongdoers, three recently released and one about to regain his freedom, who might conceivably bear Jack ill will. Maisie wanted to know more but, unfortunately, just then, their train got a lot busier and Jack had to put his confidential papers away.

The train pulled out and there were still people roaming the corridors, looking for spare seats. Through the internal window, Maisie saw a harassed man with a lush moustache, wearing a cricket blazer and cap, peer in to their six-person compartment. He mouthed an expression of relief – she thought it was 'Thank heavens for that' – and called over his shoulder for his companions. Politely, Jack stood up and slid open the door.

'Thank you,' the cricketer said. 'That's a relief. I thought we'd be standing all the way to London.'

'Glad to help.'

The man's companions arrived, three small boys in shorts and blazers, shirts and ties, carrying cricket bags that he lifted into the luggage racks. The man's blazer was plain beige, but the boys' jackets had blue and pink stripes. The boys were very quiet until the man – who Maisie assumed to be their schoolmaster and coach – told them: 'You are at liberty to chat but, if you disturb me, you are disturbing others, too.'

The three boys replied in unison using a Latin phrase: '*Magister dixit.*'

Hearing it gave Maisie a flashback to her own experience of attending a minor public school where relations with the staff were peppered with old-fashioned phrases. This one meant: 'The master has spoken.' It was an acknowledgement of intellectual authority, from the life of Aristotle.

Maisie exchanged a smile with Jack and recognised that he, too, had been struck by the phrase from their shared teenage years. They hadn't often been in the same class-room, the girls and boys being strenuously kept apart until they were cast together as sixth-formers in the school play, *The Beggar's Opera*. Jack had attended Westbrook College as a scholarship boy whereas Maisie's parents had scrimped and saved to send her and Stephen there. Some of the less well-brought-up children of wealthier parents had contemp-tuously referred to Jack as 'Charity Wingard'.

The master sat by the internal corridor window and pulled his cap down over his eyes to rest, with one of the boys between him and Maisie. The other two young cricketers sat next to Jack, meaning all six seats were now taken, to the disappointment of several more fleeting faces of passengers who had walked the length of the train in the hope of finding somewhere to land. Maisie was frustrated that she and Jack would no longer be able to converse openly but, to her surprise, she found the youngsters' reading matter surprisingly entertaining.

The boy next to her had a copy of *Look and Learn*, a sort of semi-educational comic that she had seen before but never read, with excellent artwork illustrating its stories. The front cover trailed an exciting drama from something called the 'Trigan Empire' which, when he opened it to read, his right forefinger following the words across the page, Maisie saw to be a combination of science fiction and the customs of ancient Greece and Rome, with antigravity vehicles and energy-ray weapons, plus worship of a 'golden lotus' that apparently had magical – or perhaps supra-scientific – powers.

The train rattled south. The boy read the story with intense focus, then swapped his issue of the magazine with the boy opposite so Maisie was able to surreptitiously learn, from the next episode, that the 'golden lotus' was a new apparition in the 'Trigan Empire' whose strong and heroic leader – drawn to resemble Jack, as it happened – believed it to be some kind of 'Trojan horse' and a 'major new threat'.

When the boy got to the end of the story he sighed and there was a brief conversation with the other two about when they would be able to get their hands on the next issue.

'That boy in the third form, Unwin Major, already has it. Perhaps we can do swapsies.'

'He never trades.'

'Do you have any pocket money left? It must be on sale in London.'

'*Magister*, can we go to a newsagent when we arrive?'

'Yes, and be quiet,' said the master, his eyes still concealed beneath his cap.

Maisie's neighbour turned to another *Look and Learn* story about a schoolboy called Rob Riley from the fictional town of Westhaven-on-Sea – somewhere in Devon or Cornwall – who seemed to be well on the way to becoming a private detective. Maisie smiled to herself, reflecting on the parallel with her own experience of contributing to the solutions of five mysteries.

There wasn't much to the Rob Riley story, so she looked away at the landscape, rushing past in glorious autumn sunshine. In her imagination, she pictured herself telling someone who knew nothing about Church Lodge or Bunting or Bitling or the Festival Theatre or Sunny View about all that she had seen and done. She pictured her flatmate, Sophie, in their top-floor apartment, under the eaves of their lovely Dutch-style building on the Place des Vosges, her eyes widening with surprise and shock at the sequence of events.

Oddly, though, it all seems very reasonable to me, in the sense that, at every step, there was always a good reason for me to be there, where I was, at the heart of the mystery, with a sound justification for being involved. I never went and sought any of them out.

The story about Rob Riley didn't hold the boy's attention any more than it held Maisie's. He put the magazine away and suggested to his friends that they play cards, bringing out a 'Happy Families' pack. The three of them crouched on the floor between the seats, their bare knees on linoleum dirtied by the ash from the previous occupants' cigarettes. Their conversation became boisterous with the competition and, without emerging from beneath the peak of his cap, the master told them: 'Moderate your excitement, microbes.'

Maisie saw that Jack had put away his papers and was watching the Midlands landscape evolving beyond the poorly washed window glass.

'Jack, I'm going to have a wander up and down the train. If I meet the trolley again, do you want anything?'

'No, thank you. Shall I come with you?'

'You look tired.'

'I was on lates all this week.'

'In that case, you stay there.'

The three boys shrank back to let her past. She slid the door open, then let it close on internal springs. In the corridor, she felt the train's side-to-side lurch much more strongly, traversing a set of points. She made her way to the end of the carriage with a rolling gait, like a sailor on board a ship, then opened a heavy door that gave access to a connecting platform. She was able to see the rails rushing past through gaps between the footplates and the concertina walls. A particularly abrupt jolt of the tracks threw her against the frame, banging the point of her left shoulder, reminding her of Jack's bruise.

We ought to be talking about all that right now.

She realised that she wished they had somehow been able to get married sooner, that she had been able to travel north to be with him, as his wife, protecting him from danger.

I should never have let him go alone.

She dismissed the thought.

I'm not sure he could be any safer than he is right now, at the very end of the train and surrounded by the cricket party.

No sooner had that idea crystalised in her mind than she wanted to touch wood or shake little fingers with someone, to dispel the 'jinx'.

NINE

Maisie pushed open the door from the noisy connecting platform into the next carriage, lurching left and right with the swinging of the train, looking into a series of six-place compartments in which every seat was taken. In a couple of them, children in over-formal uniforms had been obliged to share spaces with one another, squeezed together on the dusty cushions. Maisie wondered if, perhaps, this weekend in September was the start of term and they were on their way back to their London boarding schools from the provinces.

It felt good to be on her feet, especially after her copious breakfast that she hadn't been able to 'walk off', due to the manager of the Northumberland kindly organising them a taxi to the station. She pressed on past some first-class compartments that didn't look so very different, except for the bright-white British Rail antimacassars on the headrests of the seats.

She crossed another rattling, swivelling, intimidating connecting platform and found herself in a dining car. As luck would have it, a young couple – with an air of being newly in love – got up from their table just as Maisie came by. She stood and waited as the waiter cleared their plates and wiped down the surface with a wet rag, leaving some damp, unhygienic smears.

Maisie ordered coffee, asking if there might be brown sugar – there wasn't – and sat down. The ride seemed smoother than it had been while she was on her feet, but the waiter still split her coffee in the saucer beneath her cup. She asked him for a paper serviette and placed it underneath to soak it up. The coffee was lukewarm and not, actually, very coffee-like, reminding her of a story she had read. In her memory, she thought it concerned the writer W Somerset Maugham who, on a cruise ship or a transatlantic liner, called out something like: 'Purser, if this is tea, bring me coffee. If, on the other hand, this is coffee, bring me tea.'

She drank, all the same, then began to regret doing so, imagining the appalling train toilets that she would prefer not to have to use. Then, to her surprise, further down the dining car, she saw a face she recognised – one of the two salesmen with whom she had shared a compartment on the way up to Newcastle the previous day. It wasn't the little man that she had helped with the heavy holdall of Target Insurance pamphlets. It was the other one, taller, with a narrow unshaven face and – she now realised – a very penetrating expression in his eyes. He wasn't exactly looking at her. She thought his focus was the door between compartments, over her left shoulder, but she also suspected that he was examining her at the same time in peripheral vision.

To disguise her sudden interest, Maisie sipped her coffee, thinking back.

Why did I assume he was a travelling salesman? He didn't have any bags of samples or anything like that, just his own small PVC holdall with the British Overseas Airways Corporation logo on the side, enough for an overnight trip but not much more.

The waiter wandered up the aisle, obscuring her view.

I think it was simply by extension from the little man who sold insurance.

The waiter asked if she would like a refill.

'No, thank you. Where are we, by the way? I've lost track.'

'Just coming in to Peterborough.'

'How long till King's Cross?'

'Fifty minutes. We're fast, now.'

59

'No more stops? This is an excellent service.'

'We do our best,' he said.

Maisie realised that she hadn't paid and found him the appropriate decimal coins from the purse in her handbag. He put them in a pouch on his belt and moved away, revealing to Maisie that the 'second salesman' was gone.

She got up and walked the length of the dining car, glancing left and right to see if he had changed position. She pulled the door open on the next connecting platform with its gusting outdoor air, just as the train began decelerating. She pushed open the heavy door into the next carriage, a simultaneous change in momentum making her stagger forward, allowing it to slam shut behind her. It took her a few moments to regain her balance. Then, through the side window, she saw that her quarry had jumped down onto the Peterborough platform and was walking quickly away from her, up the line.

She felt a desperate need to get down herself to see where he might go, but the corridor was blocked by a family of five clumsily trying to organise their heap of miscellaneous luggage – suitcases and rucksacks and a wooden travel chest – heaving it all on board. Not twenty seconds later she heard a whistle and realised there would be no protracted halt before they were once again on their way.

Reluctantly, Maisie returned to the front of the train, wondering what it was that had unnerved her in seeing the 'second salesman' again.

It's the idea of going up to Newcastle from London in a single day, only to return on the next morning's train. Doing so seems normal to me because I hadn't seen Jack for so long and I've been missing him so terribly. Thinking logically, though, why would anyone else make such a long trip for so short a time?

Maisie hesitated outside her and Jack's compartment. The schoolboys had left off playing Happy Families and were reading what looked like Latin primers, their *magister* asking them questions. Jack's eyes were not quite closed and he remained upright in his seat, his face angled slightly away from her, watching the suburbs of Peterborough slide away from the accelerating train.

He got off, though, the 'second salesman'. It's just a coincidence. Maisie frowned.

Yes, he got off, but who's to say he didn't do that because he noticed me noticing him. And I knew his face because he was on the up train with me all the way from London. So why would he get off at Peterborough on the way down? But I can't be sure he didn't run down the platform and get back on again. When we arrive at King's Cross, I'll have to keep an eye out.

Maisie tried to quell her anxiety by gazing on the countryside outside the corridor windows. Because it was now around lunchtime, she saw – as Philip Larkin had done in the trip that provided the inspiration for 'The Whitsun Weddings' – dozens of somnolent cows and two separate village-green cricket matches.

The trouble is, that makes three things. First, there's the apparent accident that, had it not been for Gary Naylor, might have been much more significant. Second, there's the mysterious Mr or Mrs X seen running away from the scene by the short-sighted neighbour. Third, there's this sharp-eyed, narrow-faced man, the 'second salesman', who might or might not be following me.

She turned and saw that Jack was watching her through the glazed portion of the sliding internal door of the compartment. She smiled at him but his face was serious – almost grave.

Where have you been? he mouthed.

'Sorry,' she told him, knowing he wouldn't be able to hear, but shaping the sounds carefully so he could read her lips.

Then came the inescapable thought: *I'm worried and he's worried, too. That can't be good.*

61

TEN

Though it was Saturday, work continued on the Petter Farm, near Selsey, eight or so miles south of Chichester. For Mick and Jez Carter – whose poor life decisions had left them with no other options – it was an endless series of back-breaking tasks, the worst of which was gleaning the potatoes left behind by the mechanical harvester, bending and straightening, lugging the sacks to the ends of the rows, standing still for a moment to ease their aching muscles, thinking about a lifetime of rash mistakes.

Mick and Jez had woken with the sun that morning in their stuffy, rickety caravan, little more than an aluminium can perched on the edge of the fast-running stream – the rife – that ran along the potato field towards the foreshore and the sea. They each knew that, in theory, they ought to be grateful. The fact that they had found gainful employment with accommodation thrown in – however rudimentary – was almost a miracle.

On their release from prison, they had been shown the advertisement in the *Chichester Observer*, seeking 'seasonal farm labour', by their probation officer who made a note for them of the address and a phone number. To save money, they had walked south along the canal and then the edges of the fields to the outskirts of Selsey, finding the rutted drive to the impressive Petter Farm with ease because it was the biggest and most prosperous round about. Walking up between the pick-your-own field on the left and a couple of dozen rows of flourishing and well-tended roses on the right, Mick had remarked: 'This'll do.'

'It might,' Jez had replied.

Interviewed in the farm kitchen, kindly given tea and garibaldi biscuits, they had met George Petter, a straight-talking man in his fifties, dressed in tweed trousers held up by braces over a flannel shirt, and muddy wellingtons.

'This is my business. It's been in my family for three generations, starting small and growing to become an important employer. People say the first generation makes the money, the second one saves it and the third one spends it. Not us. With money comes responsibility. I know what you did and why you've got no references. I'm prepared to give you both a chance but I'll not stand for any nonsense. Do you understand me?'

'Yes, Mr Petter,' they had both replied in the voices they had been in the habit of using when, occasionally, they were spoken to by the governor of Ford Open Prison.

At that moment, George's daughter Liz Petter had come in with a basket of roses, looking strong and healthy, dressed becomingly in jeans and a man's white T-shirt.

'What's this then?' she asked.

'These here are Michael and Jeremy Carter,' her father told her. 'They've been inside and we're giving them a chance to get themselves back on the right path. They'll be sleeping in the caravan down on the potato field because they've nowhere else. You'll need to direct them and keep them busy.'

'Yes, Father.'

That had been ten days before. Since then, they hadn't met George Petter a second time to speak to, but they had learned from his daughter that he was chair of the Rotary Club and was involved in several other local charities. They had seen Liz every day and judged her 'fair and fair of face'. On this particular Saturday, she had told them that they could 'come in for their money at lunchtime', having completed the five and a half days of their working week.

Next to their caravan was a plastic bowser of water, warmed by the sun, that they used for washing. With their hair wet and their clothes brushed, they crossed the field to the farmhouse to pick up their wages. Then they walked three-quarters of a mile into Selsey to the 'turf accountant', the betting shop on the high street, perching themselves on stools to consult the *Racing Post* and the dedicated pages in the *Daily Mirror*, listening to radio reports from several alternating meetings.

By teatime, Mick had lost a third of his week's wages and Jez about half. They came out, spent some of what remained on bread, cheese and cheap bottled cider, and walked back along the deep-running rife, talking about the old days when they'd had a thriving business and life wasn't an endless drudge.

'Whose fault's that?' asked Mick, rhetorically.

'Jack-bloody-Wingard,' replied Jez, unnecessarily. 'That's who.'

ELEVEN

Maisie slipped back into the compartment and retook her window seat opposite her fiancé. Despite their copious breakfast, she and Jack agreed that they would both soon be hungry.

'It's travel,' she said. 'It was just the same when I took the train down to Sunny View. I ate the sandwiches Florence made me before I was halfway there.'

They were still unable to talk openly because of the schoolmaster and his three small charges. The cricket bags had all been wrestled down from the luggage racks and the master was delivering a pre-arrival lecture.

'It can be dangerous on the underground trains, what people call the Tube. There are lots of twists and turns in the tunnels and it's easy to get lost. If there are delays, the platforms can become very crowded, especially for microbes like you three. Stay close to me at all times and no talking while we find our way.'

'*Magister dixit*,' they all replied, unenthusiastically. Then one added: 'I looked at a map of London. Could we walk? It doesn't look far.'

'What was the scale on your map?' replied the master, dismissively.

Maisie had learned from their conversation that they were going to Lord's Cricket Ground in St John's Wood. She told the boy: 'It's a very easy journey, changing at Baker Street, and the roads aren't that nice for walking, anyway.'

'Thank you,' said the master. 'What do you say, boys?'

'Thank you, miss,' they chorused.

Because the school party was closer to the door, Maisie and Jack let them go first as the train came to a halt. Maisie stayed by the window, looking out for the 'second salesman', but didn't spot him in the crowd.

If he's there at all. Perhaps he's gone innocently home to his wife and children in Peterborough.

She and Jack went out into the corridor, along to the end of the carriage, and climbed down, then joined the sluggish flow towards the barrier, encumbered by their luggage. They handed in their return tickets – there was no need for them to be clipped and retained – and walked through the busy concourse and out into the sunshine.

Maisie was struck by how seedy the King's Cross neighbourhood seemed. It was the middle of the day, just after lunch, but there were prostitutes ostentatiously positioned at several street corners. Two vagrants were going through two adjacent street bins, as if in tandem, looking for discarded food or, perhaps, cigarette ends to rebuild into bitter, tar-soaked roll-ups. A double-decker bus had been taken out of service and the ejected passengers were fractious, forming a disorderly crowd at the stop, instead of a tidy queue.

'I'm looking forward to being home in Sussex,' said Maisie.

'Yes,' said Jack. 'I've had enough of big cities, too.'

They located the entrance to the Tube and descended into its stuffy passageways, queueing for a few minutes to buy their cross-town tickets. The Victoria line was deep underground, accessed via two long escalators. Jack saw a copy of the *Evening News* and snatched it up on the way past. Maisie put it in the outside pocket of her suitcase just as they reached the bottom, where the metal treads disappeared into the bowels of the machinery.

They followed another pedestrian tunnel to the platform, which was – as the schoolmaster had warned his 'microbes' – extremely crowded. Jack asked a member of staff when the next train was due, receiving only a shrug in answer. Maisie suggested moving to the far end, to the rear of the train, as there seemed to be more room. When they got there, Jack put a five-pence piece in a slot machine and they shared a small bar of Cadbury's Dairy Milk chocolate.

They became hemmed in as more and more people arrived, many of them tourists or business travellers, laden and awkward. Maisie and Jack were forced uncomfortably close to the platform edge, until it no longer seemed there was anywhere safe to stand.

The air pressure in the tunnel changed, announcing from a distance the approach of the next southbound train. Then she heard it, menacing and loud, steel wheels rattling on the junctions between steel rails, noisy brakes squealing with effort and strain. A big man with an oversized canvas rucksack pushed his way between them and Maisie felt suddenly panicked that Jack had been separated from her, that she could barely even see him any longer.

Then there was a shout and a lurch in the crowd and several people gasped and everything changed. The big man with the rucksack was leaning forward, two strong hands grasping the lapels of Jack's pale-grey suit jacket as the underground train surged into the station. It struck Jack's kitbag, spinning them both round so Jack was swung away from the edge and the big man was on his tiptoes, trying to make sure the train didn't strike him, too. All around them, people had shrunk back, fear making them indifferent to invading one another's personal space, leaving a kind of *cordon sanitaire* between the drama and themselves.

The train came to a complete stop and the doors opened, disgorging – with great difficulty – one-third of its occupants, insinuating themselves through the waiting crowd. Jack did his best to step aside, silently taking Maisie's hand, simultaneously thanking the man with the rucksack.

'I don't know what you were playing at, mate.'

'Please go ahead,' said Jack. 'Thank you, again.'

The man pushed his way on board, shaking his head with a kind of bemused contempt. Maisie felt appalled that the crisis had unfolded just feet away, with her unable to help.

'What happened, Jack?' she asked.

The platform attendant called out: 'All aboard. Move down inside. Next service on approach.'

Mollified by this encouraging information, those passengers who had not been able to mount stood back, allowing the automatic doors to close. The train pulled out with people squeezed against the window glass, leaving the platform no more than one-third full.

'Jack?'

'Let's get on board and away from here,' he told her.

Maisie realised that he was scanning the people still left around them.

'What are you looking for?'

'Someone who might have seen what happened.'

'How will you know?'

'Someone unsure, who doesn't know whether to approach me or who won't meet my eye.'

'Because?'

'Because I think I may have been pushed.'

TWELVE

Jack's words sounded preposterous. Maisie made him repeat them.

'Actually, I'm sure of it. I was pushed.'

'No,' she gasped.

'It's all okay, though. I'm fine – look.'

'This is awful. Is it my fault?'

'How can it be your fault?'

'Because—'

Maisie had no time to explain what she was thinking – that it was her investigations that had made Jack a fearsome enemy, one who wanted him dead in revenge, punishing both him and her – because another underground train came rushing in with the same cacophonous symphony of metal on metal and squealing rubber brakes. They climbed aboard, finding themselves a semi-private corner away from the doors, jammed up against one another as this service was almost as crowded as the previous one.

Maisie was glad to be close to Jack but, as the service lurched through five juddering stops, she developed a woozy motion sickness from the heaving accelerations and decelerations. Finally able to get off, they made their way gratefully through the fresher air of more tunnels, up another long escalator, then a wide set of stairs to a tall stone arch that gave access to the enormous concourse of London Victoria railway station.

Maisie took a deep breath, looked at her watch and told Jack: 'If we rush, I think we'll find a service on the point of departure.'

They hurried through the crowds to a set of platforms set slightly apart in the far corner, expressing their gratitude to the train guard who, seeing them running towards him, held the train a few extra seconds so that they could climb on board, slamming the door behind them and blowing his whistle.

Maisie and Jack moved along the carriage, finding another semi-private corner where they hoped they could sit and converse without anyone eavesdropping. Jack put their luggage in the racks above their heads.

'Tell me what you meant by it being your fault,' he said.

'No, you tell me precisely what happened first,' she countered.

He shook his head, looking down at the grimy floor. When he raised his eyes, he appeared unsure.

'Look, Maisie, I suppose I should have been more circumspect. I can't be certain, but it felt like I was shoved. You know how it was with all those people, and lots more, pushing to get on the platform from the corridors.'

'But that was just a press and a crush, not a shove.'

'True,' he said, with an air of reluctance.

'You must be able to tell if it was deliberate.' He looked pained but he didn't argue. 'And,' she told him, 'it happened just as the train was coming into the station. You might have been crushed or torn apart under the wheels.'

'But I wasn't.'

'If that big man hadn't grabbed hold of you and—'

'It was lucky he was there, yes, whether or not it was deliberate.'

'How are you so calm?' Maisie demanded, keeping her voice low, so as not to encourage anyone to listen in. The intensity of their quiet conversation had already drawn glances from a middle-aged couple who were just starting on their train picnic of fish-paste sandwiches and a Thermos of tea. 'You

70

were the victim of a blatant attempt at . . .' She stopped, not wanting to say the word 'murder' out loud, but knowing he would understand. She glanced at the picknickers, sighed and sat back. 'Didn't we agree we were hungry? Maybe we should have eaten at Victoria and waited for the next train.'

'No, I can cope and I'll be glad to be home.'

As the train pulled away from its first halt at Clapham Junction, she told him, in a low voice, about the 'second salesman' that she had seen in the dining car and how she had tried to follow him.

'I think he noticed me noticing him and slipped away.'

'Did you recognise him from anywhere else, from some-where other than the Newcastle-bound train, I mean?'

'Not as far as I recall. I just saw him those two times.'

'And you're wondering if he might have got back on again. You didn't see him when we got off at King's Cross?'

'No.'

'Or down in the underground tunnels?'

'If I had, I would have drawn you aside and told you there and then. You know that.'

Jack asked her for a detailed description, pre-empting her answer with: 'I know it's not easy.'

Maisie found she had a helpful reference point. 'You remember the confectioner in East Bitling? You met him after the murder at Bitling Fair – Arthur Tate?'

'Yes, I know Mr Tate very well.'

'My man has a narrow face like Arthur's. I'm afraid he's not very distinctive otherwise: medium build, medium height, dark hair with a side parting, cut in a short back and sides.'

'Severe? Ex-military?'

Maisie nodded. 'Perhaps. And he was one of those men who has to shave twice a day if he's going out of an evening, you know? When we pulled into Newcastle Central, he already had a five o'clock shadow.'

'Like Arthur Tate?'

Maisie frowned and told him: 'I think perhaps that's right. Why do you ask?'

'I'm wondering if that's why he made an impression on you, because you seemed to recognise him, rather than for a suspicious reason.'

'Is there something more to your question? Arthur has no reason to think badly of me or of you.'

'No one told you that it was I who put him in prison where he had a breakdown?'

'No. I mean yes about the breakdown but not that it was you who got him convicted. You're wondering if this man might be connected to Arthur?'

'Or, given their resemblance, related to him.'

'And there are the other candidates – people who bear a grudge against you from your past.' Maisie remembered the papers from Fred Nairn that Jack had been reading when they got on the train, only just having time to show them to her before their compartment was invaded by the tiny cricketers and their '*magister*'. They had spoken about the recent or imminent release of several criminals, including a couple of ne'er-do-wells from a breaker's yard, a female fraudster and her violent son. She went on: 'Plus, I've been thinking about the last six months and the five mysteries I've been involved in solving, but you have a decade of active police work and . . .' She sighed, then asked: 'What about these people? Why have they been released?'

'They've "paid their debt to society", but they are, each in their own way, not the sort to let sleeping dogs lie,' said Jack, looking grim.

'I want to hear all about that.'

The train slowed and stopped at East Croydon and their carriage became more crowded. With reluctance, Maisie realised they would have to wait once more before discussing more fully what each of them – she thought – had reason to fear. She took out her new book, *When in Rome*, and gave Jack the copy of the *Evening News* he had snatched up from beside the escalator.

Maisie found it hard to concentrate but, making an effort, she finally became absorbed in the story. Then, later, at Horsham, the train was shunted back and forth several times as carriages were added or taken away, breaking her out of Ngaio Marsh's imaginary world.

'Would you like to swap for a while?' she asked Jack.

'Go on, then. I've finished with this newspaper, anyway.'

'When your clever brain works out whodunnit after twenty pages, don't tell me,' she warned him.

'You're more likely to do that than I,' he replied, smiling.

Maisie found little to catch her attention in the *Evening News* and didn't enjoy the fact that the ink rubbed off the cheap newsprint onto her fingers. She was about to put it aside when she discovered, on an inside page, a substantial review of a BBC television drama series called *The Lotus Eaters* and remembered the coincidence of the mural on the hospital wall and the powerful 'golden lotus' in the little boys' *Look and Learn* comics.

The story of *The Lotus Eaters* concerned the lives of British expats, sunseekers living on the island of Crete. Maisie didn't quite follow the story because the reviewer assumed her readers were watching the programme and knew all about it, but it seemed to involve an unlikely scenario in which a woman called Ann, the owner of a bar, was actually a sleeper agent for British Intelligence. The review did explain where the title came from, however. The lotus eaters of Greek mythology were members of Odysseus' company who, having eaten the fruit of the lotus tree, lost all desire to return home, becoming indolent and purposeless.

Maisie considered her fiancé. His eyes were flicking across the pages of *When in Rome*.

That could never be said of either of us. Once we're home, we're going to get to the bottom of all these suspicious events.

Then, she frowned, thinking about what else awaited them.

And our wedding, of course. That's just seven days away. How could I have forgotten that?

II

Peonies

Signifying bravery and good fortune, but also anger

THIRTEEN

On the final stretch of the train journey, Jack stopped reading, his mind turning to the previous afternoon, the Friday, while Maisie had been on the train up to Newcastle. He had been feeling a sense of achievement, having received official confirmation that he had done well in his studies and could expect an excellent report, making his promotion far more likely than if he had simply 'passed' without making much of an impression.

Over the two months he had spent in the north-eastern city, Jack had enjoyed getting to know the 'Geordie nation', as Gary Naylor referred to it. His experience of community policing in Chichester had, happily, prepared him well for the challenge of establishing authority over a community that didn't know him and found his accent 'foreign'. Within a week or so of his arrival on the Tyne, he had even found himself adopting some of the local vernacular, calming boisterous drunks or settling disputes over city-centre parking rights and issuing cautions to shoplifters.

That sort of work was the bread and butter of a uniformed officer, but not the meat of why he had been away from Maisie for two months. The 'promotion path' was a way to become better paid, a career move that would make marriage – and, who knew, perhaps children? – financially viable rather than a struggle.

Packing his things at the hostel on that Friday afternoon, ready for transfer to the city-centre Northumberland Hotel later that day, he had also been thinking about the five murder investigations that Maisie had become involved with. He found it extraordinary, above all, that she had somehow found the time to solve two whole mysteries in the brief period since he had proposed to her at the Market Cross in the centre of Chichester, a public romantic gesture that he looked back on with a mixture of pride and embarrassment.

She said 'yes', though ...

The marriage proposal had been the signal to finally take the plunge and embark on the pathway of career advancement, taking him down to Exeter around the time of the murder at the fair and up to Newcastle before the murder at Sunny View.

In future, I need to keep her by me. That's what would be best. The thought didn't arise from lack of trust.

I definitely don't want to clip her wings. I just always want to be on hand to help.

Jack wondered if Maisie's life would, one way or another, continue to draw her into mysteries, that she would always find herself attracted to solving puzzles of human motivation and action. He thought he had made peace with the idea. It was precisely as he had told her after the murder at the fair, when he had come upon her in the willow arbour next to Bitling Pond.

You must never be sorry for being yourself, Maisie. You are who you are, and that's enough for me, wherever it leads.

She had admitted: *I was worried you'd be unhappy with me.*

He had told her, with emotion in his voice: *You, Maisie, are what makes me happy.*

At that point in his musings, reassured by the romantic memory, Jack had sat down on his lumpy hostel bed, indulging in a dream of a little house somewhere not too far from the centre of town, with room for a swing on the pocket-handkerchief lawn and—

'Are you coming?'

Gary Naylor's strong voice had broken the spell of his imagination. Together, they had left the hostel and, then, everything had changed with the 'accident' of the falling equipment from the scaffolding on the building next door.

*

Jack's reminiscences were brought to an abrupt close by arrival in Chichester. He and Maisie took a Dunnaways taxi from Chichester railway station to Parklands Road and his grandmother's modest bungalow, painted pastel pink.

They came to a halt outside number 147. Jack climbed out with his luggage, delighted that Maisie got down too, if only for a moment, so that they might properly embrace before she got back in to be driven on to Phyl Pascal's manor house in the village of Bunting, in a quiet green fold of the Sussex Downs. He felt frustrated by the fact that they had been unable to converse frankly because of the presence of the Dunnaways driver.

Maisie believes she's been followed and I've never known her to be wrong.

For a few moments, standing at the side of the road, watching the cab disappear out of town, he thought about the fact that Maisie was a very beautiful young woman and that it was commonplace for her to draw the eye of a stranger, especially one with the good fortune to come across her twice in two days, like the 'second salesman' on the train.

But that doesn't come close to explaining why someone might have shoved me on purpose on the underground platform. I'll be glad to talk all that through with Fred.

Lugging his bags to the front door of number 147, finding it ajar, he pushed inside, past the heavy, black rotary telephone on the shelf to the left, turning sharply right into his small bedroom at the front of the house. He dumped his things on the narrow single bed, noticing a pair of jeans left untidily on the floor, and a very hot smell of apples, brown sugar, nutmeg and cinnamon pervading the small bungalow.

He headed for the tiny square kitchen at the rear where he found a large saucepan of sliced Bramleys that were busy turning themselves into a frothy compote on the electric stove. Laid out on clean newspaper on the kitchen table were two dozen jam jars with discs of greaseproof paper and pre-cut lengths of string ready to seal them to preserve the fruit for the winter.

Where is she, though? It's not like her to leave the hotplate unattended.

Jack turned down the heat under the Bramleys and went out into the back garden, following a path that ran the length of Florence's vegetable patch. He found her sitting on a bench beneath a pergola through which a gnarled plum tree had been trained. She looked very small and unnaturally still.

'Grandma?' She didn't move or answer. Jack felt a surge of anxiety, came quickly close and touched her shoulder. It felt very spare and bony beneath her cardigan, but she shifted in response. 'I'm back, look.'

She turned her face to his, her eyes vague.

'Ah, there you are at last. How nice.'

'Are you all right? Did you fall asleep?'

'No, I don't think so, but I was in a bit of a daze.' She took a deep breath. 'You have been gone a long time.'

'Two months. People have been looking in on you, like we planned?'

'Everyone's been very kind.'

'You've wanted for nothing?'

'Now and then I'd have been glad of more peace and quiet. A little of Fred Nairn's wife Mavis goes a long way, don't you think?'

There was a glimmer of good-natured malice in Florence's eye that Jack found reassuring.

'Do you need tea?'

'What time is it? Sherry, I think, don't you?'

'Yes,' said Jack, smiling. 'Good idea.'

They went slowly indoors and Jack fetched two schooners of Harveys Bristol Cream from the living room. Back in the kitchen, he found Florence decanting the apple compote with a ladle. He lent a hand, positioning the discs of greaseproof paper and tying the top papers with the lengths of string. Florence, he noticed, was moving very gingerly.

'What's happened?'

'Well,' she said with a small sigh, 'you'll find out soon enough so I suppose I'd better tell you.'

'What are you talking about?' he insisted.

'It seems so silly. I don't really know where to start. There was such a good handful of them, onionskins and aggies and alleys. I didn't see them because it's shadowy in the porch, even though they were shiny.'

'Are you talking about marbles?'

'The onionskins have swirls and the aggies are made of stone – agate, I suppose, or they used to be – and the alleys are the big ones.'

'Why were there marbles in the porch?'

'You know how it is. They sort of slip and slide under your feet and I went down.'

'You mean you fell over?'

'Like a sack of potatoes. There's a bruise on my bottom like a dinner plate,' said Florence, continuing the ladling out. 'Luckily, I caught hold of the door knocker or I might have gone over backwards and hit my head. Still, I went down "plop". Someone brought them for the jumble, I expect. You know we're having a fundraising sale at the hall on Sherbourne Road where we have the whist club? No, you don't though. You've been away. Anyway, we are and they were in a paper bag on the mat and I suppose it must have tipped over and they all came rolling out. It might have happened to anyone.'

'What did the doctor say?' She didn't answer. 'Have you seen a doctor?'

'No.'

'Grandma, you need—'

'I rang young Zoe at the Dolphin and Anchor and she came round. She's done a first-aid course for her work and she's more than competent. I showed her my bruised bottom and she agreed.'

'When was this? I'll give her a piece of my mind—'

'Stop, Jack.' Florence's voice was unusually sharp. She held his gaze for a moment, then picked up her sherry and sipped. 'Zoe's been on late shifts so it helped her out to stay in your room for a few nights, Wednesday and Thursday and Friday, just to be sure. I imagine you've seen some of her bits and pieces in there. She's a dear little thing. But I told you, I didn't hit my head or anything. I just went down.'

'You are the limit, Grandma.'

'I don't know what you mean. By the way, Phyllis Pascal came round with a lovely bunch of peonies from Marks and Spencer's for my bedroom. She's a thoughtful sort of person, despite appearances. And she didn't interrogate me. You should go and have a look. Their blooms are almost as big as a baby's head.'

'Don't change the subject.'

'I'm not changing it. I'm moving on. The topic of marbles is closed.'

Florence seemed so determined that Jack decided to leave it at that for the time being. He was also troubled by a nasty, unspoken premonition that Maisie might be discovering some equally disconcerting 'accident' at Bunting Manor, perhaps befalling Phyl Pascal, Maisie's mother's sister, which might mean . . .

No, none of these events are connected. We just think they are because they happen to have come at once.

Together, he and Florence finished decanting and sealing the compote, making short work of it with four hands, and put the jars in the bottom of the pantry – a brick-built cupboard on the north side of the kitchen with marble shelves and airbricks to the outside to keep it cool.

'I'll go and have a sit-down,' said Florence.

Jack washed up the saucepan and other utensils in the big white sink, leaving them on the wooden draining board. He dried his hands on the tea towel, absent-mindedly carrying it through to the living room. He found Florence in her chair beside the unlit open fireplace, propped up with pillows from her bed as well as her usual cushions, presumably to relieve the pressure on her dinner-plate-sized bruise. She was asleep.

Uncertain what to do, Jack briefly considered calling the doctor behind her back, then decided that getting the GP out on a Saturday to respond to what was only a vague disquiet about something that had happened the previous Wednesday wasn't really fair.

The trouble is, though, it's Sunday tomorrow and what then?

Jack went back down the garden to hang the tea towel on the washing line, came back in and rootled about under the sink for Florence's string shopping bag. On a hook on the wall was a small blackboard for shopping lists and reminders on which he wrote her a message with a stub of white chalk.

Just popping into town. I'll bring back sausages for tea.

Closing the front door very quietly, he found the late afternoon was what the weather forecasters called 'pleasant', but with most of the heat gone out of the intermittent sun.

He walked down St Paul's Road, slowing a little as he passed Old Man Strickland's abandoned second-hand furniture warehouse.

That's one of the places it all began, with the murder at Church Lodge and Maisie facing—

He made a deliberate effort to stop himself dwelling on events that, after all, had turned out well.

He pushed on into town, up North Street towards the medieval Market Cross, making a detour into the pork butcher's shop for half a pound of chipolatas. The butcher asked why he hadn't seen Jack at the last two Rotary Club meetings.

'Chairman Petter wants your help setting up a schools concert for Christmas.'

Jack explained that he had been away on police business. On being questioned more closely, Jack admitted that he was in training, that he hoped to achieve promotion to inspector.

'If you want my advice, you should stay as you are. This city needs proper community policing, like you give us. There's not enough of your old-fashioned "Dixon of Dock Green" sort. Where were you, then?'

'Newcastle.'

'The north-east is better for sheep than it is for pigs,' said the butcher. 'Sussex is the place for pigs. I won't hear any different.'

'Fair enough,' Jack agreed.

'And you're right to take the chipolatas. Bangers look good on the plate, but the thinner ones are quicker to cook through without burning the outsides. If you want my advice and you don't mind the extravagance, cook them in the oven.'

'I'll pass it on,' said Jack. 'Thank you.'

Emerging onto North Street, busy with the bustle of late-afternoon shoppers, he set off for the police station on the canal at the bottom of the town.

I need to talk through Fred's news. Ronan Kemp is coming up for release. His mother, Peggy, and Mick and Jez Carter are already back on the streets.

As he passed the greengrocer's, he began thinking about the potential for a Christmas concert bringing together all the school choirs.

It's a good idea. Charging just a couple of shillings per ticket, we should make a tidy sum for the Rotary Club charities, if all the mums and dads and uncles and aunts and grannies and grandpas decide to come.

He determined to give 'Chairman Petter' – a very prosperous farmer from down Selsey way whose first name was George – a ring to discuss it.

I hope he's not still got a bee in his bonnet about Liz, though.

Jack's stride shortened as he realised something else.

I'd better talk to Maisie about Liz Petter, too.

FOURTEEN

Continuing her journey from Chichester out into the countryside, Maisie was disconcerted by several competing ideas. First, she somehow felt that she had badly let herself down by forgetting that, in just a week's time, she and Jack were to be married.

How could that have receded so far from the front of my mind?

Second, the rural outskirts of Chichester looked like a series of lovely landscape paintings, resplendent in the picturesque autumn weather, giving her a sense that all unhappiness and unpleasantness had been left behind in the big cities of Newcastle and London.

But that's ridiculous. It's in Chichester and the villages round about that I've had to confront the worst of human frailties – greed, anger, envy, pride and the rest.

The third idea was more subtle.

Jack tells me that he's not worried by everything we've so far been unable properly to discuss – and he said it with such earnest emphasis that, obviously, I can't possibly believe him.

The Dunnaways driver swung a little too fast through the S-bends at Bitling and, further on, took the sharp right turn out of Framlington with undue haste. In both villages, Maisie caught glimpses of people she knew, none of whom, she thought, bore her or Jack any malice.

But there are others . . .

Following a potato lorry along the narrow country road, she pictured the church in Framlington that she knew Florence and her friend Kinori were planning to decorate with flowers on Friday 29th September, the eve of the wedding. That reconnected her thoughts with the first mystery she had come across – the murder at Church Lodge in which she had investigated the death of her brother, Stephen. It had begun, by coincidence, with a 'floral' clue, linked in her imagination to the odd ubiquity of lotuses in her recent journeys.

In that frigid February of 1972, made memorable also by power cuts and sudden darknesses, someone had left a small bunch of modest winter flowers on Stephen's coffin, itself standing on trestles in the nave of St Mary's church. Maisie had only seen the posy at the end of the service, the flowers wrapped in a sheet of thick paper with writing on the inside. She had unwrapped them and discovered a stanza of poetry, written in a swirly, flowing hand, from a work by Percy Bysshe Shelley entitled 'On Death'.

> *The secret things of the grave are there,*
> *Where all but this frame must surely be,*
> *Though the fine-wrought eye and the wondrous ear*
> *No longer will live to hear or to see*
> *All that is great and all that is strange*
> *In the boundless realm of unending change.*

She remembered the almost supernatural quiet in the church, the low February sun disappearing from the stained-glass windows, leaving the light flat and grey. And she remembered seeing the poem as a puzzle.

What are, exactly, the 'secret things of the grave'?

Maisie's taxi made a final uncomfortable right turn, in through the narrow gap between Phyl's ancient gate pillars, each surmounted by a stone acorn, and up an untidy gravel drive in sore need of weeding. They came to a halt in front of the ugly Jacobean manor house and the driver politely got out to open the rear door for her, carrying her bag up the few steps to the impressive front door. Through the tiny diamond-shaped leaded panes either side it was too gloomy to see if anyone was about.

To Maisie's surprise, the front door was locked. As the taxi driver pulled away, more than content with a generous tip, she lugged her small suitcase round the side, through the walled herb garden to the kitchen door. It stood open, which was much more usual. Before going in, she took in the fact that edible-herb borders were all weeded and deadheaded, some having been replaced with newer, more verdant specimens. The central space was now occupied by a sturdy set of brand-new oak chairs around an oak table. At the far end, against the courtyard wall, stood the innovation of a brick-built barbecue with a shallow bed of ash beneath its charred metal grill.

What on earth has been going on?

Maisie went inside. On the kitchen table was the usual mess of post, newspapers, parish newsletters, shopping that needed putting away and, inevitably, a part-finished bottle of wine whose cork had been forced back into its neck, clumsily narrowed with a knife. There was also a bouquet of peonies in a large clay jug, impressive pink blooms, each one seven or eight inches across.

'Are you there, Phyl?'

No answer came. Maisie left her suitcase and crossed the impressive, dark-panelled hallway and through another doorway into a library room with tall windows on the north, west and south sides. Two-thirds of the walls were lined with books and the ancient floorboards were covered with three or four overlapping rugs, plus a few sagging sofas and armchairs. Two of the latter had built-in bookshelves under the armrests and Maisie smiled to herself.

I'm almost impatient for winter, with the fire burning in the huge hearth, sitting quietly and reading.

That had been her experience back in April, before the investigation into the murder at Bunting Manor took over both Phyl's life and her own.

But Bunting Manor will no longer be my home once I'm Mrs Wingard. I do feel very unprepared.

The corner of one of the rugs was pulled back, revealing an open trapdoor to the wine cellar.

'Are you down there?' she called.

'Maisie, is that you?' came Phyl's surprised voice in reply. 'Don't come down. I'll come up.'

With a certain amount of grunting and heavy breathing, Phyl emerged, looking short-tempered – which wasn't unusual – a heavily built country woman wearing moleskin trousers and a waxed jacket. They briefly embraced then returned to the kitchen where Phyl got busy drawing the cork from a dusty bottle of red wine.

'This is a noble vintage, a nineteen sixty-one burgundy from the Côte de Beaune.'

'What's wrong with this one?' Maisie asked, indicating the unfinished bottle on the table.

'It's white,' said Phyl, 'suitable as an apéritif but not for a celebration.'

'I've only been away thirty-six hours.'

'All the same. Pass me those glasses.'

As usual, there were several poorly washed tumblers on the wooden draining board. They were little better than old mustard pots, washed out and recycled, because Phyl – though wealthy – was frugal in her habits and always maintained: '*Good wine doesn't need posh glasses.*' Maisie polished the tumblers clean with a tea towel and Phyl poured. They both drank. Phyl raised an eyebrow, wanting Maisie's opinion.

'For what it's worth, I'd say we're just in time.'

'Meaning?' asked Phyl, looking impressed.

'It's about to go over and lose body. You may have cellared it for too long.'

'Clever Maisie,' said Phyl. 'Spot on.'

Maisie drank again and said: 'Those peonies are wonderful.'

'They are,' said Phyl. 'Imported, of course. I got them from Marks and Spencer's in Chichester. Did you read the label? The variety is "Sarah Bernhardt", you know, the famous French actress with one leg and extraordinary magnetism. That made me think of you. Have you begun to miss Paris?'

Taken by surprise, Maisie replied honestly: 'From time to time – more, just recently, than before.'

'That'll be the prospect of marriage. However much you may feel you want to be a wife – and I'm not saying you're wrong – on the other side, you know you'll be trapped.'

'Really, Phyl, that's a bit strong,' Maisie protested.

'You mark my words. Ah well. It may pass. Now, tell me everything that's happened.'

They sat down on the hard kitchen chairs and Maisie described London's galleries and theatres and her 'progress up north'. When she got to the part about Jack's accident, she hesitated.

Do I want to make my suspicions more real by speaking them aloud?

She decided not and changed the subject.

'Oh, I wanted to ask what prompted the refurbishment of the walled kitchen garden.'

'Littlegreen Sawmill, up at Bitling. They've started making furniture instead of just logs for burning and I thought I'd give them some encouragement.'

'That was kind of you. And the barbecue?'

'Zoe wanted it and Archie built it Wednesday morning, just after you left.' Archie Close was Phyl's farm manager and had been there at the climax of the investigation into the murder at Bunting Manor. His brother, Bert, had played an important role in providing information about the murder at Church Lodge. 'On Friday, we had a rib of beef, which wouldn't have fitted in the oven anyway and invited a handful of people in – you know, from the village.' She grinned. 'Those you haven't put in prison.'

'Don't say that,' complained Maisie. 'Not even in jest.'

'I'm only joshing because you have that look in your eye, Maisie. Something's going on. Out with it.'

Reluctantly, Maisie told her tale. As it turned out, Phyl was unimpressed by the sequence of events.

'Did Jack really delegate this new recruit, this Donaldson man, to go from door to door?'

'Don't you think we ought to find out who was up on the scaffolding?'

'I expect it was one of the decorators come to add some bits and pieces for the work due to begin on Monday, and he caused the things to fall with sheer clumsiness and then ran away, not wanting to take the blame.'

'Strangely,' said Maisie, 'that hadn't crossed my mind.'

'That's because life has been busy training you to expect the worst.'

'I don't like that idea either.' Maisie went on to tell Phyl the story of the 'second salesman', the sequence of events seeming more tenuous the further she got. 'But the thing that worries me is that he might have been the person who gave Jack a shove on the underground platform at King's Cross.'

'Yes, he might have been,' Phyl retorted, 'or it could have been some other clumsy oaf or even a kind of chain reaction through the crowd with people pushing onto the platform from behind.'

'That's what Jack tried to convince me of.'

'Had your "second salesman" been there, wouldn't you have noticed him? How tall did you say he was?'

'Medium height and unremarkable, expect for his narrow features. And, remember, there was the big man with the huge rucksack on his back. He was like a barrier beyond whom . . .' Maisie stopped. 'This is getting us nowhere. Tell me your news.'

'Oh, you know . . .'

'Go on.'

Phyl went into considerable detail about the difficulty of bringing in the harvests of autumn fruit and vegetables in the absence of enough casual labour.

'I've been wondering if officially joining the European Economic Community next January might help. We're suffering terribly with the flight from the countryside. All I'm left with is Harold Farr and his slow-witted nephew.'

'Rural depopulation is an issue in France as well,' said Maisie.

'I'm told wages in Britain are higher than on the Continent.'

'The cost of living, too, however. Are there any letters for me?'

'On the telephone hallstand.'

Maisie went to fetch two envelopes with French stamps. Though each had been sent from Paris, their subjects were unrelated. The first was from Adélaïde Amour, an actress who had been a central figure in the Chichester Festival Theatre mystery.

'She wants me to come and work alongside her at a festival in Avignon where she is to perform in a bilingual production, in French and in English on alternate nights.' Maisie showed Phyl, who was able to read it fluently. 'You remember, she asked me before and I prevaricated.'

'Interesting,' said Phyl. 'Are you keen?'

Maisie harboured certain suspicions about Adélaïde's behaviour that she had shared with no one, not even Jack.

92

'I suppose it might be fun,' she said, doubtfully, then noticed the gleam in Phyl's eye. 'What are you plotting?'

'I was just asking myself, if you don't want to do it, why shouldn't Zoe go instead?'

Ever since the preparations for Bitling Fair, Maisie had been teaching the vivacious sixteen-year-old French and Zoe had been making excellent progress.

'Surely she's not old enough to go away on her own?'

'She'll be seventeen in November, in less than two months.'

'But so young, still.'

'Perhaps, but she needs to get away from this awful backwater. It's all right for fogies like me, but Zoe needs to get out and see the world,' said Phyl. 'Or, if you go, perhaps she could accompany you?'

'You know I'm getting married?' said Maisie, changing the subject. 'Where is she now?'

'In Chichester. She's stayed with Florence for a few nights.'

'Because she's been on late shifts at the Dolphin and Anchor?'

'No,' said Phyl with a frown. 'Because Florence had a bit of a fall.'

Maisie knew that Jack's grandmother had, coincidentally, been rushed into hospital during the investigation into the murder at the theatre, having cut herself in a kitchen accident and fainted.

'Do we know why? Is she anaemic again?'

'It was an accident, apparently.'

'Poor Florence,' said Maisie. 'Poor Jack, too. I left him there with no idea what he was about to find . . .' Maisie shook her head, then realised that Phyl had something else on her mind. 'What is it?'

Phyl poured them both a second tumbler of wine, her own to the brim and Maisie's just halfway up.

'It's how it happened.'

93

'What does that mean?'

'I wish I had the details. I tried to find out from Zoe but Florence apparently made Zoe promise not to pass on the exact circumstances.'

'Perhaps it was clumsiness and Florence just felt foolish?'

'Zoe said it was more than that, but she wouldn't divulge,' insisted Phyl with an air of frustration.

'Some kind of mystery?'

'I got the impression,' said Phyl, 'that it was something meant.'

'Meant?'

'You know, an ambush or a trap. But that's absurd, isn't it?'

'Obviously, it's absurd,' said Maisie, not wanting to reveal that the idea actually made her feel cold inside. To dispel the shadow of the unsettling moment, she opened her second letter. 'Oh, it's from my Paris boss, Madame de Rosette. She's planning "*une fête fabuleuse*" in a country house not far from the capital. She always talks about this kind of thing as "a fabulous party", though they're always very hard work for us. She wonders if there is "any chance at all" that I might be able to "help out with the organisation". There's a bolt from the blue.'

'Are you tempted?' asked Phyl.

'It does sound fun and it would be nice to see everyone again, all my colleagues.'

'If you accept, I hope there isn't a murder.'

'Phyl, please don't make light of things like that.'

'Sorry.' Phyl emptied her glass. 'But if you can't laugh at life, what's the point of any of it?'

'I expect I'm oversensitive. I'll think about both ideas, including the possibility of Zoe coming. You never know, it might coincide with Jack's next posting away from Chichester.' Maisie put the clay jug under the cold tap. 'These peonies could do with some more water.'

'Shall we have a turn round the woods?'
'Will I need wellingtons?'
'Probably. Or do you want a lie-down?'
'No, thank you. I'm not a wilting flower.'

FIFTEEN

In the kitchen at Bunting Manor, Maisie put the freshened jug of peonies back on the table and covered her unfinished glass of wine with an unopened utility bill. Phyl tossed hers back, despite it being, as she claimed, a 'noble vintage'.

They went outside, through the rejuvenated kitchen courtyard garden, round the manor house and the recessed outside door into the wine cellar, then up the lane into the woods, past the place where Phyl had welcomed her 'lodger', an anonymous woman who had set up camp in a clearing and who had turned out to be central to the Bunting Manor mystery. Phyl asked if Maisie would be prepared to help bringing in bales of straw to the barn.

'Of course. When?'

'Tomorrow or the next day or the next. We're terribly short-handed.'

'I'll be happy to help.'

From the clearing, they branched off through the trees on a slippery, uneven path that linked with the pilgrim trail across the Downs, with Maisie telling Phyl about the play she and Jack had seen in Newcastle. Then they veered left, down through the woods into the village of Bunting proper, with its cottages and church and shop and so on, clustered around a sodden green.

'It's been wet for weeks,' said Maisie.

'I was listening to the farming programme this morning on the radio,' said Phyl. 'They give more rain for the weekend.'

Maisie smiled at the familiar colloquialism – 'they give more rain' – then her mind went back to the posy and the poem on her brother Stephen's coffin. She reminded Phyl of the story.

'And?' asked the older woman.

'I can't get that phrase out of my mind.'

'Which phrase?'

'The one about the "secret things of the grave".'

'Do you think Percy Bysshe Shelley has something to tell you about your current circumstances? You do get some fanciful ideas.'

'You have to admit that the most unlikely things sometimes turn out to be connected. They sort of resonate with one another. I'm not saying that Shelley is directing my thoughts from beyond the grave, just that . . .'

She stopped and, perhaps because of the seriousness of her expression, Phyl left off mocking and suggested: 'In hindsight, everything looks meant or predetermined. Surely that's all there is to it? Otherwise—'

'In hindsight, there's always a pattern,' agreed Maisie. 'But isn't it better if you can see it coming? It doesn't matter how you find it, what your methods are. And the reason for finding it is to prevent the bad things happening.'

Phyl didn't answer and, as they walked on, Maisie wondered if she had spoken too dogmatically, her tone too peremptory.

As the accidental investigator of five unconnected capital crimes, am I becoming 'fanciful'?

'Maisie,' said Phyl, in a different tone.

'Mm?' she replied, distracted.

'I had a letter myself.'

'Good news, I hope,' said Maisie, vaguely.

'A threatening letter.'

'What?'

'Now, don't worry or start imagining things. I almost didn't tell you. I'm sure it's nothing.'

'What did it say?'

They had reached the door of the Dancing Hare. The pub wasn't yet open because licensing hours hadn't commenced for the evening. Phyl sat down on a stone bench beneath one of the pub windows and Maisie followed suit. From an inside pocket of her disreputable wax jacket, Phyl produced a crumpled brown envelope of the sort used by people whose priority was economy. It had a second-class stamp, part obscured with a smudged postmark that indicated it had been sent from Chichester, addressed only to 'Bunting Manor'.

Maisie didn't take it, asking instead: 'How much have you handled this? Jack's colleagues, Sergeants Tindall and Wilson, might be able to find fingerprints on the paper.'

'I doubt it, not poor-quality stuff like this.' Phyl folded back the flap and took out a single sheet of equally cheap writing paper. 'It's soft and absorbent. See how the ink has smudged of its own accord.'

It was true, both the envelope and the writing paper were almost fabric-like, with no sheen of china clay on the surface that might have given the forensics officers a chance of working their magic.

'All right, show me.'

Phyl gave her the note and, all the same, Maisie held it carefully at the very corners. The shaping of the letters was clumsy, all in capitals. Maisie wondered if its author had used their wrong hand to disguise their writing.

YOU SHOULD MIND YOUR OWN BUSINESS OR SOMEONE WILL GET HURT

Maisie turned the sheet over, looking for something more helpful.

'I'm sure it's nothing,' said Phyl again with determination. 'I bet it's someone who doesn't like the idea that I'm turning Bunting Manor into a respite home. You know how people are.'

'Perhaps,' said Maisie. 'I remember when you announced it to the parish council meeting and in church. It's a natural extension to your other charitable work.'

'And would mean this big old house was properly used. You'd think people would be all for it.' Phyl sighed. 'You agree, about the note, that there's nothing to worry about?'

Maisie argued: 'How can I tell you that? And it could just as well be for me as for you.' Then she remembered not being able to get in the front door. 'Phyl, you've taken it seriously, though. You're worried, aren't you? I've never known you keep Bunting Manor locked up.'

'Actually, I did that to impress you,' said Phyl, her creased countrywoman's face broadening into a smile that Maisie couldn't return.

'This is one thing too many,' she said with determination. 'It isn't possible that all these events – the accident in Newcastle, the man who might or might not have got off the train at Peterborough, the near-disaster on the Tube, this threatening note, the circumstances around Florence's fall – it can't all simply be a coincidence and it can't also be random. There's a root cause.'

'What does that mean?'

'I'm not a detective. Mysteries keep finding me. Do you see what I mean?'

'I don't think I do,' said Phyl. 'What are you saying, that this is a sixth mystery and, in contrast, it is random?'

'No, completely the opposite. It's meant.'

'Meant how? Meant why?'

'Because of something I've done.'

'You're going to need to spell it out.'

'Phyl, someone wants revenge, someone I've helped to bring to justice, or someone close to someone I've helped convict. That's what this note means. "Mind your own business." Well, I haven't, have I? It's directed at me, not you.'

For a few seconds, Maisie watched the idea sort of settle in Phyl's eyes, becoming a reality rather than a theory. Then, Phyl asked: 'What will you do now?'

'I'll share this with Jack and we'll talk it through, of course.'

'And then?'

'I will definitely not,' said Maisie with a determined expression, 'be minding my own business.'

Phyl said nothing in reply. They both sat in silence for a time on the stone bench beneath the pub window. Archie Close went by, driving his tractor, dragging a wagon piled high with a load of hay.

'What's Archie's brother up to?' she asked. 'Can he not help with your harvests?'

'He's not been well,' said Phyl, then lapsed back into silence.

Maisie remembered how Bert Close had provided information that completely undermined Old Man Strickland's alibi in the murder at Church Lodge and helped her solve the crime. It gave her a tiny boost. Then her mind returned to the present and her creeping, insidious sense of imminent threat.

Not so much the 'secret things of the grave'. More, the 'secret desire for revenge' – with me or anyone close to me as victim.

SIXTEEN

No sooner had Jack decided that the police station should be his next port of call, than he changed his mind, remembering what Florence had said about Zoe's schedule at the Dolphin and Anchor Hotel.

Zoe's been on late shifts so it helped her out to stay in your room for the next few nights, Wednesday and Thursday and Friday, just to be sure. She's a dear little thing.

Though Jack liked and, even, admired Zoe very much, he didn't find this information entirely reassuring. Just sixteen years old, the young woman had bounced back remarkably well from the upset and danger of the murder at Bunting Manor. But he thought he would describe her as 'precocious' or 'spontaneous', rather than a 'dear little thing'.

He found his way to the Dolphin and Anchor on West Street, opposite the cathedral green, an ancient establishment whose façade was still pierced by a picturesque brick-paved alleyway leading beneath the first-floor accommodation, through which, in olden days, horses could be led to stabling and refreshment. The lobby was empty and quiet, but for the rattle of a typewriter, the percussive sound coming from an office concealed behind a wood-panelled hatch. He leaned in over the counter and saw Zoe, confidently striking keys that were covered with plastic caps in different colours to obscure the letters printed upon them.

'Your typing's coming on,' he told her. 'Can you do it blindfolded?'

She spun round in her chair, smiling, looking surprisingly grown-up in her grey pencil skirt and crisp white blouse.

'Hello, Sergeant-soon-to-be-Inspector. Let me just finish this. It's the menu for this evening and I need to put it through the Roneo machine for copies. Come round.'

Jack did so, entering the office via a door at the rear. Zoe completed her typing and pulled the special paper from the machine, crossing the office to insert it into the Roneo device with its pervasive odours of spirits and oil. She turned the handle, printing out thirty copies of the menu, laying them out on the desk and the top of the filing cabinet, one by one, to make sure they didn't smudge before the ink dried. Because the machine was noisy, they didn't speak till it was done. Then Zoe said: 'You'll want to know about your grandma. I'm a bit worried about her, actually. Has she always been so tiny?'

'Yes, always. I'm forever on at her to eat more but what can you do if someone doesn't have the appetite?'

'Food is medicine,' said Zoe, firmly. 'What's in your string bag?'

'Chipolatas.'

'Good idea. Wholesome. Shall I tell you what happened?'

Zoe told the story with what Jack thought was misplaced enthusiasm. At the end, he remarked: 'I should never have gone away.'

'You can't always be standing by in case something happens. Maisie wants you to get your promotion and Maisie's always right.'

Jack laughed at Zoe's dogmatic tone.

'You think a lot of my fiancée, don't you?'

'She's my sister, too.'

'In a way.'

'Anyway, she saved me in the Bunting murder and she's going to take me to Paris and show me there's life outside this one-horse town.'

Jack laughed again, thinking about how different Zoe was from the frightened and uncertain child he had met six months before, lonely and traumatised by a difficult life in care.

And she's right. It's all down to Maisie. Me, too. I'm a different person since she's been back. I'll not let anyone take that away from me.

He remembered Fred's paperwork, sent up to Newcastle, informing him that he ought to be on the lookout for—

'What are you thinking about?' asked Zoe.

Jack realised he had drifted away inside his own head.

'Just work. I need to get on top of things, now I'm back,' he told her.

Zoe was sharp enough to see through his evasion and told him: 'Maisie says it's important to talk things through out loud. It clarifies your ideas. She says it's been difficult sleuthing when she's not had an ally to bounce her ideas off. When that's happened, she's made lists and character notes and things and that's been almost as helpful. And she likes to draw a map.'

'She showed me the one of Bitling. It was charming.'

'Did you know that, in the Bunting mystery, she wondered at one point if I might have done something bad?'

'She told you that?'

'You know, using poison. Then she worked out that I couldn't have,' said the young woman, as if being suspected of a capital crime was an everyday occurrence. 'She was right, to be fair.'

'You are very special, Zoe.'

'Thank you. By the way, I think I might have left my jeans on the floor of your room. Sorry.'

A hotel guest came downstairs, wondering if there was a programme for the Granada cinema available. Zoe said they should find it in the first-floor sitting room where she had served afternoon tea: 'In the *Chichester Observer*.'

The guest – a twittery, genteel lady in a pale-grey jacket and skirt – seemed baffled by these simple instructions. Zoe went upstairs with her, pulling her pencil skirt above her knee to climb the steps. Jack dialled nine for an outside line on the heavy office telephone and, from memory, spun the rotary mechanism six times for Fred Nairn's home number. Fred's wife answered in a clipped tone that had very little to do with her working-class origins.

'This is Mavis Nairn. To whom do I have the pleasure of speaking?' Once she knew who it was, she launched into a lengthy complaint about Fred working multiple extra shifts due to Jack's absence. 'And without so much as a "thank you", if the past is any guide.'

'I'm sorry to have been a trouble. I take it he's not in. Can you tell me where he is, Mavis?'

'At the station, I expect. I'm surprised you didn't try that first. He lives there more than he lives here.'

Jack didn't speak aloud his own conclusion – that Fred was perhaps glad of the excuse not to be too often 'at home', if this was the general tenor of his wife's conversation.

'Thank you very much, Mavis,' said Jack. 'That's very helpful.'

'Give him my best,' she replied in an acid tone.

'I will,' said Jack, not rising to the bait. 'Goodbye, Mavis.'

Jack hung up by pressing down on the cradle, spun the nine again, waited for the change in dial tone, then composed the station number, also from memory. Soon, he had been put through and had Fred on the other end.

'I'm back and I'm at the Dolphin.'

'Well, that's grand. I'll drive up, Jack,' Fred told him. 'You stay where you are. See you shortly, depending on the railway gates.'

'Thanks.'

Glad to be making progress, Jack still felt uneasy at the idea of even a few minutes' idleness. Checking his watch, he wondered if PC Donaldson might be available, coming on duty for his own late shift at the station in the centre of Newcastle. The number was another he was able to dial from memory, beginning with the city area code. A different officer picked up, answering with the traditional 'How can I help you, sir?', but with the charming cadence of the local accent. It turned out PC Donaldson was, indeed, on duty and was soon available and 'making his report' in a disappointed tone of voice.

'The thing is, Sergeant Wingard, I think I told you it was an away game for the Toon,' said Donaldson, using the local nickname for Newcastle United Football Club. 'And that area round the hostel's a neighbourhood with a powerful following for the lads, home and away.'

'No one was about?' Jack guessed. 'Was that the problem?'

'They were down in Coventry,' said Donaldson.

'Fair enough. Did you speak to anyone at all?'

'Three, but none with any knowledge of the unknown ladder-climber. The fans will soon be on their way home, on the coaches and the trains, but it's a dreadful long way from Coventry. They'll be lucky if they're in bed by midnight. I'll go back again tomorrow and have a chat with any as don't mind being questioned on a Sunday.'

'Not "questioned", Constable. Just a friendly chat.'

'No, Sergeant. I take your point. Just casual-like.'

'What was the result of today's match, by the way?' asked Jack, assuming Donaldson would know. 'Will people be in a good mood?'

'They will, Sergeant. I heard it on the radio as I came in. Three-nil to the Toon. Hat-trick for Malcolm Macdonald. Away from home as well. We'll be in Europe next season if we carry on like that. Supermac should be England's number nine.'

'I expect he will be in time,' said Jack, taking care to share Donaldson's enthusiasm. 'Thank you, Constable.'

'Will I need your own number, Sergeant?'

'I'll call you at the same time. You're on duty again on Sunday evening?'

'Yes, Sergeant.'

'Then it'll be at my expense. I'm imposing on your free time, as it is.'

'I don't mind. I've always wanted to be a detective and this is the proper business. Give my best to your fiancée.'

Jack smiled to himself. He was beginning to like PC Donaldson.

'Thanks, again. Till tomorrow.'

He hung up just as Fred was entering the lobby. At the same time, Zoe was on her way down the impressive stairs with the demanding hotel guest on her arm.

'The bar will soon be open, madam. Just through there.'

'Thank you, dear. And, may I say, you have the loveliest smile.'

'Thank you, madam,' said Zoe.

Jack did a kind of double take.

It's true. Zoe does have a lovely smile. She and Maisie don't look alike, but they do have the same open, engaging charm.

The hotel manager, Mr Hume, arrived from his accommodation in the rear annex, getting ready to take over from Zoe at the front desk. Zoe fetched her bag of clothes and overnight things and Jack led her and Fred outside. Fred's beloved Mark II Jaguar was parked at the kerb, with a green-and-cream double-decker Southdown bus creeping past.

'Where shall we go,' Fred asked, 'for a catch-up?'

'I need to run. That's my bus,' said Zoe.

'You're going out to Bunting?' asked Jack.

'Are you going that way, too, Jack?' asked Fred. 'How about I give you both a lift and we can have a bit of a chat on the way?'

That hadn't been Jack's intention but, of course, it would make sense. And they could pop in for a bit and make Maisie a part of his and Fred's discussion.

'Are you sure you don't mind?'

'It would be a blessing,' said Fred, wearily. 'Mavis wants me to decorate the spare room.'

'Why is that important?' asked Zoe.

'Again,' said Fred, meaningfully.

'And you want us to be your excuse,' said Jack, smiling. 'All right, but I'll have you know, I'm in Mavis's bad books as it is.'

They all got in, stopping briefly on Parklands Road for Zoe to retrieve her crumpled jeans and for Jack to go in and give Florence her chipolatas. Happily, he found his grandma on her feet in the kitchen, stringing a handful of runner beans from her own garden, quite refreshed by her nap.

'Don't worry about me. I'll watch the telly and go to bed early.'

'All right. If you're sure.'

'I am. Be off with you.'

Outside, Jack found that Zoe had taken his place in the front passenger seat.

'We can swap back again,' she told him. 'I was just trying it out.'

'You stay there,' Jack told her. 'I don't mind.'

Fred pulled away, turning left out of Parklands, onto the Framlington road, winding through wooded private land and then the S-bends between East and West Bitling. On the straight, between arable fields, post-harvest stubble-burning had already begun, leaving the ground scorched and black.

In Framlington itself they had to wait while someone reversed into a coveted parking space in front of the pub, the Fox-in-Flight. Then Fred turned right up the narrower road into the Downs. All the while, Zoe was telling Fred amusing anecdotes from her work at the hotel, leading on to learning French and her ambition to 'go abroad, like Maisie'. Fred – clearly charmed – was agreeing with her every word. Jack, meanwhile, was wondering if he was doing the right thing.

I didn't ring to tell Maisie I was coming. Turning up out of the blue is going to give the wrong impression. Our 'bit of a chat' is going to end up looking like a sort of council of war. It's going to make everything seem a lot more serious.

Fred turned right onto the final country road, the little-used way through Harden to the village of Bunting.

Not only will it make things seem more serious, it'll give Maisie an excuse to go off investigating on her own – running once more towards the danger.

SEVENTEEN

The man that Maisie thought of as the 'second salesman' had also arrived in Sussex. He had followed her and her fiancé into London, climbing back on board the train at Peterborough then hesitating at King's Cross so that they wouldn't catch sight of him. Then, of course, he had followed them into the Tube tunnels where the kerfuffle on the platform had taken place.

It had even been possible to travel across London to Victoria Station on the same underground train, two carriages ahead. Then, his quarry had surprised him by suddenly running across the busy concourse to catch the Chichester train with only seconds to spare, something he was unable to do because it would have drawn too much attention. He had watched them pull out, bought himself a cup of tea and waited twenty minutes for the subsequent service.

He didn't consider his mission a complete failure. He had succeeded, he thought, in evading notice.

Except, perhaps, in the restaurant car. She gave me a close look that one time. But I slipped away sharpish . . .

He arrived in Chichester towards the end of the afternoon and went into the centre of town for a Wimpy and another tea, asking for it 'good and stewed'. His food came as he was turning his teaspoon, dissolving an ounce of white sugar, thinking about the odd sort of job he'd been given.

When it's done, I wonder what I'll find next.

Having eaten, he went to stand outside the cathedral on West Street, waiting for a Southdown bus to take him out into the villages.

No rest for the wicked, he thought.

Then he laughed aloud.

EIGHTEEN

By chance, it was Maisie who answered the front door because Phyl was busy putting three potatoes in the Calor Gas oven for baking, to which she intended, later on, to add some shop-bought pies. Maisie heard Zoe's happy voice outside on the steps and saw, in silhouette, Jack's unmistakable outline through the diamond-shaped panes of the Jacobean windows.

She opened up, a delighted smile on her face, beginning: 'How lovely of you to give Zoe a lift—' She stopped short, recognising Fred Nairn standing a little behind and two steps lower. 'What's happened? It's not bad news, is it?'

'No, Maisie, all is well,' said Jack, 'but I thought it might be a good idea for us all to pool resources.'

'In what sense?'

'To pool information, I mean.'

'It's worked in the past,' said Fred, earnestly. 'You and I made a good team for Bitling Fair.'

'Can I go in, though?' asked Zoe, impatiently.

'Yes, go ahead.' Maisie stepped aside and Zoe brushed past, kissing her on the cheek. Feeling her fiancé's tension, Maisie insisted: 'There's really nothing else I ought to be worried about?'

'I don't think there's necessarily anything to make us fret, but we ought to just talk things over.'

'What things?'

'Everything – Newcastle, the Tube, Grandma, the papers that Fred sent me—'

'But you said nothing had happened—'

'Nothing new has happened.'

'What about Florence? Phyl told me the bare bones. How is she?'

'She's absolutely fine, Maisie,' said Jack, using – as she recognised from having been able to watch him with witnesses – his most soothing voice. 'Please, Maisie, believe me when I tell you that there's no reason to imagine all kinds of horrors. We just thought we might have—'

'A council of war,' interrupted Fred.

Jack groaned and complained: 'Is that how you defuse the tension, Inspector?'

'I meant it in jest,' said Fred, apologetically.

'All right,' Maisie told them. 'You'd better come in, but it all feels very hasty. We only left Newcastle Central Station after breakfast this morning and here we are—'

'Do you trust me, Maisie?' interrupted Jack. He raised his right hand and laid it gently against her cheek. 'Really trust me?'

'I think we trust one another,' she told him, not wanting to smile but unable to conceal the warm feeling of belonging that was immediately coursing through her. 'Yes, I do. You know I do.'

'Good,' he told her.

'And,' she insisted, 'if you ever steered us wrong, I'd tell you.'

He laughed. 'I know you would.'

She took hold of his hand and – as he had done to her on the lawn in front of Newcastle General Hospital – kissed his palm. Then she said: 'I will consider this visit an act of chivalry from a devoted knight errant. You may enter, fair sir, you and your fellow chevalier.'

'I do love you, Maisie Cooper.' He climbed up to the top step, put his other arm round her back and drew her close. 'Nothing will ever change that.'

'Why should it?' she asked quietly, pressed against his broad chest, her face in his neck.

For Maisie, everything else retreated – the pleasant evening, the door left ajar, the birdsong. Time stretched out and she sensed herself drifting into a kind of nowhere place, like a dream but, at the same time, very real. She could feel Jack's heart beating and wondered if he was experiencing something similar. Then, abruptly – unkindly – she was drawn back to the present by Fred Nairn coughing for their attention.

'This is all very well for you young lovers, but perhaps we've spent long enough on the threshold?'

Maisie and Jack pulled apart, not without reluctance. She apologised for both of them, then led the two men across the hallway and into the library, with its comfortable low chairs and book-lined walls. Zoe joined them, having had enough time to climb to the top of the house and change out of her pencil skirt and white blouse, into a garish, loose-fitting kaftan with a loud pattern of shellfish.

'I know,' she told them, seeing their surprised faces. 'But it's the most comfortable garment I've ever owned and I got it at the jumble and it was only fifty pence.'

'Did they pay you that to take it away?' enquired Phyl, entering with a tray on which stood the two unfinished bottles of wine from the kitchen, one red and one white, plus a little tower of mismatched tumblers. 'I'd have asked for more.'

Zoe stuck out her tongue and flopped down in one of two armchairs with bookshelf armrests, asking: 'What are we going to talk about? Not the harvest and the rain making it impossible to bring it in, please.'

'Lack of rain or too much, we farmers are never satisfied,' said Phyl, putting the tray on the coffee table.

'And not the racing at Goodwood, either,' Zoe complained. 'There must be some other topics of conversation.

Maisie, tell me about where we'll go and what we'll see when you take me to Paris.'

'Actually,' said Fred, 'this is sort of a private conversation, if you don't mind, Miss Pascal. Zoe, I mean.'

Fred – despite being the same age as Jack – was much more middle-aged and fussier in speech.

'Surely not private from me,' said Zoe, looking crushed.

Maisie took charge. 'Fred, Zoe's seen enough in her short life to cope with whatever we've got to say. And, not one of us knows where any of this might lead. She won't get all silly or go off blabbering and being indiscreet. You know that.'

'What's more,' said Jack, 'Zoe's been looking after Grandma and that may have a bearing.'

'I still don't know enough about that,' protested Maisie. 'Have you two men been plotting and confabbing without me?'

'No, not at all,' said Fred. 'But my Mavis has been round to Florence and says all's well.'

The carriage clock on the mantelpiece chimed six and Phyl told them: 'The baked potatoes aren't very big. I put in extra when I heard your voices. They'll be ready at seven. Someone needs to remind me to put in the pies at twenty-five to.'

'They're not Wall's "special gristle variety", are they?' complained Zoe.

'No, they are not. They come from the Dancing Hare – Bunting's finest.'

Zoe smiled and nodded, saying: 'Ah, that's different.'

Maisie, too, was reassured. The Dancing Hare was run by the reformed alcoholic Ernest Sumner, assisted by Jenny Brook, the village shopkeeper, who had – as Grandma Florence had more than once confirmed with her connoisseur's palate – 'a lovely light hand for pastry'.

114

'Shall we gather round,' said Jack. 'Give me a hand, will you, Fred?'

Under normal circumstances, the library chairs all pointed towards the cavernous open hearth, but there was no need for a fire because the mid-September evening remained warm. The two men arranged them in a rough circle, nudging the coffee table more central. Phyl leaned in and poured herself a glass of red wine, telling the others to make their own choices. Jack, who was generally abstemious, poured small glasses of red for Fred and for himself, as Zoe filled tumblers for her and for Maisie almost to the brim.

'Good health,' said Phyl and she drank off her entire measure in a single draught. 'Top me up, Zoe.' The young woman did as she was told. Meanwhile, Phyl demanded: 'I have to be brought up to speed. Maisie and I have been talking, obviously, as have all of you. My poor old brain can't cope with a muddle.'

'That's what a mystery is,' said Maisie. 'It's a muddle until you get it all straight.'

'Is that the territory, then?' asked Phyl. 'A murder or some such?'

'No, no, Mrs Pascal,' said Jack, employing his 'soothing' voice once more. 'We've just discovered a few odd threads that we need to try and pull together, just so that we can work out if there is, after all, anything to worry about.'

'That's just what I'm saying,' said Phyl. 'What are these threads? Who's in possession of them and, more important, who's pulling on them?'

'This is a very haphazard way of going about things,' said Fred with a frown. 'I don't know if it's quite regular.'

'Don't worry, Fred,' said Jack.

'If we're going to share police business—' he insisted.

'Where should we start?' interrupted Zoe. 'I mean, everyone always tells me how Sussex is such a lovely safe place to live, that I should be grateful instead of bored, that all the extraordinary things that have happened are just coincidences.'

'That's right,' said Jack. 'They are. You start with what happened with Grandma.'

'Again? Do I have to?'

'Just start at the beginning,' said Maisie, 'then I'll take you through all of my adventures on the way to Newcastle and back.'

It didn't take Zoe long – despite interruptions from Phyl and Maisie for clarification or additional details – to tell the odd story of the rogue marbles and their unfortunate aftermath. Then Maisie narrated her and Jack's last forty-eight hours. Jack didn't need to prompt her or chip in himself because Maisie was very good at organising her thoughts. When she had finished, Fred complimented her.

'I've said it before and I'll say it again, there's no one like Maisie Cooper for laying it out neat and tidy.'

'Thank you, Fred,' Maisie replied. 'Now, I had a glance at the papers you sent Jack when we were on the train earlier today, but we were very overlooked and easily eavesdropped on, so I could only pick up on the bare essentials.'

'Yes, that would make sense,' said Fred. He looked at his colleague. 'But I don't know if this is in the same league as everything that's gone before, Jack. Like I said, this is police business.'

'You mean I shouldn't have shared it?' Jack asked.

'I'm not sure you should have, really.' Fred looked very serious. 'I wouldn't want it to come out that you'd done something against regulations and for that to queer your pitch for promotion.'

'But surely it's all in the public domain?' asked Maisie. 'We're talking about people Jack's arrested who have been tried in court by a judge and a jury of their peers. All the evidence has been heard.'

'What evidence?' asked Phyl with an edge of frustration.

'Yes,' said Zoe, equally impatiently. 'This is all very dramatic but also quite annoying. What do you all mean?'

'The evidence we're talking about,' said Maisie, carefully, 'might suggest why someone could bear a grudge against my fiancé or against me.'

'Oh dear,' said Zoe, looking deflated. 'So, Sussex isn't as safe as you keep telling me. Jack has lots of enemies.'

'By extension,' said Phyl, frowning, 'so does his fiancée, with an extra e.'

'What does that mean?' asked Fred, who wasn't gifted for languages.

'I mean,' said Phyl, 'as well as Maisie accumulating grudges from bringing guilty people to justice, Jack's enemies are Maisie's enemies, too.'

NINETEEN

Maisie was relieved when Fred insisted to Zoe – who had begun to imagine dozens of dramas in Jack's policing past – that they had only a pair of stories to tell, though they each concerned 'two individuals'. For clarification, Zoe asked: 'Directly connected to recent releases from jail and the papers Jack was looking at on the train?'

'Recent and imminent,' said Jack.

Fred took up the tale. His narration was quite roundabout, going well beyond bare fact. Maisie listened, with an increasing sense of foreboding, trying to resist the temptation to interrupt, knowing that would slow the process down. She told herself she could question Jack privately about the characters of the people involved later on.

'It's a coincidence, really,' Fred mused, 'the two things coming together like this – in time, I mean, September and the wedding and all. I'll start with the Carters because they happened more recent in my memory and Jack maybe will help me out with the Kemps.'

'One thing at a time, Fred,' admonished Phyl. 'Focus.'

'Yes, ma'am. I'll do my best though it'll be a poor second to Maisie.'

'Come on, Fred,' said Jack.

'Right, Mick and Jez Carter, brothers. They had a scrapyard over at Fitwell where they broke up old cars and shared out the parts for repairs. Previously, there'd been a father who was, by all accounts, a half-decent human being, but I never met him and perhaps that's just people not wanting to speak ill of the dead. Anyway, he left his sons, the two brothers, to fly close to the wind and argue and moan at one another all the live-long day. First time I had to go over there, it was on account of late-night noise complaints with them working with angle grinders and I don't know what at all hours.'

'Breaking up stolen cars for their anonymous parts,' explained Jack. 'But we didn't see that at first.'

'That's it,' said Fred. 'So, I knew them and like ferrets in a bag, they were, and not so careful with their trade, sometimes using components that didn't really go, like a shock absorber from an Austin into a Hillman, leaving the vehicle on the slant and unsafe for customers that knew no better. Now and then, Jack would make them a visit to try and keep them on the straight and narrow, you know, as a community officer, and get them to take care. I didn't have any hard evidence of them breaking any laws and, as they told my friend here on more than one occasion: "If you get a complaint from a customer, come back and see us. Till then, sling your hook." Isn't that right, Jack? Perhaps you others can imagine the type?'

'They're reminding me of Old Man Strickland,' said Maisie, referring to an important person in the mystery of the murder at Church Lodge, 'the one with the second-hand furniture business. But he's still safely locked up.'

'That's the profile,' agreed Fred. 'Old Sussex family, not big on education, suspicious of outsiders, jealous of their privacy, quick to take offence, self-righteous and apt to climb up on their high horses if they ever thought someone gave them disrespect.' Fred's eyes glazed over. 'That's not so uncommon, though . . .' Maisie thought he was probably running through a sequence of similar miscreants in his mind. He resumed: 'Now, the only thing Mick and Jez Carter agreed upon was the gee-gees and that was where all their spare money went – and the money that wasn't rightly spare, too – most commonly every time there was a meeting at Fitwell race course.

They'd save up for it, with all kinds of big dreams for what they'd do with their winnings. Then, like most gamblers, the more they squandered the more they wagered, trying to claw back their losses. It never worked, of course, and they got to the point where they were being threatened with eviction.'

'Zoe, drinks, please,' said Phyl.

The young woman obliged.

'So,' said Fred, decisively, 'you'll need to know who their landlord was. You'll have known him, Mrs Pascal, Bill Meacher, a farmer whose dad had made a bit of money from potatoes on some suitable fields and put all his savings into picking up extra scraps of land round about from people who were selling because money was very tight after the war. I think Bill was a bit ashamed of his dad, for all that his strategy had left Bill on easy street, because it gave him the feeling his family had profited like the spivs and black-marketeers. Their land's mostly on the north side of the A27, with the scrapyard to the south. He'd be in his fifties, now, old Bill, and he's as kind-hearted a man as you could hope to meet.'

'Why are we digressing into the character of the Carters' landlord?' asked Phyl.

'Give me time,' said Fred. 'So, I was saying, Mick and Jez were behind in their rent and rates and bills, too, I shouldn't wonder, and were facing eviction. That wasn't the worst of it, though, for them, because they'd also have the cost of cleaning up the site, the scrapyard, I mean, and leaving the place tidy. It came out that they hadn't ever had permission to convert what ought to have been a nursery or a market garden into a dirty industrial site.' Fred gave a disappointed shake of his head: 'They took advantage, really, though it seems foolish to put it like that, with them unhappy and bitter and living hand to mouth, ending every day trying to get the dirty engine oil out of the creases in their hands with Swarfega. I mean they took advantage of Bill Meacher.'

'If he was too soft, it was his lookout,' snapped Phyl. 'He let them misuse good growing land – a crime in itself, though there might not be a law – and he let them get away with not paying their rent.'

'That's right – and a modest rent it was, too.'

'So, why the sympathy?' Phyl insisted.

'Fred knew the boys at school,' said Jack, 'even before they started coming to the attention of the police. They had a bad start in life.'

'So did I have a bad start,' began Zoe, self-righteously, 'and I'm not—'

'Shall we let Fred finish?' interrupted Maisie.

'Yes, sorry,' said Zoe.

'It's true I felt bad for them from their poor home lives. Nothing's as important as getting off on the right footing, and Mick and Jez stumbled out of their secondary modern school – not one of the best – badly prepared for adulthood at fourteen years old, taking every wrong turn, drinking their cider under-age and driving the old bangers round the yard and, sometimes, even on the public highway. In the end, Bill Meacher – who, I repeat, was the mildest of men – had to come and speak to us at the station and ask our advice about getting rid of Mick and Jez for good, he'd had that many complaints from neighbours on all sides.' Fred looked rueful. 'Now, I was newly promoted and busy with other things and I think I rather gave him short shrift, merely repeating chapter and verse about taking the eviction through the courts and getting an order against them. But that upset Bill and his tender sympathies, not wanting them to end up with a criminal record, so he said he'd have another go at persuading the Carters to pack up and move on. I should have told him not to. He even let on he would promise them to deal with the polluted ground himself, at his own expense.'

'Silly man,' said Phyl. 'Is he dead?'

'Hang on a minute,' said Fred. 'We're nearly there. This is where Jack comes into it.'

Maisie glanced at her fiancé. His wine tumbler was in his hand but he wasn't drinking. His eyes were down, as if he was closely examining the Persian pattern on the rug beneath his feet.

'You were suspicious of them, the Carters?' she asked.

'I was,' said Jack, raising his eyes. 'It was something that happened when I went over for another noise complaint. I got the impression that they'd made a decision of some kind that meant they were careless of the future, that they didn't have to bother what they said to me.'

'It might help at this point,' Fred added, 'to say that Bill Meacher never married, that he had no close heirs, just an older brother who'd emigrated to Canada after his wartime service. What the Carters were banking on was this. You know how the law of probate is, perhaps? The wheels grind very slowly. The Carters thought they could get themselves a stay of execution if Bill was out of the way – in an "accident" – and no one was in charge any longer, except an estranged relative thousands of miles away who like as not didn't care either way.'

'And you saw the danger, Jack?' asked Maisie.

'It just so happened that I met Fred and saw he was fussed with all his new responsibilities and I asked how I could help and, between us, we thought Bill might need a little back-up.'

'And we were right,' agreed Fred.

Jack took up the story.

'This was a few years ago and we weren't so well equipped as we are today. I definitely didn't have access to a patrol car. Bill had driven off from the station in his farm truck and I had to get the bus to follow, worrying all the way if, on the one hand, I was on a wild-goose chase and, on the other, if I was going to be too late. Luckily, the bus had been ready, waiting to leave. Every time we stopped to let people off or on, though, I felt myself getting more and more nervous for what I would find.'

'How tense,' said Zoe, enthralled.

'In Tangmere, there was a whole school party waiting to climb aboard and it seemed to take an age, though time is always very relative when you're worried. Anyway, I got off at the Fitwell roundabout and made straight for the yard. The gates were shut – sheets of corrugated iron on timber frames – but they weren't locked or anything. I pushed on one of them and it sort of swayed out of the way and I slipped through. That was when I saw something that made me sure I was right to be worried.'

'Were they manhandling Mr Meacher?' asked Zoe, wide-eyed.

'No,' said Jack. 'Quite the opposite. Mick was talking to him politely, making his apologies, promising to mend his ways. Later, I discovered that Bill had gone home to park his truck then walked over, which was why I wasn't too late. The thing was, I could see, even with less experience than I have today, that it was all a ruse. Mick being polite – well, that was some kind of trick. Then Mick led Bill by the arm to a particular spot and told him to hang on a minute while he went into the office to fetch him a down payment in cash on what was owed. At that moment, I knew we'd come to a crisis.'

'You have to imagine the place,' said Fred, 'with rusty old jalopies piled on top of one another in teetering heaps, organised with the big claw crane.'

'That was their idea, you see,' said Jack, 'to make it look like an accident.'

'You mean,' said Maisie, seeing the scene evolve in her mind's eye, 'that Jez Carter was somewhere close by, ready to use the claw crane to tip over a pile of cars on top of poor Bill Meacher.'

'That's right,' said Jack. 'And Mick had put him in the perfect spot to be crushed.'

'Oh no,' said Zoe.

Jack continued: 'I saw it happening just in time, hearing the revving of the diesel engine from behind the heaps of scrapped cars, and I ran forward and got to Bill in the nick, dragging him clear as the heap of sharp metal came crashing down in the oily dirt precisely where Mick had insisted that he stand and wait. Mick came out of the office, the silly idiot, calling to his brother: "Did you get him?" I got myself up out of the dirt and told him he was under arrest.'

'So, they went to prison for attempted murder?' asked Zoe.

'No,' said Fred, with an expression of disgust. 'The Crown Prosecution Service bungled it and couldn't make that stick, but they both went inside for a series of lesser offences, including criminal negligence in relation to the near-accident, plus all the other misdemeanours we could pin on them. They've spent most of it in HMP Ford.'

'The open prison,' Jack clarified.

'And now,' said Maisie, 'they've been released.'

'And would have come out sooner with good behaviour,' Fred confirmed, 'but it seems they're not capable of learning their lesson, poor buggers, so they both served their full tariffs.'

'And,' said Maisie, 'you think they might bear Jack a grudge.'

'That's in character for them, as I hope I described,' said Fred. 'I'm sorry I'm not as clever at telling the tale as you are, Maisie.'

'No,' she told him, quietly. 'No need to apologise. I think I have a good sense of them and everything that happened. What did Bill Meacher do next? Is he still about? I think you spoke of him in the past tense or did I imagine it?'

'That's because he upped sticks and left – went to join his elder brother in Canada and is very happy out there by all accounts.'

'He sold up?'

'Yes, to a house developer who was in a position to clean up the land and the council was only too pleased to give the planning permission and to have the eyesore off their books.'

'I see,' said Maisie. 'So, there aren't any other repercussions or recriminations for the Carters? If they wanted revenge, it would only be on Jack, because he was the one who was there.'

'Because he shopped them,' said Fred.

'And because, in court, I did my best to get them convicted on the more serious charge,' said Jack. 'They had their eyes on me throughout the trial. I know what they were dreaming about.'

Maisie had a horrible feeling that she knew, too.

TWENTY

Before Fred embarked on his second story, Phyl asked Zoe to go and put the pies in the oven, alongside the baked potatoes, and to boil the kettle: 'So there's hot water ready for peas on the side. There's fresh from the field in a blue-and-white bowl in the fridge. Bring them in and we'll shuck them together.' Zoe did as she was told and Phyl refilled her own glass. 'Anyone else?'

Fred accepted but Jack covered his tumbler with his hand. Maisie was glad to see that Zoe's glass was still half full. She didn't want the young woman to get into bad habits.

'Where are they, Mick and Jez Carter?' she asked. 'Does the prison service keep track?'

'That's a good question,' said Fred. 'If they'd been released on licence, ahead of term, they'd have the probation service looking over their shoulders. But their "debt is paid", as people say, and the idea is they know better now, for having been punished, and won't think of doing it again.'

'Fat chance,' said Phyl. 'So, they're free and clear.'

'I believe Maisie was wondering if they're living close by,' prompted Jack, mildly.

'Oh, yes,' said Fred. 'We've taken an interest, of course. They've washed up down near Selsey, finding casual work on the Petter Farm. In a way, they're lucky it's harvest time, otherwise they've a reputation that would put most employers off.'

'Labour's hard to find,' said Phyl. 'You can't be too picky.'

From the kitchen, Maisie heard the kettle whistling, the sound quickly extinguished. Then Zoe came through with the bowl of new-season peas in their pods and a saucepan to shuck them into. She put both receptacles on the coffee table. Jack leaned in to take part in the process of popping the pods and pushing the peas out with a thumbnail. Doing so, he gave Maisie a look that suggested he had something he wanted to discuss with her alone.

Is it something about the Petter Farm?

But he, didn't get the chance because Fred was asking: 'Shall I go on?'

'Yes,' said Phyl. 'You told us there was a coincidence. What did you mean by that?'

'A coincidence of dates, with two things happening at the same time.'

'You mean the release of the Carter brothers and another potential enemy?'

'I do.'

Maisie asked: 'How worried should we all be, do you think?'

Jack insisted: 'All will be well. This conversation is a precaution, that's all. It sounds much more serious than it probably is.'

'I don't like "probably",' Maisie replied, quietly. 'I would prefer "definitely".'

'I know,' said Jack. 'As would I. Go on, Fred.'

'Right, here we go, then. I want to sort of set the scene but I don't want to confuse everyone with too much background.'

'Pies are in. Don't dawdle,' said Phyl. 'Try and make it fit the gap.'

'Good point, I will.' Fred pursed his lips. Maisie thought he was looking for the right place to start. 'Perhaps you should tell it, Jack? You were the one who saw what was going on.

I only got the credit because I was the senior investigating officer.'

'Does that mean the grudge is against you, Inspector Nairn?' asked Zoe, her agile fingers popping and shucking the pea pods.

'No,' said Jack. 'I'm the one she would want revenge upon.'

'Did you say "she"?' asked Phyl who had been busy drinking.

'I did, yes. She and her son.'

'How exciting,' said Zoe.

Maisie felt her habitual stirring of unease whenever anyone took such things too lightly or in jest. Jack sat back, took a deep breath and began.

'It will sound melodramatic at first; then it was all horribly sordid. You know there's a lifeboat station down at Selsey, a timber jetty with a boathouse at the end and a ramp to launch the lifeboat swiftly into the water? Perhaps you don't know that there's a place nearby where the bodies of convicted criminals used to be suspended on a gibbet to be pecked at by birds, their skeletons picked clean? It was a sort of eternal punishment from vengeful Christian morality – so their bodies might never be resurrected at the Last Judgement.'

'How awful but also how wonderful,' said Zoe. 'You do mean many years ago, don't you?'

'I do. Famously, some of the Hawkhurst smuggling gang ended up on the gibbet on Selsey beach, in seventeen forty-nine, I think it was.'

'I don't understand. What's the connection between the lifeboat station and the gibbet?' demanded Phyl.

'It's the setting,' said Jack, patiently. 'There's a bit of an atmosphere, especially if you know the smugglers' story. That's why she chose the place, perhaps.'

'She?' demanded Phyl, again.

'I'm getting there,' said Jack, unperturbed. 'Nearby, there's a row of converted railway carriages that people live in, you know? They ended up there after the war when lots of people were glad to find shelter of any kind. Some of the wagons have been made very nice with their gardens well kept and the timbers painted fresh each summer. One in particular was dressed up like a Romany traveller's caravan, you know, with garlands of coloured cloth and lanterns that were lit after dark each evening. The owner was a woman who, so she said, had settled in Selsey "after a lifetime of wandering". I met her on my rounds. I spent six months in Selsey as a beat constable and didn't think too much about her, except that I thought she was much more likely to have washed up there having been bombed out from the East End of London, rather than being a genuine Romany.'

'Why was that?' asked Maisie.

'Accent, above all. She tried to hide it but couldn't keep it up. And she used London colloquialisms.'

'I know what you mean,' said Maisie. 'That came up in the investigation of the murder at Sunny View.'

'At that point,' Jack continued, 'back in nineteen sixty-two or sixty-three, I'm not sure which, there didn't seem any reason to give her obvious posing any more thought. A few years later, though, there was a very sad event when a middle-aged spinster named Keltie walked into the sea, late one night in winter, when the cold might well have done for her as much as the drowning.'

'She died?' gasped Zoe.

'She did. In the course of my investigation, I discovered that she had been visiting this supposed Romany character in her converted railway carriage.'

'What was her name?' asked Zoe, shucking the final pod of peas.

'Well,' said Jack with a shake of the head, 'she always introduced herself as "Esmeralda". I subsequently discovered that her real name was Peggy Kemp and that I'd been right. She was from Poplar in the East End.'

'Had she been telling people's fortunes?' asked Maisie.

'She had.'

'And she used that as a subterfuge to deceive and gain control and defraud people?'

'Yes,' said Jack, smiling. 'You really are very remarkable, Maisie.'

'No, I'm not. It's obvious, isn't it? Otherwise, why would we be talking about her?'

'All the same,' said Fred, 'Jack's right. You do seem to get there quicker than everyone else.'

'All right, I take the compliment,' Maisie told them. 'How did it all come out?'

'The usual way,' said Jack. 'Interviews, cross-checking and plodding.'

In his tuneful voice, Fred sang a line from a popular comic song: '*A policeman's lot is not a happy one.*'

'Had it been going on long when it came to your attention?' Maisie asked.

'Yes, unfortunately,' Jack told her. 'In the end, we uncovered seven confirmed cases where she had drawn people in, at first with her crystal ball, would you believe, then with cartomancy, you know, the illustrated Tarot deck, plus some other nicely stage-managed methods of divination, including the Chinese one. What's it called?'

'The I Ching,' said Zoe. 'With sticks.'

'How do you know about that?' asked Phyl.

'Sneaky Steve told me about it.'

They all knew that 'Sneaky Steve' was Zoe's nickname for her nosy social worker – an oddly sympathetic hippy who once gave Zoe a smelly Afghan coat and, later, provided

Maisie with a couple of important clues towards the end of the Bunting Manor investigation.

'How exactly did she use these stage-managed predictions?' Maisie asked.

'The people she chose were all credulous,' said Jack. 'I don't mean to criticise them. I'm not saying that there can't be anything in any of that rigmarole. Who am I to judge? But I think it's obvious that people who visit fortune tellers are, by definition, looking for something intangible – reassurance, certitude, forgiveness – meaning that they are ready to be persuaded, vulnerable.'

'Shall we take this next door?' asked Phyl. She got up, leaning heavily on the arms of her chair. 'We don't want Jenny Brook's pies to burn.'

'What did you get?' asked Fred, looking keen.

'Three steak-and-kidney and three chicken-and-ham.' She addressed the gentlemen. 'There's five of us but you two will want more than one each, I'd wager.'

'Up and at 'em,' said Fred.

'Zoe, bring those peas through.'

They all got to their feet and hurried across the impressive hallway. Once installed round the kitchen table, Maisie thought they made an interesting composition, Jack and Fred on one side and she and Zoe opposite, with Phyl at the end, piling up her unopened post, moving it to the seat of her kitchen chair and sitting on it for safekeeping. Zoe poured the hot water from the kettle into a saucepan and set it to boil, turning off the oven and leaving the door ajar, with five dinner plates on the lowest shelf. Zoe tipped in the peas plus some mint from the newly tidied kitchen garden, giving Phyl the idea that they should all decamp outside.

'Or why in heaven's name did I go to the expense of buying that new outdoor furniture?'

They did so, Maisie finding that the oak table was still a little sappy from not having had time fully to dry out and season. But it was delightful to be surrounded by garden herbs and autumn flowers in the walled courtyard. Zoe brought the baked potatoes and pies and peas through on a big wooden tray and put it all in the middle of the table. Jack brought the plates, protecting his hands with a tea towel, and Maisie went back in to collect salt, pepper, butter and cutlery. They set to, all of them glad to be eating at last.

'Lovely,' Fred soon said, his mouth full of steak and kidney.

Jack nodded and Maisie approved him not speaking until he had swallowed. Phyl had also chosen red meat and was too focused on it to reply. Everyone, Maisie thought, was a little 'talked out', and the meal was a touch dry because the pies didn't contain very much gravy. They all ate with appetite, though, except Zoe who daintily served herself only half a chicken-and-ham, the smallest baked potato without butter and only a handful of peas.

'You're not on a diet, are you?' Maisie asked, lightly.

'Me? No, of course not. It's just that there was this lady at the hotel who ordered a cream tea and had no one to eat it with, so I shared with her up in the TV room because she seemed so sad.'

'Ah, that's why you were so long upstairs,' said Jack. 'You are a delightful young person, Zoe.'

'Thank you, Sergeant,' said Zoe with a twinkle. 'You see, Maisie, I'm just a bit full up already.'

Phyl was a very quick eater, so she finished first and regaled the others with news from the villages round about. Several of her stories concerned, obviously, the aftermath and repercussions of Maisie's investigations – a topic that Maisie knew she would have to confront sooner or later. Phyl made the events seem comic, with blundering police officers and rural stereotypes, including the 'drunken publican', the 'horny-handed blacksmith' and the 'high-handed landowner'. Eventually, she ran out of steam and Jack asked: 'Shall I go on?'

Maisie was about to say 'yes' when she realised that he might well want seconds, but he had perceived she would be glad if Phyl's comic monologue were curtailed.

'Are you sure you've had enough?' she asked.

'Absolutely. Would that be all right, Mrs Pascal?'

'Go right ahead.'

'You won't mind,' asked Fred, 'if I have that other chicken-and-ham?'

'Tuck in, man,' said Phyl.

'So,' said Jack, 'I'd got as far as the idea that people who visit fortune tellers are "seekers" and, in the experience of the police, apt to be easily taken in by a con artist with a convincing tale and a steadfast gaze. Confidence breeds confidence, you know? I don't think I could do it. You have to be a salesman for yourself, if you see what I mean. You're selling your charisma and your strength of mind. "Esmeralda" – Peggy Kemp in real life – had it in spades.'

'You haven't said,' Maisie guessed, 'but I'm imagining that Peggy convinced people to pay more and more for her services with ever greater elaboration in her staging.'

'Yes and, doing so, she got some of her victims to part with their savings for spurious reasons – bogus investment opportunities, wagers informed by her knowledge of the future, that sort of thing.'

'Did she not get any comeback from those she duped?'

'Yes, she did, of course. But, even then, she managed it very cleverly. She was softly spoken in manner, though magnetic and almost mesmerising in her way of looking at you and finding the right words to draw you in to her way of seeing the world, as if you and she shared a special secret.

Even I felt it. And, when she did get someone inclined to fight back, she was always able to calm them down and – as we eventually discovered – get them to make an appointment to "come and talk things through properly", at which point she was accompanied by her son, an evil-looking youth called Ronan, with muscles like steel wire and tattoos on more or less every inch of his sunburnt skin. People soon got the message – that it wasn't Peggy's fault if things didn't pan out. If they wanted to discuss it alone with Ronan, that was an option they could take.'

'Nasty piece of work, the son,' said Fred who had finally got himself outside of his second pie. 'He'd caught the attention of several forces along the south coast, but no one had ever been able to make anything stick.'

'Witnesses were always strangely unforthcoming?' asked Maisie.

'Precisely.'

'And where are the Kemps now?'

'Peggy and Ronan weren't anywhere near so well represented in court as Mick and Jez Carter,' said Jack. 'I think Peggy had an idea that wouldn't matter, that she would just use an everyday solicitor and rely on her own intelligence and charisma. That backfired, of course. You need to know the law, and confidence easily looks like arrogance to a jury in the harsh light of cross-examination. She was put away for a longer term than the Carter boys. She had the sense to keep her nose clean inside, however, and came out at the same time with good behaviour. Ronan's due for release on Monday.'

'In two days?' asked Maisie, keen to know precisely when this new potential danger might rear its ugly head.

'That's right and that's the reason why Fred wrote to me – you know, Maisie, the notes I showed you on the train

– because the date of his being on the street again had just been confirmed.'

'How did he get pinched in the end?' asked Zoe.

'Ah, that was Jack's work, too,' said Fred. 'Constable Wingard, as he was back then, was sent to fetch Peggy in for further questioning with a view to arresting her on arrival at the station. He found her climbing up with her shawls and veils – and her crystal ball, I don't doubt – onto the bench seat of a horse and cart with Ronan beside her holding the reins. Jack took hold of the bridle and spoke calmly to the nag and, no matter how he twitched the leathers, Ronan couldn't get the beast to move on. Furious, he jumped down and—'

'All right, Fred,' said Jack. 'No need for all the gory details. Let's just say that Ronan went down for "assaulting a police officer" and the south-coast forces all breathed a sigh of relief.'

'A temporary sigh of relief,' said Phyl, 'because now he's back out.'

'He'll shortly be back out,' corrected Fred. 'Monday morning at eight o'clock.'

Maisie wanted to get it all straight in her mind. 'The Carters ended up in Ford Open Prison. What's that? Just east of Chichester?'

'Six or seven miles,' confirmed Fred.

'Where did the Kemps find themselves?' she asked. 'In different establishments, obviously.'

'Ronan ended up in the men's prison, HMP Parkhurst on the Isle of Wight. His mother was detained in . . .' Fred stopped. 'Give me a hand, Jack. Where was it?'

'Holloway, first, then East Sutton Park. It's a women's open prison near Maidstone. She took care not to attack me, but there were sufficient grounds.'

'And Ronan – and maybe his mother, who's been out already for a spell – they'll be looking for you, Jack,' said Maisie.

'If I read his character right,' Jack replied, 'Ronan will have been thinking about me first thing each morning and last thing each night, every day since he was sent down.'

TWENTY-ONE

Seated round the lovely new oak table in the kitchen court-yard garden, with the night scents of pittosporum and jasmine heavy on the air, Maisie and Jack each kept their counsel as Fred, Phyl and Zoe discussed the details of the two stories: the Carter brothers, Jez and Mick, from the Fitwell scrapyard; the bogus fortune teller Peggy Kemp, from the converted Selsey railway carriages, and her combustible son, Ronan. At one point, she considered raising the threatening note, but refrained because she had an idea she might be able to get to the bottom of that on her own.

As the conversation began to go round in circles, Maisie appreciated that there was a double connection with the town of Selsey at the tip of the peninsula south of Chichester. It was where 'Esmeralda' had set up and it was where Mick and Jez were now working as casual labourers on Petter Farm. She interrupted the flow of debate to ask: 'If we're truly worried, wouldn't it be a good idea for me to know what they look like?'

'Who do you mean?' asked Fred.

'All of them – Mick, Jez, Peggy, Ronan when he gets out. Do any of the men have sort of squashed faces, you know, narrow?'

Phyl saw what she was getting at: 'You're thinking of your man on the train again, aren't you. I don't think there's anything in that,' she said, firmly. 'Jack, you agree, don't you?'

'I don't like to take anything for granted,' said Jack. 'Maisie, I can see why you're asking.'

'But it's all coincidence,' Phyl insisted. 'Maisie, you said so yourself, that he was probably getting off in Derby or Peterborough or wherever it was and going home for his tea.'

'I know you don't want to see me worrying, Phyl,' said Maisie, 'but, if it's a possibility that he bears any of us ill will, we should face it.'

Zoe burst out: 'This isn't fair. You're arguing about things I don't know about. Do you want me to go up to bed because I'm too young and silly?'

'No, Zoe,' said Maisie. 'I'm sorry. Fred's not completely following either, I can see. We're talking about the man on the train, you know, the second salesman? I told you about him earlier on, before we embarked on Fred's tales of Jack's early-career derring-do. Perhaps you were busy with the dinner.'

'Oh, yes, I remember,' said Zoe.

Fred nodded ponderously and Maisie wondered if perhaps both he and Zoe were tipsy and vague from the wine.

'So,' insisted Maisie, 'do any of the men – Mick, Jez or Ronan – have a kind of "narrow" physiognomy?'

'Not one,' said Jack.

'And, if you happened to come across him,' said Fred, his eyes unfocused as if picturing Peggy Kemp's dangerous son in memory, 'you'd find that Ronan has tattoos that make him unmistakable, even above his collar.'

'Not if he had a polo neck,' said Zoe, wanting to be a part of things.

'In my opinion,' said Phyl, decisively, 'we need more wine and we also need to consider the people left behind by the five mysteries that Maisie has solved, rather than the "second salesman".'

'How do you mean, "left behind"?' asked Fred.

'Phyl means the family and friends or even accomplices of the . . .' Maisie stopped, unable to find the right word from the technical vocabulary of legal retribution. 'What's the word?'

'The friends and relatives of the perpetrators,' said Fred, with relish.

'Oh, I'm lost again,' said Zoe. 'I don't think I'll have any more wine myself but I'll run and get another bottle, Phyl, if you want me to.'

'No, I'll go,' said Phyl, quickly, heaving herself upright.

Zoe went on: 'You're saying maybe the wife or the husband or the son or the brother of someone that Maisie has brought to justice might be ready to act on their own grudge.'

'Yes, obviously,' said Phyl. 'Now, don't say anything else until I'm back.'

Phyl got up and wove away indoors. Zoe followed with a stack of crockery and cutlery on the big wooden tray.

Maisie told Jack: 'I know I ought to wait for Phyl and Zoe to come back, but I've been thinking things through and I'm not convinced. The murderers I've helped to reveal just aren't that sort. They deserved what came to them and everyone agreed. Outside of their awful deeds, the places I've visited were happy, placid, normal.'

'Abnormal things happen in the most unremarkable places, Maisie,' Jack told her.

Maisie brushed a midge away from her face and told him: 'Back in a minute.'

She went inside to pull aside the curtain beneath the sink, looking for the citronella candles she had bought earlier in the summer to drive away biting insects. Phyl's leathery country woman's skin meant she hadn't been aware that there were any midges in her garden. Fred – who was a pipe smoker – gave Maisie a light and she put the two candles at opposite ends of the table. Soon, their fragrant smoke was hanging hazily in the air because the courtyard was completely sheltered from any evening breezes.

Zoe came back out with news that the washing-up was 'having a good soak'. Phyl returned with bottle and corkscrew and 'did the honours', refilling all the glasses. Maisie thought it was Fred and Phyl's fifth while she and Jack had limited themselves to just three measures. Phyl showed no ill effects but Fred was drooping. Noticing her gaze, he apologised.

'It's true what Mavis said. I've found it hard without Jack to back me up at the station and I've had to put in more hours than my old bones would really like. This evening's been an unexpected release, despite the tricky subject matter of our conversation, and I've over-egged the relaxation.'

Maisie knew that Fred was in his thirties, more or less her own contemporary, and wondered why he liked to pretend to be older and more fogey-ish than he really was.

'Have a cup of coffee and then drink up that last glass for the road,' said Phyl.

'I wouldn't mind tea,' said Fred. 'Would that be all right?'

Ever helpful, Zoe went to make it and Jack told a couple of his Newcastle stories to pass the time, including one that Maisie hadn't yet heard about a tourist launch that got stuck sideways in a canal and brought all other pleasure-seeking and trading narrowboats to a halt.

'Sugar?' called Zoe.

'Lots, please,' said Fred.

Zoe brought a cup and saucer outside and put it in front of him, then retook her seat. Maisie recommenced in a calm voice – not enjoying herself but determined to go through with it – presenting the characters involved in her brother's death, the murder at Church Lodge, in a coherent sequence, explaining how she had, by turns, suspected them and then moved on, in one case, coming back to her first idea in order to solve the mystery.

'What do you think?'

No one had any clear sense of what Fred called, enunciating very carefully, 'an aggrieved third party' who would 'want revenge for the rightful punishment handed down for such a dreadful act'. Jack said nothing.

Maisie went on to her second investigation, the murder at Bunting Manor, with similar results.

'No one's got any reason to think you did the wrong thing, Maisie,' said Zoe. 'You were a servant of justice.'

'That's a very highfaluting way of saying someone got their comeuppance,' said Phyl. 'But I agree, I suppose. I've actually sympathy for our Bunting murderer, as you all know, though their strategy wasn't one I would recommend.'

The conversation became a little confused as Fred, Phyl and Zoe became more impatient, asking questions at random, meaning Maisie's storytelling got twisted out of order and she began to worry that she might fail to mention something important. The individuals in the murders at the theatre, at Bitling Fair and at Sunny View in central Devon started to mingle in her imagination, making her frown and hesitate.

'I think,' said Jack, 'we've got as far as we're likely to go this evening.'

'Yes,' said Maisie, grateful once more that he was so uncannily able to read her mind – or, perhaps, her mood. 'We can talk again another time.'

'Soon, though,' said Zoe. 'Because the wedding's in just a week. In seven days, about this time, the two of you will be changing out of your glad rags into your everyday clothes, ready to drive off on your honeymoon.'

Maisie shut her eyes, visualising the calendar.

It's true. Seen in that context, this seems a lot of fuss about nothing.

She opened them again to see Fred finishing his very sweet tea, then tossing back his final measure of red wine – his 'one for the road', as Phyl had put it.

'Coming, Sergeant Wingard?' he asked, lurching to his feet.

'Have a turn about the manor grounds, would you, Fred, for the fresh air before we drive?' Jack requested. 'Perhaps Mrs Pascal will go with you, and Zoe, too.'

'Oh,' said Phyl. 'Young love needs a little space.' She hauled herself up. 'Come along, fellow gooseberries. This will do us good. But I say this: come back tomorrow at twelve sharp and I'll pay for lunch at the Dancing Hare. Jack, bring Florence. Fred, bring Mavis.'

'That would be lovely,' said Jack. 'Florence will be so pleased.'

'I can't,' said Fred, looking disappointed. 'Mavis already has plans.'

'To do what?' challenged Phyl.

'I fear I can't say. I wasn't listening to her.'

'All right then. Have it your own way. And no "murder talk". Agreed?'

Everyone murmured approval, then Phyl led Fred and Zoe away for 'a trot'. Jack stayed where he was, at the opposite end of the long oak table from Maisie.

'Littlegreen Sawmill, where this table was made, was at the heart of the Bitling Fair mystery,' he said. 'The people left behind there might be said to owe you a debt, rather than bear you ill will.'

'I know,' said Maisie.

'So, why do you look so careworn?'

'I'm not sure. Is it because I've spent so much of this year thinking about awful people and awful crimes?' She told him about the note and he took it in his stride, declaring that it was much more likely to have been for Phyl than for her. She asked him: 'How do you do it? How do you leave the bad things behind and not find them eating away at you?'

'It's as if I have compartments in my brain. That was one of the reasons I thought there was no hope for us, because your presence forced me to cross over those boundaries with your brilliant sleuthing, making it impossible for me to keep the two worlds apart – Jack the police sergeant and Jack the man.'

'But you don't think that any more?'

'I've told you, Maisie, absolutely not. But I can't be surprised that it's taking you longer to find a new equilibrium than I. You've only just started on this pathway.'

Maisie pondered the calendar of her year.

'Yes, in January, I was working hard with visitors to Paris from New York and Madrid and even Japan, unaware of how my life was about to change. Then, in February, I got Stephen's message.'

'Go on,' he encouraged.

'In March, I was astonished to hear from my mother's long-lost sister, Phyl, and to learn about why they fell out and . . .'

Maisie stopped, surprised by how deeply she was suddenly feeling her parents' loss – caused by a foolish traffic accident in a London 'pea-souper' fog.

'Keep going,' said Jack. 'Bring us up to date.'

'The murder at the theatre was at the end of April, just tipping over into the beginning of May, with the opening play of the new summer season. Then Bitling Fair was the week of midsummer, in mid-June. Finally, Sunny View was when the schools broke up, late July.'

'Do you see what I'm getting at,' Jack asked.

'Yes, I think I do. You want me to take a step back and recognise that all five mysteries were quite separate adventures, with their own distinct causes, sequential in time but not continuous.'

'That's right. Does that help? In my experience, it's letting the bad things feel like a tide that makes them hard to navigate. They aren't a tide. They're occasional drops of rain in a life of sunshine.'

'Do you believe that, really?'

'I do,' he told her. 'I mean, I didn't use to, but I do now. Thanks to you.'

144

TWENTY-TWO

The others suddenly came tumbling back in from their discreet constitutional stroll, giving Maisie the impression that Jack had something else to say but would no longer have time. Zoe was first to climb the stairs to her bedroom – a garret in the roof of the manor – in order, so she said, 'to listen to my new album'. Phyl asked her what it was and seemed confused by the gnomic answer: 'It's *Zeit* by Tangerine Dream.'

Once Zoe was gone, the conversation lost some of its fizz. Maisie realised that the young woman's – by turns – naïve and then obstreperous interventions had provided a welcome counterpoint to the more sober commentaries that she, Jack, Fred and Phyl had provided. In fact, Maisie found herself wishing that she, too, could slip away to think.

No, not to think. To drift off.

Of course, there was too much in her head to imagine she might find herself instantly embraced in 'the arms of Lethe'. Jack asked her what was in her mind and she told him, quoting Hamlet: '*To sleep, perchance to dream.*'

'I know what you mean, but Hamlet is talking about being troubled by bad dreams in death, not common-or-garden insomnia from stress and anxiety.'

Phyl surprised Maisie by making a big effort to turn everyone's minds to the wedding itself. Fred spoke enthusiastically about the guard of honour that he had organised from the other police officers from Chichester station who were primed to form up in two smart rows, dressed in their best uniforms with white gloves and other accoutrements of 'high days and holidays'.

'Thank you so much, Fred,' said Maisie. 'We appreciate it very deeply.'

'Will it be full, do you think?' asked Phyl, referring to the church of St Mary's, Framlington. The conversation moved on to practicalities, including the flowers. Phyl told Maisie: 'I've been talking to that nice Japanese woman from West Dean who has a remarkable life story and some very complex ideas about the meanings of the blooms she's chosen.'

'In what way?' asked Maisie.

'There's a language of flowers, apparently. I told her about my peonies from Marks and Spencer's and she said I should beware – you know, with a smile and a wink, not seriously – because they signify bravery and good fortune, but also anger.'

'I don't like that idea,' said Maisie. 'Anger is what we've been discussing – at least, enough anger to provoke revenge.'

'It's just a silly sort of symbolism, Maisie,' said Phyl, shortly.

'She's Grandma's friend,' said Jack. 'Florence volunteers in the posh West Dean gardens and they're bosom pals. They intend to do the arrangements together on Friday, the eve of the wedding.'

Maisie saw that thinking about his grandma had made Jack frown. She asked: 'Will that be hard work physically? Should someone help them?'

'Let's wait and see,' said Jack. 'If we butt in, she'll feel that we don't think she's capable and that will hurt her feelings. And it's a few days off, still.'

'Just around the corner,' argued Phyl. 'It'll be on us before you know it. Now, before you leave, gentlemen, what are we going to do? Are we intending to keep in touch and have another conflab.'

'For what reason?' asked Maisie.

'Should anything else happen.'

'Do we expect something to happen?' Maisie insisted.

'Expect the worst and you won't be disappointed,' said Phyl. 'But not tomorrow at lunch. That's purely social.'

Jack agreed that they should all 'keep in touch', then suggested to Fred that he should drive and his friend agreed, handing over the key of the Jaguar. Maisie bid her fiancé a tender good-bye and watched him pull away, executing a tidy three-point turn on the overgrown gravel and disappearing down the drive, through the hydrangea bushes, back towards the road.

She returned to the kitchen garden and found Phyl was just bringing in the last bits and pieces from dinner. Maisie lent a hand by wiping down the table, complimenting Phyl on her choice, receiving no reply.

'What are you thinking, now?' Maisie asked.

'I want to protect you,' said Phyl, in the gruff tone Maisie had heard several times already that evening.

'Thank you,' she replied, lightly.

'But it isn't easy. You're already thinking about going off into the wilds of this business, tracking down potential miscreants, heedless of danger. I didn't like the story of how you went off from Sunny View after the murderer, through sleeping fields in the pitch-dark countryside.'

'I took precautions,' Maisie argued.

'Such as?' Phyl asked, belligerently.

Maisie admitted: 'Well, not "precautions", exactly, but I was careful, approaching very quietly, making sure I knew what was happening before they did.'

'That's just my point,' said Phyl with exasperation. 'How is anyone to keep you safe if you will insist on seeking danger?'

'Maybe it's not your responsibility to keep me safe?' Maisie suggested, then instantly regretted it. 'I'm sorry, I didn't mean—'

'Don't worry, I won't take offence. You're a grown-up and you know what's what and can look after yourself. But, after

Irene and I . . . Well, after your mother decided she didn't want anything to do with me any longer and I lost you and . . .' Phyl stopped, sniffed and wiped her nose with the back of her hand. 'I lost you for so long and I've only just got you back.'

'Got me back for good,' said Maisie. She took Phyl's hand – the clean one, not the one she had wiped her nose with – and insisted: 'I will be careful. I could have kept all my suspicions from Newcastle and London to myself, but I didn't. I brought them out in the open to see if they might sort of evaporate in the light. But they haven't. You agree?'

'I do agree,' said Phyl with a cunning look in her eye. 'So, you accept that I have the right to protect you.'

Maisie laughed. 'Yes, all right, I do.'

Phyl insisted they should leave all the dirty things in their soapy water to soak overnight, which felt slovenly to Maisie but she was pleased to climb the impressive wooden staircase to her delightful bedroom on the first floor, overlooking the drive, to prepare for bed. The actual quotation she had been groping for – a better one than Hamlet's contemplation of escape into death – came into her mind, a line from 'Book Two' of John Milton's *Paradise Lost* that she had studied in school at Westbrook College, before she and Jack had properly met. She opened the window and spoke the words quietly into the night.

'Lethè, the river of oblivion, rolls
Her watery labyrinth, whereof who drinks
Forthwith his former state and being forgets,
Forgets both joy and grief, pleasure and pain . . .'

She stayed for a minute or so with her hands on the window-sill, wishing she could remember more of the stately phrases. Her mind drifted to the apathetic 'lotus eaters' and to the idea of flowers having their own language which – naturally

– linked to poppies which, by providing opium, also promised 'forgetful oblivion'.

Is 'forgetful oblivion' a quotation as well? It ought to be, or am I becoming fanciful, like Phyl said, 'flowery' in thought and speech.

She stayed where she was for a couple of minutes more, smelling the night flowers, greeting a broad white moth that landed on the back of her hand and spread its wings, still as stone.

It seeks the warmth, I suppose, of the blood beneath my skin.

She waited for the moth to move on, the darkness surprisingly noisy with bird calls and a yapping dog somewhere further off. A breeze came gusting through the trees whose rustling autumn leaves were already drying out, almost ready to fall. Before she knew it had happened, the moth took flight, wavering and uncertain.

This won't do. I must be decisive. That's worked for me in the past.

She got ready for bed, undressing in the bathroom on the corridor, brushing her teeth and putting a brush through her short curly hair without turning on the light. Her face, however, was visible in the mirror, very pale with an almost exaggerated darkness to the mouth and eyes, like an expressionist portrait.

In the past, though, I've been trying to protect other people, not myself.

*

The next morning, Sunday, Maisie woke with the sun, turned over, away from the open window, and willed herself back into sleep. Some indeterminate length of time later, she opened her eyes on lovely dappled light across her sheet and thin counterpane, feeling refreshed and optimistic.

Once washed and dressed, finding herself alone in the chilly kitchen with its stone-flagged floor, she put on the kettle then ran the hot tap to flush away the dirty water and the remains of last night's meals from the plates and dishes. She refilled the sink, adding a good glug of Fairy Liquid to cut through the grease, and found the water too hot to put her hands into. The kettle whistled so she made herself a cup of coffee, using two heaped spoonfuls of Maxwell House and two rectangular brown sugar lumps, plus the top of the milk from an unopened bottle in the fridge. She went back into the hall and opened the front door, drawing the heavy bolt and letting in the sun, still dappled and lovely through the encroaching trees that she had several times suggested to Phyl might be cut back – without success.

She drank her coffee, realising she was very much looking forward to lunch at the Dancing Hare.

We will all be together again but, in public, no one will talk about sad or threatening things.

Phyl appeared, announcing that she would be glad if Maisie would accompany Zoe and her to church.

'Because it's expected of you as lady of Bunting Manor?'

'I feel I ought to be setting Zoe a good example and, as my manners and my habits can't be said to offer an unblemished pattern of existence, I am falling back on the dubious example of modern-day Christianity.' Maisie laughed. 'Now I have my tea,' Phyl continued, 'I'll drink it in the bath and see you in an hour.'

'A good soak,' approved Maisie.

'My Sunday routine,' said Phyl. 'I don't like being wet, except on the Lord's Day.'

Maisie laughed again and returned to the kitchen to complete the washing up, drying everything with Phyl's tattered tea towels, then draping the damp cloths on the outdoor furniture.

Zoe appeared in her ostentatiously patterned kaftan, refusing tea and mixing instead a strange powder from a sachet.

'What's that?'

'It's "Rise & Shine" powdered orange juice. We've had a trial pack from Kellogg's at the hotel. I love it.'

Zoe whisked the mixture with a fork in her glass.

'Dehydrated orange juice?'

'Yes, try it.'

Maisie took it and sipped. 'It's very sweet.'

'And very acid,' said Zoe. 'The perfect combination. Do you get it in Paris? Perhaps not yet. Ours is a trial, I think, from the Cash-&-Carry, to see if people like it.'

'Behind every Parisian bar is an electric juicer to make *citron pressé* and *orange pressée*, meaning—'

'I know what *pressé* means – "squeezed".'

'That's right. It's all natural.'

'Paris is better in every way,' said Zoe with a sigh. Maisie broke it to her that they were going to church in little more than an hour. Zoe groaned and said: 'I'll go and get changed.'

Left alone once more, Maisie went for a walk through the woods, climbing the hill to the pilgrim trail at a fast pace to get her blood moving. Then she picked her way down to the stream on the far side where Phyl's estate manager, Archie Close, had discovered a body, face down in the trickling water. Looking at the idyllic place, with the stream running much wider and deeper than she remembered, Maisie found it hard to recapture the sense of horror and confusion that she and Phyl had experienced at the time.

I'm becoming inured to death. I'm not sure I like that.

She returned home, visiting the bathroom to make sure she didn't have any twigs or leaves in her hair from yomping between the trees. Unsatisfied with her polka-dot dress as suitable for church, she put on her more sober mustard-yellow one and met Phyl and Zoe in the hall.

The church in Bunting was dedicated to St Andrew – Maisie wasn't sure which St Andrew – and had an interesting though slightly intimidating architectural detail, a platform to one side of the nave that belonged to Bunting Manor. It was one of the many reasons that Archie Close could legitimately refer to Phyl's Jacobean pile as the 'Big House', not without pride but also with humour. The platform had been added to the church's interior by the same seventeenth-century nobleman who built Bunting Manor, presumably wanting to set himself apart from the hoi polloi of his feudal domain in his moments of ostentatious worship.

From her raised vantage point, alongside Phyl and Zoe, Maisie had a view over the whole church. Pretty much the whole village was in attendance for the eleven o'clock matins, including all of what Maisie thought of as her '*dramatis personae*' from the Bunting mystery. The villagers had all become used to her in the six months that had passed since those dramatic events and no one was paying her any special attention – no guilty glances or whispered comments or acid looks.

Canon Dander delivered a sprightly 'family service', meaning there were more hymns than laborious readings or long-winded exegeses on the meaning of the scriptures. Even with everyone trooping up to the altar rail for Holy Communion, they were all out again in under fifty minutes, finding the day had darkened with heavy cloud, though the temperature was still warm.

Just then, Maisie saw someone who, she felt, might well bear her – and, by extension, Zoe and Phyl and Jack – ill will. She hadn't noticed him from the platform, looking down on the nave, because he was an occasional organist and had been seated out of sight. She knew this because he had a sheaf of musical scores in his thick hands, with plump, sausagey fingers. As usual, he was dressed – or rather 'encased' – in a heavy three-piece woollen suit, also resembling a sausage, with a monocle on a black ribbon tied to the buttonhole on his left lapel. His name was Commander Kimmings.

An ex-naval officer, he was crossing the green to the front door of his primped and pretty cottage.

I wouldn't be surprised to discover that he's been stewing ever since I brought his bad behaviour out into the open in the Bunting Manor investigation – his dodgy house-building deal and his unkindness to Zoe.

'Come on, Maisie,' said Phyl. 'Don't dawdle.'

Reluctantly, Maisie followed the other two along past the green and the dismal shop to the pub, looking for all the world like three generations of the same family – which, in a sense, Maisie reflected, they were.

The Dancing Hare was still locked up so they sat on the stone bench beneath one of the front windows. Despite having shelter from the eaves of the roof, Maisie felt a few raindrops beginning to fall and enjoyed the developing pattern of dark splotches on the already dark tarmac of the road. Then, just in time, before the sprinkling became a downpour, she heard the bolts being drawn and had a happy thought.

Jack and Florence will be here soon.

Then, before going inside, she felt a new tremor of anxiety.

If opening time is twelve o'clock, why aren't they already here?

There was no need to worry. Her fiancé and his grandma arrived soon after, having been delayed by farming traffic, even on a Sunday, as everyone was busy trying to get in their crops before the weather turned for good. They ate a delicious lunch, the five of them, avoiding topics related to 'any kind of unpleasantness', as Phyl put it, hanging around over desserts and coffees until nearly two. Then, the Wingards returned to Chichester by car for Jack to read up on the work that awaited him on Monday morning at the police station and Florence promised herself a nap in her chair.

For Maisie, the rest of Sunday passed in a blur of inconsequential pleasures. Because lunch had been excellent and far too big, she spent an hour chopping wood for kindling, stacking it neatly under cover in a corner of the barn. Then she took another walk beside harvested fields, seeing the stacks of straw bales ready to be brought in, then back along the woodland paths she knew from pheasant shoots she had worked on as a beater in childhood. A good strong pot of tea in the kitchen garden followed, plus half an hour conversing carefully in French with Zoe, at the young woman's urgent request.

Neither she nor Phyl nor Zoe was in the mood for a cooked dinner. Maisie devoted her evening to sitting in an armchair in the library, reading a fairly good Margery Allingham novel, one of a series with a hero named after a flower, the campion, a hardy herbaceous perennial. She had seen lots of them on her walk, five-petalled rose-pink blooms, competing for light and moisture in the hedgerows. She would have liked to finish Ngaio Marsh's *When in Rome*, but somehow it had ended up in Jack's luggage, not hers.

Halfway through the Allingham novel, she and Phyl and Zoe ate a little cheese with pickle and crackers at the kitchen table, all of them still feeling full from lunch but knowing they 'ought to have something'.

Maisie was the last to go up, turning off all the lights and making sure every door was locked, the windows properly closed, not leaning open on their stays. She climbed the stairs, hearing the familiar creaks and groans of an ancient building adjusting to the cool of the evening. She got ready for bed, then hesitated at the desk in her room, wondering if it might be time to set all her thoughts down on paper, in order to clarify the sequence of events thus far – and perhaps spy a pattern she and the others had so far missed.

I should give some thought to how I'm going to put Commander Kimmings on the spot.

Yawning, she changed her mind.

Tomorrow is another day.

III

ROSES

SIGNIFYING LOVE AND PURITY, BUT ALSO JEALOUSY

TWENTY-THREE

The Isle of Wight, visible on a clear day from high points on the pilgrim trail, was a substantial island a couple of miles off the south coast of England, across an arm of the English Channel known as the Solent. Getting on for twenty-three miles wide and twelve or thirteen miles deep, it provided good arable and pastoral land to many small-to-medium farms, plus woods to support forestry trades and harbours to encourage boatbuilding and sailmaking and fishing. Most of the important settlements were perched on the edges, some with flat beaches, many with steep drops down into the waves, a few of these also the locations of important discoveries in the field of dinosaur-fossil hunting. In the centre of the island was the city of Newport. Not far from Newport was another significant landmark.

Her Majesty's Prison Parkhurst.

The Isle of Wight had history as a place of confinement. Fleeing the roundhead army of Oliver Cromwell, the cavalier King Charles I thought he might take refuge there, but instead found himself incarcerated, unable to travel on and find asylum in Catholic France, due to the grey and forbidding seas and a governor who judged that he owed allegiance to Parliament, not the Crown – to the will of the people, not to the Stuart household's unilateral assertion of 'divine right'. Later, the Isle of Wight became the final home of another monarch, Queen Victoria, who endured the undignified metaphorical incarceration of advanced age in her summer residence of Osborne House.

Early on Monday morning, the 25th of September, after the Saturday evening conflab at Bunting Manor and the Sunday lunch at the Dancing Hare, with just five days to go until Maisie and Jack's wedding, Phyllis Pascal, philanthropist, supporter of several significant charities, was present on the island. She knew the place well from pre-war holidays in her youth, as well as through her voluntary work as a prison visitor, doing her best to help men who had lost their way to find a path back to becoming 'useful members of society', as she liked to put it. Phyl had a strong moral code, backed up by a – contrasting – forgiving nature. Her sharp tongue was moderated by her soft heart.

As a prison visitor, Phyl's main preoccupation was assisting in teaching the men to read and write, knowing full well that there was a strong correlation between illiteracy and wrongdoing. Her journey to HMP Parkhurst for each of these charitable – and, to be fair, personally rewarding – visits required driving south out of the Downs to Portsmouth, onto a small car ferry, across the Solent and then twenty minutes or so on winding island roads. Then, she would endure the tedious rigmarole of security identity checks, despite being well known to almost every member of the prison staff, before being allowed inside, each time hearing the doors clang shut behind her with an uncomfortable note of finality.

Phyl vaguely knew the prison pastor, a clever man with a wry manner that, she thought, helped him to stand above the disappointments and frustrations of his difficult ministry. Once, waiting together to be admitted, she had asked him what his motivation was.

'Love, Mrs Pascal. That is the basis of all Christian ministry. The mystics compared it to the closed bud of the blood-red rose, ready to open out and receive God's bounty of understanding.'

'Love for all, whatever their guilt?'

'Whatever their deeds, however dark their hearts,' he had confirmed.

'And their confessions and prayers, your absolutions and your blessings – is all that sufficient to purify their souls?'

'For a time, perhaps, until the next jealous thought, the next betrayal of trust or kindness.'

'When it all begins again,' Phyl had agreed, earnestly.

'It all begins again,' he had repeated, sadly.

Since that first conversation, they had not spoken privately again, pursuing their individual purposes – didactic and spiritual – on parallel lines.

On this particular Monday morning, Phyl had set out very early, just as the sun was rising, in order to be at the gates of HMP Parkhurst even before access to visitors became permissible. It was, of course, Fred Nairn's news about Ronan Kemp being released that had prompted her to make the trip. And she had decided to do so without telling Maisie or Jack.

They would have told me to leave well alone. I can't do that.

Phyl still wondered if she oughtn't to have told Maisie where she was going and why. She had left an indeterminate note on the kitchen table.

Gone out for some things. Back mid-morning.

On reflection, she judged that the phrase 'some things' was likely to make Maisie suspicious, so vague did it now seem.

She parked and – waiting nervously behind her Land Rover's steering wheel, glad that she was too early rather than too late – stared at the wire-topped walls and fell to thinking about the philosophical implications of the 'denial of liberty' as a method of punishment.

The old traditions of forced labour – though they were often taken much too far – surely constituted a more productive way for offenders to 'pay their debt to society'.

Because Phyl's relationship with HMP Parkhurst was a long one, she knew its history, beginning as a military hospital before – dispiritingly – being transformed into a children's asylum. Worse still, by the time the young Queen Victoria was on the throne, it had been reclassified as a children's prison, a place of punishment not care, from which many boys were sent abroad, 'transported' to the colonies of New Zealand and Australia – out of sight, out of mind. The idea was, Phyl supposed, that the pioneering colonial life would 'put them straight', teaching them the virtues of honesty, hard work, prudence and so on.

The Victorian miscreants who remained behind were also purposefully employed. Taught the craft of brick-making, their wares were put to punitive use, extending the prison campus by adding new wings to the growing complex, ready to 'welcome' an ever-growing population, the vast majority of whom came from the most disadvantaged segments of society.

But that's not so very unusual.

The morning was grey and so was Phyl's mood.

Do we not, all of us, build our own prisons in our hearts and in our minds, with the way we choose to see the world, the guilts we can't assuage, the regrets for which we can't forgive ourselves?

Phyl had chosen Parkhurst as the theatre of her charitable work because it was close at hand and, despite having to cross the Solent, reasonably easy to get to. A second argument in its favour – Phyl having melodramatic tastes in some ways – had been its deliciously sinister reputation as one of the country's toughest jails. Just six years earlier, in 1966, it had been given special status as one of a handful of 'top-security' jails, suitable for the 'dispersal' of the most disruptive and intractable offenders.

Another car pulled up, a beaten-up Ford Escort with one wing a different colour from the rest of the bodywork.

A woman got out, dressed in a beaded skirt and what looked like several shawls. Despite having never before seen her in person, Phyl deduced that this must be 'Esmeralda', Peggy Kemp, recently released from a women's detention centre near Maidstone whose name she couldn't remember, although she knew that either Fred or Jack had mentioned it.

Phyl watched Peggy reach into her car, scrabbling on the dashboard for a gold packet of Benson & Hedges cigarettes, lighting one with a petrol-filled Zippo lighter and smoking greedily, as if she had refrained while driving and felt the lack of nicotine very deeply.

More time passed. Peggy lit a second cigarette from the butt of the first, half sitting on the mismatched fender. The sun rose a little higher behind the screen of cloud and then Phyl saw Peggy drop the filter of her second B&H and squash it underfoot. She was wearing sensible black shoes with one-inch heels, probably issued to her on release, along with the return of her fortune teller's garb.

Phyl wound down the window of the Land Rover and heard sounds of inner barriers being unlocked and swung back, clanging and banging. Then, in the huge outer double doors, wide enough to allow a bus or a truck to enter, a smaller pedestrian access swung inwards.

A prison guard emerged, wearing dark trousers and a grey shirt with insignia that, at a distance of thirty yards or so, Phyl couldn't read, though she had seen it many times up close. The guard looked left and right as if checking that no one was waiting for this moment to surge inside the prison and, perhaps, take the place by storm. Then he leaned back inside, his voice too faint for Phyl's straining ear. She got out of the Land Rover, assailed by doubts.

Am I being foolish? Perhaps, but I couldn't just stand by and do nothing . . .

161

A second prison guard emerged and they stood, one on either side of the small door. A strongly built man followed, stumbling slightly as he lifted his foot over the sill because the opening didn't go all the way down to the ground. Phyl knew who he was because she could see his neck tattoos above the neckline of his grey-white shirt and because Peggy Kemp ran towards him, calling out: 'My Ronan, my boy.'

Phyl watched mother and son embrace for fully a minute, Ronan's strong arms about his mother's shoulders, his hard hands clasped together. There were tattoos on his arms, as well, that Phyl could see because his sleeves were rolled up. They moved towards the Ford Escort. Soon it would be too late. She took her courage in both hands and approached.

'Good morning, Ronan. Congratulations on your release.'

The two Kemps sprung apart, both on their heels, as if preparing to flee.

'Who are you?' asked the mother.

'Hang on. You're the reading lady,' said the son.

'Yes, I'm the "reading lady". I wonder, could I speak to you? Do you have a few minutes?'

'My boy's time is his own, now,' said Peggy. 'Are you here to try and find him more trouble?'

'Not at all – the opposite,' said Phyl. 'I want to offer some advice.'

'What kind of advice?' Ronan demanded. 'I don't need no book learning. I've got on fine without it for twenty-six years.'

'Have you?' asked Phyl. 'Are you sure?'

'I know my own life better than you do, I reckon.'

'The decisions you've made mean you've spent a good stretch locked up in this awful place. Was that always the plan?'

'What do you want?' snapped Peggy. 'Out with it.'

Phyl took a deep breath, then delivered a version of the speech she had been rehearsing in her head, all the way down from Bunting to Pompey – Portsmouth – and across the chilly neck of water of the Solent, then through the island's woods and fields.

'I'm not here to talk to you about rehabilitation or studying to read and write and reintegrating into society. I imagine you've had enough of that from do-gooders of my caste. If you haven't paid any attention to well-meaning people trying to help, year on year, inside the prison, I don't suppose you're going to start now you've regained your liberty. You never came to any of my classes, even though I'm sure other inmates will have told you that I wasn't there to judge, only to help. Well, because you never came, you don't really know me, which means I have the advantage over you because I've recently learned quite a lot about your background. Just for the record, my name is Phyllis Pascal and, by a sequence of coincidences that I won't go into right now, I have some close contacts in the police force.'

Phyl hesitated, realising she had gone off script, that she hadn't got to the point anywhere near as quickly as she meant. Her pause allowed Peggy Kemp to interrupt.

'Why are you here, poking your nose into our business? Are you trying to spoil Ronan's day? We've got places to go, people to see.'

'Pints to sink,' added the son.

'I'm not surprised and that's fair enough,' said Phyl. 'I'm aware that you, too, have been released only recently, Mrs Kemp. I have this to say to you. Sergeant Jack Wingard and his fiancée, Maisie Cooper, are very close friends of mine. I came across this morning to give you a warning, do you understand? I'm advising you not to do anything that you will later regret because, I promise you, everything you do and everywhere you go will be known to the police.'

The mother and the son exchanged glances. It seemed to Phyl that her words had struck home.

'Are you telling us that we're being watched?' asked Ronan, a suspicious gleam in his eyes.

'That's right.'

'Where are they then?' he demanded with a dismissive wave of his hand. 'I don't see them?'

Phyl sighed with frustration. 'Look, I came here because I'm aware that you have a grudge against Sergeant Wingard. I'm warning you not to act on that grudge in any way.'

'We don't know you,' said Peggy. 'Leave us alone.'

'This is for your own good.'

'I reckon we can decide that,' said the son.

'I'm just trying to prevent—'

'This is harassment,' said the mother. 'You've no business—'

'All right. I'm sorry. I realise I'm intruding on an important moment but I wanted you to know because, surely, it's better for all concerned?' Phyl heard her voice almost pleading. 'You don't want more trouble, I'm sure, and doing anything to harm Jack or Maisie will see you back inside these prison walls before you can say "sixpence".'

Phyl could see that her words had had an impact but she was unsure what precisely it might be.

Have I hardened them in their desire for revenge, or have I managed convincingly to forewarn them that nothing they do will go unnoticed?

She noticed that the two prison guards were still outside the small open doorway, observing the conversation. She supposed she had spoken with enough emphasis and emotion to be heard by them and wondered if that might queer her pitch and preclude her from visiting any longer on the literacy scheme.

I wouldn't be surprised. They'll probably decide I've become a loose cannon.

She turned away, feeling foolish, and went and climbed back into the Land Rover.

Which I suppose I have.

She put the car in motion, crunching the gears in her distracted, unsettled state, reversing out of the parking space and swinging away towards the junction with the main road where a quarry truck went barrelling past just two feet from her front bumper. She drew a sharp intake of breath, shrinking back in her seat, then exhaled and pulled away.

The road ran uphill and she soon caught up behind the heavily laden lorry, grinding slowly along with no passing places in sight. Now she had done what she had set out to do, all she wanted was to be back home, imagining that it had never happened.

Have I made it all worse?

She thought about other steps she had taken, incognito, without discussing them with Maisie or anyone else, not even her faithful Archie.

Is it just as likely that this presumptuous attempt to forestall unpleasantness will rebound on those closest to me?

The truck pulled off into a building site and she was able to accelerate, heading for the ferry back to the mainland.

I'm a silly old woman. The world would be a better place if, in future, I stopped home and kept myself to myself.

TWENTY-FOUR

That same Monday morning, the 25th of September, Maisie had also risen early, intending to borrow Phyl's Land Rover to set off on an errand of her own. Finding Phyl's vague note on the kitchen table and the car not available, she went to find Archie. Luckily, he was clearing the barn of some bits and pieces of farm machinery, moving them to a smaller timber storage unit close by. She asked if there was any other means of transport available, perhaps Zoe's moped.

'You ladies are up and about very early today,' he commented. 'Thanks for getting that kindling chopped, by the way. You know I was hoping for all hands on deck later in the week to get the straw bales into the barn?'

'Yes, Phyl mentioned it. I'll be happy to help. How's Bert?'

'Not had a peep from him.'

'Are you worried?'

'No, he hates bother. He wouldn't thank me for fussing round with the honey-and-lemon linctus.'

Archie went on to assure her that, yes, Zoe's moped was in good working order and 'fuelled to the brim' with an appropriate mixture of oil and petrol. 'She'll be right.'

'Zoe won't mind if I take it?'

'Mrs Pascal doesn't like the maid using it. She says it's too dangerous to be out on that frail thing in traffic.'

'Phyl worries a lot about both of us, Zoe and me, doesn't she?'

'She does, but you'll take care, won't you? I'll run the lass down to the main road through Framlington in the tractor and she can take the bus. She'll not be late.' He took out his rolling tobacco and Maisie realised that he had more to say. 'Mrs Pascal frets something chronic over you, Miss Maisie, that's where 'tis. You're not silly. You'll have seen it. Is there anything I can do to help?'

'I'm not sure, Archie, but thank you.'

He licked his Rizla paper and twizzled the hand-made cigarette between thumb and forefinger.

'You and Miss Zoe have made this a happy place after some dark times. You know that, don't you? I wouldn't like to see the clock turned back.'

'I promise you, Archie, I'm aware and I appreciate your devotion to Phyl. She's a good woman and she deserves you. That's what I think.'

'She's always after doing good, and sometimes at a cost,' said Archie. Then he repeated his favourite – inconclusive – Sussex vernacular expression: 'That's where 'tis.'

Maisie was surprised to see how sombre was Archie's expression, his eyes wet, as if he already foresaw some awful consequence of Phyl's philanthropy. That made her think about the threatening letter and reconsider who it was really aimed at.

'I promise, if anything happens that I think you can help with, I'll not hesitate to let you know.'

'Fair enough.' With a sigh, he put the roll-up behind his ear. 'Looking forward to it, are you?'

'What's that?'

'The wedding, Miss Maisie. Not long now. He's a lucky man, Jack Wingard.'

Mentally rebuking herself for not realising what he must mean, she hastily replied: 'Thank you, Archie. I'll be delighted to see both you and your brother in the congregation. Do you think Bert will make it?'

'I've not seen him this fortnight. I expect he'll make an effort for Saturday, though.'

'If you do speak, give him my best. Tell me, is Petter's Farm easy to find?'

'Oh, yes. Big place. Just before the Selsey sign, on the left.' With a sort of twitch of his chin, Archie mooched away, perhaps embarrassed at having revealed such depth of emotion, calling over his shoulder: 'Key to the moped is on one of them kitchen hooks.'

Maisie went back inside for some long trousers, instead of her dress. The only real option she had was a boiler suit that she wore whenever she was engaged in helping out with manual tasks on the estate. She rather liked it, the most practical apparel possible in thick white cotton that didn't have to be kept clean or ironed, under which she could wear as many layers as the season required.

Despite the mild weather – apart from the after-church shower – Maisie thought she might well be cold on the road with the wind whipping past, even though the moped's tiny 50cc engine would limit her speed to only about forty miles per hour. She put on a pair of winter tights, plus a vest and a jumper under her boiler suit. Then she pushed her feet into her wellingtons.

The key was, as Archie had promised, on one of a vertical row of hooks screwed untidily into the architrave frame of the kitchen door. Maisie recognised it from the fob that gave the name of the motorbike shop in Chichester, CMW Motors, where Phyl had it serviced.

She located the moped in a corner of the barn, under a tarpaulin, with the helmet perched on the seat. She squeezed it on over her ears, adjusting the strap under her chin, swung her leg over and – with the moped still on its stand – turned the key and pedalled furiously to kick the motor into life. Once it was ticking over, she paddled out with her feet then revved the engine to carry her away onto the gravel and down the drive, between the hydrangeas.

This won't take long. I'll drive to Selsey and have a quick look at the Carter brothers just so that I can recognise them should I come across them anywhere – and make sure neither of them can be my 'second salesman'. I'm not going to do anything silly.

As usual, there was little traffic on the country roads. Once she got down through Framlington, though, she became nervous of commuting cars and thundering lorries, desperate to overtake on roads that didn't really allow it. Twice she felt herself squeezed into the gutter, so she took the strategic decision to ride fully in the middle of her lane, so as not to allow the unsettling experience to be repeated.

In Chichester, the roads were busy, too, and the railway gates next to the station very slow to open. She sat, waiting for three trains to go by, before being released with a platoon of cars onto the road south. A mile or so further on, she passed the turning for Chichester Marina on the right, then wound on a couple of miles through Sindlesham and Nunton, beginning to feel the cold from the rush of air – her helmet had no face shield and her cheeks were stinging – before finally seeing the turning she wanted on the left.

The entrance to Petter's Farm was a sticky lane made of wet clay and chalk, beside which were three brick-and-flint workers' cottages with untidy gardens. Maisie thought they could easily be spruced up and become very desirable, but they were uncared for and sad.

She turned up the lane, finding a pick-your-own field on the left with rows of soft fruits under ragged netting to protect the crops from birds. There were crows and seagulls circling, plus a dozen or so on the ground, searching for a way in. On the right-hand side were a dozen impressive rows of rose bushes with vivid blooms in red, white and yellow. Maisie wondered what those colours might mean in 'the language of flowers' and thought she might ask Florence and her friend, Kinori.

She could taste salt on the air because the sea was now very close. Noticing a woman walking between the roses, Maisie stopped her moped and got off, removing her helmet out of politeness – also with relief because she wasn't enjoying the sensation of her head being compressed by its tight cushioned lining.

'Good morning,' she called. 'Do you work here?'

The woman looked up, a quizzical expression in her eyes. She was dressed like a man, in jeans and a tartan bomber jacket over a white T-shirt, a wicker basket of long-stemmed blooms over her arm and a pair of secateurs in her right hand.

'What's that?'

'I mean,' said Maisie, 'of course you do, unless the roses are pick-your-own as well?'

'No, I work here. Can I help you?'

Now that she had reached the moment of crisis, Maisie wasn't sure what to say. She still felt cold and stiff from the early start on the moped through the chilly air. She pushed her fingers through her short curly hair that felt unbecomingly crushed against her scalp. The woman simply watched. Her expression was neutral and her pose very still.

'Do you perhaps employ Mick and Jez Carter? Someone told me . . .' Maisie began weakly, wishing she had prepared a pretext for her enquiry. 'Are they about?'

'They are. What have they done?'

'Nothing – or, I mean, I just . . .' Maisie felt very foolish. The woman had a very direct gaze and seemed content to wait for more information before committing herself. 'Look, I realise this must seem very odd. Let me introduce myself. My name is Maisie Cooper. Would you tell me your name?'

'Liz Petter.'

'Pleased to meet you. Can I speak frankly?'

Liz Petter left a pause. Standing still, Maisie was beginning to thaw, feeling a little wan sun on her face and neck, even smelling the delicious rose-fragrances, drawn out by the growing warmth.

'That's always best, in my experience,' the woman replied.

'This is going to sound silly, but I want to get a look at the Carter brothers because I want to be able to recognise them.'

'Why's that, then?'

Maisie glanced round. Because of the distance between them – two alleyways of opulent rose bushes – she was having to raise her voice. She felt very exposed on the edge of the muddy lane, even though there seemed to be no one else about. She decided that she had no alternative to the truth, however bizarre it might sound.

'You must know they've been inside?'

'I do.'

'My fiancé is the policeman who put them in jail. I'm worried that they might bear him a grudge.'

'I know Jack Wingard. And you said your name is Maisie Cooper?'

'I did.'

Liz Petter half closed her eyes, as if searching her memory for something deliberately forgotten, then told her: 'You look very different from last I saw you. And from your picture, after, when I read about you in the paper.'

'Oh.' Internally, Maisie sighed, hoping the woman wouldn't quiz her interminably about being an 'amateur sleuth'. Brightening her smile, she said: 'You may well have done but I hope you didn't believe it all.'

'I'm not the credulous type. Why don't you come along with me.'

Liz Petter walked up her row of rose bushes towards a large, red-brick farmhouse at the top of the drive. Maisie was obliged to walk parallel on the rutted clay, pushing the moped alongside, the left-hand pedal several times catching on the flapping trouser of her boiler suit, before she decided to lower its stand and leave it behind.

At the top of the field of roses, Maisie found herself in a concrete yard with scatterings of dirty straw and heaps of horse and cow mess lying around. She followed Liz inside the house, through a back door into a spacious but dark kitchen with pots and pans hanging from a frame over a heavy table and an Aga lodged tightly in an enormous, old-fashioned fireplace, its warmth beckoning.

'Come and stand against it,' said Liz, thoughtfully.

'Thank you,' said Maisie. 'That's so kind, but I don't want to take over your morning. I really just want to take a look at them.'

'At Mick and Jez?'

'Yes.'

'You don't want to talk to them?'

'Not at this stage,' said Maisie, wondering if that were true. 'Or perhaps I should. What do you think?'

'I really couldn't say. Please, make yourself comfortable.'

'No, of course. Silly question.'

Maisie moved round the heavy table and leaned back against the chrome rail of the Aga. Liz Petter put her basket on the draining board and reached up to a high timber shelf for a vase that she filled with water from an iron tap whose spout was encrusted with limescale. Maisie noticed a large gauze cloche on the table and lifted a corner, expecting to see a cake or, perhaps, a fresh-baked loaf. Instead, she recognised the ugly flaccid form of a fresh-plucked pheasant, the greyish skin puckered and loose, with a small puddle of blood round its tiny head.

She put the cloche back and, to break the silence, told her host: 'This is an impressive old building. Do you work the farm alone?'

'It's my father's and my mother's.' Liz finished what she was doing and turned back towards Maisie. 'But I have no brothers or sisters so I suppose it'll be mine in the end.'

'I wonder, have we met before? I have an idea we might have done, but I'm terrible with names and faces.'

'Not met, exactly. At least, not recently.'

'Go on, please? I'm sorry if I seem rude. I've been living abroad for quite a few years and only came back to Sussex in February. Memories of my childhood and teenage years are very distant.'

'Oh, I wasn't talking only about all that time ago, though I did know who you were, even then, because you were in the Westbrook College cadet force and you carried the flag at Remembrance Day and things like that. All the boys fancied you in your smart uniform.'

'Oh,' said Maisie. 'That's not how I remember it. You weren't at Westbrook College, too?'

'No, the high school. But, like I said, I've seen you more recently. I was in the theatre that night.'

'That night . . .' said Maisie, confused. Then she understood. 'Good heavens, you mean when the . . .'

She stopped, trapped for a few seconds in the awful memory of the hero of *The Beggar's Opera* choking to death in front of an entire audience, a full house.

'Yes,' said Liz. 'That's right. What the *Chichester Observer* called the "Murder at the Theatre". We were there when it happened, Mum and Dad and I, and I saw you talking to Jack Wingard as we were being ushered out. Dorothy Dean, the theatre manager, gets roses from us to put in the stars' dressing rooms and we take adverts in the programmes, so we get complimentary tickets.'

Leaning against the chrome rail of the Aga, Maisie was – thankfully – no longer tense with cold. She asked: 'You know Jack as well?'

'I've lived round here all my life. Everyone knows good old Jack.'

She said it lightly, but Maisie felt a frisson of some deeper emotion behind the words, as if she was saying: '*Some know him better than others.*'

'I feel I should explain. Jack and I are engaged and—'

'Congratulations,' interrupted the other woman with the same peculiar – almost dismissive – tone.

'Thank you. We're very happy. But, given Mick and Jez Carter might well bear a grudge I just wanted—'

'It makes sense,' said Liz.

She smiled and the effect was dramatic. Maisie felt glad that she seemed to have finally broken through the woman's reserve.

'I'm so glad to hear you say that. Are they working this morning?'

'They will be. I've got them gleaning in the potato fields – picking up the tubers left behind by the mechanical harvester.'

'That sounds like hard work.'

'Back-breaking. I don't envy them.'

'My impression of them, from the stories I've been told, suggests they won't last long at something like that. Am I wrong?'

'If they had the choice, but where else can they go?' said Liz, evenly. 'I've got a caravan down by the rife, so they're housed as well as earning a crust.'

'The rife?'

'The stream.'

'I see. Well, a roof over their heads must be welcome after a stretch in prison.'

'Better than being homeless and on the streets, yes.'

'I feel sorry for them, too, you know,' Maisie insisted. 'And I'm not absolutely certain that I should be worrying about what they might do. It's just . . .' Maisie frowned, telling herself not to share too much. 'I'm sorry, Liz, I know this is an imposition and you must be very busy. What farmer isn't? Just to be clear, you didn't recognise me at first, then you worked out—'

In the same odd tone, Liz broke in: 'You looked very different in your Balmain dress. Like an actress, in fact.'

Maisie had another vivid flashback to Adélaïde Amour, the star of *The Beggar's Opera*, railroading her into wearing a clinging long dress with a vivid and colourful pattern.

'Oh, yes. That wasn't my idea. The management insisted I had to . . .' Maisie shook her head. 'I could barely breathe.'

'It fitted you like a glove.'

'Very different from this old boiler suit,' said Maisie, uncomfortable with the direction the conversation was taking. 'Anyway, if you tell me where to go, I'll just walk out and take a glimpse at the Carters and be on my way. Would that be all right?'

'I'll come with you. That'll look less peculiar.'

'You're sure?'

'I am.'

Without another word, Liz led Maisie outside, across the dirty yard and between two outbuildings, one a traditional timber barn and the other a larger corrugated-aluminium one. They crossed a first narrow stream – running deep with clear water – that Maisie had been reminded should be called a 'rife' in Sussex vernacular. Then they were on the edge of an enormous potato field measuring at least six or seven acres. The soil had been turned over and was by turns being wetted and drying in heavy clumps in the mixed September weather. On the far side of the field, she could see a hedge line, beneath which another rife probably flowed, indicated by the lush grass beneath the hawthorn. The caravan Liz had mentioned was in the far corner, where the field met the foreshore and the sea.

'What a wonderful location,' said Maisie.

'Yes,' said Liz. 'If we go down this path, we'll pass close by them.'

They set off along the edge of the field, towards the water. Not far from the caravan, two men were working, repeatedly bending to pick up the gleanings – left-behind spuds – dropping them into hessian sacks. At the ends of several rows were other sacks, left for collection, already filled. Liz led Maisie by them, calling out: 'Morning, Mick; morning, Jez.'

Both men stood up, mirroring one another's gestures by putting a hand into the small of their backs to relieve the pressure of the work.

'Morning, Miss Petter,' said one of them, the taller of the two. He had very short dark hair, cut close to his scalp. 'We'll soon be done with this field.'

'Today?' Liz asked.

'No,' said the other. He was a hand shorter with the same tight crew cut. 'Not today but maybe tomorrow.'

'When you get to lunchtime, take a break from spuds and you can come and hose down the yard.'

'Thank you, Miss Petter,' they both replied, clearly grateful.

Liz walked on and Maisie kept herself on her far side, half hidden from the two Carter brothers who appeared not to be paying her any attention in any case. When they reached the water, Liz turned right.

'We can come back to the farmhouse this way, through the flower garden. Did you get a good look?'

'Yes, I did. Thank you.'

'What was your impression?'

'Nothing's easier than doing the wrong thing. The trick is to get back on the right path afterwards. I hope they aren't plotting doing something silly, but I've got several other—'

Maisie stopped, realising it would be entirely inappropriate to be talking openly to this stranger about her suspicions, even though she had apparently vaguely known Liz Petter in childhood.

'You don't have to go on,' said Liz, sounding uninterested. 'I hope you feel reassured.'

'Time will tell,' said Maisie, then realised it sounded rather portentous. 'I mean, yes, I do, in fact. I would definitely recognise them if I saw them in town or anywhere.'

'Good.'

Liz pushed open a gate into a formal garden laid out with multiple flower beds. Maisie recognised sparse blooms of peonies, carnations, chrysanthemums and dahlias, scrupulously deadheaded to extend their season, plus woody plants including rosemary and lavender, and camellias whose blooms were long past. There were also brown and withered spears of daffodil and tulip, bent double and tied with string to keep them tidy.

Soon, they were back in the filthy yard. Uncomfortable with the lack of conversation, Maisie thanked Liz once more.

'Give my regards to Jack,' said Liz, then she smiled her broad and disconcerting smile for a second time.

'I will,' said Maisie, wondering precisely what Liz meant by that. 'Goodbye.'

Liz turned away without another word, heading back inside the kitchen. Maisie strolled out of the yard and down the sticky lane to her moped. Before climbing on and pedalling like a mad thing to get the motor started, she squeezed her helmet over her ears and stood for a moment in the muffled quiet, lost in thought.

Am I right? Is there a connection there, too?

As well as everything else that was swirling through her mind, she began to wonder if the threatening letter Phyl had received – that might well have actually been for her – had come from Liz.

Warning me off – telling me not to get between her and Jack.

TWENTY-FIVE

Before going home, Maisie decided to drive on through Selsey to the shoreline, to see the lifeboat station on its timber-framed jetty, like a pier.

And perhaps there will be a memorial to the place of execution near to where Peggy Kemp ran her evil and manipulative confidence trickster's business.

The town was wide awake, with tradesmen's vans and delivery lorries busy round the shops on the high street. A café close to the beach was doing good business providing teas and breakfasts to late-season tourists as well as to working men and women.

Seeing the lifeboat jetty in the distance, Maisie drove towards it and parked by a stylish Sixties concrete-and-glass beachside house and tramped along a promenade that lay half concealed beneath shingle thrown up by the waves. Further along, she found herself close to the row of converted railway carriages where Peggy had lived, noticing one with tattered garlands around the front window, its timber porch subsiding and its garden overgrown.

Thinking that was rather sad, despite the reason for its dilapidation – the owner spending several years in prison – Maisie walked on, unsure where she should look for a marker of the location of the smugglers' gibbet. She saw a woman in a bright waterproof cagoule coming the other way, walking a pair of sedate black Labradors. Because she looked local, Maisie spoke to her.

'I beg your pardon. Are you from round here?'

'Born and bred,' said the woman. 'Are you lost?'

'Not exactly. I wonder if you're aware of the history of this place?'

'I should say so. Most folks are. Is it the gibbet you're thinking about?'

'Actually, yes,' said Maisie.

'You'll be disappointed, I'm afraid. The "gibbet field", as was, is mostly gone under the sea.'

'Oh, I suppose it was a long time ago. Do you know the story?'

'I do. It was the constant fighting with France and the rest of the continent that made the English government impose high taxes on imported goods to pay for their wars – on things people wanted like brandy, wine, gin, lace, tobacco and tea. Smuggling became a huge business. It probably sounds romantic.'

'No,' said Maisie. 'Not to me.'

'Are you in the police or the coastguards, perhaps?'

'I do have experience of criminal investigations,' Maisie told the woman. 'Please go on.'

'The culprit on this occasion was tea, which was incredibly expensive and sought after in the middle of the eighteenth century. The Hawkhurst smugglers, knowing that they'd been found out, took the decision to murder a customs officer and his chief witness in the most brutal manner imaginable. They were tried in Chichester in the Guildhall – you know, the old Franciscan chapel in Priory Park. Two of the Hawkhurst men came from near Selsey, so they were hanged in chains down here so their bodies could be seen far out to sea.'

'Good heavens. It was brutal, wasn't it?'

'What they deserved,' said the woman. Her placid Labradors were lying on the shingle at her feet and seemed asleep. 'Does that help?'

179

'Oh, it was just idle curiosity,' Maisie fibbed. 'Thank you so much.'

She said goodbye and returned to her moped, spinning the pedals to fire the engine and pulling away, none the wiser, she thought, for her trip to the beach.

There didn't seem to be any special atmosphere to me. Peggy Kemp must have been very good at creating her own spooky mood.

★

By the time she was back at Bunting Manor, Maisie had come to a firm conclusion about Liz Petter – one she would have to take up with Jack because, obviously, it concerned him as well – that, at some point in the recent past, they had been 'an item'. Pursuing that, however, wouldn't be possible for the time being because, until the end of the day, he would be hard at work at the police station and it would be quite wrong to disturb him when he had a huge amount to catch up with, following his two-month absence.

Maisie found Phyl at the kitchen table, opening her post, a task she knew Phyl undertook only periodically, when the pressure of the accumulating envelopes became too great to ignore. Maisie told Phyl the story of her early morning outing, expecting Phyl to return the compliment and narrate her own crack-of-dawn adventure, but she didn't, gesturing to her post and saying instead: 'Do you mind if I just get on with all this? I'm embarked, now. Archie, by the way, took Zoe into Framlington twenty minutes ago and he'll be back in a moment to go through the sheep and the forestry books with me.'

'I don't mind at all.'

Maisie went upstairs and took off her boiler suit, folding it up and putting it away in the floor of her wardrobe, removing her winter tights and her jumper, slipping her mustard-yellow dress over her head. She remembered Liz Petter's jeans and bomber jacket – an incongruous match with the basket on her arm that was much more suited to an elderly Miss Marple–type character with grey hair and pink cheeks, innocently pruning her roses whilst eavesdropping on her neighbours.

Maybe I ought to get some jeans? They might be useful, especially as the weather turns.

She pictured herself side by side with Liz, dressed similarly.

What would Jack have to say about that?

A broad smile on her face, Maisie went back downstairs and rang Florence Wingard from the phone in the hall, by the front door. She ascertained that all was well.

'You shouldn't worry about me,' Florence told her. 'Worrying just brings more worries.'

'Is that right?'

'Take it from an old woman.'

'Sixty-eight is not old,' Maisie told her. 'Do you need any shopping?'

'I'm quite capable of popping round the corner to the parade.'

'Good,' said Maisie, who found Florence's independence bracing and encouraging. 'Glad to hear it. If Jack comes in for lunch, tell him I called, please?'

'Urgent?'

'Not especially, no,' Maisie told her. 'And do I need to drop in for another measure for my dress?'

'Yes, you do. How about tomorrow at ten?'

'Splendid.'

Maisie went outside, realising that she had forgotten to put the tarpaulin over the moped in the barn. Having remedied that oversight, she stood in the outer doorway, wondering what she should do next with her day. The imminent wedding had put her in a kind of limbo, unable to make any decisions about what should come next.

Was I right to rush it through after the end of the Sunny View mystery? Should we have waited in a civilised manner for next spring to do it properly?

She ran back upstairs to look at her own post, including the two unanswered letters from France. She wrote replies to both, explaining her situation, using very similar words in each – that she couldn't make any plans until after she was married and the honeymoon complete.

'*Mais ça m'intéresse.*'

But I am interested.

She put them in envelopes and addressed them, then went downstairs to scrounge a couple of stamps. Phyl didn't have any suitable for France. Maisie decided to go into Chichester to the main post office, asking Phyl if she could borrow the Land Rover and if she should do any shopping while out.

'Yes, you can, and no shopping required,' said Phyl. 'Unless there are things you need.'

'I'll have a think on the way.'

Before setting off, Maisie wound both windows down, having to lean far across for the passenger one, meaning that she was moving quite slowly along the drive. To her surprise, she caught sight of a figure half concealed in the tall hydrangea bushes, dressed in dark clothes and impossible to make out because of a bright shaft of sunlight on the windscreen, meaning the shape in the shadows beneath the trees was indistinct.

Not thinking, acting purely on instinct, Maisie took the car out of gear, put on the hand brake and got out.

Where have they gone?

Standing still, she could hear rapid crunching footsteps, hastily retreating through the undergrowth, and set off in the same direction. The stiff branches of the hydrangeas pulled at the skirts of her mustard-yellow dress. After twenty paces, she stopped. The sound was still there, but further away.

Maisie pressed on, passing more easily through a stand of fir trees with little undergrowth, just a carpet of their acid needles lying thick on the ground. She was able to accelerate, almost sprinting to the far side, into a coppiced section of hazels, cut down almost to the ground. Beyond that, maybe two hundred yards away now, she caught a glimpse of the same dark figure disappearing into thicker woods, tall chestnuts and beech trees.

With renewed energy, she danced through the coppiced hazels – new growth sprouting from the stumps in multiple shafts. Half a minute later she was on the edge of the shadows, her heart thumping and her breath coming in quick pants, listening for her quarry.

I was too slow.

Nothing – no hint of the direction she should now take.

I've lost him – or her.

Disappointed, she turned and made her way back, less hurriedly. On the drive, she found the postman had been and, unable to get past the Land Rover, he had left a few envelopes on the bonnet. Maisie picked them up and got in, tossing them onto the passenger seat. She started the engine and nosed very carefully out onto the road through the village because the large stone gate pillars, topped with stone acorns, did their best to obscure her view.

Nothing was coming. She turned left towards Harden, wondering if she oughtn't to stay home.

Is Phyl quite safe with a dark-clad stranger roaming through the undergrowth, perhaps delivering another threatening, anonymous note?

She drove slowly, her eyes on the left-hand verge and the trees beyond, wondering if she might catch another glimpse of whoever it was.

They were up to no good, obviously, or why would they have run from me?

She dabbed the brake, progressing now at little more than walking pace.

Or did I frighten them, perhaps? Could they have been an innocent walker? Were they just worried they'd be had up for trespassing? I never got a good look at them . . .

She stopped the Land Rover at the side of the road, crunching some gravel washed down by heavy rains from the fields, opposite Canon Dander's vicarage in Harden.

Phyl said Archie was about to come in and go through some accounts. She's not on her own.

There was a fingerpost in the left-hand verge, indicating a bridleway into the trees. Maisie got out and went to stand at its entrance, peering up the overgrown path. The ground showed hoofprints in the sticky mud between the flints. She felt the countryside was eerily quiet, without even the flap of a bird's wings to disturb the silence. The air was heavy and humid. She wondered if that meant more rain or if it was simply moisture drawn up from deep in the ground by the trees.

Phyl will be okay with Archie. Zoe is on her way to Chichester on the bus. Florence is off to do her bit of shopping on streets where most people know her face, if not her name. Jack is at work at the police station. Everyone's fine. Nothing bad can happen.

She returned to the Land Rover and pulled away, not believing it for a second.

Twenty-Six

Maisie queued at the main Chichester post office for five minutes – behind people renewing their television licences and asking questions about how to fill out their passport applications – to buy half a dozen stamps suitable for letters to France plus half a dozen 'Air Mail' labels. She licked two of each and stuck them down, then put her envelopes in the 'foreign' posting box, folding the spare stamps inside her purse.

Out of doors, the weather was still humid but the rain – that a heavy sky surely promised – had not yet decided to fall or it was falling elsewhere, perhaps up on top of the Downs, ready to filter down through the chalk and flint into the valleys below, swelling the rivers and streams.

The obvious next step is to talk to the only people I know who hear all the legal gossip – and who are my friends, so they won't keep back.

Maisie walked along West Street, past the cathedral bell tower, to the office of her solicitor, Maurice Ryan, where she found Maurice's striking wife and assistant, Charity Clement, busy with the post at her enormous typewriter. Charity broke off to hug Maisie, told her Maurice was in court, then insisted on hearing the whole story of the murder at Sunny View while she made tea in the rudimentary office kitchen. Maisie obliged, but felt she told the tale badly, feeling distracted, and – of course – Charity noticed.

'Qu'est-ce qu'il y a?'

What's the matter?

They continued the conversation in French and Maisie felt a benefit from expressing herself in her second language because it became easier to distance herself from the emotions that all the unexplained events had provoked. Once she had finished, Charity looked unimpressed.

'*Mais tu as dû t'attendre à quelque chose de la sorte tôt ou tard, non?*'

You must have expected something like this sooner or later?

'No, I didn't. I suppose I was naïve, thinking I could get involved in other people's lives, putting things right, explaining their motivations and their mistakes and then, you know . . .'

'Bringing them to justice and moving on?'

'Yes, that's it.' Maisie frowned. 'I convinced myself that solving each mystery could be the end of the affair, like in a book or in a film, even though it clearly wouldn't be. Haven't I had to endure all kinds of frustrating court appearances and the rest of it, so that the police and the Crown Prosecution Service can complete the . . .'

'For the wheels of justice to turn.'

Maisie sighed and switched back to English. 'I've been naïve, haven't I?'

'Idealistic, perhaps.'

'Do you have time for a longer talk? You're very clear-sighted. You won't get het up over nothing.'

'What does "het up" mean?' Charity asked.

'Hot and bothered, you know?'

'*Ah, je comprends.*'

'So, do you have time?'

'*On peut aller manger si tu veux. Il est presque midi, tu sais.*'

'Is it midday already? Okay, splendid, yes. Let's go and get something in the café opposite, above the department store?'

'Too crowded if you have secrets to share.'

'Then a visit to the baker in the Butter Market for sandwiches and a pastry that we can take to the Bishop's Palace Gardens?'

'Perfect.'

The Butter Market was on North Street, built by 'royal assent' in 1807, designed by the celebrated architect John Nash, with a portico of six doric columns. It had originally been conceived as a place for market traders to shelter from inclement weather. On one wall, the 'toll board' was still visible, announcing – for example – that a butcher or cheesemonger must pay a *per diem* of 'one shilling' for use of the premises.

Maisie and Charity both chose freshly made cheese-and-tomato sandwiches and a piece of bread pudding, served with a paper serviette in brown paper bags, and took them through the cathedral cloister to the delightful gardens beyond, full of mature specimen trees, some of them brought back from the southern hemisphere by explorers and botanists. The sky remained dark but the rain held off.

They found an unoccupied bench in a quiet corner and sat down. Maisie told Charity her story with economy – in French because that was an extra barrier to being eavesdropped – including the visit to Petter Farm, at which point Charity had finished her sandwich and admonished: 'That was perhaps not wise, to show yourself in that way. If you are wrong and they had no ill will, no thoughts of revenge, your visit may have provoked them.'

'I know, but I can't just sit still, can I?'

'Yes, you can. That's exactly what you should do. Worrying at things more often causes upset than letting a situation evolve in its own time.'

Charity's expression was very serious.

'That's the natural conservatism of the legal profession,' Maisie told her, attempting to lighten the tone.

'There is wisdom in patience, in not precipitating things. Now, eat your sandwich at last.'

Maisie did so and Charity told her quietly about the complicated aftermath of the murder at Bitling Fair where her husband, Maurice, was involved in a professional capacity.

'But, having solved that one, Maisie, you went off elsewhere seeking new challenges? I would have thought you'd have had enough of mysteries by now,' Charity told her, once again with a critical tone.

'My friends in Sunny View wrote to ask for my help,' said Maisie, weakly, between bites. 'I couldn't simply refuse.'

'You might have, but you didn't.'

'It never crossed my mind,' said Maisie, honestly.

'So, you are embracing this life? Will it continue after you are married?'

'I don't know.'

'You have considered the repercussions on Jack's career? It will be different when he is an inspector, in charge of important investigations, rather than a lowly community sergeant.'

'I know.'

'What does he say?'

'That I should be myself, you know, follow my own star.'

'Of course he does. That is his love for you speaking. He may not be right.'

'But my involvement in each mystery has been an accident.'

'Because, each time, you decided not to look the other way.'

'I can't, Charity,' Maisie protested in a tone of frustration. 'It's not in my nature.'

'I'm sorry.' Charity switched to English. 'Don't be "het up". I'm just thinking aloud about what is best for you, my dear friend.'

'I know.'

188

They sat in silence for a minute or two, eating their stodgy cubes of bread pudding. When they had finished, Charity remarked: 'Imagine trying to sell these lumps of wet, recycled leftovers in Paris, Maisie. Can you picture the confusion? "Is it to eat or to mend a hole in the wall?" But I have grown to like traditional English food and it seems normal to me, now.'

Maisie considered her friend – very much an 'exotic' in Chichester with her dark Guadeloupian skin and colourful twin-sets and scarves. It made her think about the wedding flowers and the lotuses and peonies and roses she kept coming across.

'I'm sorry if I sounded short-tempered with you.'

'You are forgiven.'

Maisie found herself saying something out loud that she hadn't known until that very moment. 'The truth is, since I finished solving these mysteries, my life has felt almost mundane. I've lost purpose. Madame de Rosette has written to me from the office in Paris to offer me a temporary job that I would love to take. And Adélaïde has asked if I might accompany her on another theatrical production, which sounds incredibly glamorous and exciting and . . .' She sighed. 'I want to marry Jack and I'm so excited for our wedding, but I don't want life to pass me by.'

'No, indeed. Why should you let it?'

'I left Chichester and joined the Women's Royal Auxiliary Corps because I wanted to be like my brother, but also because I'd been dreaming of getting get away from this stifling provincial life with so many people who just do the same things every day, barely looking beyond their garden gate.'

'Like Florence Wingard, for example?'

Maisie was about to argue, then realised that Charity was right.

I don't want to live like Florence, pottering about in the garden, going to the shops, playing whist with her friends on a Thursday evening, organising the raffle for the community centre.

'I love Florence but surely there are bigger things she could be doing?'

Charity shrugged and suggested: 'She's happy. She doesn't want to.'

'I suppose I can see a risk in being content with a very narrow future,' Maisie agreed, grudgingly. 'And I don't like it.'

'You would rather have big dreams and projects, like Madame Pascal turning Bunting Manor into a respite home.'

'Yes,' said Maisie, wistfully. 'I want always to have big dreams.'

'And family?'

'You mean children.'

'That's right.'

'Yes, and children, too,' said Maisie, slowly. 'Perhaps that's it.'

'But for that, too, you have to wait. It isn't entirely in your control. That is the heart of it.'

'The heart of what?'

'Oh, Maisie, do you not see? It is not a compliment to tell you that you are very clever. Everyone knows this. And clever in many ways – with numbers and languages and organising events and with your pentathlon skills and all the rest of it. But, most of all, you see through people and put together clues and work out the connections that others miss. But the reason you are good at all that is because you are trying to shape the world to your will.'

'I don't know where you're going with this,' Maisie protested.

I do, really, though.

'The desire to understand,' Charity patiently explained, 'is very close to the desire to control. Just now, in this difficult time while you wait for an enormous change of life, you feel out of control. So, these suspicions that you perceive – left, right and centre – are a reaction to your feeling of distress that life is carrying you along like a cork in a stream, you understand?'

Maisie knew precisely what Charity was describing.

'I felt that the other day when the train started moving and it looked like the world was sliding away without me.'

'Yes, that's another good example.'

'Am I really that passive?'

'No, you are fighting the movement, the current, every step of the way and your feelings of frustration come from being unsure you will prevail.'

'You make me sound like a complete megalomanic.'

'No,' said Charity. 'Not if you are aware of who you are. And, of course, you are focused on helping other people.'

'But you think I should "look the other way".'

'No,' said Charity, her tone very serious. 'I'm saying you "could" have done, in the past. But not now, not any more. In the previous mysteries, it was always about someone else. This time, it's about you.'

'Yes, it is.'

'So, you must observe and reflect and stay ahead of the danger to yourself.'

Maisie bit her lip, her eyes down, fighting an unaccustomed flare of anger. When she spoke, it was in a fierce undertone.

'And the danger to Jack and to Phyl and to Zoe and to Florence.' Maisie could hear the tension in her own voice. She felt a coil of pressure, like an overwound spring, deep inside herself. 'The idea makes me feel quite wild.'

'Yes,' said Charity. 'I know.'

Mais qui est-ce que je deviens?' Maisie asked, quietly.

Who am I becoming?

Twenty-Seven

When Maisie had met him, back in February, during the investigation into the murder at Church Lodge, Derek Field-house had been a well-kept, bullet-headed, barrel-chested man, puffed up with good food and alcohol and his own sense of self-worth. Since then, though, his circumstances had changed. Failure and prison had knocked the stuffing out of him.

Had Maisie met him on that same Monday morning, skulking around the stables in Framlington having spent the night wrapped in horse blankets in the tack room, prickly with straw, she'd have had to look twice. His head was stubbly with a sporadic growth of grey-brown hair, his face deeply lined, his physique and posture deflated.

Back in February, Derek had been taken into custody in a smart suit that fitted him as the peel of an orange fits its plump flesh. Today, dressed in the same smart tweeds – plus a once-crisp white shirt and what looked like a regimental tie but which was, in fact, something of similar design available to all and sundry from Marks and Spencer's – the wiry woollen fabric hung about him as if he had borrowed it from a much bigger man.

The stables belonged to Framlington Manor – to Derek's wife, Daphne, in fact, whom, as a distant cousin of the same surname, he had married. Sometime soon, a *decree nisi* would be delivered into his hands, a severer punishment for his transgressions than his brief jail time. His acceptance thereof would be the signal for Daphne's lawyer, Maurice Ryan, to make a significant payment into Derek's bank account on the proviso that Daphne 'never have to look upon his foolish face again'.

Had Daphne said those dismissive words with venom or, at the very least, anger, Derek would have been happier. But, on her sole prison visit, she had uttered them in the same wan tone of disinterest with which she had spoken to him throughout their joyless, childless, shared pilgrimage as husband and wife.

Mistress and dogsbody, more like, he thought.

The stables were not currently in use because it had been a good few months since they had provided shelter to any horses. Daphne, of course, had no interest. Even the fine grey stallion that, Derek knew from the tale told in court, had more or less saved Maisie Cooper's life, had been sold and shipped out. In July, therefore, Bert Close, the Fieldhouses' farmhand, had been delegated to other tasks – no more mucking out, rubbing down, saddle-soaping leathers or soaking cob nuts, though Bert continued to sometimes eat his lunch in the quiet yard.

Using the horse brushes, Derek did his best to smarten himself up, improvising with the shiny underside of a tin of saddle-soap as a mirror. Then he slipped out of the stable, across the concrete hardstanding of the yard and up into the field, crossing two stiles and coming out behind the Fox-in-Flight, on the road that separated the forge from Framlington Manor. For a minute or so he stood still in the shadow of the hedge, waiting for two cars and a farm lorry to pass, then listening for silence to return. Once it had, Derek crossed the road and slipped into the grounds of the fine house he used to inhabit, from which he had been banished, through the pedestrian side gate, hesitating once more as he listened for any signs of life.

Nothing. Good.

During his married life, it hadn't been unknown for Daphne to lock Derek out on days when he failed to return on time from the pub or from a meeting of one of the business clubs in town, the Rotary or the Masons. On these occasions, he waited for her to go to bed, then found the key he had secreted under a clay pot containing a large rosemary bush that she, with her infirmity, would never be able to move, then crept in to sleep downstairs on the sofa in the lounge. In the morning, he would slip out before she was up in order to make a pretence of having painfully slumbered – oh, how uncomfortably – in his car, a shiny MG Midget sports car in British racing green.

Sure enough, the key to the kitchen door was still there, among the frightened woodlice that scattered as he tipped up the heavy pot. The key turned with barely a click and, with a sense of relief that Daphne hadn't changed the lock, he slipped inside.

The house was warm, the central heating on despite the mild weather. He could hear faint voices from the first floor where Daphne was probably chiding her physiotherapy nurse for imagined clumsiness.

Derek pulled a kitchen chair away from the table, moving it close to the counter and the cupboards above. He climbed up and reached into the nearest one. On the top shelf were some Tupperware boxes of dry goods – flour, sugar, pasta, rice, dried pulses and so on. He took down a tall plastic container of rice, removed the lid and pushed his stubby fingers into the grains, not at first finding what he was looking for, feeling a surge of panic, then exhaling with relief as he retrieved a tight roll of banknotes.

Enough to keep body and soul together.

It was a roll of twenties, enough for someone careful to start a new life.

But I don't care to be careful.

He replaced the Tupperware, climbed down and slid the chair back into position. At the sound of voices on the landing and the whir of the Stannah stairlift thrumming into life, he slipped outside with just time to relock the kitchen door, hide the key, and disappear through the pedestrian gate into the lane, crossing to conceal himself once more in the shadows of the hedge, smiling to himself with satisfaction.

Can't keep a good man down, he thought.

Then he chuckled, humourlessly.

Nor a bad man, neither.

TWENTY-EIGHT

Charity only had ten minutes left before she needed to be back at her desk. Maisie accompanied her through the cloister on to West Street, hesitating at the door of the office to ask: 'Just one other thing. Do you know the Petter family?'

'Maurice and I know all the wealthy people. The Petters have many acres and many interests. The father is the chairman of the Rotary Club. Do you know what I mean?'

Maisie did know what she meant. However stuffy and old-fashioned it was, she had great respect for an organisation whose motto was 'Service Above Self'. She said: 'They get successful people to do good works and, meanwhile, encourage a sort of mutually beneficial network of business and social contacts.'

'That's right, but not silly and secret like the Masons.'

'No,' said Maisie, momentarily taken back to the Masonic Hall in Kirton where one of the most important meetings in the investigation into the murder at Sunny View had taken place.

'Jack is a member of the Rotary Club,' said Charity, meaningfully.

'I know. He runs their poetry competition for school-children in spring each year. He was busy with the preparations back in February when I first came back.'

Charity tilted her head. 'What is your interest in the Petters?'

'It isn't them, or it wasn't. I told you, that was where I went this morning.' She added some more details from the story of the scrapyard in Fitwell. 'I know you judge that was a mistake, but I'm glad to think I'd know Mick or Jez if I ran into them. I also met the daughter of the family, the only child, apparently, called Liz.'

'Ah, yes,' said Charity. 'The lovely Liz.'

'Is she lovely?'

'Definitely. Not stunning like you, Maisie, but certainly a head-turner. Is that the right expression?'

'Should I know her?' Maisie asked, aware that Charity had something else to add. 'She told me we have childhood things in common, but I have no memory of them. And she was at the theatre when the murder happened on stage . . . Well, you know. You were there as well.'

'And you have no memories of her? That is perhaps another way of making her feel small.'

'What does that mean?'

'Why do you not recall her?'

'I sometimes wonder if it's because my parents died. That sort of drew a veil over my past.'

'I think it might be a good idea if you were aware of who she is – who she was,' said Charity. 'Or can you guess?'

'Yes, I think I can,' said Maisie. 'As I was riding away on my borrowed moped, it did cross my mind.'

'Liz Petter and Jack Wingard,' Charity confirmed. 'A very handsome couple. And the parents would have been over the moon, I think. The father is a very traditional man, old-school, survived the war by being in a reserved profession on the family farm, ended up very "tweeds and wellingtons" as Maurice calls it, smart but still in touch with the soil.'

'How serious was her and Jack's relationship?' Maisie asked, uninterested at this point in the character of the father.

Charity pondered and Maisie waited, feeling disloyal to Jack, knowing that these were questions she ought to be asking him directly, not ferreting around for information from a mutual friend. Eventually, Charity admitted: 'It seemed to last a considerable time. This and many other things happened while you were away. Maurice and I sometimes ran into them at events, you know, the summer season at the theatre, concerts in the assembly rooms, special services in the cathedral.'

'Were they ever engaged?' asked Maisie in a small voice.

'I don't believe so. I used to wonder if it was more a sort of . . .' Charity frowned. 'I don't know the word in English. In my family, we talk about "*cousinage*", meaning going to parties with your cousins because you don't have a boyfriend or a girlfriend, but perhaps one or the other felt more strongly than that.'

Maisie wanted dearly to ask how the relationship ended, but a Daimler with a very long bonnet pulled up beside them and Maisie understood that it was Charity's next appointment.

'Thank you for talking it all through with me.'

They kissed one another on both cheeks and Maisie slipped away before the man – another 'tweeds and wellingtons' type – extracted his corpulent self from behind the wheel of his ostentatious motor.

*

Maisie didn't want to dwell on all she had learned, in particular how she was going to broach with Jack the subject of his . . .

What would be the word? Entanglement? Liaison? Understanding?

She drove back out of town, stopping halfway home in Bitling, parking on the forecourt of the turkey barn, a part of Phyl's farming interests supervised by Harold and Adam Farr. No one was about.

She walked across a field into the main part of the village, coming out close to the pub, the Silver Garter, just as it came on to rain – a sharp downpour. Of course, she had the option of ducking inside but, now she was here, she found she didn't want to talk to anyone after all.

She crossed the narrow street and skipped through the small graveyard beside the chapel, coming out onto another lane lined with low houses, and the entrance to Bitling Green. She ducked under the canopy of the wide-spreading weeping willow beside the pond, its waters encroaching on the turf beneath the dangling branches. Sheltered from the rain shower, she sat on a tree trunk, dragged into position for just that purpose, her knees drawn up, her arms folded.

This is normal. Jack is entitled to have had romantic attachments in the past, as I am – as I have.

Maisie adjusted her position because there was a heavy drip-drip falling on her right shoulder.

But none of mine were ever serious. I always used to wonder what it was people meant when they talked about the coup de foudre, *the bolt of lightning, of falling 'head over heels' and all that. Of course, I know now. It means you've found someone you didn't know you were looking for – and you don't ever want to lose them.*

She squeezed herself further over to the end of the tree stump.

How about Liz Petter as a vengeful, spurned woman? Is that conceivable?

Maisie turned her mind to the reason why she had decided to turn off the Framlington road.

I wanted to think through the protagonists in the murder at Bitling Fair and – stimulated by being on the spot – try and find one who might be out for revenge.

Being 'on the spot' made no difference. Just as she had thought when talking it all through with Jack and Fred and Zoe and Phyl, the answer was no one.

I'm sure it's Jack's past that matters, not mine.

As the rain grew heavier, the willow proved incapable of providing good shelter. Its narrow fronds didn't work like the generous leaves of a chestnut or sycamore, creating a proper roof. She slipped out and jogged back through the graveyard and across the field to the turkey barn. Jumping back into the Land Rover, with the windscreen wipers working away, she drove across the main road into West Bitling, the new 'development' that had enormously expanded the village with around a hundred houses, a small school and a little retail parade – a butcher, a fish-and-chip shop and a confectioner.

She parked in front of the sweet shop and ran quickly inside. Arthur Tate was behind the counter, licking a pencil and making notes in an accounts book. The shop looked prosperous, well stocked with tobacco as well as the many jars of sweets. He looked up at the sound of the doorbell, vibrating on its coil of steel.

'Good afternoon, Arthur.'

'Miss Cooper, hello there. What a surprise and a pleasure, of course. How are you, then?'

'Business seems to be booming?'

'I don't complain and I'm very grateful for Mrs Pascal's support, of course. Please tell her. I've done my best, but she doesn't like to hear it. Do you know what I mean?'

'I do, Arthur. Phyl doesn't enjoy being complimented.'

'In response to your other question, the cigarettes are making all the difference, that's for sure, despite the regulations these days that mean they all have a label that says: "Smoking can damage your health." It doesn't seem to put anyone off, thank heavens, because it's hard to make a living on gobstoppers and liquorice.'

'I'm glad you're doing well.'

'And might be on the street if Mrs Pascal hadn't taken pity when I was released.'

Maisie was glad to have been presented with an excellent conversational gambit for the question in the back of her mind.

And I also know that it was Jack who put Arthur inside.

'I've often wondered, Arthur, how it was in prison. I know you had your faith, but it must have been very hard. Did you get many visitors?'

'I don't have much family. My brother came when he could.'

'Am I right that you spent time in Ford Open Prison?'

'Yes, Miss Cooper. I started in HMP Parkhurst on the Isle of Wight. Then I was moved to the kinder environment in preparation for release.'

'In either Parkhurst or Ford, did you meet anyone called Carter?'

Arthur frowned and mulled the name aloud: 'Carter? Did I, though . . . ?'

'One would have been Mick or Michael, the other Jez or Jeremy?'

He shook his head, accentuating how narrow his face was. 'I've got no memory of them but Parkhurst has several wings, mostly kept quite separate. Would they have been in Bible study? Those were the people I spent time with, as you know.'

'I'm not sure they would have been.'

'Is there some trouble?' he asked, humbly. 'I don't like to think back on those times.'

'No, of course not. To change the subject, could I have four ounces of sherbet strawberries and the same of sherbet lemons, please?'

'Ah, Mrs Pascal's favourites. I'll do that for you sharpish.' He selected two big glass jars, removed the lids and began tipping the hard-boiled sweets into a steel dish on his scales, reverting to their previous topic. 'I think people should be able to decide for themselves. Can't a man have a smoke when he wants one, without being told he oughtn't? Goodness knows, they'll be telling us not to eat bread and butter, next.'

'It is nicer to go to a cinema and not find it hard to see the screen,' Maisie suggested.

'If I'm not allowed to smoke at the pictures, I won't go no more. It's as simple as that.'

'Not all of them have a smoking ban, I don't think,' Maisie reassured him.

'It should be like the seat belts. Harold Wilson made it the law that cars had to have them fitted, but left it up to the driver and passenger if they wanted to use them. Some people don't find them comfortable.'

'I know what you mean, but I always do. You never know what's round the corner.'

Arthur decanted the sweets into two small paper bags. Maisie paid and bid him goodbye, reflecting on the fact that he was much more confident and forthcoming than she had known him during the Bitling Fair mystery. Back then, he'd reminded Maisie of Uriah Heep in the Charles Dickens' novel *David Copperfield*, who repeatedly – and unconvincingly – claimed: 'I'm a very 'umble person.' Uriah Heep turned out to be full of self-important malice, even after he got his comeuppance and became a prisoner awaiting transportation. Maisie hoped that there wouldn't turn out to be a similar dark side to Arthur.

She drove away with the windscreen wipers once again sweeping back and forth, looking forward to discussing with Phyl all she had discovered on her jaunt into town and into Bitling.

It'll be interesting to know if Phyl knows that Arthur has a brother. I didn't make anything of it just now because I didn't want to put him on his guard. We don't have a better explanation, though, of the 'second salesman'. Of course, there's no direct reason why Arthur would bear me ill will, except for a possible grudge against Jack.

Maisie knew about the nature of Arthur's crime, a scam involving antiques and insurance fraud. She thought back to the moment on the Chichester-bound train, down from London Victoria, somewhere around Clapham Junction, when she had asked Jack about it. At the time, she hadn't paid attention to the very deliberate way Jack had answered, perhaps unable to be more forthcoming because of the picnicking couple close by.

Yes, I know Mr Tate very well.

Later, approaching East Corydon, he had told her, quite clearly, why.

No one told you that it was I who put him in prison where he had a breakdown?

Maisie deeply regretted that they had never found time to come back to the question. Then, she asked herself something else.

Should I believe in the show of friendly respect that Arthur just showed me? He seemed on edge, as if his ranting about cigarette laws and seat belts was a way of covering up what he was really thinking.

Maisie drove on, taking care negotiating the narrow and winding country road, the tarmac wet and treacherous, full of respect for the sound advice she had given Arthur.

You never know what's round the corner.

TWENTY-NINE

Back at Bunting Manor, Maisie wanted to take her mind off things by cooking dinner for Phyl, Zoe and herself. Archie provided aubergines, courgettes, onions and tomatoes from the manor's own produce, and introduced her to four large trays of mushrooms flourishing under sheets of carboard in a gloomy corner of the barn.

'Wouldn't these have been better in the wine cellar?' she asked.

'Mrs Pascal didn't want them down there.'

Maisie made quite a thing of her ratatouille, glad to have something do that took her mind off her worries, and it was a big success, even without the garlic that she would have added had she been in her Paris apartment, able to shop for extra ingredients on the nearby Rue Saint-Antoine. After dinner, she and Zoe washed up, combining that useful activity with some more French conversation. Then, Zoe wanted to know: 'Is there any news, you know, about the other stuff?'

Maisie told her breezily: 'None at all.'

She offered Zoe a choice of sherbet strawberries and sherbet lemons. After sampling one of each, Zoe went upstairs and Maisie found Phyl in the library, reading and listening to a classical concert – a re-broadcast of Mahler and Brahms from the summer season of Proms concerts at the Albert Hall. Maisie passed on Arthur Tate's message of thanks and Phyl ate most of the boiled sweets while Maisie finished her Margery Allingham novel, finding herself reassured by spending a couple of hours without talking or trying to predict the future or unlock the secrets of the past.

They both went to bed at ten without a phone call from Jack, with Maisie trying not to think the worst.

Time has got away from him, that's all, and now it's too late.

★

Despite the lack of communication from her fiancé, Maisie slept '*comme une bûche*' – like a log – and woke slightly groggy.

The next morning, Tuesday, was another overcast day with an unfulfilled threat of rain. Maisie drove Zoe into Chichester for work, arriving at half past eight at the Dolphin and Anchor Hotel. Then, although she would be very early, Maisie decided to go straight to 147 Parklands Road where, she imagined, Florence would already be up.

If not, I've got my swimsuit and towel in the car so I can go to the swimming baths for an hour.

She parked, feeling a little ashamed of how she had dismissed Florence's 'pottering' way of life in conversation with Charity. There was tragedy in Florence's past, too, related to Jack's mother, Pamela. It was a story that Maisie had never fully been told.

It isn't for me to judge. Everyone's different. Who knows what impact that might have had?

To Maisie's delight, she encountered Jack on his way out, ready to walk down through the town to the police station. They embraced and he gladly accepted her offer of a lift, remembering to fetch her the unfinished Ngaio Marsh novel from his bedroom.

'I didn't guess whodunnit or how,' he told her, getting in and tossing the book onto the back seat beside Maisie's swimming kit. 'I imagine you will. I'm sorry I didn't call last night. I lost track of time and then it was too late.'

She thought about quizzing him playfully on the subject of Liz Petter, but thought better of it. It clearly wasn't a good moment. Although he was pleased to see her, his mind was largely elsewhere, contemplating his and Fred's backlog of work. Maisie parked just past the police station, beside the greasy water of the canal basin.

'Any news from PC Donaldson?'

'No one he's spoken to saw anything material.'

'Good,' she said. 'It might have been an accident, then. Phyl suggested a labourer who came back, dislodged the timber and ran away because they were worried about getting into trouble.'

'Yes, that was always the most likely explanation,' he told her.

Maisie thought about telling him about the trespasser she had encountered and chased from Phyl's drive but it might also resurrect the drama of the threatening note – and he looked so wearied that she didn't have the heart.

That, too, is most likely a coincidence, someone walking the pilgrim trail who took a wrong turn on private land and then panicked.

'Back to the grind,' he told her with a sigh.

'How is everything?' she asked.

'Complicated,' he told her.

'More bad news?'

'No, just Fred's been overstretched and the paperwork is very behind. It'll be the same late finish today, I'm afraid.'

'Never mind. It has to be done.'

'It does. What are your plans?'

'I'm seeing Florence for a dress fitting, then I have an appointment to meet her friend Kinori at Framlington Church to discuss flowers, though I'm not sure why. I don't think I'll have any kind of useful opinion.'

'Both meetings are a kind of tribute,' he told her.

'In what way?'

'A way for you to express our appreciation, yours and mine, to the people helping to prepare our upcoming nuptials,' he said with a smile. 'Perhaps a recognition of their importance – to them as well as to us? I wish I could come with you.'

'I wish you could, too.'

There was a steady stream of green-blazered boys filing past the Land Rover, meaning any kind of intimate show of affection was out of the question. Jack squeezed her hand and got out, striding up the road to the imposing brick-built police station, then disappeared inside.

Maisie drove back to Parklands and found Florence up and washed and dressed, having cleared a space in the cluttered living room for a low stool. Maisie was obliged to undress, stand on it and pull the ivory-coloured, hand-me-down wedding gown over her head, taking care not to be pricked by the many dressmaker's pins or to catch her toenails in the appliqué lace.

'I'm very grateful to you for agreeing to alter your own dress,' she told Florence. 'You've kept it beautifully.'

'My chest of drawers is cedar, to keep off the moths.'

'How did you manage to make it bigger?'

'The seams were quite generous so I was able to let it out.'

'It still feels snug.'

'That's because you're such a lovely shape,' Florence insisted, checking the drape of the fabric and the hem. 'I think we're there. You are dismissed.'

'Thank you.'

For several days, Maisie had been unable to get any proper exercise so she went directly from Parklands Road to the swimming baths at the end of East Street and bought a ticket for the main, twenty-five-metre pool, finding it cold at first, then refreshing as she ploughed up and down for four hundred metres, sixteen lengths.

She arrived in Framlington with a headache from the damp, enclosed atmosphere of the swimming baths. Having twenty minutes before she was expected, she parked in the gravel area at the end of Church Lane, next to a tiny Mini, then took a stroll through the village and up Running Lane, so called for the streams that trickled either side. With all the rain that had fallen, they were well on their way to merging, drowning the tarmac completely.

At the top of Running Lane, she reached a mill pond for a watermill that no longer functioned and was in a state of dangerous disrepair, the water wheel broken with protruding sharp shards of timber from its split paddles. Just in front of the wheel was a rusty grille set between two round steel posts, choked with branches and leaves, washed down on the streams that channelled rainwater from the Downs to the sea. She could hear the water rushing through concealed gaps and see the current moving across the surface.

Maisie wondered why the whole mill couldn't be redeveloped as something useful and picturesque – workshops or perhaps even rudimentary homes for people with nowhere better, like Mick and Jez Carter or the hand-to-mouth Bitling labourers that Phyl supported, Harold and Adam Farr.

Two white geese appeared out of nowhere, gliding down to merge with the surface of the deep water, graceful and impressive. Maisie wondered if they were a couple and if they mated for life.

As I have, she thought, *and nothing anyone can do will change that.*

Then, for a second time in just a few days, she looked round for a piece of wood to touch in order to ward off the 'jinx'.

THIRTY

Unknown to Maisie, Kinori Osaka was already in Framlington. She had parked her tiny Mini on the gravel at the end of Church Lane, a cul-de-sac. As Maisie contemplated the geese breaking the mirror-like surface of the brimming mill pond, Kinori was already inside St Mary's church, making notes in a little leather-bound jotter about the dominant colours in the stained-glass windows, to help decide the ideal positions for the various flowers she was intending to use. She heard footsteps and a scrape of furniture being moved or a door being opened, telling her that someone else was in the building somewhere, but she didn't think she was in anyone's way or likely to be intruding on a private service or prayer.

Not all of St Mary's colourful stained glass had survived Henry VIII's Reformation – or, perhaps, it had been damaged by simple wear and tear from centuries of weather and the clumsiness of parishioners. That which remained was principally red, green, yellow and blue – plus sections of clear glass – some of the panels engraved, some noble enough to have been signed by their makers.

Because her preparation was always assiduous, Kinori knew about St Mary's thirteenth-century arcades and chancels, the fifteenth-century tower and the 1858 reconstruction. She had read about – but not retained – the meaning of other technical vocabulary such as the 'double-chamfered arch'. This was, in the end, not important. The key was that there were sufficient ledges and stands to support enough floral displays to change the character of the austere interior into a place of celebration.

Kinori completed her 'colour notes' and went to sit in the porch, sketching a bird's-eye-view plan of the building as another form of *aide-mémoire*. It wasn't really necessary as, if truth were told, one church was much like another. In the end, the design questions were always resolved by money: how many blooms the father of the bride could afford or could bring himself to afford. In this case, though, there was no father of the bride. Instead, the cost of the decoration of the church would be met by Mrs Phyllis Pascal, 'the bride's mother's sister' as Florence had somewhat laboriously described her.

Her sketch complete, Kinori checked the time, noting that Maisie Cooper – about whom she had several times read in the *Chichester Observer* – was about to be late. Deciding to go down and meet her at the end of the path, at the bottom of the dead end of Church Lane, she stood up, listening for the sound of whoever had shared her visit with her.

The silence was complete.

'Odd,' she said aloud to herself.

She moved to the threshold and looked out across the gravestones and the wiry late-summer grass to the yew tree, a little uneasy at the idea of so many generations of Framlington residents piled up underground. It was a thought that most people were reluctant to acknowledge, that the space beneath the sods of the churchyard was finite. Digging a new grave inevitably disturbed the last resting place of a previous occupant – perhaps even more than one – however little of their clothes and flesh and skeleton remained.

Behind the yew tree, the sky looks like an enormous bruise – the same colour, in fact, as the dinner-plate one on Florence's backside.

Kinori had been raised by her Japanese-American parents in the Shintō religion, one with neither formal structure nor doctrine, derived from the veneration of roadside shrines and the agricultural rites of rural families. From it, she had inherited a feeling that death – although it must be spoken of and acknowledged – was something impure, reinforced by the fact that cemeteries were not built near Shintō shrines.

Beyond the far hedge, Kinori caught a glimpse of Maisie coming down the path between the potato plants in the unharvested fields, recognising her from images in the newspaper.

I think the editor probably thanks his lucky stars each time he finds a pretext to put a picture of Florence's future granddaughter-in-law in its pages. She's famous, these days, as well as very lovely. I wouldn't be surprised if there's a journalist and a photographer at the wedding.

Kinori stepped outside, not noticing the iron boot scraper set firmly in the flagstones and stumbled, lurching to the left, leaning a hand on the rough stonework for balance. At the same moment, a blurred, indeterminate object came whistling down from the roof of the tower and crashed into sharp-edged fragments beside her feet.

THIRTY-ONE

Maisie returned to Framlington across another potato field, smaller than Liz Petter's one, planted later and not yet harvested, the haulms standing tall. Two men and one woman were cutting off the greenery in order, Maisie knew, to encourage the tubers beneath the ground to develop thicker skins for winter storage. She hurried on, not wanting to get caught up in conversation because she would soon be late.

Kinori Osaka was waiting at the lychgate – a small woman with black hair cut in a severe fringe, the sides and back just resting on her shoulders. Her skin was very pale, her eyes darting this way and that.

'Good afternoon,' said Maisie, making Kinori jump. 'I'm sorry, I didn't mean to startle you.'

'Oh, yes, excuse me. I feel . . .'

Maisie realised that Kinori was holding on to the timbers of the lychgate for balance or support.

'Can I help you? Have you hurt yourself?'

'No, not at all, just . . .' Kinori seemed to pull herself together. 'It's all right now. I had a shock and panicked, running down the path and . . . I'll be fine. I just need to get my breath back.'

'What was it?' Maisie asked.

'I'm not sure. Something fell from the roof and crashed at my feet. I felt the wind of it pass me by so very close.'

'What was this something?'

'I wish I could tell you. You know what Florence would say? "Well, I never did." It was a shock, that's all. I'm quite all right.'

As was common at the end of a church path, the lychgate was equipped with a shallow bench to either side, sheltered by the timber roof. Kinori sat down then tried to get up again.

'We've never been introduced—' she began.

'Never mind that,' interrupted Maisie, putting her hand gently on Kinori's shoulder. 'Please stay where you are. I'm Maisie Cooper, obviously, and you, equally obviously, are Kinori Osaka. Florence has told me so much about your cleverness and your excellent eye. Jack and I are very grateful to you for helping us celebrate our wedding.'

'Florence is a special person. I've met her grandson, your fiancé, only twice, but he seems a fine man.'

'He is,' said Maisie, trying not to sound self-satisfied. 'But, tell me again. What happened?'

'I was just coming out and a slate, perhaps it was, came whistling past and smashed on the flagstones just where I'd been standing a moment before.'

Maisie frowned but kept her voice light. 'Would you mind if I go and have a look?'

'Not at all.'

The church pathway was beaten earth beneath a layer of fine gravel, through which no weeds grew because the churchyard was well kept. It curved round the building, taking Maisie out of sight of Kinori. She stopped a few paces from the porch.

It was, indeed, a slate that had fallen and shattered into tiny fragments. Maisie looked up at the roof and the tower.

I suppose it could have fallen by accident, but it's not windy. It seems an unlikely coincidence.

Maisie stepped round the broken slate and went inside, her eyes adjusting slowly to the relative gloom, recognising the slightly damp, stuffy smell she associated with St Mary's from early childhood. She stood still and listened, hearing a creak as if from a loose tread on a wooden staircase. She advanced into the nave, her ears attentive to every faint sound, and heard it again.

I know where that's coming from.

At the west end, at the base of the church tower, was a robing room lined with oak cupboards, containing cassocks and surplices. It was in this room that she and her brother Stephen had dressed for appearances in the church choir in their youth. One of Maisie's earliest memories was of their mother, Irene, making her a tiny red cassock to take part in a service of commemoration and celebration for the end of the war, when she had been seven years old and could barely hold a tune.

Maisie advanced on the robing room and pushed open the door. The space smelt of incense because it was here that the thurifer set light to his coals beneath fragrant crystals for each Eucharist. Set in a frame on the right-hand wall were the ropes that the verger would pluck in order to activate the bells, high above. The ropes disappeared through a slot in the wooden ceiling. In the corner of the robing room was a low arched door that gave access to the spiral staircase that led to the belfry and the roof.

Maisie pulled the door open and looked inside. The stone steps were both narrower and shallower than she remembered them, turning around a central column, against which her shoulder brushed as she began to climb. There was a faint updraught from the nave of the church, presumably because of the breeze running across the roof, drawing the air out of the shaft.

Which means that the hatch is open at the top.

Maisie counted the steps as she went, with an idea in the back of her mind, a vague memory, that there might be seventy of them, each one six inches deep, climbing therefore about thirty-five feet. Pausing to listen once more, she identified the harsh call of a rook coming from above.

The hatch is definitely open. I should have asked Kinori if she heard anything while she was inside.

The spiral stair took Maisie on another three circuits of the central pillar. She decided that it felt narrower and more claustrophobic than in memory because she, herself, was bigger. Then the stone steps ended at a wooden platform in whose centre the three church bells hung suspended. Far below, their ropes disappeared through the slot in the wooden ceiling of the robing room.

Looking down gave Maisie a moment of dizziness. She pressed herself back against the cold wall of the tower and got her first glimpse of the sky. There was a square opening at the top of a wooden ladder, itself lashed to a large iron staple set firmly into the stonework. She embarked, turning her knees to one side because it was almost vertical. At the lip of the opening, the hatch itself standing upright, she felt the strength of the breeze, much more noticeable than on the ground.

She climbed another step, anxious at the idea of confronting someone while in a position of inferiority. The square roof of the tower had a parapet about two feet tall all the way round. Inside the parapet was a lead gulley to channel away rainwater then almost all of the space was taken up by a pyramid of slates surmounted by a weather vane.

Maisie emerged from the hatch. Now she was out, she could hear a duet of harsh cries as two black birds, twenty yards away in the canopy of a sycamore, also thirty-five feet off the ground, complained at her presence.

She stood up. The footing was awkward in the gulley. She edged round one corner of the roof, heading for the north side overlooking the porch. The labourers in the potato field, diminished by distance, gave her a cheery wave. She leaned out to glance down at the flagstones, then drew back, a queasy moment of vertigo taking hold of her with the parapet only just higher than her knees.

Calm down, now. You're quite safe.

Turning away from the drop, she saw a blemish in the otherwise regular pattern of good-quality slates on the south side of the pyramid roof. One was missing, the patch beneath where it had lain quite clean, indicating that it hadn't long been exposed to the weather.

Could it have been prised out by strong winds? Have there been high winds? Perhaps while I was away in London and Newcastle ...

Maisie edged clumsily along, with her back to the pyramid roof, her hands outstretched for balance, her feet in the awkward gulley, towards the next corner. As she reached it, there was a sudden commotion from the far side, scuffling and scraping.

Is that more rooks?

She turned to face the slates and tried to hurry round to the hatch.

Or is someone else up here?

She rounded the corner just in time to see the hatch slam shut.

As quickly as she dared, she crept along and bent down to examine the mechanism, a hoop of metal that she thought could be prised up and pulled to release a catch of some kind. She broke a fingernail trying to do so but the hoop was either rusted in place or, more likely, it required a particular tool. She looked round for a piece of wire or an old nail to use instead, but there was nothing.

Maisie edged back to the south side of the battlements, looking down towards the porch.

I shouldn't have messed about trying to get the hatch open; I should have looked down straight away. If it was someone, I might have seen whoever it was escaping.

There was no one there. The churchyard and the potato fields beyond were empty, apart from the same labourers – looking tiny with height and distance – cutting their haulms.

★

It took Maisie a full minute of calling before she managed to attract Kinori's attention. The woman came into view, her pale face angled up to see where the noise was coming from.

'Could you come up and free me, please?'

'How?' Kinori called.

'In the corner of the robing room is a spiral staircase with a ladder at the top. I'm sure the hatch opens easily from the inside.'

'I'll come now,' called Kinori, sensibly.

Waiting for her rescue, Maisie looked down on the village of Framlington and, beyond, across to the soft shapes of the wooded Downs. Born and raised in south-west Sussex, she could name many of them. She dropped her eyes to the graveyard, seeking out, somewhere at the edge of the spreading branches of the yew tree, her parents' shared grave. It stood out because the stone was relatively new. For reasons she couldn't fathom, an unexpected thought came into her mind.

It's such a shame they'll never meet my children.

IV

WHEAT

SIGNIFYING THE COEXISTENCE OF GOOD AND EVIL,
SACRIFICE AND RESURRECTION

THIRTY-TWO

It was Maisie's responsibility to bring Zoe home to Bunting Manor from work at the Dolphin and Anchor Hotel at the end of the day, but that was a few hours off, still. Once she and Kinori had parted – with Maisie allowing the florist to believe that the wind had closed the hatch at the top of the church tower and that it was possible that a slate had been dislodged by accident – Maisie went to look at her parents' gravestone close up, rather than from the level of the adjacent rookery.

At the time of her parents' deaths, Maisie had been more than a hundred and fifty miles away, working at Sunny View in Devon. She had felt, ever since, a deep well of guilt that she hadn't been close at hand, somehow able to . . .

To save them.

Maisie decided it would be foolish to ever say those words aloud.

But that's my problem, isn't it? Charity is right. I want to save everyone. Meaning I stick my nose into affairs that aren't my business, perhaps in the end doing more harm than good.

The gravestone was a modest one – because neither she nor Stephen had been able to afford anything better or bigger – in black basalt. Though her parents' deaths had been nothing but a stupid accident, the impact on Maisie had been severe. She had come to regret leaving the Women's Royal Auxiliary Corps, despite the low ceiling to her career in the army, unsettled by the sudden lack of a sense of service and purpose. Her life became directionless, only saved by the whim that took her to Paris – a happy accident, rather than a tragic one.

Maisie left the graveyard and, because she had time, wandered back up Church Lane on foot to the main road through the village. There, she paused to contemplate the big ugly house, Church Lodge, in which her brother Stephen had lived and – foolishly – schemed. It appeared that there were no new tenants, but a local building firm that she knew from work they had done for Phyl in Bunting – Singer's – had erected scaffolding at the front of the house. A cement mixer was churning away on the gravel drive and there was a pile of construction timber peeking out from beneath a large blue tarpaulin.

Feeling unsettled by the idea that Stephen's home was being remodelled, somehow erasing his memory a little further, she wandered on, past the tiny rented cottage occupied by the elderly poets, Mr and Mrs Casemore, and along in front of the village shop. In a gap in traffic, she jogged across the road to the forecourt of the pub, the Fox-in-Flight, hoping to look in on the blacksmith's forge next door. The place was shut up with no smoke rising from its chimney, suggesting the farrier, her robust and practical friend Jon Wilkes, must be out in his van, working with horses in the fields.

With no particular destination in mind, she wandered on, along a very narrow pavement in front of the roadside wall of Framlington Manor, a lovely Georgian house of brick and flint. When she came to the opening for the drive, she was surprised to see someone she recognised tending to a bank of colourful autumn flowers, planted in raised borders beside smooth modern tarmac that was at odds with the mellow materials of the imposing old house. Maisie would have walked on, but the woman saw her and spoke.

'You look surprised,' said Daphne Fieldhouse in her wan, unemphatic voice. 'I am not entirely physically incapable.'

★

Standing with her back to the sink in the kitchen of Framlington Manor, Maisie watched Daphne Fieldhouse manoeuvre her wheelchair into a position where the warmth of the sun through the windows could strike her face.

Daphne Fieldhouse was, Maisie reflected, a kind of polar opposite to Phyl, despite the similarities in their positions, each in their own manor house, dominating the affairs of two separate downland villages. Where Phyl was loud and demonstrative, Daphne was – on the surface, at least – vague and withdrawn. Phyl was unapologetically judgemental, though also generous and philanthropic. Daphne kept her cards close to her chest and ran her business affairs without sympathy for those at the mercy of her arbitrary decision-making.

For several reasons, Daphne had been at the heart of Maisie's investigation into Stephen's death in the murder at Church Lodge. Invited to come into the Framlington Manor kitchen 'for a word or two', Maisie was surprised when Daphne chose to speak openly about her disability, her eyes unfocused, not meeting Maisie's gaze.

'I garden, a little, especially now Bert Close has apparently taken to his bed. But my scope of action is paltry. Since the events around your brother's death, I have begun to wonder how my confinement in this wheelchair might have shaped my patterns of thought.'

'I think I would wonder that, too. Have you ever been able to walk?'

'I was a county-level cyclist as a junior. I held the one-hour record for my age group for six consecutive years.'

'Was it a cycling accident?' asked Maisie.

'In a sense. There are accidents that occur because they have been planned. There are others that occur because no one thinks to prevent them. "Accident" is a very broad term, when you think about it.'

'Do you want to tell me about it?'

'No, I don't think I do.'

'Then what do you want to talk about? Would you like me to make some tea?'

'Ah, "tea", the English panacea. You haven't grown out of that, living in Paris?'

'Or coffee?'

'No, thank you.' Daphne's hands were gloved to help her grip the rails on the wheels of her chair. She pulled each one tighter and Maisie thought it was in preparation for some important revelation. Daphne went on: 'It was fortuitous that you should pass by. I have been hankering after an opportunity to speak to you, though perhaps you might feel that I haven't the right?'

'I needn't pay any attention if I don't want to.'

Daphne breathed a shallow sigh, her eyes still vague.

'You are a very pretty woman,' she said. 'I can see that you always have been. And you have that other indefinable quality, a kind of charisma. You were an athlete, isn't that right, a swordswoman and horsewoman, and so on?'

'In a small way.'

'You are habitually modest, too. I read your remarks in the paper about the murders at Bitling Fair and at the Festival Theatre of which I am a patron. Why didn't you decline to be interviewed? Knowing you a little, as I do, I imagine you found that painful.'

'I could have done, but that would have seemed more ostentatious than allowing the journalist to ask me a few routine questions.'

'You don't like your notoriety?'

'I wouldn't call it notoriety. I don't enjoy being recognised or pointed out.'

Daphne turned her wheelchair to face Maisie, tilting her head to one side.

'It would be reasonable for me, don't you think, to resent your continued presence in my village? Unravelling your brother's murder had a considerable impact on my affairs.'

'I realise that,' said Maisie evenly. 'It also brought to light a number of decisions that I hope you have come to regret.'

Daphne looked away and told her: 'You have your opinions and I have mine. Perhaps it would be better not to speak of the past, though it is hard to avoid, I suppose. I invited you in as a kind of . . .' Daphne glanced up. 'As a kind of apology, I suppose – something I do not make a habit of.'

'Is that right?' asked Maisie, surprised.

'It is. And you are not making this easy.'

Maisie wasn't enjoying the odd conversational dance. 'I wasn't aware of being anything but patient and polite.'

'Let me get to the point. I understand you are to be married here in just a few days. I wanted to tell you that the man you had put away – whose name I won't mention for reasons you know well – has managed to have his conviction declared unsafe.'

'On what grounds?' asked Maisie, shocked.

'I see your beloved Sergeant Wingard hasn't told you,' said Daphne, slyly. 'How remiss of him.'

'Never mind what Jack may or may not have told me,' Maisie snapped. Then she added, unconvincingly: 'He is restricted by his professional code of conduct in what he can share. Do you mean that your husband has been released?'

'I regret to tell you, on your account, as well as my own, that he has.'

'Do you know where he is?'

'I do not.'

'Has he come to you?'

'That neither.'

'Then how do you know? How long has he been out?'

'In answer to your first question, because I make it my business to know. In answer to your second, two weeks ago.' Daphne glanced up and, in her eyes, Maisie thought she saw genuine sympathy. 'I have told you before that, despite his foolish schemes, I found your brother sympathetic and amusing. I am sorry for your loss and for my connection to it.'

'You needn't feel any responsibility—' Maisie began.

'Will you let me finish, Miss Cooper?' Daphne asked, without emphasis.

'Go ahead.'

'The man I mean – as I said, I will not name him – must bear you a grudge. You see that.'

'I do,' said Maisie in an undertone.

'I would advise you to take care.'

'I will, Mrs Fieldhouse. Have no fear.'

'Oh, it's all the same to me. I'm mostly a bystander in life – in this story, in particular – whereas you are condemned to play the leading role. Will it be hero or victim, I wonder?'

★

Maisie left Daphne Fieldhouse soon after, annoyed that she had, as always, allowed the woman to get under her skin.

It would have been a good deal easier if Jack had forewarned me and—

She shook her head.

No, that's not fair for two reasons. There's the question of professional secrets, plus he wouldn't want to worry me.

She walked quickly back to the Land Rover that waited patiently on the gravel pull-in at the end of the cul-de-sac of Church Lane. She got in and, on a reflex, pressed down the buttons to lock both doors, abruptly nervous lest someone jump in next to her.

But that's ridiculous. Pull yourself together.

THIRTY-THREE

The events at St Mary's church in Framlington were serious enough for Maisie to think she had the right to interrupt Jack's afternoon. She drove into Chichester and parked on the canal basin once more, getting out into a crowd of schoolchildren whose day had come to an end, many of them with the fresh-scrubbed look of new boys wearing brand-new blazers that were too big for them, their parents clearly hoping that they wouldn't need to buy a new one next year as well.

Maisie made her way through the car park in front of the police station, climbing a couple of steps to the lobby – a depressing space lined with generic printed messages on ill-kept noticeboards – intending to wait there until Jack became free. To her surprise, the elderly Sergeant William Dodd was on duty, squeezed into a worn but well-kept blue uniform, looking very much at home behind the counter.

'How nice to see you,' he told her.

'You, too,' she told him truthfully. 'What's happened to retirement?'

'A small staffing crisis. The powers-that-be asked me to stay on an extra fortnight and here I am.'

'How's life in Bitling?'

'Very much improved thanks to you, for reasons you can imagine.'

'Good,' said Maisie, not feeling she had time to go into the precise circumstances. 'Then that's an investigation you and I can both be proud of.'

'Oh, it wasn't me,' William argued. 'I was caught up in my own foolishness.'

'You underestimate your contribution. Tell me, is Jack in? Might he be available?'

'No, he isn't, I'm afraid.'

'Do you know where he's gone and when he'll be back?'

'For the first question, he's gone to speak to the governor at HMP Ford. I happened to hear him telling Fred Nairn. But I can't tell you why.'

'Can't or won't?'

'Can't because I don't know. Now, Maisie, because of staying on that bit longer, this weekend at your wedding will be the last time I wear this uniform – plus the white gloves and so on. Isn't that grand? I know it's your day but it'll be my day, too, in a way. Everyone from Bitling's looking forward to coming – and to the party afterwards. Will it be in the Fox-in-Flight?'

For a second, Maisie wondered to herself: *Yes, will it?* Then she realised that it would only happen if she organised it and, somehow, in all the other bits and pieces in the rushed nuptials, she hadn't given it a thought.

I need to get a grip. First things, first, however.

'Yes, of course. We'll all troop up to the Fox-in-Flight afterwards. But do you know what he's doing at the open prison?' she asked.

'Jack's a careful sort of person, isn't he, so it wouldn't be unlike him to want to find out how someone he's put inside is getting along. He's not one of those people who thinks offenders can't change and he's right. I've seen people transformed under their own steam or by discovering something inside themselves. Take Arthur Tate. I had a downer on poor Arthur and thought he wouldn't be able to leave behind a lifetime of . . . Well, no need to drag all that up. But he's a sidesman for me now at the chapel in Bitling and there's no one has a bad word to say about him.'

'Good,' said Maisie, distractedly, thinking of people she considered more likely enemies. 'Can I ask you about Derek Fieldhouse, Daphne Fieldhouse's husband?'

'That's a miserable business, but it happens now and then. There's a mistake in procedure and a clever lawyer is able to get someone off.'

'Do you know what it was that had the conviction declared unsafe?'

'I don't, but I do know that's not the end of the story. Fred's been looking for a way to get Derek Fieldhouse back under lock and key on a lesser charge.'

'I met his wife, Daphne, earlier today and she claimed not to know where he was or how he was living.'

'Didn't she disown him when it all came out?'

'So she says, though I'm not certain she can be trusted.'

Maisie left William Dodd and went and parked behind Boots the Chemist with half an hour to kill before Zoe would be out. She ran along West Street to the solicitor's office where she found Charity preparing to leave.

'Is Maurice in? Can we have a conflab? It's urgent.'

'Yes, go through. I'll join you once I've put these letters in their envelopes.'

The door to the inner office was ajar, revealing Maurice's desk in the centre and low bookcases round the walls in dark wood. She thought it was mahogany but she had never asked. As usual, Maurice's desk was very tidy – nothing but a heavy beige rotary telephone, a green-shaded desk lamp and a leather blotter with a little-used piece of absorbent paper.

Maurice himself was slotting a legal tome back in the bookshelves and didn't notice her until he turned round, exclaiming: 'If it isn't my favourite detective!' A big man with expansive gestures, he crossed the room and embraced her, then stepped back, holding her hands. 'What's happened?'

'Nothing yet,' she told him. Then she realised that wasn't true. 'Nothing absolutely definite.'

'Want to tell me about it?'

Charity came in and Maisie flopped down in one of two club armchairs in tan leather. Charity sat poised in the other as if preparing to take notes.

'When Stephen died,' she began, 'when he was murdered, Maurice, you were the first person to tell me the truth, not to keep me in the dark.'

'Yes, but you know Jack would have come clean sooner had he been able. And there was the added complication of you and Jack knowing one another from school and he'd been holding a candle for you for ten years—'

'I know, Maurice,' she interrupted. 'I'm not criticising Jack. I'm saying that I would never have got to the bottom of it without your support, pointing me in the right direction.'

'Did I? I don't remember that. I think it was all you.'

'Have it your own way.' Maisie smiled. 'Modesty doesn't suit you, by the way.'

'Maisie,' said Charity, 'are we getting sidetracked? You said it was urgent.'

'Yes, it is.' She collected her thoughts, aware that Maurice was weighing her up, running a fleshy hand over his hair. She told him: 'I spoke to Daphne Fieldhouse, about Derek, her husband. I know there was more to Stephen's murder than just Derek's involvement, but I was surprised to learn that he's no longer in prison. Were you aware?'

'I was. Small-town life.'

'And what's your opinion?'

'It's a lawyer's job to do their best by their client, whoever they may be.'

'But Derek was – is – guilty.'

'I know, Maisie,' said Maurice soothingly. 'It's the nature of our adversarial legal system, however. The police and the Crown Prosecution Service try to get people put away and defence lawyers try to preserve their liberty.'

'It's not a joke, though.'

'Maurice knows it's not a joke, Maisie,' said Charity. 'He's trying to explain—'

'I know,' said Maisie, frustrated with herself for being peevish. 'I'm sorry. Do you know what he might be up to, by any chance?'

'I do know something, as it happens,' said Maurice.

'Really?'

'You won't be surprised to hear that Daphne Fieldhouse is divorcing him. It's for her money, after all, that he married into at Framlington Manor.'

'Are you acting on her behalf?'

'I have that honour,' said Maurice, complacently. 'Most of the great families trust me with their affairs.'

'I've often wondered, Maurice, how you get so much done with just you in the office?'

'I took the trouble to marry an expert. Charity is a qualified lawyer, too. Did you not know?'

'Of course. I'm sorry, Charity. I think I did. I've always known you must be much more than secretary. But to come back to Derek, if you're acting in the divorce, do you have an address for him?'

'The initial papers were served while he was still incarcerated. Now, though, I have no idea. The *decree nisi* ought to be delivered into his hands.'

'Maurice, I am already so much in your debt,' she told him. 'And you, too, Charity. Should you discover where he's staying, will you tell me?'

'I suppose I might, though with the hope you won't do something foolish, however,' Maurice chided.

'Husband,' said Charity, 'if you were able to tell Maisie where Derek is, your "something foolish" would become . . .' she switched to French for emphasis '. . . *inévitable.*'

★

Maisie left them, feeling irked that they, like Jack, thought her irresponsible, likely to 'run into danger'.

Zoe was ready and wating, leaning against the bonnet of the Land Rover. On the way home, vertical rain began to fall. They passed the time with Zoe describing the countryside in French and asking Maisie how to say the names of the trees – with little success. Maisie didn't know the names of very many trees in English and couldn't help with most of them.

'I've never known something you're not good at,' said Zoe, bantering. 'My confidence is shattered.'

Maisie stopped on the small forecourt in front of the Fox-in-Flight in Framlington, telling Zoe: 'I just have to run in.'

'What's up?'

'I forgot to organise a party for after the wedding. There has to be something, however pitiful.'

'Phyl's done that,' said Zoe. 'She got on to them the moment she heard. It's all paid for and everything.'

'She hasn't said,' said Maisie, astonished.

'Yes, well, obviously she hasn't. If she had, you'd be all grateful and huggy and she wouldn't want that, would she? It's not her style. Jenny Brook's helping so it won't be just dismal sandwiches and shop-bought sausage rolls.'

Maisie was very relieved to hear that. She had a depressing memory of the awful wake she'd organised for after Stephen's service of commemoration, also in the Fox-in-Flight, overwhelmed by the idea that all the villagers were

232

looking at her quizzically, wondering whether she knew how and why Stephen had died.

If our wedding party had turned out equally depressing, even with all we've got on, I'd never have forgiven myself.

She pulled back out, took the sharp right by Framlington Manor and headed across country.

'What else are you worrying about?' asked Zoe.

'Nothing.'

'Why lie?' asked Zoe, sounding hurt. 'I can tell, you know.'

'I'm sorry,' Maisie told her, feeling that she was apologising a lot these days. 'Derek Fieldhouse is out of jail.'

'Oh, blimey. How come?'

'Some technicality. It doesn't matter but I just—'

'You began to wonder if he might be behind the things we were discussing the other night.'

'Yes,' said Maisie.

They had come up behind a tractor turning slowly into a field. Maisie waited, thinking hard.

'Have you written down a list of enemies?' asked Zoe.

The tractor pulled off.

'No,' said Maisie, accelerating. 'But I think I should.'

THIRTY-FOUR

Coming into Bunting, Maisie was still thinking hard, grateful that Zoe had read her mood and wasn't interrupting.

I need to put some order in my thoughts, even though there's a risk it will make it all more frightening.

Indoors, it seemed that Phyl and Zoe were of one mind, determined not to dwell on upsetting news. Between the three of them, they prepared dinner. Maisie washed the lettuce and mixed some fresh vinaigrette dressing, including two anchovies that she chopped very fine. Zoe carefully fried some cubes of stale bread into croutons with salt and pepper and butter. Phyl pulled some chicken meat from a carcass in the fridge, assuring Maisie: 'This is from only two days ago.'

They ate without mentioning their worries. Maisie stayed quiet while Zoe told them about Mr Hume, the manager of the Dolphin and Anchor, who had suggested that she might do half a day a week of accountancy and management at the college of further education.

'At the hotel's expense.'

'Very kind of him,' said Phyl. 'What did you reply?'

'He genuinely believes I want his job in twenty years' time and need to start preparing, now. I think I'd rather die.'

'Don't say that,' said Phyl.

'It's just a figure of speech.'

'An ugly one.'

'All right,' Zoe replied, not taking offence, used to Phyl's abruptness. 'Would you like to hear about the new second chef instead? He thinks he's an absolute charmer, you know, like in Jack's grandma's expression: "He really fancies himself." I saw him adjusting his chef's hat, looking at his own reflection in the steel of the big fridge, sort of preening. And he wears one of those corset-type things, you know, with Velcro under his whites to keep his belly tucked in.'

'Silly man,' said Phyl.

The conversation never quite became fluent, but the Caesar salad was a success. Once they'd washed up, Maisie excused herself, saying she had some letters to write and would do so upstairs. She left the kitchen and crossed the hallway, hearing Zoe's precise and energetic voice behind her.

'I hope Maisie's making a list of everyone she's suspicious of. I think it's a good idea.'

Already embarked on the staircase, Maisie didn't catch Phyl's reply. Then she realised that she had been so preoccupied that she hadn't thanked Phyl for organising the wedding party on her behalf.

Feeling ungrateful, she trudged on to her room and took a seat at the desk in the window. The time was getting on for eight and the sun had already gone down behind the tall trees that loomed over Bunting Manor. She put on the table lamp – a forty-watt bulb beneath a grubby brown-and-orange shade – but sufficient to illuminate the Bunting Manor-headed notepaper from the drawer.

She took up her pen with a feeling of *déjà vu*. In reality, it was a memory. The moment she was suddenly reliving was from the investigation into the murder at Bitling Fair – the one that had closely concerned Sergeant William Dodd, the elderly officer on reception at the police station, on the verge of retirement. Jack had been away on a brief training course and she had written to him, beginning her letter:

Dear Jack,

You've only been gone a few hours, so please don't assume, when you read this, that I'm about to become a desperate and clinging wife. It's just that I'm awake and no one else is and I feel a need for conversation, even if it's only with the ghost of you on this page and I'm not going to get any reply . . .

She was in the same position now, needing to talk things through but unwilling to burden either Zoe or Phyl – and she didn't know where to start. Then, before putting pen to paper, she remembered something that had happened on the train that she had paid no attention to at the time.

Her attention had been caught by Jack's very serious expression, reading the papers Fred Nairn had sent, and she had asked: 'What's the matter?'

Without a word, Jack had folded one of the sheets of paper and put it away in the inside pocket of his jacket, passing her only the second sheet, the one that concerned sparse information on the Carters and the Kemps.

The first sheet must have been the news about Derek Field-house being released. Jack didn't want to worry me. 'Sly' Daphne was right.

She sighed, confirming an idea that had come to her several days before.

The fact that he tried to hide it worries me more than anything else.

Maisie thought about going downstairs to the telephone to ring the station and find out if Jack had returned from HMP Ford, but changed her mind.

He more or less asked me straight out not to do that, knowing that he would be working very late with Fred once more, trying to get everything caught up. And these things are much better discussed in person.

Maisie frowned, realising something else that she hadn't considered – something that ought to be a delightful idea but which actually felt oppressive and difficult.

We're about to go away together for our fortnight's honeymoon at Sunny View. I bet Jack is trying to make sure that this second extended absence doesn't turn out to be an additional burden on his colleagues. I wouldn't be surprised if he works till ten every night this week, trying to get everything shipshape.

Maisie had slumped in her chair so she made herself straighten her back and focus.

I'll do what I did before – what I've done several times. I'll make a list and try and see if there's a pattern.

She frowned.

Except, on this occasion, it's a different sort of mystery. I'm not putting together evidence about a thing that's happened, trying to work out the whys and wherefores and assign the guilt from the past. I'm trying to prevent something bad from occurring in the future – in my future. It seems to me that's a lot harder.

Beneath the table lamp was a charming stainless-steel Art Deco calendar with white cards that flipped over to reveal each day and date. She had got into the habit of using it because life in the countryside was oddly undifferentiated, one day very much like the next, with nature not caring whether it was Wednesday or Sunday. Today, the calendar told her, was Tuesday. She counted back to Newcastle to make sure that was accurate, then yawned.

I'm not sure I have the focus for this. Maybe I'll leave it for the morning.

She spent a few minutes doodling a map of the area around St Mary's, Framlington, then remembered her Ngaio Marsh novel, *When in Rome,* that she had bought at the W H Smith & Sons on the Newcastle railway station forecourt and then lent to Jack. He had given it back, leaving it on the back seat of the Land Rover.

She went quickly downstairs to fetch it, taking care not to disturb anyone because she didn't want any more conversation. Back upstairs, she found the page where she had left off and read for twenty minutes at the little desk in the window. Then she saw that the time was nearly nine o'clock and decided it would be quite reasonable to get into bed and continue reading there. By the time she had washed and undressed and brushed her teeth, however, she didn't have the energy.

I'm becoming a proper countrywoman – up with the lark and back in bed with the setting of the sun. Perhaps things will seem clearer in the morning.

★

Because she had gone to sleep so early, Maisie woke completely refreshed, before the Wednesday sun was fully up. Not wanting to rouse the household by fussing about in the kitchen, she stayed in her room, pulling on a thick tartan dressing gown because the room had become cold overnight, with the window open four or five inches for fresh air. She drank the glass of water she always kept beside her bed and began writing.

Mick and Jez Carter, brothers, scrap dealers; grudge against Jack; working on Petter Farm, the home of another potential enemy?

Liz Petter – should I call her 'a woman spurned'? – with a grudge against Jack and resentful of me, too? Is it just a coincidence that she's providing employment and accommodation to Mick and Jez, or could they have a shared goal?

Peggy Kemp, bogus fortune teller; confidence trickster who took advantage of vulnerable people; grudge against Jack (who uncovered her frauds) on her own behalf and also her son's ...

Ronan Kemp, Peggy's son and 'muscle'; terrible temper; assaulted Jack then arrested by him; definite grudge.

Derek Fieldhouse, involved in Stephen's murder, grudge against Jack and against me.

The 'second salesman' who may or may not be following me; connection to Arthur Tate? Perhaps brother? Arthur was put in prison by Jack.

Someone, like Commander Kimmings, the part-time organist, who didn't end up in prison but who may have been festering for months, getting angrier and angrier.

Maisie came up with another idea, one that didn't help at all.

Someone I don't know in Newcastle; a new enemy Jack's made while away?

Maisie contemplated the list. It didn't seem very clever or penetrating, just a set of uninspiring conjectures. Rereading the paragraph about Liz Petter, she felt obliged to add another.

A far-fetched possibility is Vaughan Quinn, the vet in Bitling who – though I didn't know it – carried a candle for me ever since school. I suppose he might have the same (potential, uncertain) malign motivation as Liz Petter, but in reverse?

Thinking about Bitling, she realised that there was someone else who lived in the almost-feudal village that she hadn't properly considered, the sister of Old Mr Strickland – he had ended up in prison thanks to Maisie's solution to the murder at Church Lodge.

Ada Strickland could bear a grudge on behalf of her brother. Might there even be some kind of evil alliance between her and Derek Fieldhouse, because he was involved, too?

She added another possible conspiracy.

Arthur Tate, Ronan Kemp and Mick and Jez Carter – or any combination of them – might have met in Parkhurst or, later on, Arthur might have encountered the Carter brothers in Ford Open Prison (though Arthur denies any memory and the dates might not work).Where was Derek Fieldhouse detained? Could he have run into – and formed an alliance with – any of the above?

She moved on to a few moments of unexplained drama.

The building materials that fell from the site next door to the hostel in Newcastle; someone seen running away; maybe an innocent accident . . .

Seeing the 'second salesman' for a second time on the London-bound train; then feeling that he ran away so as not to be challenged.

Attempted 'murder by Tube train' on the underground platform at King's Cross – but it might have been an accident due to the crush in the crowd.

The marbles on Florence's front step as a sort of sideways attack on Jack (and, therefore, on me, too). Has Florence discovered who left them?

The threatening letter that might have been for Phyl but also might have been for me, from more or less any of these people, including Liz Petter.

The slate that fell − or was thrown − from the roof of the tower at St Mary's, Framlington. I need to tell Jack about that.

Maisie sat back, visualising the sequence of events. She wasn't sure that there had been someone on the roof with her. The scuffling she had heard might have been the flapping of a rook's wings. Also, she had a memory − from childhood − that the verger often left the hatch open in good weather in order to create an updraught of air from the nave to remove the smell of damp. The hatch falling closed might have been an accident, a change in the direction of the breeze or even the bird − if there was a bird − unbalancing it.

Because it shut with a slam, I didn't actually hear any footsteps going down the ladder and the spiral staircase. When I looked over, no one was in sight. I asked Kinori and she saw no one running away.

Maisie knew that wasn't a definitive answer, though. The south porch was out of sight of where Kinori had been sitting under the timber roof of the lychgate.

An intruder could have simply scampered off in the other direction.

Maisie visualised the scene from the opposite point of view, with the unlikely presence of an enemy at the top of the tower, and expanded her note.

Why would they make an attack on Kinori? Only if they were utterly deranged, surely, would they fling a roof slate at the florist for our wedding and think that was a legitimate target?

She hesitated, her pen poised above the paper, thinking about the possibility of someone 'deranged', finding the idea more frightening than any of the other possibilities. In investigating all five mysteries – Church Lodge, Bunting Manor, the theatre, the fair, Sunny View – she had encountered misunderstandings and confusion, but never madness.

I've seen people driven to terrible acts out of desperation or greed or misunderstanding or jealousy, but no one who has utterly lost their grip on reality. Therefore, I've been able to solve the puzzles with logic and an understanding of human nature. But, if there's a mad person out there, it's impossible to say what they might think or do.

Maisie heard someone else stirring in the big house and remembered the plaintive words uttered by Lewis Caroll's Alice, trapped in Wonderland: *'I don't want to go among mad people.'*

THIRTY-FIVE

Downstairs in the kitchen, Maisie discovered from Phyl that today was the day, trailed by her and by Archie, 'to get the straw bales into the barn'.

'Good, some proper exercise at last. I feel like I just drive around, doing the shopping, picking up and dropping off, with nothing really energetic.'

'You may regret that thought later,' Phyl told her.

'I know it can be pretty back-breaking. Who else is helping?'

'Harold and Adam Farr will come over once they've completed their early duties at the turkey barn.'

'Oh, good. I'll be glad to see them,' said Maisie.

She knew Harold from the investigation into the murder at the theatre and both he and Adam from the mystery of the murder at Bitling Fair. Harold had been an unhappy case, with no fixed home or income until Phyl took a chance and gave him a job at her turkey business, alongside his nephew. 'Has Harold proved reliable?'

'Utterly.'

'And Adam?'

'A hundred years ago people would have thought of him as the village idiot,' said Phyl, brutally. 'But he just needs a role. Anyway, he and his uncle are helping. The slaughterer wanted to come today but I put him off.'

Maisie hid her shudder at the idea of the 'slaughterer' coming to end the lives of several hundred plump birds. Zoe arrived, her hair mussed and her eyes vague.

'What time is it?'

'Ten minutes then we're off,' said Phyl. 'Thank you for giving up your day off.'

'That's okay,' said Zoe in a small voice, sitting down on one of the hard kitchen chairs, looking like she wasn't sure why she was there, even though she was dressed for physical labour in jeans and a flannel shirt. 'Is there tea?'

Maisie had already poured out a mug, decorated with a Union Jack and the slogan 'I'm buying British'. She asked the young woman: 'Toast?'

'I couldn't – not yet.'

While Phyl dressed and Zoe drank in silence, Maisie made three rounds of cheese-and-pickle sandwiches for them to take with them, then ran upstairs to wash and brush her teeth and change into her boiler suit. When she got back downstairs, Zoe was, after all, munching a doorstop slice of toast, dripping with butter and Bovril. Maisie ate a banana from the fruit bowl. Phyl joined them and they left Bunting Manor in the direction of the barn where Archie was waiting with a trailer rigged up behind his tractor.

They climbed in and rattled off down the chalk and flint lane through the woods, in the direction of the south-facing fields between Bunting and Harden. Zoe insisted on eating her cheese-and-pickle sandwich *en route* and Maisie and Phyl were soon doing the same.

'We'll get something more substantial in the Dancing Hare at lunchtime,' said Phyl, her mouth full.

At the field, the combine harvester had already been through, cutting the crop and separating the ears of wheat – that would, once dried, be ground to flour for making bread – from the tall yellow stalks. The lengths of straw had been bound, by the same remarkable machine, with nylon twine in rectangular bales, each one about the size of a large suitcase. Very considerately, Archie had bought two pairs of old and dirty farm gloves for Maisie and Zoe, though his horny hands and Phyl's required no protection.

The work was hard – loading the trailer in the field and unloading at the barn – but it was broken up by the back-and-forth journeys. Harold and Adam Farr arrived at half past eleven and Phyl said that she and 'the other girls' would 'go and bang on the pub door and we can each have a shepherd's pie'. Maisie was very pleased with that idea as the hard work had made her very hungry, despite her sandwich. Even Zoe – who had been known to flirt with vegetarianism – was delighted. Because they had been up with the sun, Harold and Adam had already eaten so they stayed with Archie in the field.

Phyl and 'the other girls' accompanied their shepherd's pies with cider as the most refreshing option available, reminding Maisie of her friends at Sunny View, Russell and Audrey Savage, and their hand-made scrumpy business, conducted out of a large shed in their garden, supplied with their own cider apples from their orchard next door. Once lunch was over, Phyl groaned and complained about her muscles seizing up with sitting still. Maisie sympathised but Zoe, with the carelessness of youth, said: 'That means you need more exercise to keep yourself supple.'

'I'll remind you of that comment when you're sixty, if I'm spared,' said Phyl. 'See how you like it.'

For the second time in a couple of days, Maisie saw the part-time organist and retired naval officer, Commander Kimmings. He was alone at the end of the bar, nursing a heavy-bottomed glass of whisky. She decided to put into action the idea she had pondered in her bedroom and spontaneously confront him.

'Wait for me here,' Maisie told the others. 'I'll just be a moment. Don't come and get involved.'

The urgency of her tone made Phyl and Zoe do as they were told. Maisie crossed the pub. Hearing her step,

Kimmings looked up with a half-smile, then his face fell when he saw who she was. He pulled himself together and asked: 'Ah, the ingenious Miss Cooper. How can I help you?'

Maisie was not deceived by his veneer of politeness. He was, after all, one of the people who had been most unkind to poor Zoe when her foster parents had thrown her out on her sixteenth birthday, around the time of the murder at Bunting Manor. She decided to take a punt, putting him on the spot.

With a broad smile to put him off his guard, she told him: 'I know you oppose Mrs Pascal turning the big house into a respite home. You've spoken against it at the parish council meetings.' His expression was wary. Maisie left a pause, then took a stab in the dark. 'But you shouldn't have sent that anonymous threatening letter.'

'I shouldn't what . . . ?' he began, feigning confusion. Maisie could see, however, that she had hit home and he was desperately calculating his next best move. He blustered: 'That seems a strange accusation—'

She felt a surge of relief that this was a mystery she could at last cross off her list and didn't let him finish.

'Well, how about that. I'm not surprised it was you. I will pass on the guilt that I can see in your eyes to Sergeant Wingard. He will, no doubt, have something to say on the matter – and perhaps some forensic evidence to put before you.'

Maisie was fairly certain that wouldn't be the case, but he wasn't to know that. Kimmings gaped like a fish, exhibiting a hint of satisfying panic. Maisie turned on her heel and rejoined the others.

'What was that about?' asked Phyl.

'I just had this intuition. I challenged him over the threatening letter and he couldn't conceal his guilt. It was he who sent it, Phyl, to you not to me.'

'How do you know?' asked Zoe innocently.

'I caught him on the hop. It was plain to see in the expression on his guilty, piggy face.'

Phyl shook her head angrily and said: 'I'm going to give him a piece of my mind.'

Maisie put a restraining hand on her arm. 'Better to let him stew. Come on, let's go.' She gestured round the pub. 'There's no need to spoil anyone else's day.'

They went outside and squeezed together on the stone bench beneath the pub window. Archie came by and they climbed up on the trailer with Harold and Adam to return to the field. Together, they made short work of what remained, completing their last trip with a half-empty trailer at just after three.

Stacking the bales in the barn had become difficult because the top of the well-organised pile – tessellated in alternating directions for balance – was high up in the rafters. Archie had directed them to make a kind of staircase of bales to reach the top.

'We need them nice and high to save space for those from the next field.'

Finally, it was done and Archie drove Harold and Adam back to Bitling. Maisie took a moment to contemplate their achievement. Then she followed the other two indoors to wash and change, before coming back downstairs to find Phyl in the kitchen, pulling the cork from a bottle of white wine. She heard the deep sound of a vehicle with a large, well-tuned engine creeping slowly up the drive, crunching the ill-weeded gravel, and went outside to see who it was.

To her delight, she recognised the official car with diplomatic plates of Stephen's best friend, Mohammed As-Sabah, from the same regiment back when they had been in the British army together, but now an important Kuwaiti diplomat. He had played a decisive role in helping Maisie to solve the murder at Church Lodge.

The Bentley slowed to a graceful halt and Mohammed got out, explaining that he had given his chauffeur a few days off.

'I drove myself down from the embassy in London, through the gorgeous autumn colours, and felt in command, for once, instead of life transporting me on its flow.'

'That's funny, I've had that same feeling myself a couple of times.'

'Which feeling?' asked Mohammed.

'Never mind. I'll tell you later. But how wonderful to see you. I didn't know if you would be able to attend. Has my wedding interrupted affairs of state?'

'Had it done so, it would have been worth it.'

They didn't embrace – Maisie thought that was an action that Mohammed wouldn't be able to reconcile with his strict Muslim upbringing – but instead shook hands.

'You look so incredibly well,' he told her, 'I feel fat and lazy beside you.'

Maisie took in his impeccable Savile Row suit, his exceptionally white shirt and his old-school regimental tie and countered: 'You look remarkably fine, as always. Will you come in? We've only recently finished work for the day and Phyl's opened a bottle of wine to celebrate.'

'I would be glad of a glass of water with perhaps a squeeze of lemon?'

'We have lemons for when Phyl needs gin and tonic rather than wine, so yes, we can do that.'

'Do you also have ice?' he asked with a twinkle.

'We do, even in this God-forsaken English valley,' she replied, in the same bantering tone.

Maisie, Mohammed and Phyl sat round the kitchen table and Maisie was obliged to tell him – as concisely as she was able – about what he referred to as 'all of her adventures'. She did so, then Zoe came to join them, wanting to know: 'What's the plan for dinner?'

Maisie introduced Zoe to Mohammed and the young woman was, Maisie thought, very taken with – and impressed by – their visitor. He told them a little about his work as a diplomat attached to the Kuwaiti embassy and shared with Phyl a long digression on a subject close to both their hearts: racehorses. Then he informed them that it was time for him to drive on into Chichester where he had taken a room at the Dolphin and Anchor and reserved a table for his evening meal.

'I'm dining with Dorothy Dean, the theatre manager. Do you remember who I mean?'

'I do, of course,' said Maisie. Mohammed had made a 'significant' charitable contribution to Chichester Festival Theatre in memory of Stephen. 'Zoe works there now.'

'At the theatre?'

'No, the hotel.'

'Do you need a lift, perhaps?' he asked.

'You are very kind, but . . .' Zoe began, politely. Then, she said: 'Actually, I'm working tomorrow, so if I stay in a room in the staff annex tonight, no one will have to drive me in through the rush hour in the morning. The bus is so slow.'

'So be it,' said Mohammed. 'Would you like to sit behind like a dignitary or beside me in front?'

'Mohammed drives a Bentley,' said Maisie.

'In front,' said Zoe, looking thrilled. 'If you don't mind.'

'I would be honoured.' Zoe ran to get a change of clothes for the morning and Mohammed asked: 'How is Sergeant Wingard?'

'He is very well but exceptionally busy,' said Maisie.

'You said he is seeking a new role?'

'Yes.'

'In the private sector?'

'No, a promotion within the police force.'

Mohammed nodded: 'It is his vocation, I understand. Yours, too, in a way, dear Maisie, as an amateur sleuth.'

'Perhaps not for long,' said Maisie, realising with a sort of internal gulp that she hadn't talked at all about the reason Mohammed was there – as a guest at the wedding on Saturday. Once again, she felt guilty that her 'big day' hadn't been in the front of her mind. 'I mean, I don't suppose I can carry on investigating mysteries once I'm married.'

'Will you not have any kind of work? I can't imagine that for you.'

No, thought Maisie. *Neither can I.*

THIRTY-SIX

Liz Petter was experiencing a sense of deep dissatisfaction, sitting in the lonely farmhouse kitchen down near Selsey, while her father, George, was out at some club or charitable function, doing good and spreading the tendrils of his business.

A business I'm supposed to inherit and love.

The truth was, Liz loved the roses – flowers of all kinds, in fact – but she didn't like farming more generally, especially not all the endless ways of making tiny chiselling tithes of extra money. To Liz, it felt mean and small-minded, 'looking after the pennies', as her father insisted: managing the labourers to get the most out of their efforts; careful book-keeping, making sure that funds stayed in the deposit account until the last possible moment; checking that the seed merchant wasn't short-changing them; driving a hard bargain when selling their beef and lamb on market days.

It never ends . . .

She looked out of the kitchen window. She now regretted giving Mick and Jez the liberty to leave the potato field and tidy up the yard instead. They had made a poor job of it, sweeping the early autumn leaves to one end and leaving them to be redistributed by the breeze. They'd run the hose across the concrete, but they hadn't scrubbed with the yard broom. Now everything was dry once more, the smears of animal excrement could clearly still be seen.

She turned away from the glass and went deeper inside the farmhouse, to a frigid television room with two rundown fabric armchairs and a leather recliner, one of her father's few extravagances, in which he liked to lean back and shout at the *Nine O'clock News*, *Panorama* and *World in Action* with a whisky and water balanced in his calloused fingers on the wide, flat arm.

Liz turned on the TV, waited a few moments for it to come to life, then switched through the channels: BBC One, BBC Two and Southern. She chose BBC One and watched a few minutes of a critical report on *Nationwide*, questioning the supposed health benefits of margarine over butter, then turned it off with a gesture of disgust.

Oh, who cares . . .

She went upstairs to her bedroom, a large attic room, still replete with mementoes of childhood and adolescence, largely unaltered for years and years.

I've never grown up – that's my problem. But it's hard to grow up on your own.

She contemplated her bed linen, washed weekly and almost threadbare, purchased back when she was in her early twenties. She contemplated the books on her few low shelves where O-level and A-level texts still outnumbered volumes purchased for grown-up enjoyment.

I bet Maisie Cooper has yards of improving literature in several languages.

Liz sat down at her white Formica desk, thinking about Maisie's visit and how it had made her feel.

Drab, stupid and unwanted.

She opened her childhood address book, a leather-bound tome in landscape format with ruled lines on thick ivory pages. Flipping through, she found very few entries.

I'd like to be social, but I seem to have left it too late.

She put the address book aside and, from the drawer to the right of her knees, pulled out a large scrapbook, bought at Woolworths on North Street. Inside were pasted and labelled the tickets to every one of the films and theatre shows she had ever attended, from six years old when she had seen her first Christmas pantomime at the King's Theatre in Southsea, through to John Gay's *The Beggar's Opera* in Chichester – the one that had ended in murder at the theatre the previous summer. Many of the previous years' tickets were pairs, bought with Jack.

She closed the scrapbook.

He won't be taking me to the theatre again any time soon.

Liz went back downstairs, thinking she ought to make herself something to eat. Her father, George, would be dining out on salmon quiche or chicken escalope or some other staple of institutional cooking. Her mother was away at a spa, being pampered.

I should make an effort. I'll feel better.

She opened the fridge, trying to imagine an enticing meal-for-one, but found it barren – a few limp vegetables past their best, a block of lard and some potatoes that had begun to sprout.

Liz felt a surge of anger.

What is this life I'm condemned to endure, the same every day, sun up to sunset? If she, Maisie Cooper, hadn't come back, Jack and I would be . . .

Her anger subsided as she asked herself if it was really true.

Would Jack and I have gone on, walking out together?

She remembered every detail of the conversation in which he had told her how happy he was to see Maisie again, as if she, Liz, were a sister or a cousin or a maiden aunt with whom he'd gone out a few times, just because one had to have someone. He hadn't quite gone so far as to tell her that she couldn't possibly feel a sense of loss that those days were gone.

Nearly, though.

253

'It isn't fair,' said Liz, aloud, still looking into the disappointing interior of the fridge. 'What's Maisie Cooper got that I haven't?'

That, though, wasn't a question she felt inclined honestly to answer.

Finally, Liz shut the fridge and went to stand outside in the rose field, seeing the sun quite low in the sky on the line of the drive. The blooms looked particularly beautiful in the slant light.

Maisie Cooper won't make him happy. Jack doesn't want a woman with ideas of joining the army and living abroad. He wants someone solid and dependable, like me, connected to the Sussex soil. I just need to make him see it.

THIRTY-SEVEN

Maisie let herself be persuaded that she should join Mohammed at dinner with the theatre manager, Dorothy Dean, who was, after all, another wedding guest. Zoe having also graciously accepted Mohammed's invitation, Maisie suggested that Phyl should come, too, and Mohammed declared himself delighted to request a bigger table.

'Come one, come all.'

Phyl refused, saying that she hadn't yet recovered from the hard work bringing in the straw bales and would go straight to bed the moment they had left.

Before setting out from Bunting Manor, Maisie rang the station to tell Jack that she could meet him there at ten o'clock so that they could 'have a private word'. Sounding distracted, he told her that nine o'clock would do.

'There's a limit to how much paperwork a man can be asked to suffer in a single day.'

Wanting to be in charge of her own movements, Maisie took the Land Rover keys and went outside, telling Mohammed and Zoe that they could follow in convoy. Finding the night chilly, she ran back inside for a cardigan from her room and, on the way back down the stairs, found Phyl on the bottom step, pulling on her wellington boots.

'I need some fresh air,' she said gruffly. 'Then it's bed.'

'All right,' Maisie told her, wondering why Phyl looked guilty. 'You're sure you won't come? I'll not be late back.'

'Quite sure. I've been eating too much anyway. I'm becoming a fat old woman.'

Maisie still hesitated, not liking the idea of Phyl tramping about through the village and the woods on her own as the sun began to set.

'I wish you had a big dog to look after you, Phyl.'

'That's because your imagination's overexcited. Tell you what, you can drop me at the Dancing Hare and I'll potter back with Archie. He's bound to be propping up the bar, eating those little salty sausages Ernie Sumner puts out to keep people drinking.'

'Good,' said Maisie with a sense of relief that she had to acknowledge seemed out of proportion to the circumstances. Then she realised why. She hadn't mentioned the trespasser she'd come across that morning. She briefly told the story and asked Phyl: 'What do you think of that?'

'Some fool peeping Tom or a nosy parker wanting to get a look at Bunting Manor.'

'Like a birdwatcher but for architecture?' said Maisie, unconvinced.

'Or they were looking for you.'

'That's not very reassuring.'

'Not with malign intent. Because you're famous,' snapped Phyl. 'And very beautiful. It's a magnetic combination.'

Maisie frowned and asked: 'Have I annoyed you, Phyl? Is there something I ought to have done or not done?'

Phyl sighed, loudly, protesting: 'Didn't I just say? I'm tired and I'm a fat old woman and neither of those things agrees with me. You've done nothing wrong and I doubt you ever will.' Phyl heaved herself up off the bottom step of the impressive staircase, her bony, veiny hands grasping the newel post, then surprised Maisie by lurching over to her with her arms wide. 'Come here.'

Maisie allowed herself to be embraced, smelling Phyl's unwashed grey hair and a slight fustiness in her clothes.

'What's happening?' she asked.

'This is me being happy,' said Phyl. 'You should know that by now. And I'll not countenance losing you.'

'Is that in the offing?'

Phyl pulled abruptly away. 'Come on. The others are waiting.'

Outside, Maisie discovered Mohammed in the passenger seat and Zoe behind the wheel of the Bentley with the windows rolled down. Maisie had been teaching Zoe to drive in the Land Rover, but only on Phyl's private farm lanes because she was too young for a driving licence.

'I know I can do it,' pleaded Zoe. 'Please let me.'

'You can reverse to the corner of the manor, then drive down to the gate,' said Mohammed. 'Then I will have to take over.'

'Zoe, we all spoil you,' said Maisie.

'Because I'm so lovely and charming,' said the young woman. 'Admit it.'

Maisie and Phyl pulled out in front. Maisie dropped Phyl at the Dancing Hare, able to see, in her rear-view mirror, Mohammed and Zoe swapping seats. Then she pulled away with the Bentley a sober distance behind all the way into Chichester.

The meal at the Dolphin and Anchor was pleasant, if unexceptional. Dorothy Dean met them in the lobby, looking as formidable as ever – short, stocky and upright, in a tight blue trouser suit with her grey hair set in tight curls. She seemed delighted to see Maisie and was – for someone Maisie considered an earnest and practical businesswoman – surprisingly interested in the wedding preparations. Moving the conversation on, Maisie mentioned the letter she had received from Adélaïde Amour and the job offer it contained.

'But that won't be possible, once you are married, surely?' Dorothy asked.

'No,' said Maisie, suppressing a sigh. 'I suppose not.'

They completed their meal with apple and raspberry sorbets, hand-made from local fruit, floating in a fizzy puddle of Babycham, an excessively sweet sparkling wine. Mohammed refused his because it contained alcohol and Maisie let hers melt without touching it. Zoe and Dorothy pronounced themselves delighted and wished there were seconds.

When Maisie heard the clock in the lobby of the hotel chime eight-forty-five, she stood up to say goodbye.

'Will you be very busy tomorrow?' Mohammed asked. 'Miss Dean has invited me to a concert. The theatre season has ended but she recommends Cleo Laine and Johnny Dankworth very highly.'

'That's very kind.'

'Maisie will have too much on her mind,' said Dorothy.

'Perhaps,' she answered.

But I don't, though. Is that bad? Maybe this could be my chance to help with preparations for the wedding?

'If you do decide to come,' said Dorothy, 'Sergeant Wingard will be welcome too, of course. And the other one, Inspector Nairn, if he feels like it. We've a good house – a good audience – but not sold out.'

'I'll ask them both. I'm on my way to the station, now.'

Maisie bid them goodbye and thanked Mohammed for his generosity. Then she slipped out into the street to find the Land Rover, parked behind Woolworths, as was her habit.

Night had fallen. She drove down through the town and stopped once more on the canal basin, the murky water sinister and slimy in the glow of the street lamps. She was about to get out when she changed her mind and moved the car to the single yellow line right outside, much closer, where it was legal out of office hours. From this vantage point, she could see the steps to the front door of the station.

She gasped.

There on the tarmac, illuminated by the traditional blue police lamp, was Jack. And, facing him, her hands grasping the lapels of his uniform jacket, was Liz Petter.

Maisie got out as quietly as she was able, hesitating at the entrance to the station forecourt, her hand on the brickwork of a gate pillar. From beyond the parked patrol cars, she could hear Jack's soothing tone, but not – at first – his words. Then Liz Petter interrupted.

'Did I mean nothing to you? Was it just convenience? Or were you trying to get in with Dad? Was that it?'

'No, Liz. You and I were just friends, that's all.'

'I wasn't "just friends". You must have known that.'

'I didn't, Liz. I'm very sorry. It never crossed my mind that—'

'Why did it never cross your mind? What's wrong with me?'

'There's nothing wrong with you.'

'But I'm not her, am I,' said Liz, letting go of Jack's lapels and bowing her head.

Maisie hadn't moved but, somehow, Jack had become aware of her presence. Their eyes met across the bonnets of the 'jam sandwich' police cars, white with orange-red horizontal stripes along their sides. His expression was apologetic, but also serious.

I should go, Maisie mouthed, gesturing with her hand.

He shook his head, then Liz spoke again.

'For a community copper that everyone supposedly likes, you're good at making enemies.'

'I hope not.'

'You should hear what Mick and Jez Carter have to say about you.'

'Their grudge should be against themselves, not me.'

'And what about my grudge?'

'I hope, in time, we'll be friends again,' said Jack, still using his professional 'soothing' tone.

Maisie thought something in his manner must have communicated itself to Liz, because she suddenly turned and looked straight at her.

'Oh my God, there she is: Miss Perfect. Isn't that marvellous.' Liz took two steps away from Jack, then turned back. 'Has she been there all this time? Have you been mocking me, both of you?'

Maisie crossed the parking area, weaving between the police cars, determined to pretend she had seen mothing amiss.

'I've just got here,' she fibbed. 'That's why I just caught Jack's eye. How are you, Liz? Thank you for your help and advice, by the way. What a wonderful farm and what wonderful roses. You must have green thumbs, as we say in French.'

Maisie stopped, equidistant from Jack and from Liz, so they formed a sort of wary triangle, Jack looking serious and sympathetic and Liz unsure whether to believe in Maisie's polite detachment. The silence went on too long, then Jack took charge.

'Come inside, Maisie,' he said. 'Goodnight, Liz. We can meet again and talk about all this, if you like. Or not, if you'd rather forget it.'

Liz didn't answer, though her expression was dark.

Jack held out an arm to let Maisie go ahead of him, through the heavy swing door. He followed and, before it fully closed behind them, resting on its latch, Jack put an eye to the crack.

'She's going,' he told Maisie with relief in his voice. 'I think I'd better tell you what that was all about.'

'Yes,' said Maisie. 'Perhaps you should.'

Thirty-Eight

Jack led Maisie from the public lobby of the police station, with its tired noticeboards and depressing notices, into a narrow corridor with unpleasant fluorescent strip lighting. From there, he showed her into a spartan interview room.

'This is where we first properly spoke,' she told him, 'when I came back in February. This is where you showed me the police file that proved, without any shadow of doubt, that Stephen had been murdered – that he hadn't simply died with the shock of the cold water of the outdoor swimming pool on a winter's morning.'

Jack apologised: 'I'm sorry. I wasn't thinking. Should we go elsewhere?'

Maisie considered. 'Perhaps not. I wouldn't put it past Liz Petter to be outside somewhere, wanting to confront us both. She seems like a very determined sort of person.'

'She's actually very nice. You didn't see the best of her—'

'Anyway, before you go on, you should know that I've met her.' Maisie told him about riding the moped down to Petter Farm. 'I sort of guessed there was something between you. She was mostly very taciturn and then, a couple of times, she just gave me this ugly smile, like the Big Bad Wolf in the story of Red Riding Hood.'

'Did Mick or Jez see you, recognise you?' asked Jack, urgently.

'No, I don't think so, but that's not the point. I mean, why shouldn't you have had a relationship with Liz? She's very attractive and I suppose you know her father very well from the Rotary and—'

'Maisie, never mind all that,' interrupted Jack. 'We didn't have "a relationship", Liz and I. Her father's a good man and, yes, we know one another well. He asked me to take Liz to a few things to get her out and about, to mix and make friends. I did my best and, obviously, she thought there was more to it.'

'You didn't canoodle?' asked Maisie, raising her eyebrows.

'No petting of any kind,' said Jack, smiling in return.

'Good,' said Maisie. 'What with everything else, I'm not sure I could stand having ripped you from the bosom of your previous love.'

'Don't, Maisie. It isn't funny.' Then, after a second or two, they both laughed. 'All right, it is, in a way. But I do feel very sorry for her.'

'I know what you mean. You remember Vaughan Quinn at the time of the murder at the fair?'

'The Bitling vet?'

'Yes. You were away and he was very taken with me and extremely disappointed when he learned about you lurking with intent in the background.'

Thinking about Vaughan Quinn prompted Maisie to visualise all the inconclusive thoughts she had noted down on the Bunting Manor–headed notepaper. She summoned them out of memory and spoke them aloud to Jack, finding them all disappointingly thin. When she got to Derek Field-house, however, she became more serious.

'You hid that from me, his release. It was in the papers Fred sent you, wasn't it?'

'It was.'

'Why wasn't I allowed to know?' she asked, with an edge.

'Because I didn't want you to go looking for him,' he told her in a serious tone. 'I know you. Somehow you don't fear the obvious danger.'

Maisie didn't answer. There was, on the tip of her tongue, a rebuke, something along the lines of: *You mustn't think you can tell me what to do once you're my husband.*

The resentment faded.

Jack held that information back to protect me from myself, not as my future husband but as any police officer ought.

'Did I do the wrong thing?' he asked.

'Perhaps it would have been better to tell me, to put me on my guard.'

'Yes, that's true. But, on the train, I was thinking that we would be together much more than we have been. I didn't realise what a desperate logjam I'd find here at the station.'

'It doesn't matter. It's done and . . .' Maisie frowned. 'Oh, I didn't tell you about the slate.'

Concisely but with attention to detail, she narrated her encounter with Kinori. When she had finished, he favoured the explanation of coincidence, as he had with the threatening letter. Then he surprised her by saying: 'There's a proverb about rooks and crows. You said there were just two black birds on separate branches of the sycamore, level with the top of the tower?'

'I did.'

'Not a rookery, then.'

'Why do you say that?'

'The proverb goes: "A crow in a crowd is a rook; a rook on its own is a crow." And do you see what that suggests?'

'Do I see what?'

'The collective noun.'

After a second's thought, Maisie told him: 'Isn't it a "parliament" of rooks?'

'Yes, it is. But that's not what I meant,' he said, with a smile that she couldn't share.

He waited and she worked it out.

'Oh, I see. You meant a "murder" of crows.'

*

Maisie drove Jack home to number 147 Parklands Road and, seeing lights on, they went inside to find Florence up late, sewing Maisie's wedding dress, enjoying herself enormously but wincing when, finally, she had finished and got up.

'How's your bruise?' Maisie asked.

'Hard to see in the bathroom mirror,' Florence told her. 'Better, though.'

'No news of who might have brought the marbles round?'

'No, but I've been busy with this.' She indicated the lovely ivory dress. 'I've not seen anyone much to ask.' She yawned. 'Actually, that's late enough for me. I'll take myself off. Lock up, won't you, Jack?'

'I will,' he told her. 'Sleep well.'

Left alone, Maisie asked Jack if there was any news from Newcastle: 'Have you spoken to Donaldson again?'

Jack shook his head. 'I have but he's not uncovered anything. It always seemed hard to tie in someone doing nefarious things in Sussex with being on the scaffolding next to the hostel on that one day.'

'I made it up and back on the train, overnight,' Maisie mused.

'True,' he accepted. 'You did. But it would have to be someone with enough ready money.'

Maisie realised she hadn't told Jack that she had also pondered a connection with Ada Strickland, the unhappy spinster from Bitling, sister of a man that she and Jack together had put in jail.

'What do you think?'

'She's quite small and frail, isn't she? Do you mean as a candidate for the scaffolding?'

'I don't know. Just someone with a grudge.'

'Unlikely,' he pronounced. 'Is she even tight with her brother?'

'You know how it is. Close relatives perhaps don't get on but, if they perceive an outsider turning on any of them, they close ranks. And I do feel like an outsider.' Maisie sighed. 'Chichester and the villages – that's where I'm from, but I've been away and seen the world and done lots of, for most people, unusual things, met unusual people. Do you think I'll always be like that, or will I sort of . . .'

'Sort of what?'

In that moment, Maisie understood that there was something more to the doubts she had shared with Charity.

'Will I simply blend in with the scenery? I think I've been worrying about becoming boring to you, Jack. You know, if I'm just a housewife and mother. Do you love me because I'm a glamorous stranger, full of mystery from my absence – and then, because I've been accidentally involved in all these crimes.'

'Maisie, there's something you're forgetting.'

'What's that?' she asked in a small voice.

'I've always loved you, even when I thought I might never see you again and you were just a memory.'

V

CARNATIONS

SIGNIFYING, IF RED, 'I LOVE YOU'; IF YELLOW,
SLIGHTED AFFECTION

THIRTY-NINE

The next day, Thursday the 28th of September, was another early start, the weather grey with a fine mizzle in the air. Maisie and Phyl met in the kitchen once again and Phyl insisted on a cooked breakfast because she thought the rain wasn't going to last. 'Let's wait it out with some wholesome food.'

Archie came in and joined them with the good news that the second field wasn't as big as the first, saying: 'We'll be done a mite quicker.'

Phyl's countrywoman's foresight proved correct. By the time they'd finished their eggs and bacon and toast, the sky was clearing with the south-west wind. They boarded the trailer, Archie fired up the noisy engine of his diesel tractor and called out: 'Hold on tight!'

Away they went, sending partridge and pheasant flying up out of the undergrowth, breaking the peace of the morning. They found Harold and Adam Farr already waiting, having walked over on the pilgrim trail, under the shelter of the trees.

The second field was steeper than the first and about three-quarters the size. They began in the top corner and took it in turns to ride in the trailer, on top of the bales, to stack them in the barn. Harold and Adam went first. When they returned, because they had all four developed a knack for the work, the trailer was soon full once more. The women climbed on top and, unloading at the barn, Phyl asked Maisie if there was any news about any of her suspicions and she replied, before realising what she was saying: 'Oh, let's just forget all that, shall we, just for an hour or two?'

The work was done by twelve, the barn full to the rafters with just a small space set aside for the moped under its tarpaulin, the mushrooms under their cardboard and the kindling. Archie offered to take the Farrs back to Bitling and Maisie reminded them that they were expected at the wedding on Saturday.

'It's in just two days.'

'But I've nothing proper to wear,' mumbled Adam.

Maisie told him: 'Come as you are for all I care. We're friends, aren't we?'

'I hope so,' said Adam, diffidently.

'Thank you,' said Harold. 'I've not been to a wedding for thirty years.'

'I haven't never,' said Adam. 'Will there be songs?'

'Yes, there will be hymns,' Maisie told him, 'like the ones at Bitling Chapel.'

'All right, then.'

Off they went, their words of goodbye covered by the cacophony of the tractor, and Maisie thought about how, coincidentally, Harold Farr had been present when, to her surprise and delight, Jack had proposed to her, kneeling on the cold stones of the Market Cross in the centre of Chichester. Maisie had given Harold a pound note for luck and, soon after, Phyl had taken pity on him and his nephew, finding them a caravan to live in and work to do, looking after the turkey shed. That, of course, led her back to Mick and Jez Carter, sleeping in a different 'aluminium can', on the edge of Liz Petter's potato field.

Before her ideas began to spiral, Phyl chivvied her to wash her hands so they could walk over to the Dancing Hare for 'a ploughman's lunch to make a change from shepherd's pie'. Then it was time for Maisie to drive into Chichester to pick up 'the Sunny View contingent' from the railway station, and Maisie felt a kind of gear change in the wedding preparations.

It's all very well Mohammed arriving under his own steam.
This is different.

She arrived a little early, expecting three of them: Canon Greig – her alternative priest, sidelining the awful Reverend Millns – and Russell and Audrey Savage, the owners of a guest house in the mid-Devon hamlet of Trout Leap. Back in early July, Russell had written to her, asking for help, concluding with the ominous phrase: '*Something has to be done before there's a murder and the police just aren't interested.*'

Maisie hadn't at first taken the idea seriously – thinking it was conversational exaggeration – but it had led to her solving her fifth mystery, the murder at Sunny View.

The train thundered in and, climbing down, Russell and Audrey looked the same as ever. He wore a sagging tweed suit with a grey shirt that had once been white, surprisingly enlivened by a loosely knotted paisley tie, his smile framed by salt-and-pepper whiskers. Audrey's grey hair was newly set and, for comfort on her travels, she had chosen a voluminous dress whose pattern was not quite as loud as Zoe's kaftan, but not far off.

They greeted one another with delight, then Maisie broke away to acknowledge Canon Greig, of the 'Collegiate Church of the Holy Cross and the Mother of Him Who Hung Thereon'.

'Thank you for coming. You bring with you a strong link to an important earlier part of my life.'

'It was in my gift and I was happy to accede,' he told her, offering his limp hand to shake. He had travelled in a dark suit with a black shirt and white ecclesiastical 'dog collar'. 'The incumbent priest will not be disappointed, I hope? The tone of his letter was neutral, but people can be so touchy.'

'I'm sure no offence has been taken,' Maisie told him, hoping that was true.

271

Then, descending from the high step of the slam-door British Rail train, she was astonished to see Paul Linton, a handsome eighteen-year-old whose Mediterranean skin was burnished deep brown by a summer of West Country sunshine.

'Hello, Miss Cooper. How do you do?' he asked.

For a second, Maisie wanted to reply: *I'm not entirely sure.*

★

Maisie found the drive home very uncomfortable, with Canon Greig beside her making insipid conversation about his theological training with her and – oddly – with Paul Linton. She could see the young man throughout in her rear-view mirror, polite and attentive, sitting between Russell and Audrey on the bench seat in the back, all their bags piled up behind.

What on earth is Paul doing here? I would very much like to know but I can't simply ask out loud ...

As they arrived in Bunting, the sun was trying to come out. Maisie didn't go directly to the manor, but instead parked in front of a more modern house, belonging to Phyl's estate, built in the mid-Fifties in slabs of concrete and, more recently, painted an unpleasant shade of salmon pink. It had been rented for a number of years by Zoe's foster parents, Mr and Mrs Beck, before she turned sixteen and they abandoned her at the bus stop by the green, with a pitiful small suitcase of belongings and without a backward glance.

Maisie located the key under the mat, opened up and discovered that the place had been aired and the storage heaters were warm. She showed Canon Greig and Paul Linton to the kitchen and invited them to make themselves a cup of tea while she took Russell and Audrey upstairs to the master bedroom, overlooking the village green, carrying their two old-fashioned cardboard suitcases herself. Once inside, she shut the door.

'Why is Paul here?' she asked in an urgent tone, but quietly, so as not to be overheard.

'He doesn't know,' murmured Russell.

'A decision was made,' whispered Audrey, 'not to tell him and his sister that—'

'Any of the ins and outs, pending the trial,' interrupted Russell.

They were talking about the murder at Sunny View.

'You can't be serious?'

'And Canon Greig wanted to bring him along,' said Audrey, 'because he has a vocation.'

Maisie knew that Paul Linton was a server in Kirton's Church of the Holy Cross but hadn't known he was destined for the clergy.

'Can that be true?' she asked.

'It seems so,' they both told her.

'But when I arrived at Sunny View, you warned me off him,' she protested to Russell, 'telling me that he was a tearaway.'

'I think I said he might turn out to be a tearaway,' Russell quibbled. 'And you know what young people are, desperate to find a direction. Well, turns out he's found one.'

'He has, Maisie,' said Audrey. 'That's where 'tis.'

Maisie took a moment to consider their words. Paul had been very close to the heart of the murder at Sunny View, albeit not guilty of any crime.

Do I have to think of him as someone else with a grudge?

'And to prove it,' said Audrey, complacently, 'coincidentally, he's just been on a retreat to a place called Blackfriars.'

Maisie knew that the 'Black Friars' referred to the Dominican order of monks, founded in the thirteenth century, the forerunners of the Inquisition. But that wasn't what was in

273

the front of her mind. Unusually, she was experiencing a kind of premonition – a sense of a connection where there ought to be none.

'And where was this retreat?'

'Well, that's the coincidence,' said Russell, comfortably, impervious to her mood. 'It's a friary they've restored where your Jack was – while you, Maisie, were with us at Sunny View, being all kinds of clever – in Newcastle.'

With exasperation in her voice – but still quietly – she asked them: 'But did you not think it might be odd for him to come here? What's his role?'

'Canon Greig has taken him under his wing,' said Audrey. 'You wouldn't begrudge him that, whatever someone else might have done—'

'All right,' said Maisie, quickly. 'But you are absolutely sure that he doesn't know what happened?'

'Perhaps you should write them all down in a book,' said Russell, attempting to lighten the mood. 'You know, *Maisie Cooper Investigates*, or some such. Perhaps they'll put it on the telly.'

Maisie heard footsteps and, not entirely reassured, went out onto the landing to find that Canon Greig and Paul Linton had brought their tea upstairs and had each found their room, equipped with small single beds because they had been used by the Becks' foster children. Canon Greig was a short man but Paul was eyeing his doubtfully.

'I'll have to curl up a bit, Miss Cooper,' he told her. 'I think I'm longer than the bed is.'

Maisie hesitated. With his dark-brown eyes and deep complexion and bright white teeth, she had to acknowledge that Paul was a very handsome young man. And there was a clarity to his gaze that, in other circumstances, she might find appealing – or, indeed, Zoe might. Today, though, it seemed like a mask.

'I'm sorry. Do you think you'll manage?'

'Oh, I've had worse. When we were expelled from Malta,' he told her, referring to a story of forced migration that she knew, 'we ended up in a reception centre for a fortnight, not far away, on Thorney Island, you know, a military base between here and Portsmouth. Those beds were awful.'

'So, you know this area?'

'A little. We weren't allowed out and about much.'

'I understand you're interested in joining the ministry?'

'Yes, I'd like to do good in the world,' he told her simply.

Maisie asked herself if it was possible that – if he had an ulterior motive – he would be able to say something so earnest with such conviction. Frustratingly, before she could probe further, Canon Greig came and interrupted, saying he would be grateful for a lift into Framlington to meet Reverend Millns.

'Yes, of course,' said Maisie. 'Let's do that straight away.'

FORTY

Driving the short distance through the Downs from Bunting to Framlington, Maisie had an uncomfortable feeling that events had spiralled out of her control, moving towards their climax. The cast of characters was assembling. All that would soon remain would be the decisive final action.

But I'm none the wiser. I have only questions, no answers.

The sky was brighter, the clouds having been torn apart by the south-west wind. Canon Greig chose the ten-minute journey as an opportunity to instruct Paul Linton in 'the sacrament of marriage', speaking over his right shoulder from the passenger seat.

Surreptitiously observing Paul in the rear-view mirror once more, Maisie had to admit that he seemed keen to learn.

Maisie knew the Framlington vicarage from childish beetle drives for the choir – of which she and Stephen had been a part – and from summer fêtes. It was an impressive red-brick Victorian house, concealed up a short drive alongside St Mark's church. Not wanting to get involved in any – potentially awkward – social niceties with Reverend Millns, Maisie parked on the gravel pull-in close to the lychgate and told Canon Greig that she would go for a walk and be back in half an hour: 'If that seems sufficient time?'

'Yes, I expect so.'

Canon Greig and Paul Linton walked away up the drive between thick laurel hedges, the priest looking small and dapper. Paul's dark suit, though, didn't quite fit. It was tight across the shoulders and she had an idea that the hems of the trousers had been let down to try – unsuccessfully – to make them cover his ankles.

The Lintons were chucked out of Malta with just fifty pounds in their pockets. They were still trying to get back on their feet when the Sunny View mystery happened. I bet he or his mother bought that suit at a charity shop in Kirton and made a botch of altering it.

Contemplating the impact sudden poverty might have on a young man, she drew a tentative conclusion.

I wonder if Paul is considering the church because it feels safe, after all the upset and ructions.

Then she was struck by another possibility.

Or because it's a cover for his malign intentions?

Maisie shook her head, remembering what Russell had said.

But that would make no sense if he doesn't know what I discovered and how I solved the murder.

Crunching the gravel underfoot, Paul and the priest disappeared round a bend in the laurel-lined drive. Maisie wandered up Church Lane into the village, uncertain what to do with her spare thirty minutes.

Not talk to people, that's for sure. I need time alone with my thoughts.

At the corner with the main road, she glanced up the drive of Church Lodge. At the foot of the scaffolding, she saw Mr Singer, the builder, supervising a young lad – probably an apprentice – who was using a shovel to put sand and cement into the drum of the rotary mixer. She surprised herself by feeling only the faintest tinge of loss that this was the place where Stephen died.

That's probably the only real benefit of sticking my nose into other people's affairs. It's sort of pushed Stephen's tragedy more quickly into the past.

Aware that her mood was becoming unnecessarily sour, she quickened her pace, following the pavement past

Halliday's restaurant and the little sweet shop to the edge of the village. She skipped across the road and made her way a short distance up a lane that led to a concrete yard and some stables belonging to Framlington Manor and the Fieldhouse family.

The yard was empty and clean, with just a few wisps of straw being shuffled by the breeze and no horse mess. She paused to gaze up the grassy gallops on which she had ridden, bareback on a grey stallion, in order to escape—

This won't do, she told herself. *How will you solve the present mystery if your mind is always on the past?*

The stable block comprised two sections: a tack room to the left that she knew to be full of all the paraphernalia of horse riding, and two horseboxes to the right, alongside one another, with double-panelled stable doors, one above and one below. She tried all the doors, wanting to see if the bridles and other tack that she had used were still all there, but found them locked.

She turned back to the yard. A gust of wind caused a few wisps of the straw to spiral in the air, as if conjured into movement by the swirl of a magician's wand. With the gust came a noxious smell of something bad, something old and rotten.

Oh dear. Is that a dead rat or a badger hit by a car or something?

She crossed the yard to the gate at the bottom of the gallops, looking up to the top of the slope where a bridleway disappeared under the canopy of Forestry Commission woods.

If I wanted to hide, that's where I'd go, like Old Man Strickland did.

She stayed where she was, her arms resting on the top rail of the fire-bar gate, her mind emptying, watching the rooks – or perhaps crows – pecking for insects in the uncut grass. After a few minutes, she became aware that a feeling of peace had come over her, something to do with the calming influence of green fields and blue-and-white skies, birdsong and a distant murmur of traffic.

Then, the feeling was gone as some demon from her subconscious woke up and asked her an unexpected question.

Why are you thinking about hiding?

*

Canon Greig emerged from his meeting with Reverend Millns in good spirits. They had apparently bonded over 'one or two burning issues of faith and the administration of the church'. Maisie didn't ask what these were but, before getting into the Land Rover, she did ask about the wedding service and if there was anything she ought to know or which needed to be decided before Saturday.

'The rehearsal should clear that up,' he told her.

'Rehearsal?' asked Maisie, surprised.

'Is no rehearsal planned?' asked Canon Greig, his voice revealing his own shock.

'The whole thing is quite last minute,' she explained, weakly. 'It was the events at Sunny View that spurred me on to—' She stopped, seeing Paul's expression of polite interest, standing just a couple of paces away. 'What I mean is, I suppose, that reconnecting with my past gave me a kind of momentum, wanting to bond more quickly with my future.'

Canon Greig told her: 'I quite understand. Perhaps we could visit the, er, venue, as the theatricals say. There will be actors among your guests, will there not? Russell told me the story of the murder at the theatre. Perhaps they will provide the readings?'

Maisie's heart sank again.

Readings. We don't have any readings. That's another way I've failed to prepare, as if this day didn't mean anything at all.

279

'Shall we go inside?' she suggested, without enthusiasm.

She led them through the lychgate and up the path, feeling uncomfortable with Paul walking behind her, as if she feared he might bash her on the head at any moment.

Though there's no reason to worry if what Russell and Audrey say is true. Can that be right, though, that he doesn't – yet – know that he has a reason to resent me interfering?

Again, she pushed the thought away, trying to focus on what was in front of her, namely, her failure to adequately plan what was supposed to be 'the biggest day' in her and Jack's lives.

They went inside and Maisie had an odd sense of *déjà vu*, watching Canon Greig stroll around the austere nave, pointing out elements of architectural or ecclesiastical interest, reminding her of how Kinori had described her own visit to plan the arrangements of flowers. Then, she had an inspiration.

'How about I get a rehearsal together for tomorrow at some point? Mrs Pascal and the Savages will be there and, I hope, my fiancé, though he is very busy at the station. Some others. Perhaps one or two of the police guard of honour might be able to attend.'

'It would no doubt help to make things run smoothly.'

'I'll see what I can do.'

'Alan told me the St Mary's choir has not been engaged.'

Maisie frowned, unaware of who 'Alan' was, then deduced it must be Reverend Millns' first name.

'No, I haven't engaged the choir. Should I have?'

'Only if you want a choir, Miss Cooper. Some people like the sense of ceremony, the ethereal charm of children's trebles. Others prefer the voices of their guests raised in joyful – though untrained – song.'

Maisie had a flashback to her two-day trip to London, before taking the train north to Newcastle.

I should have spent that time organising the wedding, not gallivanting around the West End.

'What's the matter, Miss Cooper?' enquired Paul. 'Is there something I can help you with?'

Maisie realised that her emotions must be playing out visibly on her face.

What can he see? Fear? Disappointment with myself? Confusion about people's motives and intentions?

'That's very kind of you to ask, but all will be well. I simply haven't managed to get on top of all that needed to be done and, with Sergeant Wingard being so . . .' She stopped, struck by a certain intensity in his eyes. 'Never mind. You don't need to know about all that.'

'Forgive me,' he told her. 'I didn't mean to pry.'

'I didn't think you were doing anything of the sort.'

'Thank you, Paul, that will do,' said Canon Greig. 'Your role is a ceremonial one. I will handle the pastoral care.'

'In what sense?' Maisie asked.

'It is customary for you and your fiancé to discuss your futures with your chosen officiant – with me, in preparation for your new lives.'

'Oh, is that right? I'm not sure when we will be able to find the time.'

'I will remain at your disposal, of course. Would you allow Paul to attend this pastoral meeting, as an observer, you understand, for the benefit of his education?'

'I suppose so.'

'At least, Miss Cooper,' he told her, 'your marriage will be blessed with a handsome acolyte. May I say how pleased I was to be invited to officiate? I had no idea that my ministry had impressed you so deeply. You attended just the one service in Kirton, I believe?'

'That's right,' said Maisie. 'You spoke very well.' She remembered the moment when the service had been disrupted by the awful grief of the railway gatekeeper, Fred Luscombe, prostrating himself at the altar and asking for forgiveness for his behaviour in relation to his daughter, Holly. 'And you took the interruption so well in your stride,' she fibbed.

He visibly preened. 'Poor Mr Luscombe. What an awful thing it was. But better we shouldn't dwell on past unhappiness with so much joy to look forward to.'

He gave a sideways glance at Paul, which Maisie supposed was designed to warn her off the subject. Paul noticed, of course, because Canon Greig wasn't subtle, but he didn't flinch or become especially interested. She couldn't help herself asking: 'You knew Holly, didn't you, Paul?'

'I did. I thought it was sad.'

'Her death?' she asked.

'Of course, but also her life.'

'In what sense?'

'In a better organised society, she would have been cared for, found a role.'

For a second, Paul reminded Maisie of the idealistic young man on the bus in Newcastle, the one with the meagre attempt at a Che Guevara moustache.

'Do you have strong political convictions?' Maisie asked.

'I am interested in liberation theology,' he told her as a frown creased Canon Greig's features. Paul went on: 'The church is nothing unless it addresses the oppression of the weak. The promise of religion can't just be an afterlife in heaven. It should be a better world in the here and now.'

'Paul has been reading about the Second Vatican Council, which is really a matter for the Roman church, above all in South America.'

In an even tone, Paul replied: 'Christianity – of whatever branch – should promote social justice and care for the poor and vulnerable.'

'I agree,' said Maisie, finding the conversation – the three of them clustered round the Land Rover on the patch of gravel at the end of Church Lane – unexpectedly stimulating. 'I don't think it's from a Christian ideal, but Mrs Pascal, one of whose houses you are staying in, is working to turn Bunting Manor into a respite home. I'm sure that what you are saying would chime with her – that those with a lot should do their best to help those with little.'

'Wealth is not only notes and coins counted by banks,' said Canon Greig, then he embarked on what he called 'the contested history of liberation theology'.

Maisie listened with increasing impatience while Paul, she had to acknowledge, remained polite and attentive, his dark-brown eyes never blinking or leaving the older man's face. As Canon Greig digressed into 'the question of evangelism more generally', Maisie gently broke in.

'I expect you would like to return to Bunting. You've had a long day already, with all the travelling.'

'Yes,' said Canon Greig, immediately diverted. 'And perhaps a bite to eat?'

*

The need to make sure her guests were adequately fed was something else to which Maisie hadn't given any thought. Happily, Phyl had, with a table booked at the Dancing Hare for six, soon after opening time, the earliest possible moment. To Maisie's delight, Jack and Florence were able to join them, in part to deliver the wedding dress. Once the meal was ended, Jack had to drop Florence home and return to the station.

'Is there any chance we can have a rehearsal tomorrow?' she asked him. 'I feel I've let us both down by not properly preparing.'

'I don't think we need to practise walking up and down and repeating the vows, do we?' he said, looking distracted.

'I suppose not.'

Once he had gone, Maisie regretted not drawing him aside to ask what was worrying him.

Has there been more news of the Kemps or the Carters or even Derek Fieldhouse? Is that what's preoccupying him? Or has Liz Petter been badgering him some more?

Once Jack and Florence had gone, Maisie wanted only for the evening to end, but Phyl was enjoying herself in company, having drunk more or less all of the expensive bottle of wine she had ordered, Paul and Canon Greig being teetotal, Russell preferring cider and Audrey opting – with delight – for Babycham, served in a frosted champagne *coupe*.

They all 'took a turn' round the green, then up one of the many pathways into Phyl's woods, with Canon Greig delighted to learn the history of the pilgrim trail across the Downs, linking the villages 'along pathways worn by immemorial feet', as he pompously put it.

Fuelled by one of Ernest Sumner's best reds, Phyl took them beyond the ridge in the trees and down the other side towards the fast-running stream where Archie Close had discovered a body face down in the crystal-clear water – not a memory Maisie wanted to confront just then. The stream had widened to a large pond, held back by a fall of timber and autumn leaves. At the last moment, though, to Maisie's relief, Phyl turned away, telling everyone: 'The ground is very steep. Let's go back.'

Maisie and Phyl left the Sunny View contingent at the ugly pink house and walked back alone through the trees to the Jacobean mansion, finding the place unlit.

'Zoe's staying in the annex at the Dolphin again. She's on early in the morning, then she'll be back because she has Saturday off, of course. What's your plan, afterwards?'

284

'After what?'

'After the wedding, Maisie,' said Phyl, impatiently, and giving Maisie another lurch of guilt. 'Anyone would think you're not looking forward to it.'

Phyl opened the front door – left unlocked, Maisie noticed, with a twinge of apprehension.

'You mean the celebration, the reception you've set up at the Fox-in-Flight. Did I remember to thank you for that? It really is very generous and—'

'No,' said Phyl impatiently. 'After that.'

'Oh, yes, of course.' Maisie frowned. 'Well, I suppose I thought Jack and I might travel down to Sunny View together with the Savages.'

'What about the wedding night?' Phyl asked.

'I suppose Jack could come here?' she suggested, reflecting in the privacy of her memory that the interlude in Jack's hotel room at the Northumberland had made that less urgent.

Not for Jack, though, perhaps?

Phyl shook her head and led Maisie through to the kitchen, slumping down on one of the hard chairs.

'For all that you understand people and can see their hidden motivations,' Phyl told her, 'I'm not sure you understand your husband.'

'What do you mean?'

'He's working all the hours God sends so that you can be together, uninterrupted, alone. Sunny View is, I'm sure, a lovely place, but it's not exactly the Ritz or a chic villa on the Riviera.'

'But everything had to happen quickly,' protested Maisie. 'I couldn't wait any longer. I wanted to get it done.'

'That, too, isn't how most people like to hear their wedding spoken of – as something that needs doing, like getting their doctor to excavate a verruca.'

'What a horrible simile.'

'Yes,' said Phyl, going to the fridge for an open bottle of white wine. 'Want some?'

'No, I think I'll just go up. Thank you for organising the meal this evening,' Maisie said, trying to change the subject. 'That was very thoughtful of you.'

Phyl wouldn't be distracted. 'You hadn't given it a thought?'

'No,' Maisie admitted. 'I'm very bad at this, aren't I?'

'Having doubts?'

'What about?'

'Marriage. I wish I'd had doubts myself but, then, I wouldn't have this house and all this land.'

Maisie knew the story of Phyl's marriage to Blaise Pascal, a very wealthy member of the Free French forces stationed in Portsmouth in World War II, and how its disintegration had led to Phyl's sumptuous divorce settlement.

'I have no doubts about my marriage,' said Maisie, wearily. 'It's everything else and how my mind has been . . .'

She stopped and sighed. Phyl pressed her so she went upstairs to fetch her notes to bring down. Together, they read through them, with Maisie adding a few more comments in her tidy cursive hand, in particular in relation to Paul Linton and to Liz Petter.

'Do you know George, her father?' she asked.

'Lovely man,' said Phyl. Then she added with a giggle: 'Nothing to fear from handsome Liz, though. She's not a patch on our Maisie.'

'This is serious,' Maisie admonished.

'I know,' said Phyl. 'I'm sorry. I'm tiddly. Let's get to bed.'

286

FORTY-ONE

It wasn't especially late and Maisie wasn't tired. She reread her notes at the kitchen table, drinking two tumblers of water from the old iron tap over the sink. More than ever before, her ideas seemed futile. She told herself to buck up.

Five times, now, I've solved – or helped solve – a murder. Why don't I believe in myself?

Thinking it through, she had to admit that she had had moments of doubt each time, more or less at the same moment in each mystery, just as events seemed to be moving towards their climax.

Are they, though? It's the wedding that makes me feel like there's a deadline. That doesn't mean that, once we're married, we'll be safe from ideas of revenge and ...

Maisie frowned.

I think, all things considered, that the idea of Liz Petter as a murderer is fanciful. Jack does, too, and he knows her better than I.

She smiled to herself.

But not too well, thank heavens.

She pondered Paul Linton's liberation theology and his idealism. She had allowed Canon Greig to rattle on out of politeness, not because any of it was new to her. As a Catholic-majority country, France's newspapers – in particular Maisie's favourite, *Le Monde* – often covered such stories. But the connection to the brutal illogic of the young man on the Newcastle bus still perturbed her.

The idea that the indiscriminate attack on the Israeli delegation at the Munich Olympics was a legitimate political act ...

Certain that sleep was still far away, she crossed the hall to the library and fiddled with the radiogram until she found an evening concert from BBC Radio Three. It was Béla Bartók, a composer whose bracing work she enjoyed in small doses, but which seemed a bit much for late on a Thursday evening when listeners, surely, were winding down, not needing complex time signatures and surprising key changes.

She was about to turn the radiogram off when the piece stuttered to an unexpected halt and the announcer moved on to a weather forecast, predicting among other things 'an unsettled forty-eight hours in central southern England, with brief bright spells and sudden downpours'.

That's all we need, a sodden marriage ceremony, just to put the tin hat on all my incompetence and lack of organisation.

Remembering Phyl opening the front door without her key, Maisie went to lock up, using the one she kept in her purse. Through the small diamond-shaped panes to one side, she could vaguely see the looming trees. Some of the higher branches, she knew, were close enough to scrape against the upper windows.

The hall light switch was beside the window. She flipped it, plunging herself into darkness, making the woods and the drive a little more distinct. At the base of one of the closest trees, she saw a darker shadow, a kind of blacker blob against the general gloom.

There's someone there.

Standing quite still, she kept her eyes trained on the spot. Seconds passed then, she thought, minutes. Finally, she noticed movement, as if someone crouching low to the ground was adjusting their position.

Maisie put a hand on the door handle, turning it very slowly. Despite her care, the mechanism creaked and the dark blob was suddenly in motion. She dragged the door open just in time to catch a glimpse of the shadowy figure pounding away down the gravel drive, disappearing round the first bend. She felt her muscles tense, ready for pursuit, and would have launched herself out into the night, were it not for a memory that stayed her – something Phyl had said with a pained expression in her eyes.

How is anyone to keep you safe if you will insist on seeking out danger?

The crunch of the intruder's footsteps on the gravel faded on the night. With regret, Maisie closed and locked the front door. Then she went round the whole ground floor, making sure all the windows were closed and the kitchen door bolted. Unsure whether the outside access to the wine cellar was secure, she pulled a heavy armchair over the trapdoor in the library – something she had done before, during the Bunting Manor investigation.

Upstairs in her room, she used a technique she had employed in her brother Stephen's ugly rented house, Church Lodge, when she had found herself frightened of shadows in the undergrowth. She moved the upright chair from the desk and wedged it under the doorknob. Then she lay, fully clothed, on the bed, her brow creased with thought.

What if I misunderstood what Phyl meant? What if it wasn't rhetorical? What if she actually wanted me to tell her what would be the right thing to do?

Then worry left her conscious mind and, instead, she sank into troubled dreams.

★

A few hours later, Maisie was roused in the middle of the night by something between a snore and a snort because she had been sleeping flat on her back.

Like Lenin in his mausoleum.

289

She got up and moved the chair away from the door. After taking a moment to listen to a few odd creaks and groans from the sleeping house, she went to the bathroom to undress and brush her teeth.

Back in bed, with the chair again wedged under the doorknob, she turned on her side and slipped into renewed oblivion.

FORTY-TWO

As the sun rose on the Friday morning, shining through a small slot in the eastern clouds that loomed over the sleeping city of Chichester, Jack Wingard was already awake, boiling the kettle in the small square kitchen at number 147 Parklands Road.

I need to get ahead of things. The wedding is tomorrow. I need to talk to the people Fred and I are worried about and warn them off. I'll not let anything spoil our day.

He took his tea back to his bedroom – which was little bigger than the compact kitchen – alongside his grandmother's room at the front of the bungalow, with a window that gave onto the tidy front garden and the road, both wet from overnight rain. Zoe had forgotten to take away her jeans, so he had folded them up and put them on the rush seat of the chair that he kept tucked under the dressing table.

Jack's tea tasted weak and too milky because he'd been impatient and hadn't left it long enough to brew in the chocolate-brown teapot. He drank it all the same. Time, he felt, was short.

He dressed quickly in his well-kept uniform, thinking that, if his promotion came through, he would miss the way the smart wool jacket and shiny buttons marked him out as a figure of authority and reassurance. Then he touched the blemish on the shoulder, wondering if Florence might be able to effect an invisible repair.

No time for that, now.

He went out into the quiet street, running through the tasks he had set himself.

Everything has to be squared away before the wedding and honeymoon. I don't want any kind of shadow hanging over me – over us.

It took him fifteen minutes to walk down through the town, most doors still closed, most windows still dark. All the same, he had to wait for a train to come through at the railway gates before crossing and entering the quiet station. Fred Nairn was already there, drinking his own disappointing cup of tea, looking bleary-eyed at his desk.

'Give me five minutes for a shave in the washroom,' said Jack. 'I didn't want to wake Grandma.'

Jack was true to his word, using the kit he kept at the station. Applying his Old Spice aftershave, he couldn't help but judge his own reflection.

I look impatient. That won't do. This has to be done carefully – not once, but three times.

He and Fred drove to Selsey in the inspector's Mark II Jaguar, the windscreen wipers scraping back and forth, with most traffic going the other way, into the city. On arrival, Fred parked very close to where Maisie had briefly left the moped – though neither he nor Jack knew that. Before getting out, they took a moment to observe the converted railway carriage.

'They've done nothing to fix it up, yet,' said Fred. 'I'm surprised she's got the gall to come back here where she was the cause of so much misery.'

'What choice did she have?'

'Family?'

'We looked into that. There's no one would welcome her – or Ronan. She's burned her bridges.'

'She'll need to mend her ways.'

'That's what I'm going to tell her.'

'And you don't want me to come in?'

'No, I'll wait for a light to come on, then take my chances.' That was the moment that a glimmer appeared in one of the side windows. 'They're in the habit of early rising from prison. Here I go.'

He crossed the road, aware of a face at the window, watching him. He knocked on the front door, sheltering under the crumbling porch from the rain. Around him, paint was peeling from timbers attacked by salt spray from the sea. There was a pause, then he heard low murmurs and a scrape of furniture.

'Who is it?' came a voice.

'You know who. You saw me clear enough.'

Peggy Kemp opened up, eyeing him through a tiny gap between door and frame.

'What have we done now?'

'Nothing, I hope. Can I come in?'

With obvious reluctance – but also curiosity – Peggy stepped aside and he was able to enter, finding the main room dimly lit with a bare bulb dangling over a dirty round table at which the muscular, tattooed form of Ronan Kemp was sitting, stirring a teaspoon in a mug, a wary expression on his face.

Jack sat down opposite him and asked: 'How are you both getting on?'

'This place is all we've got,' said Ronan. 'Have you come to take it away from us?'

'How would I do that?'

'I don't know, do I? I'm not the police.'

'You might lose it if you don't pay your bills.'

'I've got money put by,' said Peggy.

'I dare say,' said Jack. 'But how long will it last?'

'We don't need much,' said Ronan.

'You can't go back to what you were doing before,' Jack told them. 'Word will get out and you'll go down for longer, next time.'

'Thanks for coming,' said Ronan, sarcastically. 'Is that it?'

'I might be able to help you,' he told them. Peggy was still on her feet, as if ready to show him out, but also interested in what he had to say. 'You both need jobs and a way back. If you keep your noses clean for a month, shall we say, I'll do my best for you.'

'How?' demanded Ronan.

'People I can talk to. You know me. If anyone hereabouts can get you back onto the straight and narrow, who else might it be?' Peggy and Ronan exchanged a glance in which Jack saw doubt and, he thought, hope. He tried to press home his advantage. 'There are charities I can speak to. You don't want to be looking over your shoulders all your lives long.'

'What about the woman who came to warn us off?' asked Peggy, unexpectedly.

Jack's heart sank.

Good grief, what's Maisie been doing now?

Soon, though, from their descriptions, he understood that it had been Phyl at the prison gates.

'Perhaps the lady shouldn't have done that, but she meant well, I expect. She's important to several local and national charities and may even be able to find some way to help you herself, once the dust has settled.'

'This isn't just talk, is it, while you find something else to pin on us?' asked Peggy.

'I give you my word it isn't.' Jack looked round the meagre room. The walls were, obviously, thin. The furniture was dusty and there was mould in the corners of the window frames. On the floor in one corner was a heap of dirty washing, including a beaded shawl. 'A month,' he repeated. 'Keep yourselves to yourselves. Maybe get this place shipshape. Then we'll speak again. I can see you've had enough trouble in your lives. Some of which you've brought on yourselves. But you can change.'

With that, he stood up and let himself out, crossing the road to the Jag, aware of Fred's anxious face through the windshield, mouthing: *At last.*

Jack opened the door and subsided in the comfortable leather passenger seat.

'Well?' Fred asked.

'There's a chance,' said Jack.

'You think they'll turn over a new leaf?'

'A chance,' Jack repeated, shutting the door. 'Let's go.'

Fred put the Jag in reverse and executed a smooth three-point turn. They left Selsey but, almost immediately, turned onto a sticky clay drive by the Petter Farm sign. Fred went carefully so as not to scrape his sump on the uneven surface, then pulled onto a pristine yard beside the farmhouse.

'You stay in the car again,' said Jack. 'And don't worry.'

He got out and went to knock on the farmhouse door. George Petter answered, dressed in tweed trousers held up by braces over his vest.

'Well, you've caught me early doors, Jack,' he said. 'To what do we owe the pleasure?'

'I want to speak to the Carter boys. They're on your land so I wanted to ask you first. Are you happy with their work?'

'Mostly, yes; sometimes, no. Liz had to rip a strip off them the other day. She'd given them an afternoon away from the gleaning to clean the yard and they made a pig's ear of it. They did a good job second time, though, once she'd told them what she expected of them.' George put his head on one side. Jack thought he looked old – unshaven and unready to face the world – and perhaps he nurtured a glimmer of hope that Jack might be here for romantic reasons. To confirm his intuition, George asked: 'Shall I call Liz, so she can tell you herself?'

'Better not,' said Jack kindly. 'She's unhappy with how things turned out between us.'

'As am I, my boy,' said George, sadly.

'But I never "led her on". You know that?'

'Yes, I do.'

'Good. Mick and Jez are in the bottom field, I think? I can go by myself. Fred Nairn's in the car, by the way. He'll just wait for me.'

'All right. You know best.'

The path along the field's edge was muddy but the rain had stopped. Mick and Jez were out of doors, standing with breakfast mugs in their hands, watching his approach. When he reached them, the conversation ran on similar lines to the one with Peggy and Ronan, with an important additional detail.

'I've visited every bookie, every betting office, in Selsey, Chichester, Barnham, Emsworth and Havant and I've given their owners copies of the police photographs of both of you.'

'Is that right?' asked Jez.

'And I've advised them against accepting any more of your wagers.'

'On what grounds?' demanded Jez.

'On the grounds of my sympathy with you as victims of your own foolishness.'

'That's pretty rich,' said Mick.

His tone combined surprise and, Jack thought, relief.

'You don't look well, either of you,' Jack told them. 'If you keep chucking your money away on the horses, you'll end up doing something seriously unwise and I'll be back here with handcuffs, not advice. Like I said, keep your noses clean for a month and I'll see if I can help in any way.'

'We've got Mr Petter on our side, haven't we?' said Jez.

'Not if you make a wrong step,' said Jack.

'That woman who came down here looking at us like we were animals in a zoo,' said Mick. 'Miss Liz says you're marrying her.'

'I am,' said Jack, trying not to bridle.

'What did she want with us?'

'It was a coincidence,' Jack lied, 'wanting flowers for the wedding.'

'Oh, right,' said Mick. Then he turned to his brother. 'Told you.'

'Aren't you clever,' retorted Jez.

Judging he had said all he needed – and fairly confident that the brothers weren't making any immediate plans for revenge – Jack left them to their mugs of tea and returned to the farmhouse, taking advantage of the boot scraper by the open back door. In the centre of the kitchen table, a striking bunch of yellow carnations stood in a tall vase. He waited a few moments, then Liz appeared from somewhere inside.

'Hello,' he told her. 'How are you? Feeling better, I hope?'

Liz had stopped moving, standing stock-still, as if caught out in some misdeed.

'How long have you been there?'

'I came down to talk to Mick and Jez on police business. I'm sorry if I startled you.'

Liz sighed. 'Dad says we can help them make good citizens. What do you think?'

Jack told her about what he had said and the fact that the local turf accountants ought not to take any more of their money.

She nodded. 'There's a chance, then. We've work for them over the winter – maybe worth a three-day week – but nowhere better than the caravan to lodge them.'

'Then that'll be a test, too. I hope they pass it.' Jack waited for Liz to reply. Her eyes were down and she looked very sad. 'I'm truly sorry,' he told her. 'I couldn't know what was going to happen—'

'The perfect Miss Cooper coming back into your life,' she interrupted him, bitterly, without meeting his gaze.

'That's right, but we never promised one another anything, did we?'

'You certainly didn't.'

'Neither did you, Liz. There was nothing spoken. I didn't mislead you.'

'I suppose not.'

Jack left a pause, wondering if the idea that had popped into his head was wise.

'If I asked you to the wedding, would you come? We could be friends again if you gave it a chance. Maisie, too. You'd like her, I'm sure.'

Liz raised her eyes and seemed to be making an enormous effort of will.

'I'll see. I'm not sure . . .' Her eyes went to the impressive yellow carnations. 'Some people always get what they want. I wonder what that's like?'

'I wouldn't know, Liz,' said Jack. 'I just hope for the best with each new step. Goodbye.'

He returned to the car and found Fred had already spread some newspaper in the footwell to protect his carpets.

'That went as well as could be expected,' Jack told his friend.

'You should be a diplomat. Turned out I was a spare part.'

'Yes, but thanks for being there in reserve. Either conversation might have turned nasty.'

Fred swung the Jag in a wide circle in the yard and picked his way back down the bumpy drive, saying: 'It's good of you to make both pairs the offer of help.'

'And I'll follow through, if they keep their end up. But my first objective isn't about in a month's time. It's about today and tomorrow. I'll not have our wedding spoiled.'

'You sound fierce, Jack. I've never heard that tone to your voice, like you might do something you'll regret if they cross you. You won't, will you?'

'Of course not,' he said. Even to his own ears, the words sounded hollow. 'Right, shall we get on?'

'Will she be up, yet, do you think?'

Jack glanced at his watch. 'Just about, perhaps.'

Twelve minutes later, Fred touched the brakes as he approached the wide vehicle entrance at Framlington Manor, pulling in slowly alongside the raised borders, designed to enable Daphne Fieldhouse access to them for weeding and deadheading from her wheelchair.

'It's looking untidy,' said Fred.

For this third visit, they both got out, climbing the steps to the front door and ringing the bell. After a pause, a middle-aged woman in a nurse's uniform opened wide, so that Daphne – who was descending on the Stannah stairlift – could see who it was.

'Ah, I've been expecting you, Sergeant. At some point, at any rate. Who is your companion?'

'My colleague, Inspector Fred Nairn, Mrs Fieldhouse.'

'Of course. We met at the evacuation from the theatre after the unfortunate incident on stage with the fake gallows – the very real gallows, as things turned out.'

'Can you spare us a moment or two?' asked Jack politely, not wanting to get sidetracked.

'Trapped as I am by this contraption, I believe I've allowed you a moment or two already.' The stairlift reached the hall and the nurse helped Daphne into her wheelchair. 'I have one chair for upstairs and one for down. A simple idea but a telling one. If we go into the living room, the nurse will bring coffee.'

Jack thought it was characteristic that Daphne would refer to 'the nurse' rather than use the woman's name. He wondered what the cost of daily visits – presumably morning and night – might be. Something well beyond the means of ninety-nine per cent of people he knew. That led his quick mind on to the fact that, in time, perhaps, Florence would need daily care. He frowned, imagining the burden that would place on Maisie and—

'Shall we, Jack?' asked Fred.

'Sorry, I was thinking of something else.'

They followed Daphne into the living room, comfortably appointed with a conspicuous space between the armchairs, facing the hearth, for the wheelchair.

'You are here because you want to know if I have had any contact with Derek,' she told them, her eyes on the ashes in the grate. 'I have not. I visited him once in prison to tell him how things would henceforward be. Since then, he wouldn't dare.'

'Not even a letter?' asked Fred.

'Not even.'

'Have you changed the locks?' asked Jack.

Daphne glanced up and then away.

'He wouldn't dare,' she repeated, quietly.

'I'm not sure I agree with you,' said Jack.

'That is your prerogative—' she began.

'The trial and the experience of incarceration will have changed him,' Jack insisted. 'He may no longer be in thrall to your personality.'

'Is that right?' Daphne raised her gaze. Jack wondered if she would bridle, but she seemed to take the idea seriously. 'Yes, I suppose you may be right. You make a good point. I am imagining the prior iteration of my husband. Though only six months have passed, I suppose it's possible that he might . . .' She stopped, her eyes wandering, vaguely. 'You have put me in mind of a test.'

'A test, Mrs Fieldhouse?' asked Fred.

'Yes, or a clue, if you prefer. Will you follow me?'

Daphne declined Fred's offer of assistance and propelled herself back across the hall into the kitchen, gripping the circular rails on her wheels with gloved hands. The back door

300

was open, through which Jack could see that the kitchen herbs had all been allowed to bolt and there were weeds growing in between, encouraged by the warmish autumn weather and the rain. Daphne saw his glance.

'Bert Close has been unwell. But he has sent no word of excuse or explanation. I am considering curtailing his employment.'

'I'm sure he'll bounce back,' said Fred.

'What did you want to show us?' said Jack.

'I cannot reach,' said Daphne. 'Derek thought he was so very clever, secreting his sordid little *cachettes* on high shelves. But characteristically, he never took enough trouble, never took pains. He grew careless and gave himself away. I observed him from the hall, through the crack at the hinge of the door.'

Jack followed her gaze to the higher cupboards. 'Up there?' he asked.

'And, being a short man with delusions of grandeur to compensate, he was obliged to balance on a chair. You can reach without such assistance.' Because it seemed her intention, Jack stretched up an arm to open the cupboard and get down two Tupperware containers from the top shelf. 'Give me the one with the rice.'

Jack did so and he and Fred watched as she balanced it in her lap, between her withered thighs, and released the lid, groping through the dried grains. 'There is nothing here. Pass me the other.' Jack took the box of rice from her hand and gave her the one of pasta.

Daphne did the same as before, combing her fingers through eight or ten ounces of dried fusilli, again coming up empty-handed.

'He has been here,' she said, simply, 'in order to retrieve the money he hid. I ought, as you suggested, to have changed the locks.'

Fred gave Jack a glance. Jack nodded to indicate agreement and Fred asked: 'If he came to you, openly, what would be your reaction?'

'I fear it might not be up to me.'

'In what way, Mrs Fieldhouse?' asked Jack.

'If you are right and prison has changed him, meaning that he is no longer – how did you put it? – "in thrall" to me, he might not give me time to react at all.'

FORTY-THREE

Maisie's morning began badly. She called the police station and discovered, although it was still early, that Jack had been in but was already 'back out'. No one knew where. She asked if either Sergeant Dodd or Police Constable Barry Goodbody might be there – who she knew to be members of the guard of honour planned for the wedding ceremony – but they were not. All the same, she decided that, even without Jack, she would comply with Canon Greig's request to practise the sequence of steps of the marriage service.

An odd sort of rehearsal this is going to be. It will be just him, with Paul Linton assisting and observing, plus Russell and Audrey, Phyl and Zoe, if she's free, perhaps Archie and maybe his brother Bert if he's feeling better.

Maisie sighed, reflecting on the fact that it was because she had asked no one for help that none had been forthcoming.

No, that's not fair. Florence has taken it upon herself to let out her own dress for me and Phyl has organised and paid for the party afterwards.

She considered asking some of the Bunting village people to come and practise with her.

Ernest Sumner and Jenny Brook will be busy in the pub, then they'll have baking ahead of tomorrow. I can't get them to come and waste an afternoon, pretending to be the congregation.

She went back upstairs, aware that she ought to try on the wedding dress one last time, after its most recent alterations. She knew that Florence would be at St Mary's, helping

Kinori Osaka with the flowers. If there were any last-minute changes required, she could ask her then.

Unfortunately, because she was so distracted, she was also clumsy and trod on the hem, tearing a length of appliqué lace from the skirts. With a shout of frustration, she ripped the dress off and threw it on the floor. The sound of her cry brought a response from Phyl's bedroom, wanting to know what was the matter.

'Nothing,' Maisie called abruptly back. 'Do you have time to do a rehearsal?'

'Of course. When?'

'Teatime, I suppose? And Zoe, too?'

'She's working,' came the disembodied reply. 'And she's not in. I told you. She stayed in the hotel annex again.'

'Never mind.'

She and Phyl met in person in the kitchen but, almost immediately, the telephone rang in the hall. Maisie went to answer and was delighted to recognise Jack's voice.

'Where have you been? I called the station good and early but—'

He broke in: 'Maisie, I have good news. PC Donaldson has been in touch. He's very sorry it's gone on so long but it took him a while to sort of befriend the decorators, you know, the ones working on the exterior of the building next to the hostel and, finally, he's got one of them to admit they were responsible for the accident. It was like we thought. The culprit was a clumsy apprentice sent back with something someone had forgotten.'

'Did we all think that?'

'One of us said it. It doesn't matter who. He ran off because he was worried about what he'd done – you know, believing he'd go to jail for assaulting an officer.'

'Is Donaldson certain? It wasn't a different event?'

'Yes, absolutely certain. There's nothing to worry about there. And he also spoke to Gary Naylor. You remember? You met him at the hospital?'

'I felt so sorry for him, poor man, but I was so glad that it was him, not you, who bore the brunt.'

'Well, he's up and about with his foot in plaster and no real harm done.'

'That's a relief,' said Maisie, her mind turning of its own accord to her handwritten list of potential enemies. 'What else—' she began.

Jack interrupted and forestalled many of her questions by telling her about making visits to the Selsey converted railway carriages and to Petter Farm, ending with: 'I think all is well, there. Neither the Kemps nor the Carters seem to me to be an immediate threat.'

'And Liz Petter? She was pretty fierce and disappointed at the police station.'

'Liz is unhappy, not vengeful,' said Jack. 'It's very common among farming folk, the difficulty of meeting someone special. It's a lonely life – long hours with the crops and the beasts, rather than people. I hope she does end up marrying one day.'

'She ought to. She's very attractive.'

'Is she?' Jack asked.

'You know she is.'

'Not my type,' he told her. 'My type is a category of only one.'

'All right,' she told him, still feeling ill at ease. 'Is there any chance you might be able to come to Framlington for a rehearsal after all? I know you think it's silly but, maybe, at the end of the day?'

'I've set a deadline of sixteen-hundred hours, four o'clock, then I'm done. So, yes. I'll be there soon after with Grandma.'

Having put the phone down, Maisie opened the front door to look out at the day. The sky beyond the encroaching trees was dark and a vertical rain was falling, undisturbed by any breeze.

Everything Jack said was encouraging – or, at the very least, not discouraging. Why do I feel worse than before?

Maisie fetched the torn dress, got herself together and drove into Chichester to admit what she'd done to Florence – who took it in good part, telling her: 'You should have waited for someone to help get you into it, dear. Never mind, I'll soon put that right.'

'I really am sorry. I feel so ungrateful.'

'Never mind. Oh, and in other news, I know who left the marbles. It was Mr Carsley from the three doors down. He must be eighty if he's a day and his grandchildren are all grown up, so he wanted someone else's kids to enjoy them, you know, selling them through the jumble.'

'That's good to know.'

Florence told her the repair to the dress wouldn't be quick: 'You needn't wait. Also, I've promised to help Kinori in St Mary's with the flowers this afternoon so I'd better get on.'

'I feel I must thank you again for all that you're doing. Is it a huge disappointment how I've rushed things?'

'It isn't perhaps what I would have wanted, but we all wish to see you happy, both of you.'

Maisie drove into town and dropped in on Maurice and Charity to see if they might be free to attend the rehearsal at four that afternoon, but they were not. At the Dolphin and Anchor, she discovered that Zoe was on a late shift and wouldn't have finished in time either.

She went to the greengrocer's shop on South Street and bought a nice green Granny Smith apple. In the distance, she saw Police Constable Barry Goodbody – once her enemy but now very much her ally. As she approached, she understood that he was supervising an elderly gentleman who had fallen on the uneven pavement. She didn't feel she had the right to interrupt for something as frivolous as a wedding rehearsal.

Returning to the Land Rover, she ran into Mavis Nairn who was wheeling a tartan shopping trolley along to the bus stop outside the cathedral. Maisie thought about pretending not to have seen her, then decided that would be unnecessarily unkind.

Mavis reiterated her complaint at seldom seeing her husband, Fred: 'With the long hours they're working, him and Jack Wingard, I wonder they don't ask for overtime. Still, it'll be done soon and, perhaps, there'll be new blood in the station once you're married and the sergeant gets his promotion and you move away.'

'Will we inevitably have to move away, Mrs Nairn?' asked Maisie, uncertainly. 'You know more about this than I, but Fred's local, isn't he? And you're living in Chichester still?'

'Yes, but he began his career elsewhere, in Brighton, then came back.'

'Oh, I didn't know.'

'Where do you think you'll end up?' Mavis asked. 'You know they don't give you a preference? But you'll understand that, having been shunted about in the army, I expect, even though you're a woman. I dare say orders came from on high and, as usual, the little people . . .' Mavis shook her head. 'Still, you have to do your best, don't you? Are you looking forward to tomorrow?'

'It can't come soon enough,' said Maisie, with a horrible feeling that was the wrong answer, that she was – once again – giving the impression that she just wanted it over and done with. And, in the same moment, she wondered if, in reality, she might like to move away from Chichester. 'I think I've come to regret getting involved in the mysteries, Mrs Nairn.

Can you understand that? I never asked to be an amateur detective. Each time, it was just circumstances and . . .'

She stopped, feeling she was sharing too much, that Mavis wasn't a close friend, just the frumpy wife of Jack's friend and—

'A wedding is so much change,' said Mavis, earnestly, 'it makes you reconsider many things.'

'Perhaps that's it.'

'Don't let doubt spoil your day.'

'No, that's good advice.'

'And, if you and Sergeant Wingard are happy together, nothing else matters.'

'But what if one's past actions make life difficult?'

'There's always got to be a hangover or two from the couple's previous lives.'

'And if the trouble comes from only one side and it's one person's fault – for getting mixed up in things that didn't properly concern her – but not the other's responsibility?'

'Then you face it together. That's what a marriage is, Maisie. Do you mind if I call you "Maisie"?'

'Of course not – you must.'

'I expect I'm not a very deep thinker, but I do know this. The future is what you make it. You should hold on to that.'

Maisie wanted to argue that, in her particular circumstances, she thought there was someone who wanted to make sure that she and Jack didn't have a future. Instead, she murmured: 'That's very wise.'

'Look, there's my bus. I must be off. We'll see you tomorrow and do our best for you.'

What does that mean?

Mavis bustled away with her shopping trolley, climbing aboard the Southdown single-decker, and Maisie realised too late that she hadn't reciprocated and called Fred's wife by her first name.

I'm a terrible person.

The bus pulled away. Maisie could see Mavis in one of the middle seats, bending the ear of her neighbour, giving a glance out of the window to indicate who she was talking about.

Oh God, she's telling that stranger all about me.

Maisie sketched a brief smile and turned away, crossing the road and heading up Tower Street to the sanctuary of the county library, an interesting circular building with book stacks arranged like the spokes of a wheel. She went to the poetry section that she had visited during the investigation into the murder at Church Lodge in order to identify the quotation about 'the secret things of the grave'. The volume was there on the shelf. She wanted to take it and retreat into its pages, but didn't feel she had the right.

I should get on. My visitors will be wondering where I've got to.

She drove back out to Bunting along wet roads with puddles in either gutter. Clearly, it had been raining heavily on the Downs while she had stayed fairly dry in town.

She pulled up outside the ugly salmon-pink village house. Shutting the car door, she noticed that the Bunting village pond was brimming. She looked up at the soft green hills, thinking about how the rain that fell on the sheep-cropped pastures didn't just flow away in streams, but also filtered down through the permeable chalk to bubble up out of the ground in the valleys below.

That must be the case at the mill pond near the Framlington church, too – fed by a spring as well as the surface streams that slosh down either side of Running Lane.

The Savages and Canon Greig appeared in the doorway, dressed for out of doors. It was their intention to walk the pilgrim trail through the woods to Bitling.

'Will you come with us?' asked Russell.

'Don't be daft,' said Audrey. 'Maisie's got far too much on to come traipsing about with us.'

'No, actually, I will. I've no duties.'

'What's the trouble?' asked Russell, perceptively.

'Nothing,' she told him.

'Have you managed to find a moment for our consultation?' asked Canon Greig. 'With your fiancé, too?'

'Perhaps after the rehearsal?' she improvised.

'That would be satisfactory.'

Maisie opened the rear of the Land Rover to find a not-quite-clean anorak in case it came on to rain again, even though they would mostly be sheltered among the trees. Phyl arrived and Maisie grasped that it was she who had suggested the expedition.

Once again filling in for my failures of organisation and hospitality.

They set off and Maisie asked Canon Greig what Paul Linton was doing.

'He went out earlier on his own, intending to go much further than our old limbs can manage.'

Maisie nodded but found herself wondering if Paul had an ulterior motive. She couldn't shake the idea that he might know more about the murder at Sunny View than the others believed. Then, unbidden, Mavis Nairn's final remark came back into Maisie's mind.

We'll see you tomorrow and do our best for you.

Maisie wished she knew who Mavis meant by 'we' and what it was 'we' were going to do. She couldn't give the question any real attention, however, because Canon Greig was talking at her, previewing what he called his 'spiritual guidance for newlyweds', making it sound as if the ideas were all his own invention, rather than predictable and commonplace.

They walked on for ten minutes with Maisie aware of another walker behind them on the path. Then, they emerged from the fringe of the trees and – though above their heads were dark clouds, heavy with unfulfilled rain – they all stopped to marvel at the view south to the distant sea, dappled with shadows and patches of brightness as the sun pierced the clouds. Phyl picked out several features of the landscape for their visitors, including the Isle of Wight, some of whose geography was clearly visible in the clear air.

As Phyl was talking, Maisie's excellent hearing discerned the much closer presence of the other walker in the woods they had just left. With a shiver of anxiety, she turned to see if Paul had followed them. But it wasn't Paul. It was the same dark shape she had encountered alongside the drive, trying foolishly to hide among the hydrangeas, who she had then run after, hunting them through the woods and fields of Bunting valley.

With a surge of anger, she ran, unwilling to allow herself to be stalked across the Sussex countryside, determined to confront whoever it was. The shadowy shape hesitated then stepped out into the bright daylight to face her. She recognised him at last – the 'second salesman' – and bent to snatch up a length of fallen timber as a weapon. She saw his mouth move but she was so intent and angry that she didn't hear what he was saying.

Then, from behind her back, Phyl's urgent voice broke in. 'Maisie, stop. Please. It's my fault, not Mr Tate's.'

FORTY-FOUR

Maisie's confrontation with the 'second salesman', on the edge of the chestnut woods, part-way along the pilgrim trail between Bunting and Bitling, caused the party to break in two. The Savages and Canon Greig continued on their way, with looks of curiosity in their eyes. Maisie, Phyl and the man Phyl had referred to as 'Mr Tate' stayed where they were, with storm clouds overhead and the bright sea in the distance.

'I'm sorry, Maisie,' Phyl began.

Maisie wouldn't allow her to finish.

'Let me tell you what I think has happened here. You've been worried about me, Phyl. I remember you almost telling me what you'd done when you asked, almost revealing your hand: "How is anyone to keep you safe if you will insist on seeking danger?" It's entirely in character and I should have seen it sooner.'

'Maisie, if you will just listen for a moment—'

'There's no need to explain. You called him "Mr Tate" just now and the resemblance to Arthur declares itself plainly.' Maisie shook her head. 'I know why you did it, how you must have come up with the plan, knowing Arthur Tate so well, as you do, as his benefactor. So this is the brother he mentioned and—'

'Forgive me interrupting,' broke in the 'second salesman'. 'Yes, that's all true, but our Arthur's got nothing to do with it. Mrs Pascal and I kept it from him, not wanting him to have to tell a lie.'

'Yes, but I think he guessed,' said Maisie. 'He was very talkative when I spoke to him in his shop, as if trying not to express the thoughts in the back of his mind.'

'That would be just like Arthur,' said the 'second salesman', nodding. He held out his hand. 'I'm Cedric Tate. I'm sorry if I frightened you. Mrs Pascal didn't want you to know.'

Maisie shook and told them both: 'You were right to conceal the idea that I needed protection. I would have refused. And I can't say I'm pleased, Phyl. You ought to have learned your lesson after the murder at Bunting Manor when you concocted—' Maisie stopped, realising that it would be very cruel to rake up old embers of guilt when Phyl had pretended to be the victim of murderous threats in order to reconnect with Maisie, having been estranged for many years. More importantly, right now, she had an opportunity to clear up one or two of her remaining questions. 'Mr Tate, you followed me up to London and then on to Newcastle. Is that right?'

'Yes, I did. London was easy because I know it pretty well. And you were mostly up the West End, seeing plays, and you can ask when they start and stop, so I could be there as you came out. But, up on the Tyne, everything was new to me. I got off the train before you, then hung about, then I lost you when you got into the taxi with the police constable. With the way you crossed the road as if you were going to walk, then dodged back to pick up a cab, I thought perhaps you'd spotted me.'

'No, I hadn't. That was a complete accident. How did you find me again?'

'I spent the night festering in my bed at the YMCA, thinking I'd perhaps failed. Then I told myself you'd be safe enough with Sergeant Wingard. But Mrs Pascal had told me that you both might be targets.'

'I see. But you didn't know where I'd gone.'

313

'Mrs Pascal had told me that you were only staying the one night, though she didn't know where. I just made sure I was at the railways station good and early the next morning. I was that relieved when the two of you turned up. I followed you and Sergeant Wingard onto the train.'

'And when I spotted you in the restaurant car and became suspicious?'

'Yes, I saw in your eyes that I'd been too slow to slip away, so I got off the train at Peterborough and hopped back on board up the back, by the guard's van, just before it pulled out.'

'And at King's Cross? Why didn't I spot you.'

'I followed you but I kept my distance – until, that is, we were down in the underground tunnels where it was so busy it was easy to keep close, yet still not be seen.'

'Then,' said Maisie, decisively, following her own train of thought, 'perhaps you can help me. On the platform, when Jack was nearly pushed onto the rails, did you see what happened? Was that an accident or was that a murderous attack?'

'I did see it, Miss Cooper. It was an accident, no question. There was a kerfuffle where someone next to me tripped up and shunted forward so as not to fall and it sort of caused a ripple, like dominos, you know, set up to fall, and it ended with Sergeant Wingard because he was close to the edge. I made it worse by trying to push through and help but, luckily, there was a big man with a rucksack on his back who—'

'Yes, I remember. I was there,' interrupted Maisie, uncomfortable with the memory. 'I'm sorry to snap. You were doing what you were asked to do and I ought to be grateful, even though it isn't what I would have wanted. Just to be clear, it was you who I chased through the woods and the fields from the drive of Bunting Manor.'

'Yes, Miss Cooper.'

'And you, Phyl, when you refused Mohammed's invitation to come to the Dolphin and Anchor, that was because you wanted to sneak out and get Mr Tate's report?'

'It was.'

Maisie turned her attention back to Cedric.

'I saw you outside the front door last night, crouched in the trees, watching over us,' she added, nodding.

'What's that?'

'Last night, just before we all went to bed, I put the hall light out and saw you in the shadows. But I didn't know it was you so I opened the front door and you ran and, well, I didn't chase you because I was in a strange mood, thinking about not seeking out danger.'

'That wasn't me, Miss Cooper.'

'Are you sure?'

'I was up above the manor when I saw the lights go out, looking down through the trees. I did hear noises but you do, at night. There's a good lot of animals out and about, making more racket than you'd think, pushing through the under-growth. Then, when all was quiet, I came by and made sure all the doors and windows were locked, before using the key Mrs Pascal gave me to creep into the wine cellar through the outside door because she'd made me up a bed.'

Maisie frowned, wondering if the shape in the trees could have been a badger or even a deer. It had been very dark under the looming trees. She turned to Phyl.

'It's because Mr Tate was down in the cellar that you didn't let me or Zoe go down there for fresh bottles of wine.'

'Yes,' said Phyl. 'I'm sorry.'

'And that's why Archie couldn't grow his mushrooms down there and had to propagate them under cardboard in the barn. I suppose you thought you were acting for the best.' Maisie's mind was racing, trying to think if Cedric Tate might be able to dispel any other worries. 'You didn't follow me to St Mary's, Framlington, when I met the florist, Kinori Osaka?'

'No, I've not been able to keep up with every trip, just those where Mrs Pascal knew in advance where I would need to be.' He frowned. 'I did worry that you might know me if you saw me, because Arthur and I have similarities in our appearance, sort of unfortunate-like.' Then he added, with his narrow smile: 'Though our mother loved us, I believe.'

'Of course she did,' said Maisie, distracted.

What does this leave? The slate from the church tower? Yes. The marbles on Florence's front step? No, that's been resolved.

'I'm sorry if I was wrong again, Maisie,' repeated Phyl.

A few fat drops of rain began to fall.

'We should get back,' she told them.

Without a word, they walked the short distance home under the trees, the thickly leaved branches of the chestnut trees creating a complete canopy from the shower. Eventually, Cedric Tate spoke, a little breathless because Maisie was walking quickly. Phyl, in fact, was lagging wearily behind.

'I couldn't get up into the library from the cellar for a glass of water or a snack last night,' he told her.

'I pushed an armchair over the trapdoor,' Maisie told him, pausing with her hand on the trunk of a beech tree, still attempting to work out which threats or unanswered questions remained.

Just the shadow outside the front door. Is that right? Once I've put all this together with what Jack told me, perhaps there's nothing to worry about after all.

'I won't go on about it,' said Phyl, coming alongside. 'This is the last time I'll say it.' She took several deep breaths then resumed. 'I'm sorry but you're too important to me to have stood back and done nothing.'

'I understand,' said Maisie, absorbed in her thoughts. Then she pulled herself together and surprised herself by saying, with great warmth: 'You know I love you, Phyl.'

They walked on, crunching through some dry, fallen leaves while under the trees, then slipping and sliding on wet ones on the final stretch of exposed path, especially where damp and greasy chalk peeked through the soil. Back at Bunting Manor, Maisie cooked Cedric Tate bacon and eggs to make up for having prevented him from getting anything to eat in the night. Though it was past midday and, therefore, 'the sun was over the yard arm', Phyl didn't seem inclined to get herself a drink. She sat in silence at the kitchen table, opening some of her neglected post.

Cedric ate with enthusiasm, polishing off three mugs of tea as well. Then Maisie took the Land Rover back out to pick up the walkers from Bitling. When she got there, she found they were enjoying their own lunch in the Silver Garter, alongside half a dozen local residents, some of whom Maisie considered her friends. She wondered about asking them to 'make up the numbers' at the rehearsal, but felt foolish.

It's all too ridiculously last minute.

Finally, leaving the pub, she ran in to Harold Farr in his disreputable brown suit, the shoulders damp because, clearly, there had been another heavy shower while the Savages and Canon Greig were eating. Harold was frowning, so she asked him what was wrong.

'I'm troubled, Miss Cooper,' he told her.

'What about?'

'It's Mr Close.'

'Archie or Bert?' she asked, knowing both brothers, Archie from his managerial work for Phyl and Bert for his day-labouring for the Fieldhouse family in Framlington.

'Well, both. That's where 'tis.'

317

'How do you mean?'

'Mr Archie should have been over with instructions for the turkeys and he's never.'

'And Bert?'

'He's not been well. I suppose you've heard?'

'Yes, and?'

'Well, I was wondering if Mr Bert Close had been taken properly sick and Mr Archie's with him in hospital or such like and does anyone know?'

'I see. When I get back to the manor, I'll ask Mrs Pascal, Harold. I'm sure all will be well.'

She gave him a bright smile as Canon Greig and the Savages climbed into the Land Rover. She got in and started the engine. Disconcertingly, Harold was still watching her with a kind of appeal in his eyes.

Gosh, he really is worried. I suppose it's true that Archie wouldn't miss an appointment on a whim. Maybe poor Bert is seriously ill.

She drove carefully down the lane to the main road and turned right towards Framlington, thinking about how Paul Linton was somewhere gadding about the countryside. She took a last-second decision to stop at the village stores.

'Russell, would you mind driving on yourself?' she asked. 'You'll want to put on dry clothes for the rehearsal and you can perhaps bring me another anorak. But I've got an hour and I'd like to pop into the shop and then I might have a mooch around the church, you know, to get my ideas in order. Would you mind returning for four o'clock for the rehearsal with Mrs Pascal?'

'No trouble, my handsome. I've been itching to have a go in this here Landy. She's brand new, isn't she?'

'Almost, yes. Mind how you go,' she warned him.

She realised that, for the third time, the advice she had given Arthur Tate was on the tip of her tongue.

You never know what's round the corner.

★

The village stores in Framlington were run by two women who, Maisie knew, had been kind to her brother, Stephen, in the period before his murder. The younger of the two, Beatrice, was serving, wearing her usual shop uniform of dungarees and hard-wearing collared shirt, because it was she who took care of deliveries and maintenance and so on.

Maisie chose a hand-made cheese-and-ham roll and a slice of flapjack and, in conversation, she discovered that Archie had been in, asking about Bert.

'That seems odd,' she replied. 'Do you know why?'

'It seems he's not at home.'

'Where does he live? I don't remember – if I ever knew.'

'A cottage about a mile up beyond the stables, where there's bluebells every April.'

'I know the place. I suppose Archie's been up there?'

'Of course,' confirmed Beatrice.

'And the stables?'

'They've been locked up since that old bugger Derek Fieldhouse was rightly put away in prison,' said Beatrice with relish.

Maisie knew that, as Alicia and Beatrice's landlord, Derek Fieldhouse had been nothing but trouble.

Does she not know he's been released on a technicality, though?

'You'd normally see Bert when he comes in for his tobacco and so on?' Maisie asked.

'Yes, but not for nearly ten days, I'd say. And, like you, he enjoys a ham roll to take and eat in the quiet of the stable yard. It really is a mystery.' Beatrice shook her head in bemusement, then said: 'Why don't you go through to our rooms and eat with Alicia. She'll be glad of the company.

You know how she hates doing the accounts and you'll give her a reason to take a break.'

'I'm tempted, but I ought to look in on Florence and Kinori. They're doing the flowers. I don't suppose you and Alicia might be free at four to do a rehearsal. I know it's rather last minute . . .'

Beatrice looked pained and told her: 'We've deliveries to bring in and we have to stay open. I'm sorry, Maisie. But you don't really need to practise walking up the aisle and saying "I do", surely?'

'Perhaps not.'

Maisie left the village stores and, before going to the church, she ran through a smattering of drizzle to the stables, thinking Beatrice was right, that it was a nice place to sit peacefully and eat.

The stable yard looked a little different, with the same few wisps of straw, but stuck to the concrete instead of being blown on the breeze, because they were wet. She tried the doors – the one to the tack room and the two stables – and found them locked. She wondered if, since Stephen's murder back in February, with all of its web of subplots and repercussions, Daphne Fieldhouse had taken the precaution of getting a locksmith in to change the mechanisms. It didn't look like it. The brass of the escutcheons and the keyholes was tarnished and weathered.

The brief drizzle had stopped. She thought about running up the lane to Bert's house in the bluebell woods, but decided it was too far. She perched herself on the edge of a large zinc water trough to eat her ham-and-cheese roll and her flapjack, doing so with enormous pleasure, discovering that she was very hungry. When she had finished, she stayed where she was, enjoying the smell of damp earth and grass and the occasional shaft of warming sunlight. Then, all of a sudden, she experienced a wave of nostalgia and affection for the powerful grey stallion that she had ridden – once for pleasure and, a second time, bareback, in fear for her life.

She got up, brushed some crumbs from her anorak and crossed the yard to put her right eye to one of the diamond-shaped holes in the upper half of one of the timber stable doors.

It took a few moments but, eventually, her pupil expanded so that she could make out the shadowy interior, only partially illuminated by bars of grey light let in through splits in the cladding. A bed of clean straw came into focus, heaped up to one side into a mound. Elsewhere on the brick-paved floor was a kind of tiny wriggling movement, as if several handfuls of grains of rice were in sinister motion.

Then, the breeze got up and brought the same smell of sickly putrefaction to her nostrils. She took a step back, screwing up her face with disgust, remembering her idea of a rat or a badger. There was a gap beneath the bottom edge of the stable door, easily tall enough for an animal to creep inside and ten or twelve more maggots visible beneath the timbers, soon, she supposed, to turn into disgusting blow-flies.

Any vermin that had eaten poison might be looking for a warmish, dry place to curl up and die.

Disappointed that she had spoiled her *al fresco* lunch, Maisie left the yard, almost dragging her feet, as if reluctant to leave.

I seem, at every step, to be out of sync with my surroundings. If, once upon a time, I had a knack for understanding what was about to happen before it came to pass, I think I've now lost it.

FORTY-FIVE

Maisie realised too late that she would have liked to talk to Florence and Kinori, to thank them for their work on her and Jack's behalf. But, as she was crossing the road to the corner of Church Lane, she saw them, pulling away in a tiny Mini, driven by the florist, with a heap of paper and wet cardboard boxes on the back seat.

Maisie checked her watch, hoping that Florence would make it back with Jack for the rehearsal at four o'clock.

But she did say there was a lot of work to do to repair the dress.

She walked up the lane to the lychgate and contemplated the damp churchyard, without entering.

This bit of land must be higher than most of the village. There's no risk of flood. I suppose all the rain runs away down Running Lane to the pond.

She set out across the potato field, because she had time to kill and nothing to do. The path through the potato field was slippery. Her wellington boots, however, were a good fit and her feet didn't slide about inside them. At the far end, the land dipped and she found herself wading through a couple of inches of running water, inundating the tarmac of the country lane because the mill pond had burst its banks. There was a noticeable current crossing the choppy surface, transporting twigs and leaves towards the outfall on the far side where, through the choked metal grille, she could hear it rushing away.

She saw a distorted reflection of herself in the ripples, reminding her of Zoe's comment about the new second chef at the Dolphin and Anchor who 'fancied himself', enjoying his own reflection in the steel door of a fridge.

I don't fancy myself. I seem to have lost track of who I really am.

FORTY-SIX

Because of the noise of rushing water, when the voice came, it was a shock, its owner's approaching footsteps – sloshing on the drowned road – obscured. The tone of the voice was mocking, almost unkind.

'Here you are, then.'

Inside, Maisie felt regret that her quiet contemplation had been interrupted, but she forced a smile and turned to greet whoever it was.

Her heart sank.

'Mr Fieldhouse,' she gasped.

'Call me "Derek",' he told her. 'You remember me telling you to do that seven months ago? Let's not stand on ceremony, not after all we've been through together – or rather, me apart but mercifully at large once more.'

'This isn't a good idea,' said Maisie. 'You'll soon be back inside if you break the requirements of your parole or whatever it is.'

'No one's about. No one's here to see.'

'See what?'

He put his head on one side, his bullet-shaped cranium glistening. His complexion was sallow, his cheeks sunken. The tweed suit she recognised from back in February was slack on his diminished frame. But there was an intensity in his eyes that was beginning to make her wary.

'When you climbed the tower of the church, I thought that was my chance, that I could simply tip you off. Did you know that?'

'Are you making that up? Did you see me go in from down below?'

'Oh, no. I was quite ready to do it, but the labourers in the potato field were watching. I dislodged a slate when I was clambering round and that got their attention. I should have been more careful. But that meant I could never have got away with it. So I scarpered, leaving you trapped.'

'Got away with what?' Maisie prevaricated, though obviously she knew.

'Before we say goodbye,' he told her, taking a step closer, so that she could see the food in his teeth, 'I just want you to know that you were just inches away from me just now. How do you feel about that?'

Maisie frowned then deduced: 'You've been hiding in the stables.'

'I watched you eat your little lunch. I tried to imagine drowning you in the water trough.'

'I'm glad you thought better of it,' said Maisie, lightly, inching away.

'But I didn't think better of it,' Derek replied. 'I just couldn't see a way of getting at you without you running away and finding help. And I know from previous experience and from reading about your further exploits in the *Chichester Observer* that you're a fine runner, better than me, no doubt. But, now, things have changed. Here I am and here you are on this quiet shoreline and there's nowhere for you to go.'

Derek was right. Maisie was standing on a sort of elbow of the tarmac road with just a narrow grass verge between her and the deep water of the pond. But she wasn't worried. She was a strong swimmer. If he pushed her in, it would be horrid and slimy, but not dangerous.

'Surely you don't want to go back to prison?' she asked.

'They won't put a hero in prison.'

'What are you talking about?'

'About me.'

'How will you be a hero?'

'I'll be the man who, despite everything, despite the conflicts of our shared past, tried to save the famous Maisie Cooper,' he told her, an odd gleam in his gaze. 'From a watery grave.'

'Derek, you're not making any sense—'

Before she had finished, he suddenly shoved her, the heels of his two hands slamming into her collarbones. She lurched backwards, her wellingtons losing traction on the narrow verge. Then she toppled and hit the surface with a cold splash, the water closing over her face and insinuating itself into every fold and wrinkle of her clothes, contracting her shocked muscles. She shut her eyes and sealed her mouth as a great weight landed on top of her, mercifully on her hips and legs rather than her torso, and she realised that Derek had leapt in after her with one intention.

He must be quite mad. He means to drown me and then try to claim that he wanted to save me from an unlikely accident.

Maisie kicked hard, pointing her toes, managing to wriggle out from under him. Her face broke the surface as he reached out for her, snatching at the sodden fabric of her quilted anorak. Her wellington boots were full of water, dragging her down, so she took a deep breath and went under, letting them slip down her calves, kicking harder, gratefully feeling them sliding off her feet, together with her sodden socks, to settle in the silt and mud.

Breaking the surface again, she back-crawled away, wanting to be able to see what he was doing, heaving against the slippery water to put distance between them. Derek launched into his own untidy thrashing stroke, quickly gaining. She rolled over in the water to employ her own smooth front crawl, swiftly crossing thirty yards of pond towards the outfall.

Reaching the dam of twigs and branches and leaves, Derek was only a few heartbeats behind. She passed her hands along the rusting old grille, which felt loose and unstable under her weight. It was set between two round steel posts so she grasped one in her left fist. It felt sturdy as she prepared to ward him off with her right, finding that she could touch the bottom and stand, though her naked feet were deep in the cloying sediment.

Derek made his last few wild strokes and was upon her, pushing her tired right arm aside and enveloping her in a bear hug. He wanted to get on top of her again to press her face down into the cold water.

Maisie realised that she had misjudged the circumstances, that she had been wrong to feel secure in her own strength, her agility and her quick-wittedness. In this awful moment, she was not stronger or cleverer than Derek Fieldhouse, not while his sole purpose in life was revenge and she was the only focus of his desperate desire for violent retribution.

She began to find it hard to breathe with his arms squeezing her chest, and the weight of him was dragging her bottom lip closer and closer to the surface of the water. It was hard to fight back with one hand grasping the steel post but, if she let go, he would soon push her under.

With weariness beginning to overcome her, she realised with an awful certainty that the dreadful smell of putrefaction at the stables must have been poor Bert Close. Even with no horses to look after, Bert would have checked up on the stables on one of the days when he was eating his lunch in the yard. He must have found Derek holed up in the tack room. The fact that Bert had been ill meant that no one had, at first, concerned themselves unduly with his absence – an absence caused by the fact that Derek had silenced him in the most brutal and definitive of ways, covering his body up with straw to be infested by maggots and blowflies.

327

For a second, the weight of Derek's body and the tightness of his arms relaxed as her attacker sought a new position, more on top of her, the quicker to push her under. She took advantage to grab a deeper breath and duck beneath the surface, trying to kick him away beneath the water. But she missed and her foot jarred against the metal grille – which gave a little.

Inspired, she repeated the action, this time aiming squarely for the rusted metal bars, succeeding in nudging it a little further out of its frame. But she was running out of oxygen, her lungs burning and weakness invading her muscles. And Derek had managed to get a foot on top of her, pressing down on her stomach, forcing her deeper into the silt.

This will be my last chance.

She squirmed to one side and, with her left hand tight around the steel post for purchase, she slammed both feet into the grille. It gave way and, suddenly, the water was in motion all around her, dragging at her sodden clothes, trying to haul her away from her desperate grip on the post.

In the same moment, to her great relief, Derek was gone.

Maisie dragged herself to the surface, hand over hand on the smooth steel, and clung for a few seconds, drawing in deep, grateful breaths, feeling colour and light return to her world. The mill pond was emptying at a rapid rate, the water churning across her shoulders then sloshing against the broken water wheel and running away past it down the channel. The grille had been flipped, end over end. Somehow, however, Derek had overtaken it.

Or, rather, Derek's body had overtaken the grille and slammed into the wrecked water wheel, impaling him on its sharp, broken paddles. A shard of timber protruded from his chest. Plus, the pointed ends of the rusting bars of the grille had impaled him from the front. His ghastly white face was slack, his mouth and eyes open with pummelling water running in and across them.

Maisie found the sight awful.

Derek Fieldhouse, however, no longer cared because, very clearly, he was dead.

FORTY-SEVEN

Looking and feeling like a drowned rat, Maisie dragged herself out of the mill pond and found a neighbour with a telephone at the top of Running Lane. She asked her – a retired schoolteacher with a calm and practical disposition – to call nine-nine-nine.

'You must get warm and dry first, my dear.'

'No,' Maisie told her. 'I'll just sit here in your porch. The day isn't cold, thankfully.'

The woman made the call, then insisted on taking Maisie to her ground-floor bathroom so that she could take off her wet things and put on an itchy tartan dressing gown. Then the woman brought her a cup of hot sweet tea.

Fifteen minutes later, an ambulance arrived from St Richard's Hospital in Chichester. It was closely followed by a police car because Jack had been on his way to Framlington for the rehearsal, bringing his Grandma Florence and the repaired dress. Instinctively, he had followed the emergency vehicle, because it was answering a call using flashing lights and sirens. Maisie called to him from the porch of the tiny cottage and, with a cry of astonishment, he came running to embrace her and ask what had happened.

'Jack, it was Derek,' she began, then found that she didn't know where to start. 'I'm sorry, my mind's all a muddle.'

The retired schoolteacher tactfully left them, each seated on a little bench either side of her welcome mat, with a scent of late carnations in the air from the cottage garden. Through patient questioning, Jack helped Maisie tell her story, then he left her, saying: 'I'll be back shortly.'

He was as good as his word. The wedding rehearsal was cancelled and, quite soon, with Maisie's sodden clothes all stuffed into two carrier bags, he drove her back to Bunting Manor where she took a hot bath and emerged, feeling much more herself. While she had been soaking, Jack had spoken to Phyl and the Savages and Canon Greig: 'They've gone out to wait for Ernie Sumner to open up the Dancing Hare, so they'll leave us in peace for a while, at least.'

Maisie found that was precisely what she wanted. She took him into her room, unwrapped herself from her towel and, for some time, neither she nor Jack spoke, as they hadn't needed to speak in their hotel room at the Northumberland in Newcastle. Then they lay beneath the covers in her comfortable bed and Jack asked her: 'Should we postpone?'

'What do you mean?'

'The wedding. We could, you know. Everyone would understand.'

'Is that what you want?'

'I want what you want.'

Maisie sat up and he did the same. They faced one another, their eyes united in love and understanding – and a firm desire from each to do what the other needed.

'I'm going to tell you,' said Maisie, 'what I told myself at the end of the murder at Sunny View investigation. "I'm not going to wait for months and months of engagement and dress fittings and banns and preparations. I've decided that I'm going to marry Jack Wingard before this summer is out." Nothing has changed. Is that all right? You don't think I'm cold-hearted and odd?'

'You are perfect in every way.'

There was another tender interlude but, eventually, they heard voices outside and the crunch of feet on the untidy gravel. With regret, Jack told her he must leave to 'go and progress formalities at the station'. From her bedroom window, Maisie heard him telling Phyl and the others: 'Maisie is tired and has already gone to bed.'

She finished her Ngaio Marsh novel, *When in Rome*, then wished she had another. Quite soon, though, to her surprise, Maisie found herself drifting into profound sleep.

EPILOGUE

Maisie woke early the next morning to a bright autumn day that would obviously begin cold – because the skies were clear – but end up lovely and warm.

Over breakfast, no one questioned her about the previous day's events, not even Zoe, though the young woman was clearly desperate to know. Eventually, Maisie took her aside to give her a very brief summary.

Florence arrived to help Maisie put on her wedding dress and Zoe shared some extraordinary ideas about make-up that Maisie politely declined. Phyl came in with a corsage of silk lotus flowers that she had worn on her own wedding day, telling her: 'This can be your "something borrowed" as well as your "something blue".'

Maisie asked about Archie, adding: 'Poor man. I feel it's my fault. I ought to have worked out what had happened sooner.'

'According to Jack, Bert must have come across Derek last week, when you were already up in London. Archie's very sad and I don't expect we'll see him today.'

'It's just too awful.'

'Yes, but it isn't your fault. Derek's next step would have been to attack his ex-wife. Jack found a kind of mad journal at the stables with his plans all written down. If you hadn't become the focus of his vengeance, he might have taken that direction first.'

When it was finally time to head off for the church, Maisie found herself feeling very glum indeed – not just for poor

Bert Close and his bereaved brother Archie, but because she thought the wedding would be a miserable affair, unrehearsed, badly planned, no choir, with nothing to make it memorable.

Arriving at the lychgate in the Land Rover, however, she was delighted to see the guard of honour provided by police officers from Chichester station who, to her surprise and amusement, sang several verses of 'Sussex by the Sea' as Phyl slowly led her up the path between the gravestones, beneath one of which her parents, Eric and Irene, lay in eternal rest.

Phyl made her hesitate at the door so the police officers could overtake and go inside, murmuring their good luck messages, including old William Dodd and young Barry Goodbody. Once the guard of honour was indoors, Maisie was surprised to see Mavis Nairn on the threshold.

'Are you ready, dear? Shall I tell the choir to begin?'

'What choir?'

'I've organised for the choir from our church in town to provide some music. I hope that was the right thing to do?'

'That was a lovely thing to do,' said Maisie, her eyes wet.

Instead of the wedding march being played on the organ, Mavis Nairn's church company gave a beautiful *a capella* rendition of the Mendelsohn classic, harmonised for soprano, alto, tenor and bass, with Fred beaming as he conducted. Maisie noticed Paul Linton in his cassock and surplice among the singers.

I'm so glad Paul's innocent of any ill will. He could turn out to be an impressive young man, I think.

Maisie advanced up the aisle on Phyl's arm, exchanging delighted smiles with her friends and Jack's, including Maurice and Charity, who were sharing a pew with Mohammed As-Sabah, and Arthur and Cedric Tate. Behind them were Harold and Adam Farr, with Alicia and Beatrice from the village shop. In front of them were Zoe, Russell and Audrey, waiting for Phyl to take her place beside them. On the other side, she saw her other Bunting and Bitling and theatre friends, plus Kinori and the members of the guard of honour.

Jack turned to greet her, the light of love in his eyes, looking chic and handsome in his dress uniform. She continued her approach, holding his gaze, seeing in his steadfast expression a kind of promise for their future together – one made up of trust and devotion and love.

The service passed in a blur but with no hint of unpreparedness – or, when there were any stumbles, no one cared. While she and Jack signed the register in the vestry, Mavis Nairn's choir sang two more Sussex folk songs, celebrating the trees and the hills, 'the fields and the beasts thereof'. They re-emerged for the final blessings and prayers and Maisie realised that Canon Greig was doing a wonderful job, providing a poised and well-balanced ritual, moving easily from the spiritual to the temporal. His remarks – that she had thought obvious and commonplace – took on new and deeper meanings.

At the end of the service, she discovered that Florence and Kinori had made sure there would be confetti made of rose petals for the photographer from the *Chichester Observer* to capture, all the congregants showering them as they descended the path and processed through the village. The party afterwards at the Fox-in-Flight was a triumph, with Jenny Brook's pastries 'setting new standards', as Florence put it. Liz Petter even looked in to give her father, George – who had done his best to drain the free bar dry – a lift home. Maisie went to speak to her.

'Please, Liz, stay and enjoy yourself,' Maisie insisted.

'I wanted to wish you all the best. I left some yellow carnations for you in the church porch yesterday. I hope you liked them.'

'I did,' said Maisie. Kinori had mentioned the mystery of the inappropriate flowers and Maisie knew that the flower expert would be glad to know the innocent reason for them. 'Have a drink with us, please.'

'All right.' Liz told her, smiling. 'If you insist.'

As the party wound down, Maisie discovered that Phyl had booked the best room at the Dolphin and Anchor for the wedding night and a Dunnaways taxi to take them there. They left with the good wishes of all their friends and neighbours from Framlington, Bunting, Bitling, Chichester and Sunny View ringing in their ears.

The next day, Jack was unable to leave first thing, as they had planned, because of the official aftermath of Derek Fieldhouse's impalement and drowning. Soon, though, Fred took over the police business and they drove off in Fred's Jaguar because, as he insisted: 'It's the least I can do as best man. I'll use the patrol car till you're back.'

The honeymoon at Sunny View was idyllic – two weeks of perfect weather, alone in the charming guest house because Russell and Audrey, supported by Phyl, had hatched a plan to stay on in Bunting to 'give the newlyweds free rein'.

It was the middle of October, therefore, before Maisie and Jack returned to Sussex – to the excellent news that Jack's promotion had been approved, 'pending a suitable post'. Maisie found she didn't mind the uncertainty because she had, over the two-week break, found herself more and more certain that the upsets and dramas – the sequence of six murder mysteries – was over. Plus, she had news to share with her husband.

She took him for a walk up on the pilgrim trail through the woods to the place where the vista opened out, across the soft rolling Sussex Downs, all the way to the sea.

'We're happy, aren't we,' he said. 'Just the two of us.'

'I think, Jack, you might mean three.'

'What's that?' he demanded, wheeling round.

'I mean – though I can't be absolutely sure, because it's only a few weeks—'

'Oh, that's the most wonderful news.'

He embraced her and they spent the next twenty minutes discussing names. Then Maisie said: 'One day, we'll look back on this year and we'll feel amazed. It'll seem like a dream.'

'I don't think so,' Jack told her. 'We'll look back and feel proud of all we accomplished – especially you.'

'Perhaps you're right,' she told him, with a tinge of regret at the idea that she would never again be caught up in drama and intrigue.

'I do love you,' he said.

'Yes, and I, you.'

'But never say never, Maisie. Who can be certain that you won't find yourself solving another mystery at some point in the future, perhaps with a baby in a pushchair beside you, or a toddler discovering clues on your behalf.'

Maisie laughed. 'That's an idea. But, in the meantime, I think that brings us full circle.'

'In what sense?'

'When I saw you, standing so solemn and so handsome under the yew tree, at the beginning of the murder at Church Lodge investigation, I ought to have known we would end up together, for always.'

'I knew – I mean, I hoped.'

'Yes, and I'm so glad. But leaving aside fanciful ideas about toddler detectives, I'm glad that the cycle is complete.'

'You mean the sequence of "Maisie Cooper mysteries", like they called them in the newspaper.'

'Yes.'

'I'm still not so sure,' he told her.

Maisie sighed, with satisfaction but also relief.

'Would it be so bad, Jack, for the murder at the wedding to be the last?'

THE END

ACKNOWLEDGEMENTS

Thanks to Luigi Bonomi whose idea it was that I should write cosy crime, and to the team at LBA; to my magnificent editor Audrey Linton, plus all her colleagues at Hodder & Stoughton; to the booksellers, festival co-ordinators, podcasters and all the others whose dedication and enthusiasm are so essential to a flourishing book industry; to all the generous writers who have supported this playwright's unexpected transition to novel writing.

And, of course, to the person from whom I learned to write books – the best and only Kate Mosse.

Don't miss the other books in the Maisie Cooper Mystery series . . .

. . . where crimes and murder abound.